# TELL ME SWEET

## LADIES LEAST LIKELY

# MISTY URBAN

OLIVERHEBERBOOKS

To Lucasta, Going to the Wars
By Richard Lovelace


Tell me not (Sweet) I am unkind,
That from the nunnery
Of thy chaste breast and quiet mind
To war and arms I fly.

True, a new mistress now I chase,
The first foe in the field;
And with a stronger faith embrace
A sword, a horse, a shield.

Yet this inconstancy is such
As you too shall adore;
I could not love thee (Dear) so much,
Lov'd I not Honour more.


(1649)

# CHAPTER ONE



There must be *some* advantages to being a poor relation.

At the moment, Lucasta Lithwick couldn't think of a single one.

Poor relations could be summoned to London on the whim of a lady aunt who had never liked them, yanked from their cherished position teaching music at Miss Gregoire's Academy for Girls in Bath to chaperone a cousin they barely knew through her first Season. Cici had turned out to be delightful; the London Season, less so.

Of course, music abounded at the routs and ridottos, masques and balls, exhibitions and promenades. Even for one standing idle night after night on the fringes of fashionable drawing rooms, London flowed with music like wine at Carlton House. Lucasta drank it in like a satyr.

But poor relations were presumptuous if they expressed an interest in taking music lessons, or calling on musical personages, or attending one of the many private concerts that seemed always on offer and in which the lady aunt had no interest. They were not in London for their own amusement, mind, but expected to focus their entire attention on the duties for which they had been summoned and to which the claims of family obliged them, all while showing some gratitude for the condescension of said family to notice the offspring of a mother who had sunk herself beyond reproach.

Also, it was expected that poor relations would meekly appreciate the ill-fitting gowns that the lady aunt so kindly provided from her wardrobe, since, as her ladyship saw fit to observe, Lucasta had only the poorest, meanest possessions of her own.

Lucasta yanked at one side of her ruffled petticoat, which didn't want to hang properly over the outmoded pannier.

"Denied," she informed her friends, crowded with her near one end of Lady Clara Bellwether's drawing room. The conversational evening was giving way to dancing, and the young women without partners were obliged to make way for those with. "Expressly forbidden."

"She couldn't." Minnie jostled Lucasta's elbow as she flipped open her fan. "Signor Marchesi is the darling of Italian opera. He'll only be in England a few months."

"One of the finest voices on the European stage, and I cannot take lessons from him. He is too much admired, in my aunt's opinion, and I should look silly dangling after him."

Minnie smirked. "They say *castrati* are skilled in the amorous arts as well as the musical. She ought to be glad you have chosen such a safe target for your infatuation."

As the daughter of the Duke of Luneburg-Zuwecken, a high-ranking and wealthy official in the Hanoverian court, Minnie would never be a poor relation. She was also, given the great liberty of not living much in her home country, prone to speaking her mind.

Lucasta snorted. "Oh, certainly, I shall present that argument to my aunt. She will take it so well."

A quartet appeared and began tuning their instruments. Lucasta itched to lay her hands on one of the violins.

"Cici is such a taking little thing, she will have an offer soon." Selina watched with longing as the dancers formed squares for a cotillion. "Then perhaps Lady Pevensey will allow you more freedom."

Upon his retirement to Britain with his Bengali wife, John Humby of the 1st Bengal Light Calvary had been granted a knighthood and a pension that made Selina highly attractive to admiring suitors. That was, before an unfortunate event earlier in the Season had quite sunk her in the eyes of the *beau monde*.

Annis watched the dancers with cool disdain. "Has your aunt said why she wanted you in particular to chaperone Cici, when she hasn't given you a thought for years?"

Anastasia Voronska, Annis to her dearest friends, was the daughter of Count Voronsky, the Russian ambassador to Britain, and her aunt, a Russian princess, was one of Catherine the Great's closest confidantes. Annis would never be a poor relation, either.

"She called for me out of pity, poor orphan that I am, and she hopes some time in London might give me polish, and perhaps a chance at a husband," Lucasta said. "You should have seen her face when I informed her that, upon my return to Bath, I am hunting up premises for my musical conservatory."

Minnie laughed and linked an arm with Lucasta's. "I hope she will keep you through the Season, at least, for what a treat to have us all together again! Miss Gregoire's girls, unleashed on London. Did you hear they are calling us the Gorgons?"

"What?" Selina exclaimed. "Who would say such a thing?"

The second violin in the quartet came in half a beat behind the rest, and Lucasta set her teeth. "Smart Jeremy, *milord* Rudyard, of course. Who else?"

"The insult isn't even fitting," Minnie remarked. "The Gorgons were three sisters. We are four."

"*Are* there any mythical groups of four women?" Annis wondered. "There always seem to be three. Fates. Furies. Harpies. Graces. Norns, in Norse mythology."

Lucasta considered. "The Hesperides?"

"Hesiod only mentions three," Minnie said. "So does Apollonius of Rhodes."

"I'm quite sure some of the later vase paintings show four," Lucasta said. "The collection at the British Museum—"

"Gorgons?" Giving a low cry, Selina drew back her skirts as a dancer twirled by. "I suppose this is because Minnie insulted Lord Ashley at the Queen's drawing room. Or because Annis did not invite his cousin and aunt to the Count's dinner?"

"His aunt and cousin are still in half-mourning," Annis replied. "I did not imagine they could accept."

"This is because it is now the fashion to regard the utterances of Lord Rudyard as the proclamation of an oracle," Lucasta said. "And to believe because he has exquisite taste in dress, he is wise in other matters."

Selina forced a smile. "My striped *robe d'anglaise* did make me look like a zebra, I suppose."

Selina had begun the season as a prime catch, gracious, educated, the daughter of a distinguished officer. Then Rudyard called her a zebra. The gossips picked up the slur about her parentage—not black, not white, but something in between—and Selina dropped from favor like a coin tossed into the Thames.

"He told me my mink pelisse made me look sallow," Annis offered.

"He informed me I was too tall to wear heeled slippers," Minnie said. "I wish he would ask me to dance, so my heeled slippers might tread on his toe."

Selina fussed with the lace at her sleeve. "If we are laughed at, there will be no more offers of marriage. Mama will be so disappointed."

Despite Selina's brave face, Lucasta knew Rudyard's remark about her gown had cut her friend deeply. Lucasta slid an arm around the girl's waist and squeezed.

"I am very glad to have these weeks with you all, and I expect that by the end of the season, you will each have a proposal in hand. Or several."

Minnie shrugged. "If Gorgons they wish to call us, then Gorgons we shall be and turn any man who looks at us into stone."

"I propose a forfeit for the first of us who accepts an offer of marriage and thereby breaks up Miss Gregoire's Girls," Annis suggested.

"Oh, a forfeit." Minnie's eyes lit. "If it is Selina, she must write up her experiments on animal surgery."

"Oh, no, I could not presume." Selina glanced around in alarm, though as usual no one was taking any notice of them.

"Annis has to give a lecture on astronomy and the celestial mechanisms," Lucasta said, for the Russian girl had her head always in the heavens.

"With pleasure," Annis said with a slow smile.

"And mine?" Minnie demanded.

"You will publish your translations, of course," Lucasta said. "What are you working on at present?"

"A long chivalric poem in Middle High German, but it is not complete," Minnie said. "Nevertheless, I accept. And you, Lucasta?"

Lucasta watched the dancers move in their figures. She stood in the shadow of her more confident, more accomplished friends, her role in their group undefined. The four of them had come together at Miss Gregoire's because they felt outcasts everywhere else, in Lucasta's case because she was an orphan, and the other girls because they were thought foreign. But in standing together against indifferent assessments of their worth, beauty, or right to belong, bonds had formed, deeper than blood.

"You shall sing," Minnie said. "In public. For money."

Lucasta's heart sank like a stone in a still pool. "Great-aunt Cornelia says it is vulgar, and Aunt Pevensey agrees. I won't be allowed."

Annis lifted a dark brow. "The rest of us have accepted our forfeits."

Lucasta swallowed the bitter taste in her mouth, left by the most recent row with her aunt. In the Pevensey's rented townhouse, Lucasta was nothing but the daughter of an obscure vicar and a well-bred young woman whose family had disowned her upon her low marriage.

Vicars' daughters were not invited to sing at courts or theaters or the finest concert halls of Europe. She was not to dream of stepping onto a wooden stage beneath glittering chandeliers and gorgeous art, nor imagine she could hold an audience in thrall with her voice alone. It was not for vicars' daughters to lift hearts, wring tears, or transport their listeners to a place of perfect beauty, just this side of heaven.

Besides, a musical vocation demanded long study and constant practice. But Lady Pevensey would not permit lessons in London, and great Continental music masters did not linger long in Bath.

After years of spinning wild hopes, Lucasta was shut out of her great dream, just as she was shunned from the world of London's fashionable. Forced, like now, to stand on the periphery looking in, the spectator and never the subject, her spirits as heavy as her skirts.

Forced, as she always had been, to expect little, make do with less, and be grateful for the scraps doled out to her.

She summoned a smile. She would not pity herself when there were real misfortunes in the world, and she would keep her spleen to herself, let it poison her own breast and not that of her friends.

"Very well, to sing my forfeit shall be. Though I am the least likely to be obliged to pay it." For what suitor would see a prize in poor, plain, undistinguished Lucasta Lithwick?

"You can cheer us with some of your epigrams," Minnie suggested. "Or the broadsheet ballads you were composing at Ranelagh Gardens."

"They were terribly clever." Annis grinned.

"Oh, do amuse us," Selina said. "I am sorry Mama needed me at home that day."

"Does it not smack of sour grapes to disparage Lady Clara's guests simply because they do not invite us to dance?" Lucasta asked.

"We shall aim only at deserving targets." Minnie surveyed the gilded drawing room, crowded with lively dancers in the middle and spectators fanning themselves about the edge. She noted the young man changing places with Cici. "Plimpton."

Lucasta glanced aside to see who might overhear them. A group of dowagers stood at their right, and to the left, a large cluster of potted palms imported for the evening.

"The most worthy Ralph Plimpton," she said *sotto voce*. "A true sprig of knighthood, but he droops without his mother to prop him."

Selina giggled. "Lord Ashley."

"A credit to his name and the country," Lucasta said, warming to the game. "He can kiss his mistress in the morning, lose a fortune at cards in the evening, ride all day like the devil is on his heels, and shoot anything that will stand long enough for him to aim at it."

"Too true." Minnie sneered.

"Mallory," Annis volunteered as the pattern changed and Cici fluttered into the major's arms.

"Fortunate he has the bearing of a military man," said Lucasta. "Nothing else could excuse that waistcoat."

"Lord Rudyard," Annis murmured. "I saw him chatting with the Duchess of Highcastle but a moment ago."

"No doubt discussing the garish ostrich plumes on her turban."

Minnie snapped her fan in mock horror. "Not even you, Queen Lucasta, could find aught to disparage of milord Rudyard."

Selina bit her lip and looked down at her gown. Lucasta lifted her chin.

"Of course there is naught to disparage," she said. "He is handsomer than he should be, and so perhaps he cannot be faulted for being no better than he is."

"You fault him for being handsome?" Annis smiled.

"We should not behave as if he accomplishes something grand simply by looking well," Lucasta said. "Here is my verse for his lordship: Many a sorry burden was less, and many a hard lot eased, because the folds of his cravat fell exactly as he pleased!"

"Cat." Minnie tapped Lucasta on the wrist with her fan. "You are top-lofty now, but should he ask you to stand up with him, you would melt at his feet like the rest of us."

"I most decidedly would not," Lucasta replied. "No one petted him when he was Mr. Jeremiah Falstead, and no one should fawn over him now that a sudden turn of events has made his father heir to a marquessate. Besides, I should be afraid to melt and soil his expensive shoes."

Annis and Minnie laughed, but Selina shook her head. "It is too bad that his cousin should die so young. Such a handsome young man."

"You are right, my dear," Lucasta said, chastened by Selina's tender-heartedness. "It must have been a terrible blow for the family."

And it had made Rudyard disagreeable, dispensing insults. She would not, like him, become cruel.

"I will be rung a peal by Aunt Pevensey," Lucasta said, striving to lighten the moment, "since I have utterly lost track of Cici's partners. Ought I allow Mr. Plimpton to lead her out for the gavotte?"

"Lucasta," Annis murmured, "I believe someone else might have enjoyed our recent conversation." She nodded toward the cluster of potted plants.

Smart Jeremy stepped from behind a lemon tree, touching his cravat as if to be sure every bleached and intricate fold was in place.

Lucasta turned to stone. "Oh, good heavens. He must have heard every word I said."

He didn't look furious. He looked supremely at ease and perfectly gorgeous, from the powdered hair pulled back into a queue to the buckles of his heeled slippers. The luxurious claret red fabric of his suit molded the kind of figure men had in fashion plates, accented with glittering buttons and beguiling embroidery on the hems of his coat and breeches.

A man who took such care with his appearance ought to have the mincing manner of a studied fop, but Smart Jeremy moved as casually as if he had simply tossed together his ensemble and strolled out the door, and it had not taken hours to achieve his dazzling effect.

Lucasta curled her shoulders into the puffed sleeves of her gown, wishing she could sink beneath the panniers holding up the too-wide skirt.

"Did he pass behind us?" Minnie demanded. "What is he doing, sneaking about the edges of the room?" She held out her fan to Lucasta.

"Because the alternative is to get plowed down by the dancers." Lucasta waved the fan, trying to ease the sudden heat in her face. Just her luck that when she decided to speak her mind, she would be caught out at it.

"Perhaps he didn't hear us," Selina said. "It is quite noisy, with the chatter and the music."

"And that dratted second violin who can't keep time." The candles and lamps poured an overbright heat into the room, and the stomacher of her gown constricted her chest.

Aunt Pevensey lectured relentlessly on this point. With no beauty, no wealth, no birth, and no accomplishments, Lucasta would always be an object of pity. She must not add to the insult of these deficiencies by being forward, unpleasant, or a fool.

Lucasta, of course, could run and bury her shame in Bath. It was not as if she had prospects anyway. But she had insulted a man who held the power, with a few words, to shatter this world, not just for her friends but for Cici.

She squeezed the words out of a tight throat. "The question is not whether he heard me, but rather, having heard me, what does he mean to do?"

# CHAPTER TWO

_No better than he was._

Jem paused beside the lemon tree, a vantage point that let him survey the room and its avenues of escape. It also allowed him to glance about with seeming casualness and identify the young woman who had at last voiced what he suspected everyone in the entire upper classes of Britain had been thinking of him for months.

He found his hand resting over his racing heart and forced his fingers to relax. Mustn't crush his cravat. His valet would give notice if Jem were careless with his work.

The four young women stood clumped like a stand of exotic flowers in a field of cultivated English blooms. Heads close, sharing whispers, they laughed as if they hadn't a care in the world. Particularly her, the slim, quick-witted one who held herself like a queen in that awful green lutestring sack that was two decades out of fashion. What else did such girls have to do with their time but loiter at fashionable London soirees and dole out jests and insults?

It was the game everyone in this room played, including himself. He was trapped in this world now, like it or not.

Judith was going to get tangled in it, too, despite his best efforts. And girls like those, who mocked and derided—they would destroy his gentle sister. Like carrion crows that pecked a carcass to clean bone.

He ought to leave now, Jem thought, before his mood had a chance to worsen. He'd accomplished what he intended. He'd acknowledged his debt to Lady Clara by appearing at her *conversazione*. He'd admired the cut of the Duchess of Hunsdon's gown and gave the Duchess of Highcastle some discreet hints about replacing her turban with something more *à la mode*. Wise to leave before he could overhear further insults, or worse.

But against his better judgment he headed toward his friends, who stood where they could catch the footmen circulating with trays of drinks and ignore the hopeful stares of young ladies who wished to dance. His friends were the reason Jem had survived thus far in the gladiatorial field that was British high society when he was nothing but a tradesman, a draper's son, suddenly vaulting into the position of marquess's heir.

"It was the balloon flight at St. George's Field," Plimpton was saying. "She told me I was shaped like one."

"We were at Astley's when she told me the bear danced better than I did," Ashley said.

"Who did?" Jem asked. If his friends, who were considered prime catches, collected insults from the assorted company, then he had even less reason to feel rankled by the supposedly clever epigram one spiteful girl had composed about him.

Yet for some reason, rankle it did. *Handsomer than he should be*, she'd said. At least he'd achieved the handsome part. Little else he was good for in the eyes of anyone in this room.

"Who else lacks the ability to appreciate such fine gentlemen?" Ashley glared across the room at the same knot of girls Jem had just overheard discussing him. "Apt that you named them the Gorgons, Rudyard. A greater set of antidotes I've never seen."

"I did?" Jem startled as a passing footman, one gloved hand clasped above the tails of his coat, bowed and offered him a tray of champagne flutes. Such ceremony belonged at the marquess's house, a place Jem had never felt comfortable. He hurried to collect a glass so the footman could straighten and move away.

The man's suit of livery was a size too large, and his silver stockings had a snag. Jem would have to ask Lady Clara what service she had used to hire extra servants for the night, then stop round the office with his card.

As if summoned, their hostess glided into place beside him. She twirled gracefully to give Jem a look at her open robe of heavy cream over a petticoat of golden silk, fabrics straight from his warehouse.

"You invented the name, Rudyard," she reminded him, confirming his suspicion that, as was rumored, Lady Clara heard everything that went on in a room. "You said it at the Queen's levee."

"The Luneburg snubbed Ashley," Plimpton said helpfully. "And then me."

"And when Mallory said they were the set calling themselves the Gregory girls, or what not, you said we might as well call them Gorgons," Ashley said.

"And it appears the term has caught on." Lady Clara smiled. "They're considered quite odd and *outré*, so of course I had to invite them."

Jem's shoulders itched inside his coat, and he knew the blame was not the fine cambric of his shirt. Good Lord, he'd said one thing in passing, a jest to lighten the mood of his friend, and now it would stick for the Season?

The same way he'd been christened Smart Jeremy. He rather suspected Lady Clara was responsible for that sobriquet.

And what would stick to Judith, were he to bow to her pleas to let her circulate in society? Girls like the Gorgons would be ruthless with her fragility. And as for his other siblings, the ones he would prefer no one in this room to ever know about—far, far worse would await them in the man-traps of aristocratic circles.

"The one in that bilious green sack, which is an offense to the eye," Jem said, affecting a casual swallow of champagne. "If they are the Gorgons, does that make her the Medusa?"

Their hostess smiled at seeing Jem perform the role she had assigned him. Lady Clara Bellwether had appeared in Jem's shop about a year ago, one of the first wave of Society matrons inspecting the Marquess of Arendale's latest heir. The daughter of an earl and emerging from mourning her wealthy baronet, Clara had taken Jem's advice on fabrics, cut, and style, and the dashing results had made her a leader of fashion.

He had little doubt she made much of him purely for her own amusement and would cut him off at the knees the moment she displeased him, for no one in London's *haut ton* would forget he was a lowly linen draper's son no matter how many estates he inherited. Still, Clara was better than *The New Peerage* for knowing the composition of every ranking family and the secrets they hid behind closed doors.

He wondered how long he could keep his own doors closed against her.

"The one in green is Pevensey's niece," Lady Clara said. "Not by blood, but by his second wife, the one he has now. His children are by his first wife, and the daughter is the darling little nuthatch dancing with Mallory."

Jem probed his knowledge of the aristocracy. Pevensey was a minor baron, a fairly new creation who, like most of his class, was in debt to his tailor. The cloth for his daughter's presentation gown had come from Dixon & Co., Jem's warehouse. Jem accepted his invitation to the daughter's coming-out ball, made a remark about her dress that had been broadcast all over town, and watched in satisfaction as orders for that fabric multiplied in the days that followed.

It made him mercenary, but better a mercenary than a fool.

"And the niece's name?" Jem wondered who had allowed the girl out of the house in such attire. What business had she cutting other people down, wearing a gown like that? Even if gossip was the favored blood sport of English drawing rooms.

Lady Clara arched thin, painted brows. "You desire an introduction, Rudyard? But you never approach a woman."

Jem shrugged, his shoulders constrained by the fit of his evening coat. "I am only wondering who has charge of the young lady's wardrobe."

Clara laughed. "That is Miss Lucasta Lithwick, and no one will make a pattern of *her*."

Lucasta. An unusual name. It had a ring of enchantment about it, though Jem would never say so aloud.

Clara went on with relish. "We all wondered why Lady Pevensey would trot her niece out from the boarding school where she'd been stowed to play companion to Miss Pevensey this Season. The family is landed—milady Pevensey's nephew is the latest Viscount Frotheringale, if you didn't know." Jem didn't.

"But her ladyship's sister was scored from the family Bible when she insisted on standing up with a poor foreign-born vicar with nothing but the clothes on her back. Can you imagine? Old Frotheringale was furious, and the dowager held her grudge even after the scandalous sister died. However, I just heard something curious from Lady Cranbury."

Ashley and Plimpton leaned in, as avid for gossip as any bored matron. Against his will Jem bent toward Clara as well.

"The girl's great-aunt, old Frotheringale's sister, Lady Evers, as she's styled now." Clara gave Jem a knowing look, and he nodded, though he had already given up trying to sort out the familial complexities. "She's amassed quite a fortune from all her marriages, and she told the Dowager Viscountess Frotheringale that she means to leave everything to her grand-niece." Clara paused dramatically. "Miss Lithwick is about to become *very* interesting."

"How large a fortune?" Plimpton demanded.

Jem blessed his friend for the question, since it would look too crass in him to ask. Titled gentlemen evaluating a lady for her dowry was acceptable in these circles; a tradesman cultivating business interests was not.

Clara paused, which meant she didn't know and was calculating exactly how interesting she wanted Miss Lucasta Lithwick to become. "A great deal."

Jem straightened. He'd gained the Pevensey custom, but he didn't know how much those coffers contained. Tradesmen talked, and Lord Pevensey was in debt everywhere.

The Frotheringales, however, were uncharted territory. If his shops were to style a viscount's cousin, that might lead to styling the viscountess, and the new viscount, and in time the new viscount's bride. And if they had friends in even higher positions of wealth and influence—there were vast opportunities there.

"Why then, someone ought to advise Miss Lithwick on matters of fashion," Jem drawled. "And who better than I?"

Lady Clara's gaze narrowed on him, and Jem detected a flash of anger. He wondered why. Because he was acting the common tradesman again?

"I suppose a linen draper's son would know," Clara said silkily. "It is such a shame your family should lose Cadmus, and so soon after that Lord Payne—the late Lord Payne, I mean to say. I am sure Lady Payne is simply devastated."

Jem jerked his head, heat choking his throat. *Cadmus.* His cousin's death still didn't feel real. Impossible to believe his friend, his champion, the bright, laughing boy he'd always looked up to was gone, and struck down by something so common as typhus.

Aunt Payne was indeed devastated, and not only to lose her heir and her hopes for a secure future. She was mortified. For now the Marquess of Arendale's third and most feckless son would inherit, the one who had injured the family by marrying a linen draper's daughter so he might continue to fund his extravagant lifestyle after his father cut him off. The son who'd been dispatched halfway across the world to be governor of Barbados, where it was hoped his excesses could be contained, was now by courtesy the Earl Payne.

And Jem was, by courtesy, the Viscount Rudyard.

His temples throbbed. He would reverse his fate if he could.

By rights and the light of a just God, Cadmus should still be alive, Arendale's heir. And Jem should be Mr. Jeremiah Falstead, linen draper and clothier, overseeing the business his mother had bequeathed him. Tending the enormous warehouse in Cheapside, running the shop in Piccadilly near the fashionable shopping districts of Bond Street and Pall Mall, traveling to Ireland and the Continent to meet wholesalers and find weavers making new types of cloth.

A year ago, he was an embarrassment to the family and to the aristocratic world at large, of no interest to those of *ton* beyond the orders their dressmakers and tailors placed with him. But now he was Smart Jeremy, fashion's leader and oracle. Now he was Arendale's eventual heir, for the new Earl Payne had no other legal sons. Now he was of great interest to the circles that had been happy to pretend he didn't exist.

"Your mourning is over, is it not, Rudyard?" Clara speculated. "High time you brought Judith out, I should say. She must be of age, and I can't think why you've hidden her from us all this time. Unless—I had heard there is some affliction?"

Jem stiffened his back. His cravat strangled. He would have a word with his valet about binding him up so tightly.

"Judith is in perfect health, thank you." He'd never mentioned his sister's name to Clara.

Ashley and Plimpton both stared, wide-eyed and ears perked. Jem never talked about his family to them, either.

"And your father—will he stay in the West Indies?" Clara lifted a glass of champagne from a passing tray. "I should suppose the new Earl Payne would be happy to return to London and his old larks. He cuts quite a figure, doesn't he?"

Jim swallowed the bile that rose every time he thought of his father. "I expect my father will continue at his post. My grandfather has competent stewards, and my father has never been interested in estate management."

Gerald Falstead had never been interested in anything but his own amusement. Not the business he'd married into; not the wife who brought him wealth; and certainly not his children, whom he considered his wife's charge.

When two of those children grew ill and died of fever, their father hadn't been there to console his wife or his remaining progeny. He'd sent regrets from the house party where he was staying for some fine shooting and, it was rumored, his latest mistress.

There were many things for which Jem would never forgive his father, but that was the first betrayal. That was the lesson that taught young Jem to have no faith that anyone else would look after him. He'd seen what little he could do to protect his darling mother, who knew what her husband was and carried on with her head held high to the end of her life. After that, Jem had no one to depend on but himself.

And he'd learned to let nothing of his vulnerabilities show to the world. Ever.

"Hmm." Lady Clara sipped from her glass. "Well, I don't doubt there is much in the Caribbean to amuse." A smile creased her rouged cheeks. "A returning ship captain, I can't remember who it was now—oh! a certain Captain Noble—he said, from what he observed, your father was enjoying the many accommodations of the island." She gave Jem a saucy wink. "*Very* accommodating."

Ashley laughed. "Some of the most beautiful women in the world, so they say." He raised his glass to the absent Falstead sire.

Jem's scalp prickled with an uncomfortable combination of pomade and powder. How much did Clara know? Jem had paid Captain Noble handsomely, along with the owner of the *Brook*, to convey certain passengers from the West Indies to Liverpool without any discussion of their origin, destination, or identities. Had Noble talked?

Or perhaps, as Aunt Payne had threatened, it truly would be impossible for Jem to keep the extent of his father's peccadillos from the prying eyes of London's gossips. She had warned him that bringing the children to London would ensure they were exposed, and she had assured Jem she would never survive the shame.

Jem downed the rest of his champagne with a quick jerk of his wrist. If the trap was about to spring around Judith and the rest of them, then he had no time to lose. He couldn't afford to be mocked or sow rancor among the higher echelons. He might be the grandson of a marquess, but his courtesy title was not enough to shield his siblings from the sneers and judgments that would surely follow their exposure to the so-called Polite World.

But if he had real power, he could protect them. The kind of power afforded by immense wealth. The slings and arrows of the narrow-minded could bruise, but as long as he had a livelihood, he could keep them from material want. The richer he was, the better chance they would be accepted, for what was reviled in the middle class was turned a blind eye in the upper.

Look at how the royal princes behaved, and no one dared cut them.

They'd dare cut any bastard children the princes sired, however.

"My thanks, Lady Clara. You've been scintillating, as usual." Jem took her empty glass and, with his, checked a passing footman to plant both flutes on his tray. The man's eyes widened as he felt the vehemence in the gesture, but he said nothing.

Jem glanced again toward the Gorgons, standing beneath an enormous portrait of the late Sir Egbert Bellwether's favorite horse.

Lucasta Lithwick. Orphaned daughter of an obscure vicar, the embarrassing fringe of an important family. Whose only weapons in this world were her wits and her tongue. And who stood, whether she knew it or not, in the path of a fortune.

She must not know, or she could never turn herself out in that awful sack gown, with its mutilating accents of burnt orange against a green that had turned sickly in the decades since it had gone out of style. Her hair was handsomely arranged in a tower of powdered curls, and she held herself well, an arrogant thrust to that pointed chin. He watched her lips curve, her eyes light as she whispered and laughed with her friends.

No doubt doling out more insults for their amusement. Jem shook off the moment of fascination and set his teeth. It was time to end this silly feud that had escalated between his friends and hers. Ashley might nurse a grudge for years if the Luneburg disparaged him, but Jem couldn't afford petty quarrels. He had been thrust unwilling into this world, but he would fight its snares as long as he could.

This world had spoiled his father and killed his mother. It would ravage Judith bit by bit until there was nothing left of her kind, sweet spirit. Unless Jem could protect her.

He skimmed a hand over his cravat, checking to ensure its precision. He might hate the name Smart Jeremy, aware of the taunt that lay within the supposedly admiring epithet. But there was a power, too, in having his every word tattled to the gossip circles and society papers. Oracles, after all, could prophesy great success or great doom. He was curious to see just how much power Smart Jeremy wielded.

"Where are you charging off to, old boy?" Plimpton called as Jem strode away from them with the briefest of bows.

"To settle a score," Jem called over his shoulder. "If the Medusa is to insult me, I want her to say it to my face."

# CHAPTER THREE

I t appeared Lord Rudyard, if he had heard Lucasta's remark, did not intend to acknowledge it.

He did, however, intercept Major Mallory as he escorted Cici from the floor. Even from a distance, Lucasta detected the light in Cici's eyes as Smart Jeremy addressed her.

She also noted the light of interest in many other stares.

"Now what is the man about?" Lucasta muttered.

Selina's eyes widened. "But everyone knows Lord Rudyard does not dance."

Lucasta gnawed a fingertip of her glove. Smart Jeremy did not flirt, he did not dangle, and he did not flatter. His gravitas was the reason his pronouncements on matters of dress were taken as objective truth. What interest could he have in Cici?

Informing her, perhaps, that Lucasta was behaving like a spiteful cat and needed to be taken in hand. Aunt Pevensey would relish the proof of Lucasta's ill breeding. No doubt she had the lecture prepared, the whip coiled and ready.

Smart Jeremy might simply be drawn to Cici's glowing vivacity. The girl was tiny and quick as a sparrow, with bright, sparkling blue eyes and curls of polished gold.

"Perhaps he is remarking how well that honey silk robe flatters her complexion," Minnie suggested.

"I would have guessed Lady P would put her in nothing but white all season," Annis said. "After Rudyard complimented her gown at her come-out ball."

"If Aunt Pevensey had her way, she would. Cici had to fight to get a gown made in anything other than ivory. I believe they bought the fabric from his shop."

That foray had transpired before his comment on Selina's gown, before Lucasta had good reason to take Smart Jeremy in dislike. She had cried off the excursion anyway, on principle that she had no need of new gowns since her aunt had so generously supplied her from her trunks in the attic. Instead she had had whisked round to the bookshop for sheet music for a cantata by Johann Christian, the son they called the London Bach, finally being published after his death.

Lady Cranbury detached herself from the group of dowagers beside them and steered in their direction. Her friends fell back in awe as her ladyship fixed her cold, sharp eye on Lucasta. Lady Cranbury was one of the more stately and terrifying matrons of London society, an established arbiter of *ton*, and in a dead heat with Lady Clara to be the town's most informed gossip.

"Miss Voronsky, I congratulate you on the Count's dinner. You laid an excellent table and did a creditable job hosting so many important guests."

Annis dipped a polite curtsey. "Thank you, milady."

"And the four of you provided a quite charming entertainment with your little quartets," her ladyship went on. "I always enjoy Haydn."

Lucasta glowed with pride. *She* had written the quartets they performed. She was a far cry from Haydn, but if Lady Cranbury could not perceive the difference, she was not about to correct her. "Thank you, milady."

"Your voice isn't terrible." Lady Cranbury studied Lucasta. "In fact I wanted you for a little musical evening I am putting together, something to amuse my nephew when he visits. But your aunt tells me you are too modest to perform before strangers."

Lucasta felt as if she'd blown too long on a hautboy and made herself light-headed. Lady Cranbury had a Cristofori pianoforte in her drawing room that Lucasta would give anything to play.

Surely vicars' daughters might perform at small, private musical evenings for genteel guests. Surely her aunt could allow her that much?

"But I am not," Lucasta said. "Overmodest, that is."

"I took the liberty of pointing out that you played the cello not half badly at Count Voronsky's dinner, and your aunt became quite querulous with me. Almost as if she'd had no idea you'd performed there. At any rate, she insisted you were unavailable."

Lady Cranbury raised her quizzing glass and inspected Selina, who wore a mantua gown of copper silk with a pattern of twining roses. No more stripes for Selina.

"Glad to see you're bearing up, girl," her ladyship said. "I told Clara she must invite you. Some pity must be shown to the daughter of an officer."

Selina's cheeks flushed with deep color. "Th-thank you, milady."

Lucasta bit her lip till it smarted. Selina had been admired, not pitied, before Smart Jeremy decided to cut her. A man could turn marquess's heir and at a stroke destroy lives with his new power, and who would stand to stop him?

And now he had Cici in his sights. She drifted toward them on the arm of the Major, Rudyard strolling alongside, a lion on the prowl, king of all he surveyed.

"Your aunt will be pleased by Rudyard's attentions to Miss Pevensey," Lady Cranbury said. "Mark me, it would make quite a conquest if your cousin snared him. I wonder if the marquess is insisting he marry? With Payne overseas, someone must be trained up as heir. I know of estates in Dorset and Wiltshire as well as the land in the West Indies, and Arendale is quite beautiful, for all it is so far in the north."

Lucasta had arrived in London prepared to find Cecilia, Baron Pevensey's daughter by his first wife, quite as vexed at the idea of having Lucasta for a chaperone as Lucasta had been vexed to leave her music. Instead, she found a charming, utterly artless girl who had won Lucasta's heart and provided a singular source of warmth under the Pevenseys' cold roof.

"Though she won't catch anyone above a second son with a dowry of five thousand pounds," Lady Cranbury said. "Pevensey should make it ten if he wants to tempt Rudyard."

"Cici is quite gifted with her watercolors," Lucasta said. "And musically inclined as well. She has perfect pitch."

"Dear girl, a woman need only cultivate her looks until the marriage contract is signed and the vows exchanged," Lady Cranbury said. "But of course you must interest yourself in how high Miss Pevensey might marry. Your future, after all, depends on how willing her husband is to support his wife's relations."

Lucasta curled her fist around the blades of Minnie's fan. "But I intend to support myself, milady, with the students in the musical conservatory I plan to establish in Bath."

Her ladyship's answer to this was a decidedly unladylike snort. "How droll. And what will Lady Evers say to see a grand niece of hers turning to trade, like a farmer." She patted Lucasta's arm. "For your sake, child, hope your cousin marries well and secures a place for you. Rudyard." Her ladyship turned her quizzing glass on the approaching trio.

Rudyard bowed. He was graceful, and that, with his height, contributed to his fine figure. He wasn't portly or stuffed into his suit, like some dandies in the room. Instead he was a tailor's dream, broad of shoulder, long of leg, with a narrow waist that some men wore corsets to achieve. Lucasta doubted that he did.

"Tell us what you think of Miss Pevensey's robe," Lady Cranbury demanded.

The corners of his eyes tightened slightly, as if he disliked the request. Lucasta found that curious. He lived for people hanging on the judgments that dripped from his poisonous lips, did he not?

Only his mouth didn't look poisonous. His lips were rather shapely, for a man's.

"The color becomes her, as I am sure she knows," Rudyard said with a small smile at Cici. Curse him for trying to enchant her!

"More so than white?" Cici peeped from behind her fan, her lips turned up in a merry smile. "For we must have this settled, you know. My stepmother wishes to feel she is exactly informed about your preference."

That tightness about his eyes again, there and gone. "I do hope your stepmother will place more value on your preferences than mine."

"You have not remarked *my* gown, Rudyard." Lady Cranbury's gown with its cascading skirts, tight bodice, and loose ruffled sleeves looked much like Lucasta's, but with a green and pink combination to insult the eye, rather than green and orange. "Yet I am quite sure you admired Clara's frock."

He bowed again. "There can be no comparison, your ladyship. Lady Clara could never carry off court dress at an informal evening."

"I'm going to tell the Duchess of Highcastle you approve of me," Lady Cranbury cackled. "I heard you hated her headdress." And she sailed off in triumph to bandy Smart Jeremy's latest decree about the room.

Rudyard's assessing gaze moved to Lucasta, and the hair on the back of her neck lifted, the sensation that hit her when she stepped before an audience to sing. That same sense of thrilling expectation, of being awake, alert, and fully alive.

"Miss Pevensey," he drawled. "I have not the honor of being known to your companion."

His rich, deep baritone sent a shiver down Lucasta's spine. He'd run her to ground, like a predator, and now the slaughter could begin.

She straightened her shoulders and waited. She'd brought this on herself, after all. And if he destroyed her gown, and her inside it, perhaps the gossips would focus on that instead of his malice about Selina.

Major Mallory undertook the courtesies. "Miss Lithwick, allow me to present to you the Viscount Rudyard. Rudyard, Miss Lithwick."

Automatically she extended her hand. "How do you do."

"A pleasure." He bent over her hand. As if she were a lady of consequence.

She wished his gloved fingers did not grip hers with such firm warmth. She wished he would not regard her so steadily. Jeremiah Falstead possessed a gaze of penetrating intensity, and his voice poured over her like warmed honey. She felt struck over the head, that voice left ringing in her ear, resonant as a bell.

A screech cut across his next words.

"I beg your pardon," Lucasta said. "That second violin. He has the most gorgeous instrument, I would guess it is an Amati, yet he plays it like a country fiddle."

"I asked if you would honor me with a dance." Rudyard led her toward the center of the room before she thought up a refusal.

He had cut her neatly away from her friends and any hope of defense. Minnie looked haughty, Annis amused, Selina full of longing, and Cici was being led out again by Major Mallory. Was that their second dance, or the third?

Rudyard stepped them into a circle with another couple before Lucasta realized. "I ought not dance, milord. I have not been presented."

"I was given to understand that such rules are relaxed if we are in a private home." He turned to face her, all feral elegance.

He did not have the powdered, polished complexion of a man who spent his days indoors, sleeping off a night of dissipation. He possessed the physique of a man who engaged in regular physical activity.

And his voice was nothing like honey. Rather a rich, creamy damask silk that she wanted to rub her hands and face in.

She must not add foolishness to her other deficiencies. Lucasta could cut her hair, throw on breeches, and run away to the stage, but this was the world Cici inhabited, that her friends needed to navigate. Lucasta could not stoop so low that they would suffer from association with her.

"I particularly do not know the allemande," Lucasta warned as the music commenced. It was a dance that would require them not only to touch but to intimately intertwine their arms. No man save her father had touched her person beyond the remotest extremities.

"Yet here we are." One of his brows rose, the color of chocolate, and she wondered if his hair was that color also. The color of the plowed fields about the vicar's cottage before the wheat was planted in the spring. The sight brought a pang to her chest, a yearning for that long-gone home.

"Ah, well. It is not as if I shall be admitted to Almack's anyway." She didn't need to glance about the room to know a great number of people were staring at them. At Lord Rudyard, dancing with *her*.

If only she knew why.

"Do you desire entrée to Almack's?" he asked.

"No. I mean, yes, as Cici wishes to go."

"But you do not?"

"The question is moot, as my aunt has not been supplied with vouchers." She concentrated on her steps, biting her lip. "What else do you wish to know about Cici?"

One corner of his mouth quirked. He did have the most pleasing arrangement of features. She'd been right to call him too handsome for his own good. "Are you interrogating me about your cousin?"

"Are you not here to learn what you can from me? Why else lead me out?"

They twined arms to turn in a figure, and Lucasta focused on her feet rather than the brief press of their bodies. She must not give rein to her sharp tongue. When the *passé* brought her about to face him, his lips quirked in a smile, unamused.

"If I wished to pursue an acquaintance with Miss Pevensey, one imagines I would address her."

His guard was up. The cool reserve he'd held with Lady Cranbury had slipped for a moment, but it was back now. He thought *she* meant to use their dance to throw Cici at his head.

For he was Rudyard now, and in possession of every virtue an ambitious mama could desire. Heir to grand estates and a title, not known to be profligate or of questionable habits, young, healthy, and not, she could grudgingly concede, a horror to the eye. Every matron in the room with a marriageable daughter would be taking a crack at him.

And he'd caught Lucasta evaluating him, but that was what one did at these functions. An insult from her could not reach him, high as he was, though through no deserving of his own. She was a flea biting the hock of a draught horse, a fly buzzing the ear of the King.

Besides, she'd merely accused him of caring too much about his appearance. He'd named Miss Gregoire's girls Gorgons.

Though she had to admit there was a certain pleasure in being thought fearsome, and the girls were like to adopt the label for themselves.

He had called Selina a zebra. Lucasta reminded herself of this as the dance turned her away from his too-keen regard. He held the common narrow bigotry of his class, and all the power with which the upper circles suffocated those of whom they disapproved.

Lucasta was glad her mother had left that shallow world for a life of deep contentment with her father. She was glad she'd been raised in what anyone in this room would consider abject poverty. The Season in London was a circus tightrope, everyone performing the same tricks, everyone watching one another, eager for a slip or a fall. And the scales weighed not one's character or actions, but one's appearance, charm, and pounds of income a year.

"I have lost you in thought," Rudyard remarked as the figure brought them together.

"I was only thinking of something Lady Cranbury said,"

Lucasta said, watching the other dancers to follow their steps. "About how high my cousin might marry. She possesses all the usual accomplishments, in spades. She sings, she plays, she paints, she embroiders, but all that others weigh of her is her dowry and her name."

"That is the way things are done, I observe. Her father, the Baron, hinted to me at her come-out ball that she would make an excellent little wife."

Lucasta frowned. "She is a dear, soft-hearted girl, and her one wish in the world is to have lots of babies. But she is seventeen, too young to be considering such a decision as marriage. Though young enough to be taken advantage of by those older and far more jaded than she."

"Suitors like me, do you mean?" His shoulders went taut, his arm stiffening as he turned about, his expression bland when he faced her once more. "Very well, if you insist, I'm afraid the Baron must be disappointed."

Lucasta could have cried with relief. He would overlook Cici. He had as much as promised, and gentlemen were absurd about keeping their word.

That did not mean anyone else was safe from him, however.

"But would you desire vouchers to Almack's nevertheless?" he said in that silky voice. "I could secure them for you."

"I was not aware you had been made a patroness of Almack's," Lucasta said without thinking.

He laughed, and she flushed with mortification as heads turned in their direction. Everyone would think she was flirting with Smart Jeremy. Her friends would think she was flirting with Smart Jeremy.

Selina would think Lucasta was flirting with Smart Jeremy. After what he had said, and done, to Selina.

"I might be able to procure you a Stranger's Ticket," Rudyard said. "Or I could speak to Lady Hillsborough about dispensing vouchers of your own. We happen to be friends."

Of course she should want vouchers to Almack's, a venue to

see and be seen, a visible stamp of approval of one's breeding and welcome among higher circles. She hoped Aunt Pevensey, or Cici, never learned that Lucasta had scorned to take a gift from Smart Jeremy's hands. But the further he stayed from her cousin, the safer she'd be.

Lucasta gave him a stony look. "I wonder what other items you are able to procure outside of the usual means, milord? Tea? Chocolate? French champagne?"

"You think me one of those wily merchants who avoids paying customs duty and excise tax?" He bared his teeth in a smile. "A shame, I suppose, that I am no better than I should be."

She was expecting the thrust, and yet his softly whispered blow took her off guard. Lucasta stumbled, right there in the steps of the allemande, before all of Lady Clara's guests. She saw the gulf of shame rising up to meet her as she began to fall—as she'd vowed she would never do—at Smart Jeremy's feet.

HE COULD HAVE his revenge right here. All he had to do was let go. Though she had managed to keep in graceful step with him, it was clear she was not practiced at the dance, though only a shade less acquainted than himself. Her hand on his arm was the lightest brush, as if she disdained to touch him. He could simply let her fall, and she would never recover from the humiliation of tripping over her feet in Clara Bellwether's parlor.

He guessed she was too proud to bear any sort of embarrassment. The gossips would feast on her, and the titters would follow her to every social function hereafter.

Just as the name Smart Jeremy followed him.

He caught her hand and stepped close, pulling her against him and into the turn. He looked down—he did not have to look far, she was so tall—to see that her cheeks had gone scarlet, as if splattered with paint.

Her face was wonderfully transparent, betraying every

emotion that dashed through her: fear, mortification, annoyance, and surprise. He waited for remorse. She might mock him for following fashion, but he was still Arendale's heir. Even Lady Cranbury, who had been one of the loudest detractors of Gerald Falstead's choice to knit himself to a tradesman's daughter, had demanded Jem's approval of her dress.

Miss Lithwick gained her balance and tried tugging her hand from his. Jem tightened his grip so she might not leave him standing alone on the dance floor. The humiliation would be his, if she did. Everyone would assume he had insulted *her*.

"You said it, and I heard you," he said softly. "So stay and face me."

He could see the calculation taking place: to grovel, beg his forgiveness, attempt to gain his favor, like all the others who scorned him behind his back and smiled to his front.

She raised her steady gaze to him, and her scowl said she wasn't the least repentant.

"You run a grave risk, milord Rudyard. Medusa turned any man she looked upon to stone."

She was going to brazen it out, the minx. To own what she said, and take the consequences. How rare, for a woman.

"Is there more you wish to say? I thought your epigram quite clever, by the by."

She did strike him as intelligent. Her eyes held a lively sparkle and an unusual blend of color, streaks of green and gold standing out among the darker brown. While her hair was powdered gray, her black brows and lashes were dark against her slightly olive skin. In poor-fitting gowns she could in no way be mistaken for a leader of fashion, but in the right dress, she could be. She had the bearing to carry off almost anything.

"I suppose none of us are as good as we could be," she said calmly, starting another *passé* before it was time. Gently he steered her back into the correct figure.

She was not inclined to about-face and grovel at his feet. Her deepening scowl said she would carry her point to the last and die upon it. Of all the people in this room, only his friends cared enough to challenge Jem on his pretensions. He couldn't hide his delight.

"Shall we call a truce? A peace between our peoples. I will stop Ashley complaining about your friends, and we will not allow people to refer to you as—" He almost said *Gorgons*. That would not go over well. "As anything less than a set of delightful young ladies."

"I do not think a truce is possible, milord," she said in a flat tone.

Alarm jumped in his chest. Her epigram *had* been clever. And gossips loved clever. If her remark were taken up and repeated everywhere—as remarks so easily were—she could lead others to decide that Smart Jeremy was another pompous, useless dandy.

The turn back to society's disapproval would be swift and devastating. He would lose custom from the upper class, so ready to sneer at him, and the ambitious middle classes followed where their betters led.

And without the barrier of wealth, he would have nothing with which to protect Judith and the others. His title offered flimsy protection, his father, none. Lady Clara's barbed probes had made that clear.

Jem set his teeth. "You cannot forgive me for caring about the folds of my cravat, I see. Or that I behave as if it were a grand accomplishment to look well?"

"I cannot forgive you for not lessening burdens where you may," she answered.

"You do not think it a service to help people turn out at their best? Or perhaps you think, with my business, I should be doing more to help the less fortunate." In fact he contributed to several charitable causes, but no one in this room cared to look past surfaces far enough to see that.

"I do not think you consider the effect of your words." Her tone was low and serious, and she looked him straight in the eye. "Any more than I did. Yet one should be judged not by appearance, but by actions. You have helped me see that, so I thank you. Milord."

A hot, white bolt of fury scorched a path through his body, as if he had been stung by some giant scorpion. Jem clenched his teeth. She knew nothing about him, had no basis for fair judgment, and yet her contempt was palpable. If she mocked him for his hypocrisy, for hating this social world even as he tried to use it to his advantage, how much harder would her scorn fall on Judith, about whom she would find even more to disdain?

*She* was the cruel one, with her petty insults and mockery. He was not out to damage but to correct. She and the Gorgons would be the first to flay Judith if he ever made the grave error of presenting her in these circles.

She shook off his hand, making him aware that his grip on her had tightened, that for some reason he was pulling her closer to him. He let go instantly.

"I do not have the power you grant me," he said, the words grating through his teeth.

The admission went against his ingrained reserve, every defense Jem had built against his father and his father's world. Why he would expose his vulnerability to this woman, Jem had no idea. It was an act of madness.

Her eyes narrowed, gold gleaming within the dark brown. "I think you mistake that, too."

The music ended and the crowd around them finished the dance, making Rudyard aware that they'd been standing, locked in battle, in the middle of the room, exposed to all eyes. He took her arm and led her back to her friends.

"Miss Lithwick," he said with a brief bow. "I strive not to give ear to the gossip of idle tongues. But I do hope I might prove, at least, I am better than you think me."

He wanted her good opinion, and hated himself for currying to anybody. But the Frotheringale fortune would be good custom for his shop. He must make himself stoop, again and again, because his wealth was Judith's shield.

Miss Lithwick drew away from him and took her cousin's hand as the Major returned. As if she feared Jem would set upon the girl despite her warnings.

"Good evening, sir," she said, and the Gorgons closed ranks about her.

Jem headed for Lady Clara, holding forth with a set of merry widows who were doing their best to become as dashing and influential as she had made herself. He nodded and smiled, a plan of revenge forming in his head. It was perfect, really. Like a Greek tragedy, the hero's destruction brought about through his own fatal flaw.

Lucasta Lithwick thought him at best useless and, at his worst, vain and petty. And yet she must know she was about to suffer the same rise as he had, vaulting from a poor vicar's daughter to an heiress. She would see what it was like to walk the hot coals of society's approval, every part of her life subjected to ruthless interrogation, whether she wanted it seen or not.

He would simply give her a nudge onto the pedestal. If, indeed, Smart Jeremy had the power to bring someone into fashion, then he would do so for her.

And if she toppled from the pedestal—if she shrank from the cold scrutiny, crumpled before the relentless gossip, bled from a thousand tiny cuts of disdain—well, it was no better than Judith could ever expect, no worse than many a debutante before her had endured, and none of his doing.

"By my word, Rudyard dancing! And in my parlor. I am quite overcome with triumph." Lady Clara swatted Jem with her fan. "And with none other than Miss Lithwick. What was it you called her again? A Gorgon? I hope she did not turn you to stone over Miss Pevensey, who is quite a taking little thing."

"I danced with Miss Lithwick on her own merits," Jem said with a lazy smile. "And as for a Gorgon, I cannot think of an epithet less fitting."

"You called her Medusa," said Clara, with a quick, sharp look. Her companions tittered, and Jem knew how the barb had already reached Lucasta Lithwick's ears. One more reason for her to spite him as she had.

He would return the favor. "If I have been transfixed," Jem said in his smoothest voice, "then it is with awe. Miss Lucasta Lithwick is the most clever, the most interesting, the most *fascinating* woman I have ever met."

# CHAPTER FOUR

He called her clever.

He called her interesting.

He called her *fascinating!*

The gossip flew with the first post across London's fashionable streets and squares, landing on the trays of matrons taking their breakfast in bed and beside the plates of debutantes searching the morning papers for admiring mentions of themselves along with descriptions of their rivals' dress.

Lady Pevensey, a pile of delicate ruffles in her morning gown and cap, wore a deepening frown as she sorted through the stack of letters growing beside her plate in the small dining parlor.

"Lord Rudyard called you clever? You, Lucasta? I own, I heard in the card room last night that someone had praised you, but I could not credit it."

Lucasta buttered a slice of toast she was determined to force down her throat to fortify herself for the round of morning calls. She eyed the stack of foolscap, wanting, and dreading, to know what tale the watchers would tell of her interactions with Lord Rudyard the evening before.

Or rather, what slant her aunt would put on Lucasta's bid to depress the pretensions of a man lauded for handing down lofty judgments. She, a vicar's daughter, twitting a marquess's heir.

At the time, she had thought herself striking a blow for Selina. But she might well have stuck a crack in the thin veneer upon which her status in this world, and her place in this family, rested.

Her hopes of a music conservatory rested on that same thin veneer.

"I would not credit that Lord Rudyard said anything of me," Lucasta said. "He was too busy making mischief for everyone else."

He had named her Medusa. Before, she had simply been invisible. Now he had made her an antidote. Prospective students would hesitate to approach her. Prospective students' wealthy parents would imagine she was difficult.

Damn, *damn* the man and his silk-thick voice and his intoxicating brandy eyes.

"He called you interesting." Aunt Pevensey moved a note to peer at the one below. "He called you *fascinating*! Good heavens, Lucasta, what did you say to him?"

Lucasta swallowed her toast like a burning sword. "Nothing of note, I vow."

Cici handed over the gossip columns she had been devouring while her father hid behind the corn prices and news. Her bright blue eyes danced with merriment.

"You did something to captivate him and everyone, cousin. Only look what else they are saying!"

Lucasta scanned the morning papers, her heart quailing with each word. Smart Jeremy had danced with and commended a woman—and not just any woman. It defied imagination to know what had caught his eye, for Miss L—L—, daughter of a vicar of unknown provenance and but the smallest distinction, had no discernable assets. She did not possess the curly hair, blue eyes, and luminescent skin that heralded beauty. She was not rich. She did not dance divinely, she did not dress in the first stare of fashion, and there had not been a single expression of interest in her by any gentlemen thus far.

Yet after one dance, something had led Lord Rudyard, whom everyone agreed had the most impeccable taste and the most beautiful manners, to pronounce Miss L— enchanting. The society columns had pounced on this latest declaration from the town's leading maker of fashion, and the cartoonists would not be far behind with their lampoons.

The bite of toast sat heavy in Lucasta's stomach. He was mocking her, knowing the town gossips would hoist her on their own petard. As usual, he had pulled his insult off beautifully.

Better all around if she had remained invisible.

A knock sounded on the front door, and a few moments later the butler proceeded into the small dining room to deliver another set of notes to his mistress. Aunt reread the latest missive, her eyes round as spoons.

"And here is a note from Clara Bellwether saying how delighted she is that her drawing room should be the scene of this riveting interchange. "For I flatter myself," Aunt read, "that I meant to introduce them, since as soon as you came through, I saw that your Lucasta has quite a queenly air. At the time I could not conscience it in a vicar's daughter, but I thought to myself, I must introduce this one to Rudyard—I should think he might take an interest. And so he did."

Scowling, Lady Pevensey laid the note aside and took up another. "And it seems Lady Cranbury credits herself for having encouraged you, Lucasta, to make the best account of yourself. 'For I said to her, indeed I did, that if she could only hope to be taken in by Miss Pevensey's eventual husband, then she should hope it were someone like Rudyard, with a secure income and status. Indeed, she must have taken my words to heart. I do wonder what she did to attract his notice, don't you?'"

Lady Pevensey regarded her stepdaughter. "Rudyard did not ask *you* to dance, Cecilia? You could not have turned him down."

"I did not, *belle-mére*." Cici smiled innocently. "Lucasta was the only young lady he asked to stand up with him."

Her aunt's basilisk stare swung to Lucasta. "He inquired about Cecilia, of course."

"Er. After a fashion." Lucasta pulled another piece of toast from the rack.

"And you encouraged him, of course."

Lucasta swallowed a dry bite. "More or less." Rather less than more, one might say.

Her ladyship nodded. "I hope I have finally impressed upon you what you owe to this family, Lucasta. You are a wayward creature, though if you would but exert yourself the least bit, you could be passably charming. Do you suppose he will offer soon, Cecilia, and we might plan a summer wedding?"

Cici pursed her lips daintily around the rim of her cup. "But he admires Lucasta, *belle-mére.*"

"Oh, the very idea," her ladyship said. "Now, let me see. The rout at Skylar House is tonight, and I am sure Rudyard shall be attending. I wonder if you should wear white again, since he favors you in it?"

She frowned at the note in her hand. "Oh. This one is for you, Lucasta."

Lucasta read the elegant missive, brief but charming. She blinked. "The Duchess of Hunsdon informs me she has a selection of Greek histories in her antiquarian bookshop, and she invites me and my friends to call on her."

Aunt Pevensey put down her egg spoon. "Her Grace the Duchess of Hunsdon?"

"Don't forget this one." Cici retrieved another folded note from the pile.

Lucasta sucked in a breath. "The Countess of Bessington hopes I and my friends will attend an afternoon salon at her home. A Miss Williams will be speaking on the topic of feminine sensibility."

"The Countess of Bessington sent you an invitation?" Her aunt picked through the remaining stock of folded foolscap. "Why should she take any note of *you*?"

Lucasta gathered her shaking courage in both hands. "As it happens, Lady Cranbury approached me about a musical evening—"

"No," her aunt said flatly.

"It would only be a small event, she said, for the entertainment of her nephew—"

"*No*, Lucasta." This accompanied by a fearsome frown.

"Lady Cranbury has a Cristofori pianoforte," Lucasta said in desperation.

Aunt Pevensey turned to her last and greatest defense, her husband. "You will make a spectacle of yourself and this family. You have begun already, with this attention, and it will end with us all looking foolish. Tell her, milord."

The baron looked up from the lampoons, for which he had put aside *The Morning Post*, and his scowl was mightier than his lady's. "How on earth did you interest Rudyard, gel?"

Why, by composing satirical verses about him, which he overheard and took exception to. Excellent way to attract a man's notice. Every overlooked maid ought to try the same.

Crumbs of toast scraped Lucasta's throat as she swallowed. "Er. He remembered you commended Cici to him, sir. He spoke of it during our dance."

"Well, take care you don't scotch her chances. Draper's son he might be, but Arendale is a fat plum." The baron reached for the *Gazette*. "My son sent a note that he is leaving Paris soon."

The lace over her ladyship's bosom fluttered with her quick, indrawn breath. "Trevor?"

"At last!" Cici cried, dropping her spoon with a clatter. "How soon might we expect him? It is long past time he came home."

"I am sure he will wish for his own quarters, Cecilia." Her ladyship forced a smile as the baron lowered his paper to stare. "I only mean, a young man of his age and—er, habits—I can't think but that he will find us too tame for his liking."

"He will put up here and save me the expense of separate lodgings." The baron snapped his paper into place. "And I expect he will be your escort to all your little functions. I do hope the other young men finding your niece *interesting* will not prove too much an obstruction."

Lucasta paused in pouring her tea. Trevor Pevensey, the baron's spoiled son and heir, had been enjoying an extended Grand Tour on the Continent. "Does that mean Cici will not require me as chaperone, sir? If her brother is home?"

If she were liberated from her duties, Lucasta could make free with London's music scene. Run riot through the symphony halls, theaters, and pleasure gardens. She could spend this last sweet season with her dearest friends until Aunt Pevensey packed her back to Bath, where Lucasta would scrape together what funds she could find and commence with her plans for a music studio.

She could duck her head, and whatever Fury Lord Rudyard had unleashed would blow past, leaving her family moored in their pride, unscathed.

The baron threw Lucasta a cold glare. "And Rudyard found you clever."

Lucasta splashed a bit of tea as she replaced the teapot. Aunt had permitted the use of fresh leaves this morning, on account of the baron's presence, though she customarily reused old leaves when it was just the three women. But her ladyship was stingy with the sugar, and if Lucasta tried to sweeten the bitter brew, there would be nothing of the brown lump left for Cici.

Lady Pevensey fiddled with her cup of cooling chocolate. "I have said before, I cannot think they would suit, milord. Lucasta is so rustic—she lacks polish. And your Trevor is such a dashing young blade. I should not wish him to be disappointed, for we both know, Pevensey, what it means when two people can deal well together in their marriage."

The baron put down his paper. "Patience, my dim pet. You told me you expect Lucasta to inherit a sizeable inheritance from your aunt."

Aunt winced. "So she has been saying, but I hardly credit it.

Aunt Cornelia enjoys wielding threats about her inheritance like a bludgeon to keep us all in heel."

The baron pushed back his chair. "She seems to have settled matters now, for I heard the gossip at my club last night. Everything that is not entailed to the Frotheringale estate, and what Lady Evers has gained from her marriages. All to Lucasta, in due time."

Lucasta froze with her teacup halfway to her mouth. This was news to her.

Her ladyship tried again. "But that does not mean she will be a fit wife for Trevor, my dear."

"If your aunt is as rich as hinted, then Lucasta is exactly the kind of wife Trevor will require. I bid you good day, my lady." The baron rose and sauntered out the door of the dining parlor, summoning the butler to bring his hat and coat and order the carriage to take him to his club.

Lucasta closed her mouth so she did not shriek. Or allow the toast to come soaring back up.

Trevor Pevensey to marry Lucasta? No. The baron could not mean it.

Her aunt's stabbing stare told Lucasta she had spoken this aloud. "It would be just like Aunt Cornelia to overlook everyone deserving and endow you with her fortune."

"But she has said nothing to me."

"Because it is vulgar for young ladies to discuss their means, and it is hardly your affair anyway." Aunt Pevensey rose from the table. "A woman's assets are for fathers and husbands to manage. Cecilia, we shall make calls this morning, and perhaps step into Lord Rudyard's shop. It will not do to let his interest in you fade, for the affections of men are all too capricious."

As Lucasta rose also, her ladyship leveled a stare full of fury.

"You shall remain home. Whatever mischief you were making last night, I won't have you continue it. Cecilia has this one Season to make a brilliant match, and I won't have you pushing your way your way in, trying to make everyone notice you. You will remain here, you will not be at home to callers, and you will, I hope, recall yourself to the duty to which you owe to this family."

She curled a hand around the large pearl at her throat and departed, but not without one final shot. "All the care I have taken with you, to be repaid in such fashion, with such ridiculous, idle gossip—I shall never escape the scandal of you, shall I?"

Cici, sparing a look of pity for Lucasta, followed at her step-mother's command.

Lucasta stood above her chair as if she were the one turned to stone.

Her mother, she'd been told again and again, had brought a stain upon the Frotheringale family, lowering herself with a marriage to a poor man and a foreigner to boot. Lucasta, as the rest of the clan made clear to her, had a great deal to do to climb out from beneath that shadow.

And now she'd gone and made an enemy of a marquess's heir.

As soon as the portal to her aunt's dressing room closed, Lucasta bolted for her music room. This refuge lay at the top of the curving stairwell of the rented house, dark with the wainscoting of a previous century. It had been a neglected sitting room where a previous tenant had begun to build a library, but the baron was not much interested in books, and Lady Pevensey preferred to impress her visitors with the formal parlor on the first floor. Lucasta paced across the broad room and threw open the heavy curtains to let the drizzle of the London morning show through.

So. Her aunt had not brought her to town out of some long-forgotten impulse of affection, nor the hope that Lucasta would make friends with Cici. Lucasta had been summoned from her safe, quiet nest in Bath and thrown to the lion-filled Coliseum that was London because the baron wanted her to marry Trevor Pevensey.

She knew him only by reputation, and if the reputation were true, then the baron's son could be relied upon to gamble his wife's dowry away at cards, expend it on drink and mistresses, and keep himself in horses and coats for as long as the money lasted.

It was a hum to say Aunt Cornelia meant to settle anything on her grand-niece, the family's black sheep. What she need not bequeath to Frotheringale, spiting his mother's expectations, Aunt Cornelia meant to leave to Miss Gregoire's school, for Miss Gregoire and Lady Evers were great friends. Aunt Cornelia had threatened to favor Lucasta in order to tease a nosy relation, and now the baron thought it a promise.

Lucasta circled to the clavichord, then ran her fingers over the harp. She would not be in this situation if her parents were still alive. That ache of grief had dulled over time but never lessened. Lucasta's sweet, beautiful mother had doted upon her only child, but died of consumption when Lucasta was seven. Her darling, distracted father, who lived among his books and invited Lucasta into that world with him, returned to the arms of his Maker when she was fourteen.

Aunt Patience, her mother's sister, had little to do with Lucasta, though she lived with them when Lucasta was young. Patience was sharp-tongued and short-tempered, often heard to say that the humble life of a vicar's family was far beneath her and her sister's birth and deserving.

Then, quite suddenly, a year or so after Lucasta's mother died, her aunt came over all smiles, and after a flurry of shop visits, fine fabrics, and a grand wedding, her calling card became a creamy slip embossed with "The Lady Pevensey."

Lucasta pulled out her piles of music and sorted through the sheets. With Aunt Cornelia in Bath providing her tuition at Miss Gregoire's Academy for Girls, Lucasta had never felt an outcast, like some other unfortunates. She'd found friends who understood and loved her, who made up for any other lack. But they were moving on now to their own worlds, their own futures.

All Lucasta had left was her music.

And it seemed Aunt Pevensey meant to deny her that, too.

Cici, dressed and ready for calls, found Lucasta at the clavichord, pounding out a stormy composition by the elder Bach. Her cousin pulled up a small upholstered stool.

"I shall not inform *belle-mére* that she has granted you a gift, leaving you at home to practice your music. She shows little enough kindness to you, my dear."

"I suppose she has no reason to. Cici, I never meant—" She stopped, for in all truth, she *had* warned Rudyard away from this bright, darling girl. "I did not mean to damage your prospects. Your plain, awkward, unfashionable cousin, an object of pity and fun. I have shadowed your sun, and that was never my intention."

Cici tossed her chin. "I have a Season before me. There are days, no, weeks of this. It will go on and on." She studied her cousin's face. "I did not know they meant you for Trevor."

Lucasta shrugged off a flicker of fear. "Surely we, the two principals, are the ones who should discuss the matter."

But she had already decided. She might have no suitors of her own, but she would not be yoked into marriage against her will, not even to a young man of tolerable morals and agreeable character, which Trevor Pevensey, to all accounts, lacked.

But she was under her aunt and uncle's roof for the duration of the Season, not expected back at Miss Gregoire's until her new term began in the fall, and so obliged to demonstrate *some* gratitude for the pains her aunt was taking with her. Short of throwing herself on Great-Aunt Cornelia's mercy, Lucasta had nowhere to flee in the meanwhile, and no means of supporting herself if she did.

And Cici adored her brother. Lucasta would have a fine line to walk, refusing him.

"Lord Rudyard has such address," Cici remarked. "And so well turned-out."

And he had caught her when she tripped in the dance. Lucasta could not seem to put that recollection from her mind. His hands warm and steady, his firm grip, the way she felt the heat of the body as he pulled her close to him through the turn. She, who most often doubled as dancing master at Miss Gregoire's when a male instructor was unavailable, had stumbled in the allemande.

A man of such fine appearance ought to have a fine character to go with.

Lucasta turned to her cousin. "I told Lord Rudyard I did not think him a good match for you."

Cici widened her eyes. "Oh, me neither. He terrifies me. I live in fear of offending his elegant sensibilities."

Lucasta had done so, freely, boldly. She had trod outright over every scruple, shred of propriety, and decorum, as well as his sensibilities.

"There will be such talk today, I don't doubt. And you will be subject to the scrutiny, all on your own."

"Which is what *belle-mére* intends, I gather. If she parades you about it should seem she is flaunting her triumph, and that would be—"

"So very vulgar," Lucasta said along with her. They shared a smile, which on Cici's side turned sly.

"But if she hides you, that will only increase the speculation. Mark you, we will visit half a dozen places, and at each we will be swamped with questions regarding you."

"With all eyes on you," Lucasta realized. "How cunning."

"She did not make herself a baron's wife by her sweet nature, that is certain." Cici rose, then paused, her gaze softening as it rested on her cousin.

"All these entertainments are quite wearying for you, aren't they, my dear? Miss Gregoire's seems a sober, gentle sort of place."

Lucasta selected another piece, wrestling with the flash of acute longing for her school, her home. At Miss Gregoire's she spent her days in quiet industry, immersed in the sciences and music and art and books, and her evenings with the other teachers and their brightest students engaged in reading, painting, dancing, and discussing the latest publications on philosophy or travel.

Their evenings out consisted of a lecture, a concert, or a ball in the Bath Assembly Rooms, which were known for being so decorous that they ended at ten of the clock. Such a life would seem dull to the Cicis and the Rudyards of the world, whose entertainments were loud, bright, and costly.

No wonder Lucasta and her friends lacked that ephemeral quality called *ton*. He was right to call them the Gorgons. She would never be accepted among the great, and it was nonsense to try.

Cici swept away, tiny nose in the air like a sparrow sniffing out crumbs. Lucasta hoped with all her heart that Cici would enjoy her Season and its pleasures and find an advantageous marriage at the end of it. She hoped that her father, with all his calculation of advantages, would at least take Cici's wishes into account.

Lucasta pulled out a stormy piece by Mozart that might relieve some of her tempestuous feelings. She could only expect a future of misery if she were given to a man like Trevor Pevensey. The prospect of becoming Lady Pevensey would cost her everything. Unable by law to possess her own property or direct her own finances, she would live on whatever her husband allowed her, and whatever credit would be extended to them by resentful tradesmen.

Her husband would dictate where she lived and whom she associated with. He would have complete control over their children. There was no custom and no law to compel a man to show fidelity or respect to his wife. He could gamble, drink, pursue other women, run the Pevensey estate into ruin and its tenants into starvation, and if the other young men of his birth and station that Lucasta had met were any pattern, that is exactly what he would do. She could not vow to honor and obey a man such as that.

Perhaps this was why Aunt Pevensey had prevented Lucasta from taking music lessons. If she had any hopes at all of supporting herself on the stage, performing at courts and concert halls, then she might be in a position to decline Trevor Pevensey's oh-so-generous offer for her hand.

She must deny him at any rate. She only needed to figure out how to do so without tying the noose around her own neck.

~

SOME HOURS LATER, immersed in dolorous communication with Handel, Lucasta didn't hear the knocker and was only warned by a lively tread on the stairs moments before the door to the music room flew open.

"He called you clever," Selina announced, a grim set to her mouth. She wore a sumptuous evening gown of French satin in a deep silver hue.

"He called you interesting." Annis tucked Lucasta's violin beneath her chin and tuned it with a few brisk notes.

"He called you *fascinating*." Minnie went to the harp and strummed a chord. Minnie's *robe à la francaise* was a pale purple silk brocade with yellow and orange flowers swarming the bodice and skirts. Smart Jeremy would certainly have something to say about that eye-watering pattern.

"Aunt told me I am not at home to callers," Lucasta warned. "I am in disgrace."

Annis shook back the cascade of lace and ruffles at the sleeves of her damask robe, a shimmering pale blue. "We are family, and so I told Possett when we climbed over him to get in. Don't you want to attend the Skylar rout? Rudyard will be there."

An odd jolt went through Lucasta at the thought, as if her friend had struck a string that sounded both dissonant and resonant at the same time. That momentary press of their bodies had been an accident, a stumble.

But there was that other odd moment when it felt he was drawing her to him, trying to convince her of something. Unlike other men who wore too much powder or cologne, Rudyard had a light, clean smell like pine and the outdoors, and that marvelous liquid voice. A thrill went through her again.

"I most emphatically do not want to see him," Lucasta said. "He overheard my epigrams and challenged me about it. Then he gave Clara Bellwether charge to make fun of me."

"Or make something else," Minne remarked. "He said Miss

Thomasina Brentleigh possessed elegance of mind and manner, and now the Earl of Avon is paying her his addresses, and she is nothing but a squire's daughter from Shropshire."

"Did he also observe that Mina has the most brilliant mathematical mind ever seen at Miss Gregoire's? The man is nothing but a narrow-minded peddler of trumpery. He called me a Medusa, which I am sure Lady Clara has also taken pains to mention."

"Then we ought to run him to ground, so you might turn him to stone." Minnie plucked out a tune on the harp.

"Is he the reason you are mewed up here like Rapunzel in her tower?" Annis played back Minnie's impromptu melody, then gestured with her bow toward Lucasta's worn day gown and old apron.

Lucasta slumped on the stool. "I learned this morning why my aunt brought me here for the Season."

Selina sat on the stool beside Lucasta, peering into her face. "Not for Cici?"

Lucasta shook her head. "The baron seems to believe that I will be heir to my great-aunt Cornelia's estate. And that makes me, therefore, a suitable bride for Trevor Pevensey."

Minnie drew a crashing chord from the harp. "Trevor Pevensey is the worst ne'er-do-well you can imagine. He gambles, he drinks, he consorts with common women—"

"Yes, I know all that. He conducts himself exactly as a son of the nobility is expected to do. And my supposed inheritance is desired to fund this lifestyle, I presume." Lucasta rubbed her sore fingertips.

"Fustian," Annis announced. "You simply decline the honor. They can't force you. You are three-and-twenty, well past the age of consent."

"Can they not? Force me?" Lucasta's laugh sounded shaky to her own ears. "I can imagine all manner of threats they might make."

A silence prevailed in the room for a moment, beyond which the traffic from the street outside could be heard: peddlers crying their wares, cart wheels and horse hooves, pedestrians hailing one another, the busy industry of the city. If she married Trevor Pevensey, Lucasta would be trapped in this room, or one just like it, for the rest of her life.

"What shall we do?" Selina whispered.

Lucasta forced a smile. "I have failed to generate any adequate ideas. Nor have Bach, Mozart, Handel, or Scarlatti, though I've been consulting them all day."

"We know what you need." Annis clapped her hands together and struck an operatic pose. "Signor Marchesi."

"But you all have invitations to the rout, and besides that, my aunt has forbidden me..." Lucasta trailed off, hearing how feeble her excuse sounded.

Minnie looked around with lifted brows. "Is her ladyship here? I see no sign of her."

Annis pulled a handbill from an interior pocket. "To be performed this evening at the King's Theatre in Haymarket: *Ifigenia in Aulide*, a serious opera, with music by Signor Bertoni, and Signor Marchesi to sing at the end a few Italian words set to music by himself." She gave Lucasta a pointed look. "Now will you dress?"

Lucasta's heart dashed against her ribs. Her aunt would be furious if Lucasta disobeyed her.

Furious enough to entomb her within the house for the remainder of the Season.

Perhaps furious enough to convince the baron that the last thing Trevor Pevensey needed was a disobedient wife.

"I've nothing suitable," Lucasta warned. Among milady's outmoded cast-offs, the only frocks fit for the opera were a muslin robe with narrow stripes of alternating yellow and lime green or a sack back of grey silk that made her look like a plague victim. The stripes occasioned much hilarity when Lucasta remarked for certain no one would accuse her of being fascinating in *those*. But without much loss of time she was robed, her hair dressed, and grinning at her three friends in her tiny handheld mirror.

"Miss Gregoire's girls," Minnie proclaimed. "We shall be a toast."

"Gorgons," Annis said grandly. "We shall terrify everyone. I confess I look forward to the prospect."

They squeezed their skirts into the Luneburg town coach and headed to Haymarket. Selina leaned over and whispered in Lucasta's ear.

"Are you certain Smart Jeremy is teasing you? For I do not think his remarks were meant to be unkind."

Lucasta's heart gave that odd patter again, and it was more than simple guilt. She *did* want to see Smart Jeremy again. For all his faults, the man had fascinated her in return. His voice, his looks, his dry wit and unfathomable expressions, all combined to make an impression that no man yet had made on Lucasta Lithwick.

All the more reason to stay as far away from him as possible.

# CHAPTER FIVE

As he dressed the morning after Clara's *conversazione,* Jem debated calling on Miss Lucasta Lithwick that day. But there was no reason to be hasty. Presenting himself in Caroline Street two days following would do quite as well.

It would only take a call or two, perhaps a drive in the park, a dance and a conversation at another society event later in the week, and he would know if the power she'd attributed to him was real. If, indeed, he had the ability to raise a vicar's daughter from obscurity by his notice alone.

And she, too, would know what it was to be the cynosure of curious eyes. To have her face, her figure, her conduct, and her conversation ruthlessly evaluated by persons who had no acquaintance with her. She would know the burden of being fashionable, the wearying and unstinting scrutiny, the desperate game of holding on to every scrap of favor.

She would understand what he faced, daily being held to standards that would never be possible for him because of his birth. Then, perhaps, she would not disdain him quite so much for being no better than he was.

Why he should long for the approval of Miss Lucasta Lithwick was a motive Jem chose not to explore. Instead he envisioned her, with her new reputation and the Frotheringale fortune, being seen in his shops, wearing his fabrics. He would be glad to advise her on matters of dress. Indeed it would be an agreeable challenge to find the gowns and styles that would bring to light Lucasta Lithwick's beauty, for he sensed it was there. She had a certain elegance in her manner that would do justice to the designs he would select for her. And if he outfitted one sudden new heiress beautifully, who else might be inclined to place themselves in his hands?

With enough success in his business, his wealth and prospects would finally outweigh any sneers he earned for being born a draper's son and a draper himself. His stature would be so great that no one would dare offer insult to anyone who stood within his protection. His siblings would be provided for. Would be safe.

Jem stood respectfully still while his valet arranged his neckcloth, wearing his customary unruffled expression. "They are saying you took it upon you to dance last night, milord," Church remarked.

"And so I did." Jem's heart gave a curious kick when he recalled the moment Miss Lithwick stumbled during the allemande, when he caught her to him.

Jem, a man of the world as these things went, was not a stranger to the feel of a woman's body pressed against his, even if tall, well-formed women who fit him well were a rarity. So it was odd that holding Lucasta Lithwick should create an impression that lingered in his memory. There lingered, too, the imprint of her long, supple arm and slender fingers intertwined with his, seared like a burn on his skin.

"Your aunt desires you to step into the drawing room when you go down," Church warned him in the same bland voice.

Jem winced as he held out his arms and Church snugged his coat into place. He'd moved into Arendale House after Cadmus's death at the command of his grandfather, who wanted a man about the place, or so his letters intimated. Lady Payne, who had grown accustomed to thinking of Arendale House as her own, had not been pleased with the move, as she was not pleased with any part of Jem's usurpation of his cousin's rights and titles.

Even before she was Lady Payne, Martha Falstead had never deigned to acknowledge Jem's mother or her children. Though she was allowed to remain Lady Payne by courtesy, and she held a life interest in the property her husband had been granted at their marriage, her son's and husband's deaths and Jem's ascension as heir was to his aunt's hopes the equivalent of a shipwreck in the Antipodes.

If she must lose all meaning to her life, Lady Payne had been heard to say, then she would very well do so in town, with the consolation of smart shops and pleasant company. But Jem rather suspected she remained at Arendale House, rather than renting a place of her own, so she might remind Jem of the duty he owed to her and their name.

His aunt was also counting the days until her half-mourning ended and she might go about in society again, since her daughter Lambertina, growing long in the tooth at the advanced age of twenty, could not afford to be kept from another Season.

"Aunt Payne. Bertie," Jem greeted them, entering the vast parlor unannounced.

He would concede that the enormous chambers and spacious dressing rooms of Arendale House made it more accommodating to a man of fashion, and Jem could not conceive of Church making do in the apartments above the draper's shop where Jem had been born and raised. But the remove made Jem feel more distant than ever from the life he had known.

Plain Jeremiah Falstead, draper, had been content to share space with his apprentices and bolts of fabric propped in every corner. Smart Jeremy, however, lived in a sprawling town house in Southampton Square and had a valet who put on more airs than he did, and dressed as exquisitely as Jem himself.

"Oh. Rudyard. Good morning." His aunt pronounced his title as if it left a bitter taste in her mouth, and Jem still felt that prickle of unease. Cadmus had been, should still be, by courtesy the

Viscount Rudyard, and Jem's boisterous uncle the Earl Payne. But the first title now belonged to Jem's father, the dissolute scoundrel passing his days in Barbados in the arms of his island mistress. And the second had passed to Jem.

"Lambertina and I were just speaking of you." Aunt Payne stabbed a needle into an embroidery cloth. "Lady Cranbury sent me a note full of the most ridiculous nonsense about some vicar's daughter she said had turned your head. I will tell her she must be mistaken, as you've never taken the least interest in any of the eligible young girls."

Bertie sent him a furtive look from her place near the window, where she was attempting a still life of a clutch of fruit. To the outside eye, everything about the scene would have appeared correct: the stately proportions of the formal parlor, the hand-painted walls clustered with expensively framed paintings, the elegant mahogany furniture, the well-adorned women at their graceful tasks.

But Bertie's artwork, rather than the bright apples and oranges of her model, looked like a sullen tomato brooding in a nest of hostile lemons. Bertie was miserable.

Jem hoped it was not on his account. Aunt Payne, as a last desperate gamble to keep her influence, felt Jem and Bertie ought to marry, though Jem harbored no such inclination, and Bertie had never given the least inkling that she fancied him. But who knew to what lengths desperation might drive a girl? Lucasta Lithwick had been reduced to making up pithy epigrams for amusement.

After he'd named her and her friends Gorgons. Jem pushed away the reminder. He'd been called much worse, before and after he'd been branded Smart Jeremy.

He folded himself onto a striped settee near Bertie's easel. "I have not had my head turned. I did, however, remark a Miss Lucasta Lithwick at Lady Clara's evening last night, where there was dancing. All of it a complete bore," he assured Bertie. "You would have hated every moment."

"Lucasta Lithwick?" His aunt lowered her tambour. "I am not familiar with the name."

"It seems the Reverend Lithwick did little to distinguish himself," Jem said, "but her maternal grandfather was the Viscount Frotheringale, and she is staying at present with the Pevenseys." As Bertie tidied away her things, he leaned over and snatched the apple, giving her a wink. "I suppose you might call upon them to show you are ready to emerge from mourning."

His aunt fixed him with a surprised stare. "Do *you* mean to call on them?"

"Yes. Tomorrow." Jem took a bite of the apple. It was past ripe and starting to shrivel.

Aunt Payne tugged her needle through the cloth. "Cecilia Pevensey has several young men dancing on a string, I have heard. The title is young—her father is only the second baron. His heir is yet unmarried, though a bit wild, they say, and abroad on the Continent to my knowledge. I do wish I could find a steady man for Lambertina. Someone older and well-established in his ways."

Bertie wiped her brushes, making no protest, but Jem caught a flash of mutiny crossing her face. Bertie feared to be a wallflower like the Gorgons. If he made a success of Lucasta Lithwick, perhaps Jem could do the same for Bertie.

"Will you bring Judith to town, Jem?" Bertie asked. "I long to see her. It is so quiet here."

"No," Jem said.

Aunt exhaled. "I should hope not. I cannot think a debut would be of any benefit to Judith. She is better where she is." She stole a glance at Jem over her embroidery frame. "You know what people would make of her. There's no reason to torture the child."

Jem munched his apple, tasting the overripe sweetness. He didn't need his aunt to remind him how Judith would be received by society hostesses like Lady Clara. Pity was the least of his worries.

"Besides," Aunt went on, tugging her thread taut, "you have

put her in a compromising position. If anyone in town knew what else you are hiding out there—"

"*Who*, Aunt Martha," Jem bit out. "They are people. Not things."

"It is a terrible idea, and I told you so from the start," his aunt flared back. "You cannot possibly expect to keep them a secret. People will talk."

"About what? My servants are loyal and run a respectable house." Jem set the apple aside. "There is nothing to talk about."

"You cannot expect to keep them hidden! Everyone will be interested in your father's doings, now that he is Payne," his aunt cried. "Pray do not pretend to be so naïve, Jeremiah. You should have left them where they were. They are better off in the place they were born, in the circumstances in which they were being raised—"

"Those circumstances are intolerable to me and to any person of the smallest moral fiber." Jem shot to his feet. "If it takes me a lifetime to correct my father's errors—and it probably will—I intend at the least to exhaust myself in the attempt." He reached for his walking stick, looking away from Bertie's pale, stricken face.

Aunt laid her embroidery in her lap and fixed him with a fierce glare. "You might also consider that *we* are your family, Jeremiah, and have a share in any shame you choose to bring upon yourself. How I could hold up my head it if became known—"

"If *what* became known, Aunt?" Jem demanded. "That I am making an effort to provide for my siblings in the manner I deem best?"

"*You* may not care for it," his aunt said in a freezing voice, "but the Falstead name is a respectable one. Why your father chose to bestow it upon someone like your mother, I'll never know. At the least you have the conscience to pity Judith, who cannot possibly pass in this world. But you so debase the honor and standing of this family by acknowledging your father's poor judgment— It is as if you truly have no concept of the breeding and nicety that is expected of the heir to a marquess. But then, how could you, raised as you were?"

It took everything in him to execute the briefest bow to his aunt and offer a stiff nod to Bertie. He would prove he could pass as a gentleman if it killed him. "Good day."

Jem gave up the thought of making calls or doing anything that might bring him in contact with the so-called Polite World. He couldn't stand it, not today. Not when his own aunt was their vile mouthpiece.

He spent the day at one of his warehouses, inspecting a shipment of new fabrics and double-checking the books. The costly chintz from India had survived its travels, the glazed fabric stiff to his hand and the intricate, hand-painted patterns gleaming with color that had held fast. There was a lustrous worsted from Norwich and bolts of sturdy broadcloth from his suppliers in Devon, along with an exquisite cassimere made of Spanish Merino wool.

He imagined the last making a shawl for Lucasta Lithwick, draping her bold shoulders and teasing the delicate skin above her bosom. He put a length aside for her, for when she called at his Pall Mall shop.

In Cheapside, the new apprentices were getting on, despite the warnings that boys from the workhouse or the lower echelons of society would make shifty employees. The Irish linen was selling well, and the cotton from the Manchester mill was increasingly popular. He found a russet-colored linen that would flatter Lucasta Lithwick's skin and a dark blue wool woven to a shine that would make a fine riding habit, if indeed she rode.

He was making no plans, of course. He knew how capricious were the whims of aristocrats, and there was no predicting what a young lady might do who learned she was coming into a fortune. But Jem whistled a popular drinking tune as he entered his dressing room to find Church laying out a new suit of fine purple broadcloth he had recently acquired and meant to advertise, along with a very fine Valenciennes lace.

While Church powdered his hair, Jem admired the lavish embroidery along the cuffs, neck, and hem of the coat and the echoing pattern in the breeches and waistcoat. His silk stockings were white as bone and his evening slippers polished to a shine. He would make the rounds this evening and with luck his ensemble would bring at least one curious gentleman or interested lady to his shop, hoping to look quite as well.

He looked forward to the Skylar rout as he had not looked forward to a society event in months, if ever. It would be amusing to cross wits with Miss Lithwick again. He couldn't remember the last time a woman had made him laugh.

She would no doubt wear something appalling. Perhaps he would drop her a hint or two about improving her style of dress. As Church arranged his cravat in a stylishly simple set of folds, Jem's hands tingled, remembering the feel of Lucasta Lithwick in his arms.

Lucasta Lithwick thought him a burden. Useless. Not someone who contributed to the world, but a parasite that fed upon it. But she had also told him he underestimated the power of his words and actions.

She was right. He had an ability, the alchemical magic to spin straw into gold. And if he could make a fortune from it, he could protect the future of Judith and the others. Protect them from the slurs on their parentage that dogged him. Shield them from the many ways they would be cut, fenced, turned away, forbidden to trespass on ground that belonged to them by right. Perhaps he could even satisfy his grim Aunt Payne and win the future she desired for Bertie.

Lucasta Lithwick had thrown down the gauntlet, and he would take it up. Jem would show them all what he could do, and he would begin with her.

## CHAPTER SIX

S he wasn't at the Skylar rout. Miss Pevensey was, and her eyes
widened when Jem appeared, but she had replaced her
distinctive cousin with her mama for chaperone. Lady Pevensey
strained to catch Jem's eye, but he did not oblige.

None of the Gorgons were in attendance, and Jem felt the lack.
Lady Clara had called it oddness, but it was some other, ineffable
essence that attended those four distinct young ladies. They added
interest to a room. Jem would like to outfit them all and have it
known they patronized his shop.

She was not at Lady Cranbury's card party, and neither was
she at Lady Hillsborough's *converzatione*. Clara Bellwether was,
and she could confirm that neither Lucasta Lithwick nor any of the
Gorgons were attending the other three parties she had looked in
on that evening. Clara met Jem's inquiry with a sly smile, and he
cursed himself for being obvious. By tomorrow, it wouldn't simply
be hinted that his head had been turned; the gossips would have
him in full pursuit.

He was furious again—he, who was generally slow to anger.
But why, he couldn't say. Only that not being able to run her to
ground felt like Lucasta Lithwick was changing the rules of
engagement. She was supposed to be at the Skylar rout so he could

single her out for his attentions, elevate her as the topic of discussion on every tongue in the *beau monde,* and then watch what she did with the sudden marks of favor.

How was he supposed to make her fashionable when she was not at any of the society 'dos, waiting breathlessly for his notice?

"Could go back to the club and have a drink," Plimpton observed, having attached himself to Jem as a welcome excuse to leave Lady Cranbury's card party, where he had been diving rather deeply into his pockets and into drink.

"Wouldn't you rather one of the theatres?" Ashley, who gratefully traded Lady Hillsborough's guests for Jem and Plimpton's company, gave Plimpton a jab in the side as they hailed a hack on the sidewalk outside Hillsborough House. "Seems to me you need a chorus girl to console you after your latest rebuff."

"New opera at the Haymarket tonight." Plimpton revived at this recollection. "Some doleful Italian bit, but an opera means opera dancers. Up for some fun, Rudyard?"

"Why not?" Jem shrugged, though he did not make a habit of getting up intrigues with chorus girls or keeping a mistress the way Ashley and other youngbloods did. For one thing, mistresses were expensive. But he was also fastidious about his sexual habits, another aspect of being raised a tradesman's son. He liked for a woman to be partial to him and not simply on the hunt for a keeper.

Nevertheless he joined his friends inside the hired coach, which smelled strongly of the last tenant's cologne, and the body odor the cologne had been intended to disguise. If the night was to be counted a loss in terms of his revenge, Jem would rather pass it watching actors shriek and fuss upon a stage than stand in a drawing room fielding speculation about his interest in Lucasta Lithwick.

His grandfather the marquess held a box at the King's Theatre, which was to Jem's advantage, since Plimpton was pockets-to-let again and Ashley had lost his purse on some stupid bet. They strolled late into the cavernous performance hall, with its massive interior space that swallowed sound.

He spotted her at once. There, crowding the stage below one of the enormous Gainsborough paintings, wearing a gown of lurid clashing stripes and a look of complete and utter captivation, stood Miss Lucasta Lithwick, her Gorgon sisters with her.

She was not at any society entertainments, clinging to the wall and waiting for him to walk through the door. She was not, as Miss Pevensey was doing and Bertie longed to do, thronging the parlors of the nobility waiting for an eligible *parti* to take an interest. Nor, as he had intended, was she trapped in a ballroom, the subject of stares and gossip.

No, Miss Lithwick had escaped to the opera, in pursuit of nothing but her own pleasure, and the expression on her fluid, expressive features said that she floated in the realm of the sublime.

Logic and calculation fled before a deeper prompting Jem could not but obey. Uncaring what his friends might think of either his tactics or his motives, he headed toward the stage, where those who desired intimate exposure to the action paid for the privilege of being close enough to touch the singers, and occasionally distract them. A miasma of perfumes surrounded him as he crossed the pit, a plethora of competing florals and musks emanating from bodies and fabrics and hair.

It was easy enough to maneuver behind the Gorgons, where he could observe but not be noticed. Standing closer than was proper to Lucasta Lithwick, Jem detected a different scent, clean, earthy, yet complex. A scent that struck him as both sweet and dark, prim and naughty at the same time. It suited her.

Despite the objectionable gown, her head was stylish, as if someone else had the care of her from the neck up. Beneath a cap of gauze and ribbons and feathers, her hair was dressed in a fashionable chignon and powdered the reddish apricot color that was all the rage at the moment. The powder was so subtle, in fact, that he smelled no powder at all, nor had turmeric fallen onto her shoulders and gown, as it did to so many other poor girls who attempted that same burnished red-gold.

"Your Signor Marchesi seems out of sorts tonight," remarked one of the Gorgons. The German duke's daughter who had snubbed Ashley at the Queen's levee, crushing his pretensions quite thoroughly. "I would have thought he'd enjoy playing a diva like Achilles."

"I wonder if he has a head-cold, the poor dear," Miss Lithwick remarked. "That cadenza he added to his last aria was not up to his usual standards."

"Iphigenia doesn't care if she lives or dies," said the other tall one, the Russian princess. Jem wondered fleetingly why the two foreign girls, who could be the toast of London for their exotic looks and their not altogether undashing style, chose not to make the effort to enchant anyone.

"She's a soubrette, and the part is written for a spinto soprano," Lucasta answered. "She's straining to reach above her range, and I don't think she understands a word of Italian."

"The chorus sounds disjointed somehow," the petite one said. She was an appealing thing, if not to Jem's taste, and he had endeavored to give her a hint when she had worn a costume one night that flattered neither her color nor her figure. It appeared she had heeded his advice, to great improvement.

"They're coming in on all the wrong cues," Miss Lithwick snapped. "Is the conductor drunk or blind?"

Jem stiffened. For a moment he saw red, and it was not Miss Lithwick's hair. The sheer arrogance of the remark, the breathless, unthinking cruelty was a mark of the upper class, no different from what he encountered a dozen times a day. It was the world they lived in.

He wanted the world to be better. He wanted *her* to be better.

He leaned close, his tone low and his nose close to the stray curl hanging behind her ear. "So a man who is castrated might master music, but a man who is blind cannot?"

She stilled, but a strange ripple passed through her, as if she were a plucked string. He felt her attention lift and focus on him before, very slowly, she turned her chin. That direct gaze had a strange effect on his insides.

He had not been mistaken about the shade of her eyes, a greenish brown flecked with gold. The dusky rose of a blush appeared on her cheeks.

"I beg your pardon, Lord Rudyard. I did not see you there."

Of course not, because he had approached her with the stealth of a poacher stalking a deer.

"Your remarks about the conductor," he prompted. It was rude to interrogate a young lady, but he wanted her prejudice out in the open. Perhaps it would finally free him of this foolish impulse to hang upon her opinions. "I gather you dislike his technique."

He watched her sort through her mind for what she had said and, as anyone would do when called to account, tried to modify the harshness of her complaint. "I was suggesting a man too far in his cups might lose track of his cues."

"I thought you had assumed he was blind, and therefore incompetent." His voice was soft, silken with fury. Lucasta Lithwick did not know him well enough to recognize this. She stared fixedly at his cravat pin, as if it fascinated her.

"They are not equivalent, and it was wrong of me to suggest it." Her brows knit in a frown. "Mr. John Stanley composes beautiful music. He is a governor of the Foundling Hospital and Master of the King's Band, and he has been almost entirely blind since childhood."

Jem knew Mr. Stanley but was surprised Miss Lithwick did. Still, her repentance was not enough to put him in charity with her.

"I thought castratos were falling out of fashion." He glanced at the stage where Achilles, in a display of musical histrionics, was lamenting the ruse that had brought Iphigenia to the port where the Greek armies gathered, her fate not marriage to him but death as a promised sacrifice for a fair wind to Troy. "Achilles seems to enjoy being the center of attention."

As she was supposed to be doing, rather than hiding here. She transferred her attention to the stage, and he was forgotten.

"Signor Marchesi is a rare talent. That *voice*! He has the most remarkable gift of timbre and range. If he adds rather too much coloratura, and enjoys his bravura performances far more than his cantabile singing, it is perhaps to be forgiven."

Jem felt jealousy sharpen its teeth on his temper. Jealousy, over a man who was not a full man! "You seem an ardent admirer. He is very handsome."

She sighed, her shoulders wilting. He liked those fine, sharp shoulders of hers, another way she did not conform to fashion, when the favored look was sloping shoulders and soft roundedness. "That is why my aunt will not allow me to take voice lessons from him."

"Because he is handsome?"

"And because he is Italian. And because—he is so ardently admired."

Castrati were said to possess legendary sexual prowess, with the added benefit of guaranteeing no pregnancy. They were much in demand by a certain set of ladies. He wondered if Miss Lithwick knew this, and jealousy bit all the harder.

"Perhaps you would enjoy the performance better from my uncle's box," Jem said. Anything to interfere with her complete fixation on the stage.

She spoke without glancing at him. "We are very comfortable here, thank you."

The tall Russian said something to Lucasta in a language Jem didn't recognize. Her native tongue? Lucasta gave a short response, and the German princess added something. All three of them looked to the fourth girl, the small brunette. She avoided Jem's eyes and, behind her fan, answered their question. Lucasta turned her eyes back to the stage.

"Perhaps when Signor Marchesi has completed his aria," she said, following the singer's every movement as he swept back and forth in majestic promenade, his perfectly shaped nose in the air.

It was not remarkable that Jem had achieved this concession. Almost certainly a box, overlooking the action, was to be preferred to craning one's head to look up at the stage. So why had Miss Lithwick not agreed instantly?

Why might she be trying to avoid him?

Because he was being as subtle as a goat, Jem reminded himself. As her promised inheritance became common knowledge, gentlemen would descend on her in hordes. He had to position himself now. As a tradesman, an artisan who wanted her custom. Not a suitor longing for a smile.

When the chorus took over, three women warbling half a beat out of time with one another and more or less drowned out by conversations among the audience, Miss Lithwick allowed Jem to lead her and her friends to the stair and the balcony where his uncle's box stood empty much of the time. Jem dropped a question in Ashley's ear.

"Did you catch what language they were speaking?"

Ashley's glare at the German girl rivaled the fabled stare of Medusa. "I couldn't say the dialect, but the Gorgons," he said grimly, "converse in Ancient Greek. Why are we sharing your box with them?"

Because Jem's aim of making Lucasta Lithwick the subject of admiration would be greatly advanced by exposing her to public view in the Marquess of Arendale's theater box. Equally speculated upon, however, would be his personal interest in this particular Gorgon.

Was he ready to risk the further scrutiny that this exercise would result in? He already walked the fine line between the *ton's* favor and their ridicule, a line sometimes too fine to see.

And Clara had already turned her attention to the rest of Jem's family. Where Clara Bellwether led, others would follow.

Jem was not like Ashley, who had borne his courtesy title since birth and had been bred to the stature he would eventually assume. Ashley's education included, in addition to hunting, shooting, gambling, racing, and taking the Grand Tour, an innate understanding of conduct, courtesy, the complicated schedule of precedent, and schooling in Latin and Greek. Jem possessed none of these skills.

But the Gorgons apparently did. At least the schooling in classical languages. What sort of girl's school taught Ancient Greek?

The box was crowded with all of them in it, but the jostling from other persons in the pit was reduced, and the sound from the stage much improved. Lucasta went straight to the balcony as if afraid she'd miss something.

The German Gorgon and Ashley stood on opposite sides of the small chamber, ignoring each other with proud emphasis, while Plimpton hung near the rear, engaging the little knight's daughter in polite conversation. The Russian joined Lucasta at the balcony, standing at her left, which yielded Jem the place at her right. He claimed it, noticing how many glances, stares, and opera glasses turned in their direction, the sudden whispers that arose behind raised gloves and fans.

While nothing could be done about Miss Lithwick's gown, Jem was pleased that at least the rest of her showed to advantage. She had a straight, proud carriage—part of her arrogant demeanor overall—and a long, elegant nose, a broad brow narrowing through prominent cheekbones to a decided chin, and a long, smooth neck that disappeared into the lace enfolding her neck.

He had the odd urge to remove the swath of fabric and unveil her décolletage. No other woman in the room failed to put hers on display. Miss Lithwick possessed a strange combination of antidote and appeal. He wanted to get to the bottom of her mystery.

Jem also did not understand a word of Italian, so he settled himself with studying how much Miss Lucasta Lithwick enjoyed the opera. The action, which to Jem's eyes was nothing but a lot of mincing and prancing, held her in thrall. Her eyes followed every gesture, every flourish of the singers. She breathed when they did, as if she were silently following along with the musical passages.

Her eyelashes were a spiky black, her eyebrows dark brown, and her complexion was a light olive, suggesting a heritage more

Mediterranean than the pale fairness frequently seen in British Isles. He couldn't discern that she had powdered her face, or in fact used any cosmetics. What an unusual girl, lacking birth and name, to forgo paint and fashion as well. No wonder the Gorgons were relegated to the perimeter for Society parties and balls.

He had not been mistaken that she held the promise of real, bewitching beauty. What a pleasure it would be to bring that out. And have others note her transformation and put themselves in Jem's hands, and in the fabrics of Dixon & Co.

The last shattering note faded, and the actors took their bows to extended applause. Lucasta clapped most enthusiastically for Signor Marchesi. The actor came out alone upon the stage to sing a solo tune, and Miss Lithwick's attitude became reverent. Even her friends refrained from attempting to talk to her during the song.

Envy slithered and hissed through Jem's chest. He wondered what it would take to turn Lucasta Lithwick's entire concentration on him.

Thunderous applause greeted the castrato's final flourish, and Miss Lithwick turned a radiant countenance toward Jem. "What a glory to have a box and hear the music pass your ears on its way to heaven," she said with a happy sigh. "Did you enjoy the performance, Lord Rudyard?"

Her glowing face and unexpected joy surprised Jem into honesty. "I didn't understand most of it," he admitted. "Except I gather there was a marriage at the end."

The Russian girl uttered what was clearly a deprecatory remark, and Lucasta laughed. The high, bright sound seemed to burst in his chest. "Yes, that was an unexpected turn of events. I gather the librettist borrowed from Gluck, who introduced that twist at the Paris Opera a few years ago. In Racine's *Iphigénie* the goddess Diana intervenes and substitutes a deer for the sacrifice, and Iphigenia is carried straight up the heavens." She sighed again. "Here, her reward is marriage to Achilles."

"You sound dubious about the merits of that reward." Jem offered her his arm as they made their way out of the box. Plimpton escorted the knight's daughter, but the other two girls strolled out arm in arm with each other, leaving Ashley to stalk behind, scowling.

Jem liked the way Lucasta Lithwick unselfconsciously placed her hand on his forearm. There was nothing coy or flirtatious about the gesture—no leaning against him, no covert squeeze. She was straightforward, practical, solid, and warm.

He was also rather surprised that she consented to touch him. Her glove was kid, not silk, and not new, but well-mended. The mystery of Lucasta Lithwick deepened.

The German Gorgon made a comment in Greek, and Lucasta smiled. "If I do not find it a reward," she said, "it is because we know Achilles sails with the Greeks, so he and Iphigenia are not likely to enjoy marital bliss. Furthermore, he will sulk in his tent after Agamemnon steals Briseis from him, and then return to battle only to kill Hector, who is the one character in all of Western literature whom Minnie devotedly loves."

She might as well be speaking Greek to Jem for all he understood these names. "I'm not familiar with the story," he said.

One of those cinnamon eyebrows arched. "You've not read the *Iliad*? I thought everyone had to read it at school."

Everyone who achieved an education beyond a few years at the dame school around the corner most likely did. Certainly boys sent to public school or taught by private tutors. Jem never had those advantages, and now he had betrayed himself to Miss Lithwick, who already saw him as nothing but a popinjay.

"Well, I like the happier ending," said the knight's daughter.

"I favor the original," Lucasta responded, as they descended the stairs and processed through the elegant foyer to the cloakroom so the gents could retrieve their overcoats and the ladies their wraps. "Euripides gives Iphigenia's sacrifice meaning. She persuades Achilles not to fight Agamemnon for her, and she chooses to sacrifice herself so the Greeks may go to war and avenge the insult to their honor. She submits to the decision of the gods and she gives her life for her country and her ideals. There's something very noble in that."

Jem helped settle her cape around Miss Lithwick's shoulders. It was a functional garment of felted wool, rust-colored and well-brushed, ornamented with dark braid running along the selvage. He would like to see her wrapped in rich silks.

"All the same, you wouldn't turn down marriage to Achilles," he said dryly.

What girl would? This season, every debutante's mama had invited Jem to her come-out, and every papa dropped a hint to Jem about how much her settlement would be. The desperation to find a suitable marriage was why Bertie was painting unhappy fruit, waiting until the moment she could be turned loose again into society.

It was the future that his sister Judith would never be offered, no matter how rich, admired, or titled Jem became.

"Wouldn't I?" Miss Lithwick turned her face up to his as they stood outside the theater before the long queue of coaches. The night shadows darkened her eyes, while the torches caught the gold in their depths. "Achilles in the *Iliad* is petulant and cruel. He is given great gifts, his mother's entire devotion, and he behaves without honor. I think I would rather be carried to the heavens in Diana's chariot."

"Indeed? Then that puts you in the minority of women of my acquaintance."

"This is us," the German girl said offhandedly as a black lacquered coach rolled up, a florid coat of arms on the door. "I apologize, gentlemen, that we don't have the seats to offer you a ride home."

"We could find a light supper somewhere," Jem suggested, and was surprised to hear himself do so. "Ham at Vauxhall. Or there might be something at Ranelagh tonight."

The girls exchanged a glance without speaking. "It is near midnight," Miss Lithwick remarked. That seemed to mean something to them, though to young fashionable gents, midnight marked the beginning of a night's revelries. Midnight often meant fire-works at one of the pleasure gardens. At balls, suppers were held at midnight, with dancing to continue to the wee hours.

But the Gorgons were clearly for home. Miss Lithwick raised the hood of her cape and settled it over her pert little cap, taking care not to crush the feather.

"Thank you for the use of your theater box, Lord Rudyard," she said with a formal politeness. "That was quite generous of you, an unlooked-for courtesy."

"I am at your service, Miss Lithwick. And I enjoyed the evening more than I expected." What he meant was, he'd enjoyed partaking in her pleasure. When was the last time he'd discussed Greek literature or opera with a woman? Never, that was when.

Her arched brows rose in a curious, imperious look. "Would you go so far as to find it *fascinating*? How fortunate for us, then."

"*Touché*, Miss Lithwick," he murmured.

He ought to have remembered she was waiting for an opportu-nity to depress his pretensions. Nevertheless, as she fumbled with the cowl of her cape, he brushed her gloved fingers aside and tied the tapes into a neat, firm bow. It was an office he had performed for a thousand customers and dress dummies. But Miss Lithwick stood quite, quite still, as if an accidental touch might burn her skin.

Her breathless whisper lacked menace, but there was a firm warning in it. "Do not trifle with me, milord Rudyard."

Jem stepped back and sketched a short bow as her friends, already in the carriage, called to her to ascend.

"I trifle with no one, Miss Lithwick."

That was true. He did not dally, loll, or dangle, nor did he wait upon the pleasure of any capricious miss. He had a business to run, and in due time he would have estates and a marquessate to over-see. Jeremiah Falstead had never trifled in his life, not from the moment he shed his infant dresses for short pants and realized a man had to work his way through the world.

And, Jem thought, as Ashley snapped the coach door shut and

rapped on the side to get the coachman moving, he was not trifling with Miss Lithwick. The evening had provided an unlooked-for momentum to his plan.

Many curious eyes had marked her at the theater in the Marquess of Arendale's box. Those same eyes had seen her on his arm. Lucasta Lithwick would set fires of curiosity about the *haut ton*. If he could lure her into his shop and let her emerge a diamond, others were sure to follow where the new heiress led.

But he hadn't forgotten his revenge, his blow for Judith. As an object of acclaim, the latest fashion, she would know how it felt to have strangers sit in judgment. He was elevating her to the same relentless scrutiny and ruthless judgment that so wearied him.

And if she tumbled out of Diana's chariot to fall among the lesser mortals, well, perhaps she would harbor a little less derision toward them, and show a little more pity.

# CHAPTER SEVEN

Signor Marchesi's song floated through Lucasta's head as she rose the next morning and went about her toilette. The melody was enchanting but simple, and she thought about a setting for the harpsichord as she washed from the basin, combed a cleansing oil into her hair, and scrubbed her teeth. While she drew a morning gown over her stays and petticoat and affixed her cap, apron, and lace fichu, she considered a set of variations for a string quartet. All of her friends played, and a new arrangement would provide pleasant occupation for a rainy afternoon. Perhaps she should make a setting for five instruments and invite Cici.

Another image surfaced from the previous night. Lord Rudyard's rich-timbred voice at her ear. The firm strength in his arm as he escorted her to and from the box, as a gentleman did a lady.

The warm brush of his hand beneath her chin as he tied the laces of her cape.

Her stomach quivered in a much different way at the memory of Rudyard's touch than it did at the thought of Signor Marchesi's music.

And quavered in another way altogether when she wondered when her aunt would learn that Lucasta had left the house without her permission to attend an entertainment she had flatly forbidden her to engage in.

She carried her basin and towel downstairs. She had a new pleasure, besides the company of her friends, to bear her through the coming weeks. A note commending Signor Marchesi's performance would not be too forward. And if she sent him an arrangement she had made of his tune, with her compliments, he might take an interest. He might consent to offer her lessons. Trevor Pevensey could squire Cici through her season, Lord Rudyard could turn his games on another, and Lucasta could focus on her music.

If Aunt Pevensey allowed. Her foray to Haymarket would not remain a secret, though she'd sneaked home before her aunt and Cici returned. If she drew notice from the gossips for associating again with Smart Jeremy, her aunt might very well come up with a more terrible punishment than relegating Lucasta to the sidelines of the Season's every ball and rout, doomed to listen to the music, but not participate.

She hummed Signor Marchesi's tune as she entered the kitchen. Her ladyship forbade the girls to take tea and toast in their rooms, for while the baron might do what he liked, unmarried girls ate in the dining parlor with her ladyship, and her ladyship did not rise before noon. Lucasta, being an early riser, would have found this fashionable schedule a trial to her constitution had she not settled, soon after her arrival in the Pevensey household, on the simple expedient of making friends with the staff.

She looked after herself and her chamber, saving the housemaid the extra effort, and Mrs. MacGowan rewarded her by sharing the servants' breakfast and occasionally sneaking meals to the music room while Lucasta practiced, with her ladyship none the wiser.

"That's a lovely tune, it is." Mrs. MacGowan, who served as housekeeper and cook, greeted Lucasta with a smile as she descended into the kitchen.

"I saw Signor Marchesi at the opera last night." Lucasta

disposed of her basin of cloudy water in the scullery, then returned to help slice a loaf of bread. Miss Gregoire insisted that her girls not scorn to turn their hands to household tasks, nor make too much of station, for Miss Gregoire knew firsthand how far a young woman might fall.

The kitchen maid hugged a jar of preserves to her chest. "I'd love to see an opera, I would."

"I'll share a bit with you, then," Lucasta said, and she sang what she remembered of Iphigenia's part while Mrs. MacGowan piled a tray with warm bread, butter, and the preserves. None of the servants being proficient in Italian, Lucasta took the liberty of composing English lyrics for their enjoyment, and no one knew to object if she adjusted the tessitura to something more suiting her natural range. Mrs. McGowan allowed the footman to idle, the housemaid to linger in the linen cupboard, and the boots boy to leave his post in the hall while Lucasta sang.

Mrs. MacGowan sighed with delight as she set her tray in Lucasta's hands. "You're fine enough for the stage yourself, miss."

"If only." Lucasta nodded her thanks as the housekeeper added a pot of tea. The opera had filled her head with visions. If she could use her time in London to acquire the training she needed, that could take her from merely passable to truly skilled.

But Rudyard replaced these visions as she whisked herself off to her music room. What cursed luck had brought him to the opera, and what misplaced gallantry had prompted him to share his box? His attention could only increase the town's speculation, and her aunt's displeasure with Lucasta.

He must know that. What possible benefit could accrue to him by being seen with the women he had named the Gorgons? What motives could he possibly have for conversing with poor, plain Lucasta Lithwick?

He had asked her about the libretto as if he were interested in her opinion.

He had tied the laces on her cloak in a manner that, even now, made her breath grow shallow and her heart thud in her chest.

No. No thinking of Rudyard. There was nothing to be gained there.

She had listened closely enough to remember every measure of Signor Marchesi's tune, and it was a simple matter to make up a notation for the harpsichord. An English translation of the lyrics, however, gave her some trouble. The theme of the ballad was a young man yearning for a lady far above his station. Nearly a rite of passage for a man coming of age, Lucasta thought with a curl of her lip.

But a girl who longed for a man far above her station was a fool. If she failed to win him, she would be taunted ever after for her vain hopes. And if she succeeded, the scorn was worse, for she would never be allowed to forget her unworthiness, her deficiencies.

Lucasta steeled herself as she entered the dining parlor for the morning gauntlet of tea, gossip, and recriminations. Aunt Pevensey had set aside her customary cup of chocolate for a dose of balsam cordial, the recommended elixir for disordered nerves in ladies of high quality. Newsprint pages lay beside her plate, which held a soft-boiled egg she demanded be made to very precise specifications and which she would likely neglect to eat.

"You were in his box," Lady Pevensey yelped. "What were you doing in the Marquess of Arendale's box?"

Lucasta perched warily in the chair the footman pulled out for her, trying to guess her aunt's complaint. That she had gone against her wishes and attended the opera, or that she was seen with Lord Rudyard?

"The Gorg—my friends invited me to the opera after you had left, and since I had spent the day indoors as you advised, mum, I thought a small outing with my friends could do no harm. It happens Lord Rudyard decided to attend the opera as well."

Lucasta poured a cup of tea and turned to Cici. "How was the rout? Were you overwhelmed by admirers, or did Major Mallory beat them all away?"

"Rudyard came to the rout," her ladyship said, attacking her egg. "But he only spoke with Cecilia long enough to ascertain that you were not present, then he took his leave of Lady Skylar *most* precipitously." She gave Lucasta an incredulous look. "He cannot have had reason to be in search of you."

"No, mum. I imagine he turned up at the theater quite by coincidence. Is there any sugar left?"

Her ladyship sat back in her chair. "What did you talk about? Did he ask after our family? It would be a great stroke for you, Cecilia, if you captured Lord Rudyard! And in your first Season, too."

"Perhaps Lord Rudyard is interested in Lucasta for herself," Cici ventured. "I'm afraid I took the last of the sugar, dear."

Cici looked a bit peaked, with violet shadows under her eyes. And the Season was only beginning. There would be weeks more of unending entertainment.

Unless Lucasta did something so deplorable as sink her cousin's chances by alienating the most fashionable man of the *ton*, one with the power to launch or scuttle maidenly prospects with a word.

She curled her toes into her slippers. She'd forgotten, last night, that Rudyard was a threat and a danger. She'd been caught up in the magnificence of the music. In the clean, sharp scent of his eau de cologne as he stood beside her in the opera box.

In the exultant thrill that raced through her body when that low, liquid baritone poured into her ear. The man had a voice that sounded like brandy tasted—rich, smoky, delicious, and quite, quite heady for one not accustomed to spirits. Did he sing? She would forget all his faults at once—saving, of course, his insult to Selina— if he did.

"Interested in Lucasta? Oh, I see." Her ladyship tapped a finger on the scandal sheet, her lips pinched as if her cordial had turned sour. "Lady Clara hinted she had also heard that your great-aunt intends to leave everything to you." Her smile showed her teeth. "Though she is my aunt also, and I might be helped just as much by her fortune. In addition, my birth cannot be quarreled with. *I*, unlike my sister, have done nothing to disgrace the family."

Lucasta stared into her weak tea. She would rather be rated for attending the opera than endure this discussion. "My aunt may change her mind, mum."

But in the meantime, gossip about her supposed inheritance would indeed account for Rudyard's interest in her. There was no other reason a man of his rank and wealth would take the slightest notice of a poor vicar's daughter.

Unless he were looking for revenge, in some fashion, for rude observations the vicar's daughter liked to sling about him and his friends. But then why not condescend to her face, as he had to Selina?

Cici frowned. "But Papa wants Lucasta for Trevor. You'll adore him, my dear. He's quite dashing."

"Far too dashing for her," her ladyship said sharply. "Cecilia, do not be a goosecap. Lucasta would not dare aspire so high, and I cannot conceive why your father should jest about such a match. Your brother and your cousin are unsuitable in every possible respect."

Lucasta winced and set her tea aside. Always the poor relation, the dowdy cousin, plain, disappointing Lucasta. Her aunt didn't approve of the Baron's plans, then. That was useful, since Lucasta didn't approve of them, either.

"Aunt Pevensey has the right of it, Cici," Lucasta said, careful to keep the bitterness from her tone. Her aunt would pounce on the opportunity to read her another juniper lecture about perceiving the generosity of her family, et cetera, though barbs about her father's foreignness and her mother's birth were slipped into every sentence. "Your brother will be a peer of the realm in good time, and I, if luck and fate are kind, will have a music studio of my own."

If she were going to be brazen, might not go for the prize. "I am much better off devoting myself to the poor sad talents that might support me at Miss Gregoire's, do you not think? And since Signor Marchesi was performing last evening, and he—"

"No," her aunt snapped. "To all of it, no, as I have told you, Lucasta! It is one thing to nurture a private talent that can prove agreeable to your friends. But no member of this family, while I live and breathe, will do something so vulgar as perform in public for pay. On that, at least, Aunt Cornelia and I agree."

Her ladyship took a deep draught of her cordial, her nostrils flaring. "Only that awful school could have given you such ideas. She ought never have let you attend it."

Lucasta forced herself to breathe evenly, all the way from her belly. It was a technique a past singing master taught her, and it was a useful trick for handling temper as well as deepening sound. How she longed for the day she could return to Miss Gregoire's. At least there she had employment, and she could play and sing as much as she liked.

"If private entertainments are acceptable, mum, then perhaps you might reconsider Lady Cranbury's invitation for me to participate in her musicale." Lucasta tried to sound diffident. Her aunt would deny her out of sheer spite if she knew how much Lucasta longed to get her hands on a pianoforte built by Cristofori.

Aunt returned to her cordial. "We have no reason to appear agreeable to Lady Cranbury, not when she is trying to match one of her grandnieces with Mr. Plimpton, and he is showing interest in Cecilia. Besides, it would appear I am pushing you forward, and I will not appear so vulgar."

She slid aside her egg in its cup. "The hairdresser is coming this afternoon, and the Baron and I are hosting a dinner this evening. I need you to make up the numbers, so pray appear on time, Lucasta, and wear the gray silk robe."

Lucasta nodded and rose, swallowing the remark that the gray robe made her look like a turned pudding, and both she and her aunt knew it. "My errands this afternoon will not take long."

"Check if Mrs. MacGowan requires anything. And Lucasta." There was ice in her ladyship's tone, though she stared straight before her, raising her cordial to her lips and not meeting her niece's eye. "There will be no more mention of your name in the gossip papers. In association with anyone, least of all Rudyard. You will avoid becoming notorious at all costs."

"There isn't the least chance of that," Lucasta said, pushing in her chair. "One has to be visible before one can be notorious."

Cici shot her a look of surprise at her bitter tone, and Lucasta left the room before she did something so foolish as to burst into frustrated tears. Only it felt a crueler loss now, to have her music denied her, after she had spent a night at the opera. She had stood in the music on its way to heaven and a man with the voice of a fallen angel had enjoyed the performance with her, conversed with her, escorted her through one of London's most beautiful theaters on his arm.

Poor, plain Lucasta Lithwick could not hope for a repeat of that experience. She had seen her last of Signor Marchesi and likely Smart Jeremy as well. He would have forgotten her already.

Until the moment he nearly ran her down in Bloomsbury Square.

## CHAPTER EIGHT

Jem made his obligatory visit to the drawing room of Arendale House to find Bertie making an impossible tangle of her netting and his aunt devouring the morning papers.

"It's everywhere, Jeremiah," Aunt Payne said with a frown. "You were seen again fawning over this mysterious Miss Lithwick. A schoolteacher, lately of Bath? Why would you let her in Arendale's box?"

"Because she wished to enjoy the opera without being jostled in the pit."

Jem glanced through the gossip sheets, wrestling down a flare of irritation at the usual fulsome, barbed praise of him. The reports wondered at Miss L—'s cleverness in beguiling the interest of that Exquisite fondly known to those of the best *ton* as Smart Jeremy. Every scandalmonger in town would be watching her next moves. And his.

That was what he had wanted, wasn't it?

"Is it because they say she is coming into money?" Aunt Payne shook her head. "Cadmus would never have stooped to fortune hunting."

Jem flinched. His own finances were sound and about to become sounder, but he couldn't say the same for his wastrel father, who was somehow managing to bleed the Arendale accounts even from halfway around the world. So said the marquess in querulous letters to Jem. His grandfather seemed to believe Jem should attempt to curb his father's excesses. When he'd never had the power to gain his father's notice or approval, much less lure him to sobriety, fidelity, or a sense of his responsibilities.

"Care to come with me to my shop, Bertie?" Jem asked casually. "I've just gotten in a new chintz from India. I'll set aside a few yards for you if you like."

It was a lovely, unusual pattern of red and brown flowers with hand-painted touches of blue, and the more Jem thought about it, the more convinced he was the fabric would make a flattering polonaise or *robe à la française* for Miss Lithwick. It would harmonize beautifully with her coloring, especially that enchanting red-gold she'd achieved for her hair.

"Bertie must be at home with me," Aunt Payne said. "We will have more callers now that we are putting off mourning." She threw Jem a warning glare. "And I will need her help to squash the gossip over your behavior."

Bertie's face fell, but she made no complaint, and Jem withdrew. He did not care to wage yet another battle over how he provided for his siblings. There was no amount of fortune, esteem, success, or social rank that would make him acceptable in his aunt's eyes, for he was not Cadmus, and never could be.

The groom brought his calash around, and as he checked that the hood was secure against the chilly air and his pair were harnessed properly, Jem considered how much attention he might pay to Lucasta Lithwick before his motives were mistaken for courtship. He should be able to accomplish his goal in another day or two. A dance at another ball, or a walk through a pleasure garden of an evening. If he could find her. As he had learned the night before, he couldn't exactly expect Miss Lithwick to appear before him.

And yet, as he clucked the horses to walk on and emerged from the mews onto Great Russell Street, there she was, traversing the great expanse before Bedford House. Another girl lagged at her elbow, he guessed a servant who had been impressed into service as companion while Miss Lucasta Lithwick strolled around town. Or rather, marched at a sustained and determined pace, clearly to some desired destination, on an expedition that according to their expressions was highly anticipated by the maiden, but not the maid.

His shop could wait, Jem decided, and guided his horses alongside.

"Miss Lithwick! Good day. Have you business at Bedford House? I am surprised to find you in my neighborhood."

He would have come up with a smoother opening, given the time, Jem told himself. But he doubted that Miss Lithwick heard a word past her name, given her look of complete astonishment.

"Milord Rudyard! You live hereabouts?" A riposte no cleverer than his sally.

"Yes, Arendale House is just there." He pointed toward the Palladian exterior of a stately townhouse standing a little apart from its neighbors, a rare privilege in crowded London. He gave her a mischievous smile. "Were you coming to call?"

The first expression to cross her face was annoyance. Jem's chest tightened. Miss Lithwick, annoyed to see him! She engaged in a short internal struggle, and then the turmoil ended in a mask of politeness.

"I am in fact on my way to the Foundling Hospital. It seems I have passed your home several times and never paid you the courtesy of a visit. How very rude of me."

"Yes, excessively. Shall I drive you?"

She regarded the vehicle with a combination of longing and suspicion. The wind carried the bite of March, cooler than usual, and he was snug beneath a thick fur. Then she glanced at the horses with trepidation, as one not accustomed to the animals.

"We are content to walk," she said firmly.

"Don't be silly. There is a seat for your maid here." Jem reached behind him and pulled down the folding bench.

"Ever so kind of you, milord," the maid said, clambering into the hooded shelter.

The dubious look Miss Lithwick gave Jem made his every contrary impulse rise to the surface. "I mentioned we are visiting the Foundling Hospital," she said, as if doubting he had ever harbored a useful notion in his life, much less a charitable one.

"I don't go there nearly enough, but I can remedy that oversight at once. Come out of the chill, Miss Lithwick. I shall hack you about where you wish today, and you shall be glad of my blanket, if nothing else."

His smile, without his planning it, turned slightly wicked. This was a perfect opportunity, as if the gods were smiling upon him. He would convey her to her errands, and then he might suggest squiring her to his shop. She was plainly in need of new gowns, particularly if she expected to be besieged by fortune-hunting suitors. He would undertake to be her advisor.

He reminded himself of the purpose for the fantasy. It was not to admire Miss Lithwick. Having more of the *haut ton* patronize his shop would forge an armor of protection around his name and status. And that armor could protect Judith, and his other siblings, when curious gossips like Lady Clara probed into his personal life.

Aunt Payne was right; it was impossible to expect he could keep his father's doings a secret. The best he could do was build strong defenses for when the attacks came.

Miss Lithwick looked anxiously into his face, that internal struggle reasserting itself. Jem was touched again by the earnest if understated beauty of her broad, intelligent brow, that determined chin, those angular cheeks and long nose, the deliciously soft lips. Society's admiration for her would not be false from those who were paying Miss Lithwick close attention.

Triumph rose in his chest as she clamped one hand on her bonnet and held out the other gloved hand to him. Winning a concession from Miss Lucasta Lithwick was no small victory.

"Very well," she said. "I suppose we can walk home when you tire of us."

"That I shall never do," Jem said.

As Miss Lithwick settled into the seat next to him, he surveyed her worn leather short boots, the kind a servant would wear, and the peek of calico skirts beneath a sensible woolen cloak. Plain attire, neat and serviceable, the garb of a woman of modest means accustomed to drawing no attention to herself.

With that striking profile, she ought to have attention. She ought to be in dress that showed her to best advantage. He would be doing her a service as much as helping his business.

"Tell me what your business is at the Founding Hospital." Jem turned the horses onto Southampton Road. She could easily have walked the short distance, but he liked having Miss Lithwick beside him. She sat stiff and alert, as if she expected at any moment that something would misbehave: the horses, the traffic, him. He wondered what it would take to win her confidence.

"It is considered quite a fashionable charity," he added. "All the ladies seem to support it in some way."

"Is that the reason for your own interest?"

"*Pax*, Miss Lithwick," Jem begged. "If you will hold off disparaging my taste, I will not presume to judge yours."

"Oh, I expect you will judge," she said, and cringed as a carter rolled past them with a heavy wagon, cracking a whip over his team of six. "But I can agree that we both might keep our cutting comments to ourselves."

Miss Lithwick was not going to flirt with him, that was clear. It made Jem all the more determined to draw her out. At the gatehouse to the Hospital she gathered herself to address the porter, but the man hailed Jem first.

"Aye now, it's Mr. Falstead! Been an age or two, it 'as. There's no guv'ners meetin' today, sir, so yer 'ere for a lookaround, then?"

"Hello, Silas. I am escorting Miss Lithwick this afternoon." Jem raked his brains for the man's last name, prepared to make an introduction, but the porter turned his genial smile on Jem's companion.

"Ullo, miss! Look at ye in a fancy carriage this day, and with these high-steppers!" He touched the brim of his cap. "Don't doubt as there's a crowd waitin' for ye. Yer one of the fav'rites, and no mistake."

"Thank you, Silas," Miss Lithwick said primly while Jem recovered from his surprise. "If you will turn right, milord Rudyard, my destination is there." She pointed to the wing with the girls' classrooms.

"But it's their midday break," Jem said. "They won't resume classes until two of the clock."

"Precisely." She clambered out of the vehicle, not exactly with grace, as he drew to a halt. "They may disperse to their own activities during this time, and some of them use it to practice their music."

Her maid opted to remain in the carriage and watch the fashionable folk promenading around the grand oval walk before the Hospital, so Jem followed Lucasta into the plain brick wing of the building. She tapped briskly down the broad hall and entered a large, spare room crowded with girls, some of them sitting at the tables used for lessons, some perched on the window ledges, many more standing around the edges of the room, talking with animation.

When Lucasta entered, they drew to attention with a welcoming chorus. "Good afternoon, Miss Lithwick!"

"Good afternoon, girls. Do say hello to my friend, Lord Rudyard."

"Good afternoon, Lord Rudyard," the girls chimed, and Jem smiled uncomfortably, aware of the immediate stir at the sight of him.

Lucasta collapsed her hooped bonnet and removed her cloak, revealing a worked muslin caraco jacket over the calico petticoat he had glimpsed before. She'd achieved that same enchanting apricot color with her hair, and the jaunty chip hat, trimmed with dark green ribbon and feathers, suggested again that she liked at least for her head to be stylish. She turned and caught him staring.

"You needn't stay, milord. We may be some time."

Jem arranged himself against the door frame in a casual pose, aware how much taller he was than she. "I've no other engagements for the nonce."

Nothing could have moved him from this spot. He was desperately curious to see what would happen next.

Several girls giggled at his remark, and at Lucasta's annoyed expression, but they silenced when she withdrew from her cloak what looked like a long, narrow violin. "Very well, let's proceed. Eliza, I believe it is your turn to play the pochette today?"

"Yes, miss," came an eager voice from the back, and a young girl stepped forward. They were all, Jem judged, between the ages of eight and fifteen, dressed in dark woolen frocks with neat white aprons and caps. The girl walked to the front of the room, trailing her fingers along the tabletops as she came. Jem stared at her face. She paused next to Lucasta and turned her palms up. Lucasta laid the instrument in one hand and the bow in the other, and the girl raised the violin to her chin.

"She's—" Jem bit off the warning. Anyone could see the girl was blind, her eyes white and scarred. Any number of diseases could have done it, as they did to so many: smallpox, scarlet fever, or a syphilitic parent were the most frequent causes.

"Becoming quite adept, aren't you, Eliza?" Lucasta adjusted the girl's posture with a gentle hand. "Middle C, please."

The girl placed her fingers and played a sound. Lucasta sang the note, and Jem blinked. Her voice was as rich and clear as sunlight, and it filled the room.

The girls sang back, not all of them in tune. Lucasta sang another note, which they repeated. There followed a set of vocal exercises, ascending and descending scales, then on to patterns that to Jem sounded random, but which the class followed with ease of familiarity. As they practiced, Lucasta moved among the girls and touched them with a gentle hand, lifting chins, pushing back shoulders, and sometimes pressing on a stomach to show them where she wanted the breath to begin.

They were a tidy group, kept clean and clothed according to the Hospital's standards, but they were not beautiful. Many of them bore the scars of smallpox or other childhood disease. Several held a cane or crutch for malformed limbs. One girl in a wheeled chair sang with extra volume, leaning forward as if she meant for her little voice to rise above them all. Their eyes followed Lucasta adoringly.

In the pauses to rest their voices, the girls chatted to their teacher as if to a dear friend, eagerly answering her questions about their lessons, their play, and their general welfare. There was no arguing, no complaining or quarreling, no posturing or henpecking as he had seen girls do. Eliza, head tilted toward the pochette, played with a blissful smile upon her face, lost in a world of beauty that Lucasta had helped create for these girls.

Something twisted and bit at the inside of Jem's chest. Judith would thrive in this circle, where defects of person were a given, not a sin. Judith was thriving where Jem had put her. But she would never survive in the treacherous world of the *beau monde*; she was no more equipped to navigate its shoals than was Miss Lucasta Lithwick.

"I believe we have time for a song," Lucasta said after the vocal exercises were over. "Have you suggestions, girls?"

"Comin' Thro' the Rye!" called an older girl with a strong Scots accent. Giggles erupted at the words.

"Far too naughty, my dear Hester," Lucasta said, though she grinned. "Matron will bar the doors against me if she hears us singing *that*. Shall we have Little Gunver, from the Danish operetta? Eliza, I believe you know the tune."

She helped the girl run through a sweet, mournful melody, adjusting the placement of her fingers and explaining the techniques for the others. Several girls positioned their hands in the air, mimicking the fingering on imaginary instruments. It would be a rare treat to get their hands on an instrument, Jem knew.

Their schooling was practical, focused on reading, writing,

household skills, talents that would earn them apprenticeship into a respectable trade when they came of age. Lucasta was an infusion of light and joy and music into their sheltered world which, while not intentionally cruel, was by necessity not adorned with luxuries.

"Now, who remembers the words? Philippa, come sing them for us, verse by verse. You sing, and we'll repeat."

A smaller girl came forward, wearing a birthmark the color of port wine across part of her face, her expression alight with joy at being singled out. She had a charming voice, clear if thin, and Lucasta chimed in with the correct pitch. As Lucasta conducted the group through the ballad, their pure, childish voices ringing out, Jem felt a deep, calm ease spread through him like medicinal balm.

It had been long, too long, since he sat like this, as within a family circle, singing together, needing nothing else in the world but this harmony that told him every evil and sorrow in the world could be smoothed over with the right melody. That he could again feel his blood run clean and light through him, like a sunbeam, and that humans could not be such terrible creatures if they were able to blend their voices in song.

After a while he realized the story was a haunted one, about a young girl lured to the bottom of the sea by a deceitful merman and then abandoned there, lost forever to the land world where she belonged, and lost to those who loved her.

The tale at the opera last night, too, had been of a woman losing her life to male whim. Jem shifted his pose in the doorframe.

Well, he did not intend to enchant Miss Lithwick, and he did not intend to harm her, either.

He had only meant to lure her, admittedly, into a position where potential harm might befall her.

When the girls finished, their faces alight with joy, Lucasta applauded them, and they clapped for her and each other. "And now," Lucasta said over their exuberant chatter, "let us ask Lord Rudyard what he thought of our song."

Jem swept a low bow. The girls wiggled in delight. "A marvelous performance," he said, and he was honest. The time had flown by. "But I confess I have one request."

Lucasta's face also glowed with delight. While she had been deplorably awkward at the ball and wary and guarded at the theater, here among her students she was in her element, relaxed, open, humming with joy. He wanted to see more of this Lucasta.

"I would like for Miss Lithwick to sing for us," Jem said.

A resounding series of affirmations met this. "Oh, yes, Miss Lithwick! Sing for us? Indeed, you must. We have been very good."

"This is your time, girls," Lucasta protested. "You don't want to spend it listening to me warble."

"Perhaps it would be instructive of them to hear a trained voice," Jem suggested.

A shadow crossed her face, a look of such longing that it tugged at Jem's heart. "I am not trained," she answered. "Not properly, at least."

"Do sing, Miss Lithwick." Eliza held out the pochette and bow, returning the instrument. "We so love to hear you."

Lucasta sent Jem a veiled look. She knew he was testing her. Jem folded his arms and leaned against the door frame. He would guess Lucasta Lithwick never backed down from a challenge.

"Very well." Lucasta picked up the pochette and faced the classroom with its rows of eager faces. The girls pressed forward. "I will sing you a hymn I am learning. It is called 'Blessed Be the Ties That Bind.' My father would have liked it, and I think Matron can approve of your hearing it."

She teased a few notes from the instrument, finding a tune, and then she drew a breath and sang.

Jem forgot to breathe.

He had no musical training. He had been raised in a warehouse and the back rooms of a draper's shop, set to work as soon as he was old enough to run errands. He learned his letters and numbers from the account books his mother kept. When she died, though he was only nine, he began his apprenticeship in earnest.

Constance Dixon had come from honest people, hardworking and upright, and they enjoyed life as much as they could. But they had not thought to give Jem the schooling of a gentleman, not when they depended on his level head and his eye for color to help with the business.

He had never learned Latin. He had never been taught an instrument. He only knew how to dance because Bertie had taught him, imparting the lessons of her dancing master. For all that his father's held a marquess, Jeremiah Falstead was a draper's son, and though he put on fashionable attire and paraded through the parlors and parks and the narrow paths of the *beau monde*, a draper's son he remained. They petted him, made much of him, teased him about his accomplishments, but they saw what he really was.

And now, for the first time, he was seeing the real Lucasta Lithwick. He didn't need musical training to understand that her voice was astonishing. The tone was as pure and clear as a waterfall on some island of paradise, like the one his father governed. Her voice made the back of his neck tingle, made his body flush with warmth. Her voice was pliable as gold, clear as sunlight, strong as spun flax, and it poured through the room like a magical elixir that cast a spell of beauty over them all.

She ended the last note and lowered the pochette. The room echoed. Jem felt hollow in his bones, in his chest. Something otherworldly had blown through him, and he might never be the same again.

Tears shone in the eyes of more than one girl. Several held hands clasped to their chins or hearts. Eliza stood with her eyes closed, an expression on her face like that Lucasta had worn when she heard Signor Marchesi sing. Complete and profound rapture.

Jem cleared his throat. "Thank you, Miss Lithwick."

Lucasta picked up her cloak and drew it about her shoulders. "Thank you, girls, for letting me spend this time with you. Shall we meet again Friday? I will bring what instruments I can, and we can practice."

"Yes, Miss Lithwick! Thank you, Miss Lithwick!" Several girls pressed forward to take her hand, sliding arms about her waist. Lucasta embraced them in return and kissed the tops of several muslin caps, generous with her affection.

Jem stared as if scales had fallen from his eyes. Or as if some veil had fallen from her, the shell she wore in society that guarded the pure, bright being beneath.

He fell into step beside her as they walked down the hallway toward the door where they had entered. "You come here often," he observed.

"As often as I can. My aunt allows it, since, as you pointed out, the Foundling Hospital is a fashionable charitable interest to have."

He regretted that sly cut. "You bring joy into their lives," he said instead. "The governors take an interest in their care and upkeep. But you bring them joy." He paused. "And you do so in their free time. I thought there was a music master?" There was at least one earning a stipend, he knew from the records.

"Several are taught singing or violin, when it may be their only possible means of support," she answered. "I'm sure you have seen the blind foundlings playing on nearly every street corner in London."

She didn't know Jem sat on the board of governors for the hospital. He was still just an idle fop to her.

Jem was very aware of those foundlings. For someone like Eliza, her opportunity for apprenticeships would be limited, and no one would take her into service. Music was one ability she did not need sight to cultivate.

The maid came awake with a soft snort as Jem helped Lucasta into his calash. He waited until she was snuggled once more into her bonnet, cloak, and the furred throw, and they had waved to Silas, before he let the question burst from him.

"Why are you not singing on the stage?"

"I'm a contralto," she said, as if that answered anything.

Jem waited. She glanced at his face, then away. "There are very few opera roles written for contraltos. And castrati often take those parts."

"But besides opera," Jem said. "I've heard singers in Ranelagh Gardens. Vauxhall. Haymarket offers more than operas. You could perform solo. You could tour the Continent and sing in the greatest courts." He didn't understand why she wasn't doing that already. A voice as divine as hers would be welcome anywhere.

She drew a long breath through her nose. He couldn't see her face beneath the bonnet, only the very tip of her nose. "I sing at Miss Gregoire's, and I've given small performances in Bath. My Aunt Cornelia likes me to perform for her friends."

"Then she should share you with broader audiences."

She shook her head. "Aunt Cornelia comes from a world where only the lower-class perform on stage. Actresses and singers are, to her, little more than common women." She chose the phrase delicately. "And Lady Pevensey is set against me training. She thinks it is vulgar. As I am only a vicar's daughter," she added in a bitter tone, "I cannot forfeit what small claim to respectability I have by performing on the stage."

"What about small venues?" he argued. "Private performances."

"Perfectly acceptable, since that supports the ease and enjoyment of my family and friends. Given that women were intended by God's design to ornament the home, not public spaces."

"Your talent should not be hidden," Jem swore. "It is a divine gift."

Her fur muff, which had been trembling as if her hands were shaking within it, stilled. "Thank you," she said softly.

Jem looked straight ahead, not daring to glance at her face. He feared her expression would unman him, as he had probed what was clearly a deep wound. Lucasta Lithwick stood on the sidelines because she was not permitted, by some absurd belief of her family, to share her astonishing talent in public. That had to be some level of crime.

She had not shrunk from Eliza, nor any of the blind children, just as she had not shrunk from the scarred, the lame, or those missing teeth. She had not treated the blind girl any differently than the others, had in fact singled her out to play for them, an honor he suspected Eliza would hold in her heart for weeks, if not months to follow. Lucasta Lithwick was not cruel.

At least, not to the vulnerable. Jem had taken it upon himself to teach her a lesson she already knew.

"Where are you bound to next?" he asked, realizing he was driving down Red Lion Street without purpose.

"Charles Street," Miss Lithwick answered. "You may set me down anywhere you wish."

"That is all the way over by Berkeley Square," Jem said, taken aback. "You cannot tell me you meant to walk?"

She gave him a quizzical look. "It's scarcely two miles. You have never lived in the country, have you?"

"You live in Bath," he retorted, turning the horses onto Holborn, which swarmed with traffic.

"I did not grow up in Bath," she replied. "But Miss Gregoire's is there, and we walk everywhere. Miss Gregoire's girls never take chairs." She added after a moment, "The Gorgons use their feet, or whatever appendages they have. Do you suppose they had human legs, or something clawed? The earlier artistic representations vary, and the mentions in Homer and elsewhere dwell mostly on the snake hair and staring eyes, et cetera. The word *gorgos* means terrible, or inspiring fear, so it's quite clear they were meant to be monsters, but one wonders—"

She broke off as Jem let loose a snort, adding pertly, "As I said, you may put me down anywhere you like."

"I will drive you," Jem repeated, "and I will call out whichever vile knave named you and your friends the Gorgons. Such a man should be driven through the street with a pitchfork."

She burst into a merry peal of laughter. It startled Jem, singing through his blood just as her voice had.

He had been wrong in more ways than one about Miss Lucasta Lithwick. One drive, one dance, one afternoon with her was not going to be enough.

And if she ever learned what he'd truly been about, with his invitations and flattery, she would have worse than taunts about his garb for him. She would consign him to the deepest circles of hell, which was no doubt where he belonged.

# CHAPTER NINE

Avoiding barreling coaches, expensive sedan chairs, and boys and dogs darting into traffic, Jem followed Lucasta's directions to a modest shop at 19 Charles Street. He couldn't have been more surprised to see the gilded sign bearing the imprint of Ignatius Sancho, Grocer.

He'd heard of the shop, but never visited. Before he had time to read the title of the books stacked in the window—*The Letters of the Late Ignatius Sancho*—Lucasta strolled inside.

Ignatius Sancho was the man whom all London had known as the noble African. He'd overcome being kidnapped and sold into enslavement to become a prominent property owner and voting citizen. Even a vicar's daughter lately of Bath must know his story.

And she must know what she was about, choosing to patronize the family's store. Nonetheless Jem walked with a cautious step into the store behind her. He'd been enjoying their stolen time together and would have, by his own lights, delayed this crucial test.

She'd been kind at the Foundling Hospital to children of every possible hue, but that was a fashionable charity. In his unfortunate stroll through Lady Clara's lemon trees, he'd overheard her disparage him for being no better than a draper's son, which was what all of England thought. Then she'd abused the conductor at the opera for possibly being blind. So far he'd seen nothing to suggest she was above the usual prejudices of her class.

He could shut his eyes to it as a business owner—he had to, if he wanted any custom in this town. But if Miss Lithwick behaved rudely in the shop of the late and much-admired Sancho, Jem would leave her to take a chair or walk alone, possibly in the rain, his reputation as a gentleman be damned.

The air smelled of tea and chocolate, spices and herbs. Lucasta strode through the neat shelves and bins to the broad wooden counter at the back of the store and greeted the woman behind it.

"Mrs. Sancho! Have you no help in the store today? What happened to the apprentice who was here last time?"

"Running an errand, so I'm teaching my William to serve customers." Mrs. Sancho was dressed far more fashionably than Lucasta in a closed robe made of chintz with dainty buff stripes. A sash tied about her waist bloomed against the skirts gathered in the back, and her sleeves were decorated with buttons as well as lace at the cuffs. Jem approved.

"What wish you today, Miss Lithwick?" Mrs. Sancho gave Jem a curious look.

"The usual." Lucasta set her muff on the counter. "Tobacco for the Baron. A pound of sugar at the least. Cici put the last of it in her tea this morning, and for that matter, we require more tea. Whatever blend my aunt commissioned is unpalatable. I suspect it is mostly ground beans and sawdust."

"Shame." Mrs. Sancho clicked her tongue. "Will, run fetch a sugar loaf for Miss Lithwick. The good loaves, my sweet."

A young boy, wearing a smart blue suit with his black curly hair pulled into a queue, ran off to attend this task with all the loose-limbed, noisy energy a young boy possessed.

"The girls are well?" Lucasta inquired. "Miss Frances? Ann? Elizabeth?"

"Well as can be," Mrs. Sancho reported as she measured tea

from the tins behind the counter. "I wish they were here. They would love to tell you how they are progressing with their music."

"I wish to hear it." Lucasta smiled as William returned with a sugar loaf wrapped in paper. "And what instrument will you take up, Master William?"

"I'm going to be a printer," the young boy declared. "And print books like Papa's."

"A noble profession," Lucasta agreed. She selected one of the books from a display on the counter and laid it next to the sugar loaf. "In that case I shall come to you for all my printed music. Your father's *Theory of Music* is quite fine, you know. I refer to it often with my students."

William beamed and ran off, content that he had discharged his duty. Mrs. Sancho rewrapped the sugar loaf and measured out the tobacco. "Now remember to tell the girls," Lucasta said as she counted coins, "they are always welcome at Miss Gregoire's. I am not sure we've ever had three sisters at one time! They would make quite a sensation."

Mrs. Sancho shook her head, smiling. "You and Miss Gregoire. I do feel she would take care of my girls. I can't say that for every school, I'm afraid." Her eyes drifted to Jem, and Lucasta turned as if recalling his presence.

"Oh! Mrs. Sancho. May I present to you the Viscount Rudyard, grandson to the Marquess of Arendale. Rudyard, this is Mrs. Sancho, widow of the extremely gifted Mr. Ignatius Sancho."

The widow's eyes narrowed slightly as she assessed Jem. "Rudyard," she said softly. "And your father is now Earl Payne. Governor of the Isle of Barbados, if I am not mistaken?"

Jem inclined his head, ashamed to admit to this woman that his father governed a colony which drew its economic profits from enslavement and exploitation. He sensed that Mrs. Sancho knew of the earl's reputation—all of it. "I'm afraid that is correct."

"Is it." She turned away. "Have you talked to your aunt about giving my girls music lessons, Miss Lithwick?"

Lucasta pulled on her muff, her face falling. "Aunt has said I will be too busy to give lessons for the foreseeable future. To anyone." She tried to rearrange her features into a brisk smile. "All the more reason to send them to Miss Gregoire's, for I shall be at liberty there, and they should be my favorite pupils. Good day, Master William, Mrs. Sancho. Please give my regards to the girls." She gathered her packages and was out the door before Jem could recall that, as a gentleman, it was his place to offer to hold them for her.

In the carriage, Lucasta seemed to be struggling to compose herself. Jem felt such a roil of his own emotions that he didn't know where to begin. He urged the horses around Chesterfield House and toward Hyde Park. It was not yet the fashionable hour, but there was a chance they would be seen. For reasons he could not satisfactorily explain to himself, he very much wanted to be seen with Miss Lucasta Lithwick.

"You frequent Sancho's," he began, keeping his eye on the team, who kicked up their heels and their spirits at Hyde Park Corner and the sight of grass beyond. "You do not mind that they are—" He searched for the word. "Africans."

She drew her brows together. "I should think they have lived here long enough to be called British," she answered. "Mr. Sancho voted in the last election, if you didn't know. But yes, I agree with Mr. Sancho's opinion that if African people are enslaved to produce our luxuries, then the family of a former slave should at the least see some of the profits of that terrible institution."

She was an abolitionist. That laid to rest one fear, but another tightened Jem's throat. She would have the same opinion of his father that Mrs. Sancho did.

"But you aren't—" For some reason words were deserting the man whose pronouncements were hung upon in polite circles. He nodded at the occupants of a passing landau, two ladies craning their necks to get a glimpse of his companion under the deep brim of her bonnet. "You didn't," he managed finally.

"Didn't what?" She tensed. "Treat them differently because of the color of their skin? As if they are less human, as the enslavers would have us believe?"

Jem's tongue felt enormous in his mouth. He had never discussed this issue with anyone, not his friends, not his family. They tiptoed around it as if circling a pit of viperous snakes.

There were thousands of Africans in England, more in the coastal towns than inland, employed at all levels of society. Too many were enslaved and denied their freedom. Others earned a salary but were denied their full humanity nonetheless.

"Not everyone believes as you do," he said hollowly.

Every line of her body went taut. "You'd best let me down here, Lord Rudyard."

They were near the reservoir. Not the greatest cad would abandon her here, leaving her and her maid to walk the miles back to Bedford Square. "You misunderstand me, Miss Lithwick. I am not—"

He was not his father, who chose to bestow his affections upon an enslaved woman, but not do her or her children the courtesy of granting their freedom. "I am not of that mind," he attempted.

"I perceive your mind, Lord Rudyard, and it makes it impossible that I can continue in your company. Mary!" she snapped at her maid, holding tight in the folding seat behind them. "We shall walk from here."

Jem denied her by the simple ploy of refusing to pause the horses. Though they went no faster than a brisk walk, she could hardly throw herself from a moving vehicle.

"I shall see you home, Miss Lithwick," he said, his tone equally sharp, "and you will do me the honor of illuminating me as to what precisely you understand my mind to be."

She refused to look at him. "I don't wish to discuss it," she said, her jaw set with anger.

His own anger sparked. "If you are accusing me of something, I'd damned well like to know what it is."

He never lost his temper. He never swore at anyone, especially not a woman. But Lucasta Lithwick burrowed under his skin in a way no one ever had.

"Your comment about Selina!" she burst out. "That said everything about your *mind*, didn't it?"

Jem raked his memory for the conversation in question. "Miss Humby? I haven't said a dozen words to her this season. I don't think our paths have crossed before the theater last night." Once, perhaps, maybe twice.

"It took less than a dozen words." She held her chin high. "You called her a zebra. No one had the least concern that her mother is Bengali until you made her out to be some circus freak. Now no one will speak to her."

Horror turned Jem's blood to ice. "I never said—"

But he had. The remark rose to his mind instantly, with the memory of those awful glaring stripes. "I meant the print of the fabric. It looked exactly like a zebra. I never thought..." He trailed off, stricken.

"You didn't mean to remind everyone that her mother has dark skin?" she challenged him. "To suggest that she is a creature half one thing, half another? Because everyone presumes that is what you meant. Everyone," she repeated.

The bitterness in her tone shook him as much as the appalling implication of her words. The style of Miss Humby's gown and the stripes, though a fashionable print, had not at all done her justice. He was sensitive to colors and prints. His taste was the basis of his success as a draper. But he had never meant to insult her heritage. He was the last person in any position to judge.

Thoughtlessness did not excuse him. He *should* have thought of it. He'd become so caught up in the role he was expected to play as Smart Jeremy, like a circus tiger himself, that he'd behaved like any driven creature, lashing back without consideration.

Lucasta had accused him of not understanding the impact of his words. She'd seen what he was doing.

He hadn't.

"I am distressed to hear that my comments should be taken in such a light." Jem managed to keep his voice calm, though his heart was dark and seething. "Please convey my most sincere apologies to Miss Humby."

"I will not," Lucasta said, hugging her muff to her middle. "It is your place to discuss any regrets you have over your remarks with her."

He would. He could not let it be assumed he despised dark skin, and for more reasons than custom for his shop. But he did not see how he could convince Lucasta Lithwick of this.

They were in Caroline Street and she had exited the calash in high dudgeon before Jem realized the only way he could make her understand. He would have to tell her everything, more than he wanted to reveal, more than anyone else in London knew. It was the only way he could redeem himself.

And yet, letting Lucasta Lithwick into his secret would risk everything he had guarded for so long, bringing the truth about himself into the cold light of her judgment.

He couldn't let her or anyone go on believing the conclusion that had been drawn from his unconsidered remarks. He might detest being Smart Jeremy, but he needed that fop. If his business suffered, Jem had no way to protect his family.

But he couldn't risk exposing that family, not even to change Miss Lucasta Lithwick's damning opinion of him. He couldn't give up his last tenuous shred of secrecy when the loss would harm far more people than just him.

# CHAPTER TEN

Lady Pevensey's correspondents hastened to inform her that Lucasta had been seen in Smart Jeremy's calash, driving through Hyde Park. In retribution, her ladyship chose not to permit Lucasta to accompany them to the Duchess of Highcastle's Venetian breakfast on Sunday.

Lucasta bore her punishment bravely and spent the hours in her music room, arranging Signor Marchesi's song for the harpsichord. She refused to speculate on what Lord Rudyard would have to say of the event, which proved an efficient use of her time, as Cici reported that he did not attend. Lady Pevensey was extremely put out, and so was Her Grace the duchess, who had apparently been hoping to learn what Rudyard thought of the arrangement of feathers on her hat.

He had been as nervous as a cat on hot bricks at Sancho's, uncomfortable to appear in an establishment run by an African family, even a prominent one. Lucasta refused to devote a moment of her mental faculties to him. He was a man who judged people by appearances, by their style or dress or the color of their skin. She had pronounced him no better than he was, and she ought not feel disappointed that she had been proven right.

On Monday, the Duchess of Hunsdon held a tea, and Lady

Pevensey left Lucasta at home again. Lucasta, having been vocal in her disapproval of Cici's many society engagements, could not now complain that she was left out of this one, though the Duchess of Hunsdon had been a student at Miss Gregoire's and Lucasta very much wanted to learn more about those Greek histories. She spent the moody hours with her violin, entertained a surprising number of callers, then ran round to her favorite stationer's for paper and ink, though she knew she would not be permitted to perform her new compositions.

She was surrounded by a symphony of more and better music than she'd ever known in her life, and was not allowed to listen, much less play a part. It was like water denied a fever patient, last rites denied a victim of the plague.

Tuesday, Lucasta fell with gratitude upon a summons from Selina. Cici was occupied by her dancing master, and it was a simple matter for Lucasta to pull on her boots, cloak, and calash bonnet, then slip from the house. She was desperate for the company of her friends.

One never knew if one invited robbery more by walking a woman alone, in unremarkable clothing, or with a servant, which indicated enough wealth to make it possible she had something worth stealing. London pickpockets were more ubiquitous, and imaginative, than ones in Bath. One heard stories of boys in baker's baskets plucking wigs off the heads of passing gentlemen, of women arriving at destinations without their pockets, never having felt the tug of their skirts nor heard the snip that cut the string.

Lucasta arrived in Brook Street without incident to find the others there before her. Minnie, in Hanover Square, had the shortest distance to cover to the Humby residence, and Annis, coming from the ambassador's quarters in Golden Square, had not much further. They gathered in Mrs. Humby's family drawing room, where the hand-painted wallpaper bloomed with plumed birds on their perches, and the hand-knotted Indian rug sprouted a profusion of vines and flowery medallions. The room was warm and inviting, a dash of rich color against the dry London gloom.

Mrs. Humby, in a satin open robe over a ruffled petticoat, with a lace cap adorning her glossy black hair, presided over the tea tray. Selina tugged Lucasta toward a cluster of boxes laid across the settee and pressed a slip of paper into Lucasta's hand.

"Lord Rudyard called upon Mama and me yesterday. And this morning, the box arrived. With a note."

Lucasta read the neat, firm hand. *I hope you will forgive my being so bold as to approach a young lady of such fashion and delicacy, but rumors of your kindness have given me the courage to inform you that I have recently established a shop at No. — Piccadilly, in which I hope to serve young ladies of distinction in a manner that does credit to their beauty and taste. I would be honored if Miss Selina Humby would care to call on me at her convenience to discuss making up a gown for her with the enclosed, which has been provided me with the compliments of Dixon & Co. I look forward with great eagerness to making Miss Humby's acquaintance, if she would be so kind as to grant us the honor of patronizing our humble establishment.*

*With deepest admiration and affection, yr servant, Mlle. Beaudoin.*

Lucasta stared as Selina lifted a length of luscious silk from the box. On a background of yellow rose brocade, exquisite pink tulips and violet asters bloomed on delicate green vines. The fabric suited Selina's coloring exactly. She would glow in it like a jewel.

Lucasta battled a wave of envy, bitter as weak tea. "Dixon & Co. is Rudyard's warehouse."

"I know," Selina said. "And Mama and I agreed that I cannot accept a gift from a gentleman. But a mantua maker who is a woman..." She glanced at the other two girls.

Annis opened a box holding a shimmering cerulean silk splashed with white and dove-gray flowers. She lifted a fold to her cheek. "This came to our house yesterday. It feels heavenly."

Minnie's box held a dark mother-of-pearl damask with rows of full-blown orange poppies. "It's Spitalfields silk." She traced the fine embroidery with her fingertips. The fabric brought out the amber undertones of her skin and flattered her dark beauty.

"So not smuggled from abroad, but made here in England," Lucasta said.

"Mama sent around to ask about Mademoiselle Beaudoin." Selina smoothed the yellow fabric with her palm. "She grew up in a place called the Sisters of Benevolence Hospital for Orphans and Women in Distressed Circumstances. It is one of Miss Gregoire's favorite charities. You know how the Foundling Hospital will only take children of married parents? The Sisters of Benevolence take anyone. The matron told Mama that a local linen draper had furnished funds to set Miss Beaudoin up in a shop of her own. She took several other girls from the institution with her as seamstresses."

Lucasta sensed her friends waited for her approval. "So while we could not accept expensive gifts from Lord Rudyard, he has designed it so we would be supporting a girl with her own shop. *You* would be supporting," she corrected herself. There had been no fabric for her. Though he had driven *her* about town, listened to *her* sing.

With that thunderstruck expression. His insistence she should be on the stage. That glow of passionate interest in his honey brown eyes, the flicker of a smile on those sculpted lips—all this layered atop the memory of his touch in the allemande, that moment he had draw her toward him, as if he meant to clasp her in his arms.

She gulped down the strange knot of longing. Perhaps she had taken a chill on the walk. "You accept his apology, then?"

Selina bit her lip with tiny white teeth and glanced at her mother. "We do."

"But is this enough to make up for the rest?" Lucasta also looked to Mrs. Humby, who poured tea into five bone china cups and picked up the sugar tongs. Selina's invitations had fallen off considerably after Rudyard's thoughtless comment.

"As Lord Rudyard's father is governor of Barbados, I don't

doubt he is exposed to certain, shall we say, attitudes. But I hope he might be brought to think more broadly about matters. Given the right influence." Mrs. Humby deposited a lump of sugar in each elegant cup and smiled at her daughter. "And only look at how well the golden damask becomes her! I cannot find it in me to refuse."

"I am content to let Jeremiah Falstead be draper to the Gorgons," Minnie said, wrapping the luscious fabric about her shoulders. "You did not receive a box, Lucasta?"

"No, and just as well, for Aunt Pevensey would never allow me to receive it, much less have a dress made up."

Lucasta, with her funds for her music conservatory locked in a bank in Bath, relied on her aunt for the season's pin money, and her aunt was not notable for her generosity. "Besides, I'm not certain I can forgive him. If we overlook his cruelty, he will go on being cruel."

Minnie and Annis could rise above being called Gorgons; they would turn it to their advantage. And Selina would make a good match to a man who loved her for herself.

Still, Rudyard's gifts suggested he had listened to Lucasta. Beyond her supposedly clever epigram.

"We are only saying we approve of his taste, not of his beliefs," Minnie reasoned. "And we can show him by example how to amend his ways."

Lucasta watched her friends enjoy their gifts, wrapping themselves in the lengths of gorgeous silk. Rudyard had chosen a fabric that complemented each girl's coloring. And by all reports, he had helped a young, friendless girl without resources set up her own shop so that she might achieve self-sufficiency, perhaps in time respectability.

That kindness sat at odds with the man who had curled up his lip upon entering Mrs. Sancho's establishment. The man who, at finding Eliza blind, had struggled to mask his shock.

"So we're to set aside our quarrel with Rudyard and his friends," she murmured. And permit him to go on as he was, splendid of form and lacking in conscience.

"I shall wear this fabric whether I like him or not," Annis exclaimed. "And furthermore, I shall pair it with the mink pelisse he hates, if only to show him that we may relent, but we are not in thrall."

"Put your new fabrics aside, girls, and take your tea while it is hot," Mrs. Humby prompted. "I have not seen you together for days! You must catch me up on everything, for Mr. Humby and I live very quietly, you know."

They settled into Mrs. Humby's new Hepplewhite chairs, and the ease of familiarity lightened the taut curl of emotion in Lucasta's chest. She had missed this, a domestic space that felt welcoming, being at liberty with her friends.

"My aunt has been approached about founding a new academy." Annis blew on her tea. "In addition to the Imperial Academy, which she already directs. I believe the goal is to support the study of the Russian language. She's asked me to assist."

"Tell her we shall all assist," Minnie exclaimed. "I should like to learn Russian. Perhaps it will help me with the translation of my poem. The Middle High German is quite different from Gothic."

"But is the work any good?" Annis wanted to know.

"Not at the moment. My knight is spending a great deal of time being beaten about by monsters and feeling sorry for himself. It's high time for some virtuous action." Minnie rolled her eyes.

"The cat I rescued from the trap survived," Selina reported, adding a second lump of sugar to her cup. "Her leg is quite mended, though part of it is now missing. I named her Nila. She earns her keep chasing rats from the mews, but I believe she may be in the family way. I shall have to try my experimental surgery on Tom, if I can catch him."

All eyes turned expectantly to Lucasta. She replaced her cup in its dish with trembling fingers, watching the milky liquid wash back and forth.

"I have been invited to get up a charity concert to benefit the Foundling Hospital."

Her friends stared. "What?" Annis blinked.

"A concert?" Selina breathed.

"We shall play for you," Minnie said immediately. "Who else shall you ask? This is your chance to become known to Signor Marchesi!"

Lucasta swallowed hard. "My aunt says I cannot accept. She says it is too large a task. I can only fail, and when I do, the shame will reflect on her and Cici."

"Lucasta!" Annis cried. "She cannot deny you this. Not when you have dreamed of such a thing. And think of all the concerts you have organized at Miss Gregoire's. There are no possible grounds upon which you could fail."

"If the governors themselves have invited you, how can she say no?" Minnie demanded.

Selina laid a warm hand on Lucasta's arm. "Oh, my dear."

Lucasta sniffed and wiped her cheeks. "Suppose she is right? I have no standing in London, no knowledge of its musical scene. I cannot imagine why the governors should approach me with such a project. And how could I, with a complete lack of connections, possibly engage anyone of note, much less a figure like Signor Marchesi..." She blinked back burning tears. "I am sure it is for the best to decline. If it did go off poorly, it should reflect on the Pevenseys, and that is a sad way to repay their charity to me."

"The governors settled on you because you've been visiting the hospital for weeks, and the girls adore you," Annis said. "They could not have chosen a better person to ask."

A sudden thought lifted the hairs on the back of Lucasta's neck. Silas, the porter at the hospital, had greeted Rudyard as if he were there for a governor's meeting. Was Rudyard somehow behind this invitation, as he was behind new gowns for the girls?

"Do they want the foundlings to perform as well?" Selina asked.

"I would adore having the girls perform a few pieces. They would enjoy it so much." Lucasta lifted her shoulders. "And if I could arrange us to perform in the chapel of the Foundling Hospital, I am sure any number of people would agree to play. Georg

Friderich Handel donated that organ, and his *Messiah* is performed there every year. It would be an honor to prepare a concert there, and an honor to perform in it."

Minnie frowned. "Then you cannot allow Aunt P to silence you. Where is our fearless Gorgon? Where is our Medusa?"

"Medusa was mortal, recall. The only sister who was. A handsome and arrogant Greek hero comes along with a sword, and that is the end of her."

She feared therein lay a metaphor too close to home. Rudyard was no Greek hero, but the more time she spent with him, the more Lucasta risked falling under the spell of his attractions and forgetting what he had shown of his nature. She would lay herself open to his cruelty, and she would not recover from his cut as Selina had.

"You belong on a stage," Annis said firmly. "You *belong* there, Lucasta. Your aunt only fears that, if you gain recognition of your own, she will no longer have the power to command you."

"It is kind of her to think about Miss Pevensey," Selina said, "but really, how could a benefit concert for foundlings be a less than noble pursuit? The effort alone speaks well of all of you."

"You must accept," Annis decided. "I will have my father speak to her if necessary. Aunt Pevensey shall find herself overruled."

Minnie nodded. "Tell her the Duke of Luneberg-Zuwecken adores charity benefits."

Annis, as a Russian count's daughter, was accustomed to overruling people, and Minnie's father, the duke, simply ignored the mutterings about German ways. Lucasta, a vicar's daughter, was not so protected.

If Aunt Pevensey turned her out for accepting, the prospect of a concert was ended, for Lucasta could not organize such an event from Bath. But if she made a hash of the event, as her aunt feared, the gossip would be scathing, and the ton might scorn Cici in rebuke. Lucasta pondered her options as she made her way through the dreamlike cloud of fog and smoke that wrapped the homes and commerce of busy London.

She found it increasingly difficult to submit to Aunt Pevensey's capricious whims. Seeing Signor Marchesi had shown her what she was missing.

Somehow, so had Rudyard.

She found the Pevenseys in the parlor, regarding a dress box much like what the other girls had received.

"It cannot be meant for Lucasta," Aunt Pevensey said. "I knew that girl must not be putting herself forward. What will be the end of it all?"

She whirled as Lucasta entered the room and pinned her with the glare of a hen regarding an insect. "Lucasta Lithwick. What is the meaning of this?"

Lucasta pushed back the folds of the box and caught her breath. The note was the same, but the fabric was not as showy as the others. It was a beautiful chintz the color of milky tea, as soft as silk to the touch. Delicate flowers hand-painted in brown and blue patterned the fabric, giving it movement and life. The colors flattered Lucasta's complexion, burnishing the olive cast to her skin.

"Lucasta," Cici breathed. "It suits you beautifully! You will be so elegant in this."

"I have never heard of Mlle. Beaudoin," Aunt Pevensey said. "We cannot be seen patronizing a new shop. It will look as though we cannot afford the best mantua-makers."

The Baron spoke from behind Lucasta, making her heart thump in surprise. She had not realized he had wandered into the room.

"Dixon & Co. is Rudyard's warehouse, isn't it?"

Aunt Pevensey smoothed a hand over the blonde lace at her bosom. "If he means to pursue Cecilia, he must rise above trade. We cannot have the Pevensey name lowered by coarse associations."

The Baron raked Lucasta with a narrow-eyed stare, the gaze of a man who assessed people by their utility to him. Rudyard's scorn seemed practically gentle in comparison.

"First he persuades the governors of the Foundling Hospital to engage you in some public scheme. Now he wants to dress you. He's heard Lady Evers plan to make you her heir, and he's trying to cozen you, the greedy pup."

Of course to the Baron, and so many others, all Lucasta had to offer could be summed up in pounds and pence. Lucasta wished she *were* Medusa and her answering glare might turn his lordship to stone.

"The heir to Arendale has no need for my aunt's fortune," Aunt Pevensey said quickly. "A knight's relict? How rich could she possibly be?"

"Well, he's cannot be interested in her person." The Baron flicked the card that had been enclosed in the box, not caring where it fell. "Cici can't be seen in a shop of Rudyard's ladybird, but you were, right, Pet, that Lucasta could use some smartening. She's not dashing enough for Trevor in your old frocks, and everyone will say I foisted your niece on my son."

"Ladybird?" Cici asked.

Aunt Patience spoke as if she were choking. "My love, as I told you, I cannot agree—"

"Let Rudyard freshen her up as his own expense. Make her a plum ripe for the plucking." His lordship rang for a servant. "Just don't let him do more than sniff around your skirts, mind."

Heat rushed from her cheeks to her ears, toes, everywhere, as if she'd been doused in boiling water. The Baron regarded her with amusement, as if he could read her look of mutiny. "I'm setting you up for life, gel. Don't bite the hand lifting you from the gutter, eh?"

As if Miss Gregoire's was a gutter. As if a career teaching and composing and singing wasn't what she dreamed about, prayed for, worked to achieve. As if a miserable marriage to Trevor Pevensey were an outcome to desire.

Lucasta lifted her chin. Her heart rapped inside her chest like a trapped bird. "I can think of a way I might come across very smart, sir."

He scowled, accepting his hat, coat, and walking stick as the butler brought them. "It's not enough I provide your gowns and fripperies, and let you roam where you wish, like a kitchen maid?" His tone was low but razor-sharp, meant to cut.

"If I am consumed with an activity—something like organizing a benefit concert, for instance—I will have no time to entertain suitors."

Aunt Pevensey hissed, watching Lucasta step around her prohibition and go directly to a higher authority. Cici held her breath.

"And there's the foreign blood coming out, isn't it?" The Baron curled his lip. "You manipulative little baggage."

"Peter. You see? You cannot ally Trevor with someone of shameful birth," Aunt wailed.

Lucasta breathed from her navel, as her music masters had taught. Control. Tone. Volume. Her aunt would never accept that her father had been a worthy man, the best of men. All they saw was that he was born abroad, and from a family of no standing.

"If I host a successful concert, all our friends might be persuaded that Mr. Pevensey looks favorably upon my talents and accomplishments, and scarcely regards my fortune."

The Baron made a sour face. Everyone of his class cared for nothing more than fortune and the status it bought. But to be transparent about this was vulgarity of the worst sort.

"Very well." The Baron met her eyes with a snarl. "But if you shame your family, like your mother did—"

*My mother was happy!* Lucasta wanted to shriek, but it would not do to behave like a kettle at full boil. The Baron would dismiss her as a hysterical woman, and that would be the end of all.

So she let the Baron have the last word. He set his brimmed hat at a rakish angle and whacked his walking stick against the paneled door as he left, off to his club. Aunt Pevensey looked as if she'd swallowed a bird, but she had no choice but to submit.

That was what marriage required of women—to submit.

"I suppose the Baron believes you might keep yourself out of mischief if you are consumed with your little charity project," Aunt said faintly. "You might go to this Miss Beaudoin tomorrow, early enough so that no one will take any note of you." She gathered up the morning correspondence with trembling hands. "You heard his lordship, I hope. There is to be no more encouraging Lord Rudyard."

"No, mum," Lucasta said.

She would trade him for a chance to organize her own concert. She would sacrifice him a thousand times. A man who bought her friends silks after he heaped them with scorn, a man who thought most of the world beneath him. It was no loss.

It was no loss, she told herself as she took the box of exquisite chintz fabric to her bedchamber, to give up foolish dreams that had no hope of coming to pass.

## CHAPTER ELEVEN

Thursday was Lady Pevensey's at-home day, and at the earliest time that could be deemed acceptable, the butler introduced an unexpected pair of callers into the green parlor where Cici sat with her embroidery. Lucasta had her nose in Jean-Philippe Rameau's *Treatise on Harmony,* and Lady Pevensey made no pretense of doing anything but wonder which important people might attend them that day.

"Lord Rudyard, mum, and Miss Lambertina Falstead, daughter of the late Lord Payne." The butler stood aside to let them enter.

Lady Pevensey dropped her copy of the *Ladies Cabinet,* trying to school her expression, which ranged from dismay to astonishment to a sly, wild hope. "Lord Rudyard! What an—unexpected pleasure."

Lucasta struggled to keep her own face from betraying the way her heart leapt straight into her throat, like a ballet dancer. He wore a beautiful suit of red-brown linen, with rows of enameled buttons lining the double-breasted waistcoat and matching frock coat, and cream-colored suede breeches buckled above the knee. He swept his cocked hat under one arm and bowed to her ladyship.

His unpowdered hair was brown as chocolate, pulled back in a queue, and his simple linen neckcloth gleamed white.

Even without the striking suit he would be handsome; it was something in his bearing, and in the character that shone through his well-arranged features. Lucasta ruthlessly tamped down a thrill as his eyes lingered on her.

It would not do to become silly over this man. She would *not* do it.

"Lady Pevensey, Miss Pevensey." He paused, and did she imagine he spoke her name like a caress? "Miss Lithwick. I wish to make my cousin known to you." He indicated the girl beside him. "She is lately emerged from mourning and hoping to meet new people."

His cousin was short and rounded, dressed in a dove-gray gown with a large picture hat pinned to her powdered wig. She looked nervous and ill at ease, and Lucasta's heart went out to her instantly. She rose and took the girl's hand.

"How kind you are to call upon us, Miss Falstead," Lucasta said. "I am new to town myself and in need of friends. Please accept our sympathies for your loss."

"Thank you, Miss Lithwick." Miss Falstead spoke in a small voice, but her grip was firm. She looked Lucasta over carefully. "How do you do."

"I don't doubt Cecilia will be a very suitable acquaintance for you, Miss Falstead." Lady Pevensey scowled at her niece, and Lucasta knew she would hear a lecture later about pushing in. "She has had the good fortune to be widely received, though this is only her first Season. You have yourself paid her several compliments, Lord Rudyard, if I am not mistaken?"

"All well-deserved," Rudyard said in the silky voice he had used with Lucasta when he accosted her at the theater. That voice made her nerve endings tingle. His eyes brushed over her as he turned to Cici.

"Perhaps Miss Pevensey will pay us a compliment in return, and reward us with her company in a drive through the park? It would be a shame not to enjoy this first glimpse of the sun in days."

"The sun is disastrous to the complexion, and Cecilia is already engaged to go driving with Major Mallory in his new high-perch phaeton." Lady Pevensey pouted. "Perhaps another time, Lord Rudyard?"

He turned to Lucasta. "Certainly. But since it is such a fine day, perhaps Miss Lithwick would care to console us. My pair needs to stretch their legs, and Bertie wishes for a companion more pleasant than I am."

"Me?" Lucasta blinked. His steady golden-brown gaze made something in her chest lift and execute a slow, unsettled turn.

*Fool!* How could she be turning into a ninnyhammer over this man, when she knew exactly what he was?

"Oh, but I can't see that Lucasta..." Aunt Pevensey trailed off as Rudyard rose to his feet.

"You won't disappoint my cousin, Miss Lithwick? Run gather a wrap. We will have her home before dinner, my lady."

"The Baron." Aunt threw a look of warning at Lucasta. Her eyes grew tight at the corners, a look of swift calculation crossing her face.

"Would approve, I hope, of seeing Miss Lithwick do a kindness to my cousin, a marquess's granddaughter," Rudyard said firmly.

Miss Falstead made a pretty show of taking her leave, and before she could come up with a reason to deny herself the good fortune of being removed from her aunt's suffocating parlor, Lucasta found herself being handed up into Rudyard's calash. Miss Falstead folded down the rear seat and arranged herself in it, while Rudyard put back the hood.

"The breeze won't bother you, will it, Miss Lithwick? Or do you find the sun disastrous to your complexion as well?"

She caught the twinkle in his eyes. "Do as you please, milord. I daresay we are all eager for sunlight after these dreary days."

She told her stomach not to leap and swirl as he mounted the carriage and settled his lean, strong body on the front seat beside her. She would keep her head at all costs. The expression on her aunt's face had been as clear as if she'd written it on paper. Aunt Pevensey *wanted* Lucasta to be in trouble with the Baron.

His lordship would punish Lucasta at the least provocation, beginning by taking away her chance to arrange the benefit concert. But a few turns around Hyde Park would not sink her, particularly if they were discussing musical arrangements. There would be no *sniffing,* as his lordship had implied, nor any other untoward activity.

Rudyard gathered the ribbons, and Lucasta considered his hands, strong, wide, long-fingered. His hold was as light and sure as Mlle. Beaudoin's skill as she had measured, draped, and pinned Lucasta at her shop.

*Was* the girl his mistress? If so, Rudyard was not an unkind protector. The young woman had been all cheer and grateful smiles at Lucasta's visit. And she spoke of Rudyard as if he had hung the stars in their constellations.

Lucasta would have no clients for lessons, no students for a musical school if she were known to consort with the mistresses of a known beau. She was about to change her mind and ask to be let down when Rudyard clicked to the horses and they set out at a sedate walk.

"Bertie, find a place for that thing on your head," he said over his shoulder. "There is not enough room in the vehicle for the three of us and that hat."

His scent nudged Lucasta's senses, as unsettling as the warmth that rose from his body. The street was clogged with traffic and vendors, and it felt very dangerous to be so close to the horses, rather than shut away in a closed carriage where one could not see the various obstacles and accidents that came at one from every part of the street. But Rudyard's hand was expert and his pair well-trained, and he guided them easily around a pair of sedan chairs whose occupants were engaged in a heated argument over right of way.

"I cannot imagine I am any consolation for Cici," Lucasta remarked.

"I wanted you," he said, and her heart gave a nervous shiver when he threw her a smile. "Mallory was bragging that he had engaged Miss Pevensey for a drive, so I saw my chance. Bertie agreed to play chaperone, because she is an obliging sort of person, and also desperate to escape the house."

"It is nice to have an airing without Mama," Miss Falstead admitted, looking about them with interest.

"You wish to discuss the concert?" Lucasta pushed away the quiver in the belly that his words produced. *I wanted you.*

They had not parted amicably after their excursion to Charles Street. But perhaps he wanted her to fawn over him about the fabrics he'd given the Gorgons. Like most men, he would assume all cruelties could be made right with a handsome gift. It was how the Baron proceeded with his marriage.

"I hope to introduce you to someone very dear to me," Rudyard said.

Lucasta glanced behind, where Miss Falstead sat cradling her enormous hat. The girl smiled.

"The pleasure would be all mine, but he is thinking of someone else," she said. "Did you tell her nothing, Jem?"

*Jem.* His family called him Jem, and now she knew that. It felt like a gift.

"Someone who might perform at the concert?" Lucasta ventured. There was no other reason he would invite her out. She had insulted this man on the occasion of their first meeting, and they had quarreled in their every interaction since.

And he had repaid her with compliments, gifts, and now a reprieve out of doors.

"This person enjoys music very much but does not get out to hear it. I thought I might as a result bring you to her," Rudyard said.

Lucasta bit her lip. He had invited her out to please another woman. Who? An admirer? Another mistress? Someone he hoped to make his mistress?

"I have missed Judith," Miss Falstead remarked as the small carriage jostled comfortably along. "Mama did not think it proper to call upon her while I was in mourning. And with the little ones there—well."

"Yes, I am well aware of how Aunt Payne feels about the rest of them." Rudyard clicked at the horses to guide them around a stopped cart. "But I hope you will call on Judith whenever you wish."

He would not bring his cousin on a visit to a mistress. Perhaps this Judith was someone he was wooing, or hoped to woo. Lucasta shied as the huge draught horses pulling a cart stamped in their harness and one snorted on her shoulder as they passed. She did her best to push her stomach out of her throat and back to its normal position.

"On the subject of music." She held one hand to her hat. "I suspect I have you to thank, milord, for the extraordinary opportunity I have been offered. The governors of the Foundling Hospital invited me to get up a benefit concert," she told Miss Falstead.

"Did they? Jem's been a governor of the Hospital for years. All the London charities want him on their boards now, of course, but this cause is dear to his heart." Miss Falstead paused, a slight frown touching her brow as she studied the back of her cousin's head. "Jem thinks very highly of you, Miss Lithwick, if he trusts you with his foundlings *and* Judith."

"Do hush, Bertie," Rudyard said, facing straight ahead. A muscle ticked in his jaw, below his ear. "Miss Lithwick won't hear praises sung of me. The governors adopted the notion at once when I suggested they would not have to pay Miss Lithwick an organizer's fee."

His guard was up, that elegant, sophisticated façade she had seen him assume at Lady Clara's. He had worn it at the theater but dropped it during their time at the Foundling Hospital and at Sancho's. He was trying to tell her—no, show her something.

That he was exactly what she thought him? Or that he wasn't?

She lifted a gloved finger to her lips for a nibble and remembered just in time that fidgeting was unladylike. She wrapped her fingers in her skirts instead, her heart doing that slow circling dance once more.

"I am surprised anyone thought an unknown vicar's daughter up to the task. When there are so many musical talents within London." She ought not let him see how deeply she feared she would fail at this.

"On the contrary, they seemed eager to call upon a music instructor employed at Miss Gregoire's. The Duke of Hunsdon, who is also on the board of governors, said his duchess has some connections to the place, and the Countess of Renwick is known to have attended."

Rudyard *had* proposed her name to the governors. He had guessed what it would mean to her to have the charge of a benefit concert. A dream come to life, in a world all too inclined not to indulge the dreams of the young, the poor, and the powerless.

"Selina appreciated the fabric that Mademoiselle Beaudoin sent." She brushed away a cloud of dirt threatening to settle on her skirts. "We all did."

"Did you visit Josie, then? I was hoping you would. She needs good patrons to make a go of her shop."

"And you suppose the Gorgons would set an example."

He raised one dark brow at her. They were the same color as his hair. She wondered whether his shoulders were truly as broad as the cut of his coat suggested.

"The Gorgons, as you call them, seem quite the rage at the moment. Everyone wants to know more about a certain Lucasta Lithwick."

"*You* named us Gorgons, I believe. And no one took the least note of Lucasta Lithwick until a certain Lord Rudyard danced with her. I suppose you did it to prove you might use your powers for good?"

Rudyard's shoulder rippled as if throwing off an unpleasant

thought, and she guessed her barb had landed. "Anyone who over-looks you is a fool," he murmured. "Did you like the chintz?"

"It is beautiful." Lucasta sighed, then caught herself. "As I am sure you are aware."

"I hope you let Miss Beaudoin choose your designs," Rudyard said. "I gave her very specific instructions."

"Why?" Lucasta turned to face him. It was her curse, being unable to hold her tongue But it was inconceivable that a man adored for his exquisite *ton* should take the least notice of a Lucasta Lithwick. "Why should Lord Rudyard curry favor from the Gorgons?" She twisted her fingers to the point of pain. "Do you not think it will reflect poorly on you if my concert is a disaster?"

It would certainly prove the Baron correct. And Aunt Pevensey. And everyone else who assumed that a plain vicar's daughter, of no birth and no fortune, had no value all on her own.

All she had was her music. It was her one gift, the solace she clung to, the one beautiful thing in her life that no one could take away. But if she proved rubbish at it, in front of a hundred people, and showed she had no business on the stage after all—what would be left for her? It was almost better to dream in the dark, in unseen corners, and not know the truth. Not have her shortcomings exposed in a way she could not deny.

Rudyard appeared to be choosing his words, his sculpted features set in an expression of studied indifference. "I do not believe any enterprise you undertake would be a disaster, Miss Lithwick."

A warm, dangerous glow sprang to life within her, like a candle flickering to life in a dark room. Rudyard, of all people, could not think well of her. Not when he judged people on their style, and she had none.

She clung to the side of the conveyance as the carriage stopped and Rudyard paid the toll for Hyde Park Gate. "Why are we leaving London?" she wondered as the gate opened for them. "Need we fear highwaymen?"

"I rarely encounter gentlemen of the road here," Rudyard

answered, which was not at all reassuring. "It is not far, and a pleasant drive, is it not, Bertie?"

"Jem, I think you could tell her a little something," Miss Falstead said. "Miss Lithwick must feel as if we are spiriting her away."

"I've never yet kidnapped a lady, and do not spoil the surprise, if you please."

They passed through Knightsbridge, and Lucasta looked about with great curiosity. She had come to London from Bath on the Great Western Road and had seen little else. It surprised her how quickly the city ended and the land turned to gentle pasture, with here and there a church spire or the façade of a great house rising in the distance. Knightsbridge was a small cluster of shops and houses lining the road, and when the lane branched, Rudyard turned southeast.

The road was decently paved, the turnpike tolls clearly being put to their intended use, but the bustle and stink of the city fell away. The scene was abruptly rustic, the shops and occasional villa hugging the road while fields and pastures stretched behind, and the air was considerably clearer and more wholesome. Lucasta drew a deep, nourishing breath as the horses picked up their pace, glad to be free of the traffic. She felt liberated from something as well.

She had no reason to trust Rudyard, but she wanted to.

They passed Queen's Elm gate and came to another cluster of buildings, many of them neat homes, and new. "Little Chelsea," Rudyard explained. "I keep a villa here, away from town. Many tradesmen are putting up some rather grand houses. I hope you will not find our little cottage too quaint."

He paused before a wooden gate set into a hawthorn hedge, and the horses snorted with approval. While Rudyard extracted his cousin from the carriage, Lucasta studied the building he had called a cottage. It rose in a neat neoclassical rectangle of yellow-gray stone, with green vines climbing the walls between evenly spaced windows. Tall shrubs flowered in soft profusion along the path leading to the front door, where Rudyard knocked briefly, then entered with a shout.

"Danny boy! There are horses at the gate that need tending, but mind you don't give them so many oats they can't move. Mrs. Cadogan, I've guests in need of refreshment. Judith, I hope you're decent—I've brought the company I promised you."

"Jem, dearest," called a gentle voice from the nearest room, "you needn't raise such a ruckus. We heard you at the gate, great stomping oaf that you are."

Rudyard led them into a front parlor filled with light, where a young woman sat on a dainty settee. She rose as they entered and held out a set of pale white hands, lady's hands. She wore a pretty gown of a light lilac hue and no wig. Lucasta stared a moment at the perfect symmetry of her face, the lustrous dark brown hair bound into a chignon, and the shade covering her eyes. She was unmistakably a Falstead relation.

Jem strode forward and took her outstretched hands, dropping a kiss on the cheek the girl turned up to him. "You brought Bertie with you?" she murmured, turning her face toward the door. "It's been an age."

Bertie advanced and kissed her other cheek. "Hullo, Judith. That frock becomes you. You've been well?"

"We've been grand," Judith confirmed. "But you did not bring Aunt Payne." She waited, still facing the door. "This is someone unknown to me. Welcome to Rose Hollow," she said politely.

"This is Miss Lucasta Lithwick, the musical acquaintance I made at the Foundling Hospital," Rudyard said. "Miss Lithwick, this is my sister, Judith."

Lucasta cleared her throat. Not his intended. Not his mistress. A sister.

Rudyard—Smart Jeremy—Jem—had brought her to meet his *sister*.

"I am delighted to meet you, Miss Falstead." Lucasta moved forward and took the girl's outstretched hand in both of hers. "I hope you do not mind that Rudyard brought me. I have only met your cousin today as well."

Rudyard watched them, his posture tense. He had told her nothing so as to test her. Lucasta resented that, and understood at the same time.

Judith smiled and waved a slight hand, as if shooing away her brother's concern. "You must sit next to me, Miss Lithwick. I am always eager to meet my brother's friends. We live very quietly here. I hope he warned you?" She slipped a finger beneath the ribbon that tied the shade about her temples and scratched.

"You may take it off if you wish, Jude," Rudyard remarked. "Miss Lithwick isn't squeamish."

Lucasta shot him a quick glance. Not a test, she realized. Another gift. He was trusting her with the person he loved most in the world.

"Oh, that's a relief. It squeezes my head." Judith untied the shade and set it aside. Her eyes, like the foundling Eliza's, were a cloudy blue beneath a white web of scar tissue.

"You smell delightful, if I may be so forward to say so," Judith remarked to Lucasta as they took their seats. "Most people wear too much scent. Yours is delicious."

"Thank you," Lucasta said, grinning as Rudyard raised a brow. She liked Judith's directness. "A classmate of mine wishes to become a perfumier, and she is ever experimenting with scents. She made this one for me."

The other girl lifted a hand near Lucasta's cheek. "I suppose it would be too bold of me to ask about your hat? Jem says I am too interested in headgear," she said shyly.

"Not bold at all, but I'm afraid mine is rather plain." Lucasta let the small, soft hand skim her chip straw bonnet. Judith smiled as she felt the velvet ribbon and the flowers on the brim. "As for the rest of me, very plain as well," Lucasta said. "Red-gold hair, very pale green eyes, and a few unfortunate freckles."

"I thought that color came from powder," Rudyard remarked. He moved about the room, inspecting various items.

"I wish it did, as I'd adopt it." Bertie placed her hat on a small table, burying a basket of embroidery, and sank gracefully onto an upholstered chair. "Judith, did you style your hair? It's very elegant."

"Is it? How relieved I am to hear that. Tressie helped, but one cannot always rely on her judgment. She likes to experiment." She tilted her head. "Jem, do stop roaming about inspecting everything. Mrs. Cadogan keeps us very well."

"It's glad to hear that, I am," the housekeeper said, entering the room with a tea tray. "Milord, I daresay that nipcheese cook of yours at Arendale House hasn't been feeding you proper, but someone knew as you were coming and made you a nice lemon-seed cake for the occasion. Now, shall Miss Bertie pour or Miss Judith?"

She managed a quick curtsy to Lucasta without breaking stride. "Welcome, miss, welcome you are. Now, Miss Judith likes her cinnamon twists, and Miss Bertie her bites of chocolate, but you just tell Mrs. Cadogan what you fancy, and I'll have it for you in a trice."

As Judith lifted her hand, the housekeeper deftly pulled a tea table before the settee and deposited the caddy upon it. "The bread's me own, made fresh this week, and the milk comes from a'down the street, so not a sour note in it," she added as she turned the tray to face Judith and straightened a few items upon it. She adjusted her apron and gave Rudyard a cheeky grin. "Does himself want coffee?"

"Tea will do, thank you, unless Miss Lithwick requires something else?"

"Tea will be delightful. I cannot imagine a greater luxury than fresh cream," Lucasta answered. "At home in Bath our dairy maid milks the cow in the street for us, but I can't say the same of what gets delivered to Caroline Street."

"Bath!" Judith exclaimed. "I want to hear all about it. Jem has promised to take me so many places, but he never has time to travel for leisure." She skimmed her fingers over the tray, checking the placement of each item, and then poured the tea. She held a fingertip at the rim to judge when each cup was full, then added sugar and cream with the ease of habit and passed Lucasta's cup to her with a smile.

The women sipped their tea and chattered at length about everything they could think of, while Rudyard lounged near the window. Ostensibly he watched the street without, but Lucasta had the sense that he missed nothing within the room. He was standing guard, and his protectiveness toward his sister tugged at her heart.

He had risked a great deal, introducing her to Judith. He had clearly feared her disdain, but hoped for better.

She had shared something of her deep, true self with him, singing before him at the Foundling Hospital, and now he had shared something precious with her. Her heart felt full and at the same time tangled. She was crossing a line with him into some territory she wasn't certain it was wise to enter.

At a natural pause, Rudyard spoke for the first time. "Ought we introduce Miss Lithwick to the rest of us, Jude? It seems so terribly quiet without them."

Judith paused, alert, and Bertie blinked quickly. "Are you certain, Jem?"

"I should like to," Judith said quietly, "if you think Miss Lithwick will not mind."

"Lucasta, please," Lucasta said. She guessed she had passed one test, in meeting Judith, but underneath Rudyard's deceptively casual demeanor she sensed a taut watchfulness. Another test awaited.

She wondered why he was testing her at all, and at the same time, she very much wanted to pass.

Judith cocked her head. "We're going to meet them whether we wish it or not," she said. "I detect the fishing expedition is over."

A door at the back of the house slammed, and three new voices began talking over one another. They were young voices, full of the enthusiasm and heedlessness of children, and engaged in a vigorous dispute about who was responsible for scaring off the fish. Mrs. Cadogan broke in with a muted order, and after a few moments of shuffling, splashing, and shushed questions, the house-keeper appeared at the door.

"Shall I bring in the children, milord? They're eager to see you, but as we have guests..." Her eyes veered to Lucasta, then away.

Lucasta sat up straight. This was definitely a test, and a tendril of trepidation curled through her stomach. They all feared her reaction, but why?

"I'd like Miss Lithwick to meet us all," Rudyard said mildly, without looking at her, "and I hope she feels the same way. And Bertie hasn't seen them in some time."

Three young faces peered around the door, and with motherly hands Mrs. Cadogan brought them in. They lined up, tallest to smallest, and stood fidgeting with excitement while Rudyard made the introductions. Tenderness filled his smile, and Lucasta's poor heart, already raw with unaccustomed activity of the day, ached as the pieces fit together in her head.

"Miss Lithwick, may I give you the rest of my brothers and sisters. This is Tressie, our resident authority on all things to do with the animal kingdom and most else. This is Starria, our future world explorer. And this is Hannibal, whom you must never chal-lenge to a footrace, as you will undoubtedly lose. Children, this is our new friend, Miss Lucasta Lithwick of Bath."

The two girls made a quick curtsy and the young boy bowed. They were beautiful children, tidily dressed, hands and faces glis-tening from their hasty wash. They shared the same smoothly curved features and vivid coloring, curled ebony hair, light brown skin, and wide, thickly lashed eyes dark as chocolate.

She caught Rudyard's eye. "This is why," she said softly. Why he had resented Mrs. Sancho's reference to his father, Earl Payne, off governing an island in the West Indies known for its barbarous practice of enslaving humans. His father had begun another family there.

A family, Lucasta guessed, that the rest of London society, who celebrated him as Smart Jeremy, did not know about.

Lucasta set aside her teacup and smiled at the solemn young faces regarding her with curiosity. "I am very pleased to meet you. Miss Tressie, Miss Starria, and Master Hannibal—are you named after the general of Carthage?"

"Yes, the one with the elephants." Hannibal, a boy of six or seven, threw himself at Rudyard, who caught him in a wrestling hold. Starria, who looked about nine or ten, ran to embrace Bertie, who gave her a buss on the cheek. Tressie, older and more dignified, perhaps around thirteen years, went to the tea tray and accepted a cup from Judith. All three converged before Lucasta to study her intently.

"Jem says you are musical," Tressie informed her. "That you sing."

"Your dress is not as fine as Bertie's. Or Judith's," Starria noted.

"Jem says the waters at Bath stink of rotten eggs, and taste the same," Hannibal reported.

Lucasta held back a laugh and smoothed her gown, consciously not looking to Rudyard for his guidance. Or approval. "All those things are true," she agreed.

Hannibal made a face. "You won't make me drink rotten water! Or bathe in it, either."

"Nevertheless you must try one cup at the Pump Room," Lucasta answered. "It is considered quite the thing." She released the laugh as Hannibal made an expression that clearly conveyed his distaste for this enterprise.

"I should like to try taking the waters," Starria announced. "And I intend to try sea-bathing as well someday. Why do you not wear a wig?"

"I detest them," Lucasta said honestly. "They itch. And they are home to vermin."

Starria nodded. "Vermin bite. Did you know that Judith had measles as a baby? That is why she is blind. And she had another brother and sister who died from it as well. I hope never to get measles. Or smallpox."

Lucasta's heart contracted. Rudyard had lost other siblings. There was so much she didn't know about him.

Couldn't have known, because she had judged him by his appearance, as she had accused him of judging everyone else.

"If you are to explore the world, I hope you will be variolated against smallpox," Lucasta said. "I was variolated while at school, and it was a great relief to me."

"What does that mean?" Starria demanded.

"It means a doctor gives you a small amount of smallpox matter, usually introduced into an incision. This gives you a very mild form of the disease, and thereafter you cannot catch it again. Lady Mary Wortley Montagu brought the practice to England years ago, but it has not become as widespread as it could."

Starria marched over to Jem, her chin set at a firm angle. "Jem, I insist on being variolated. I cannot carry smallpox to unknown parts of the world on my travels. Only look what happened to the West Indians when the Europeans came."

Rudyard nodded and caught Lucasta's eye. She read relief and a warmth that made her toes curl. "I will see to it," he told the child. "I confess you all should have been variolated years ago. Judith and I were, by our mother, after the measles— May we speak of something that does not involve disease?"

Tressie, with the unselfconsciousness of a girl who knows she is loved, seated herself in a chair near Bertie and regarded Lucasta with cool interest. "Jem says I might take music lessons," she said. "I must choose my instrument, though, as we cannot clutter up the place with everything that takes my fancy."

Rudyard winced to hear his words parroted back at him. Lucasta understood his concern, however, with not crowding a space that Judith moved about in.

"With permission, perhaps I can help you decide on an instrument," she offered. "I am familiar with several."

Belatedly she realized she was again pushing in. She guessed that Rudyard had brought her here only to prove that he had not passed the judgment she had accused him of making on Selina or the Sancho family. Some men would not acknowledge siblings from a different parent, much less a different race. Jem housed and fed his.

He did not speak of them about town, just as he did not speak of Judith.

Yet he had introduced them to Lucasta. Her eyes pricked with tears.

Judith sighed. "I would so love to learn music, but we have been unable to engage a tutor. They all say they can do nothing, since—" She pointed to her unseeing eyes.

"How absurd," Lucasta said. "There's a blind violinist in every square of London, playing for coin. I have heard of an Austrian singer, Maria Theresia von Paradis, who is blind. She is much admired in Vienna, and she composes and performs on the pianoforte. Then there is Mélanie de Salignac, who devised a way to read and write using raised print, and she uses it to record and read music as well."

"And Mr. Stanley, at the Foundling Hospital, is accomplished on the organ, the harpsichord, and the violin. I told you as much, Jude," Rudyard added softly.

"And I daresay you would have an advantage in learning music, as your ear seems to be extraordinary," Lucasta added.

She couldn't bear to look at Rudyard's face any longer. His tenderness, concern, hope, and fear for his sister were all writ clearly on his countenance, and the depth of his emotion tapped at that aching place inside her chest.

Lucasta had no siblings, and while she would claim the girls of Miss Gregoire's as being as close as sisters, and Cici was growing dear to her as well, she had never had a brother to demonstrate such protectiveness and solicitude. What a marvelous thing it must be to have a man like Jeremiah Falstead so dedicated to one's well-being.

Judith smiled sadly. "But who would have the patience to teach me?"

"I would," Lucasta said. "If your brother permits it."

It was unadvisable to offer such a thing, she realized at once. Having no command of transportation, how was she to get herself to Little Chelsea for regular instruction? Rudyard had brought her to meet his family, not insinuate herself into their lives. But she would find a way, if just to see the joy spreading over Judith's face.

"And me?" Bertie ventured. "I would adore lessons as well, Miss Lithwick, but my mother is deathly afraid that a male music master would press an advantage. She has heard too much gossip to that effect, I'm afraid."

"I should leap at the opportunity," Lucasta said. "If Rudyard does not disapprove."

Offering to give Bertie lessons was even less wise, for then she would be frequenting Arendale House and risking too much contact with Rudyard, whose power to unsettle her would only grow with each exposure. Even now her eyes could not stop straying to him, noting that bold-featured face that grew more handsome each time she looked upon it, the leashed strength and grace of his powerful form.

She recognized the tendrils of infatuation taking root and knew she must stand guard against them. She might be in need of funds and self-sufficiency, two problems giving music lessons could remedy, but she could not afford to be a fool.

"That is," she added belatedly, "if you think I might be of any use as a teacher."

"Perhaps," Rudyard said in a seemingly idle tone, looking out the window instead of into the room, "you might entertain us with some music, Miss Lithwick. It would be a treat for the children."

She recognized his casualness was forced. The man was becoming as easy to read as a musical score.

He wanted to hear her perform. And she wanted him to hear her.

"Are you certain it would be a treat?" Lucasta could not resist teasing him, hoping to poke past that veil of assumed indifference. "You have not heard me play, Lord Rudyard. In fact you persuaded the governors of the Foundling Hospital to give over their precious concert to a musician whose skill you have never heard tested."

His eyes glowed with an answering challenge. "Do you think I was sleeping that afternoon at the Hospital, like your maid? I assure you I was listening."

Judith paused, her head tilted as she listened to the exchange. "Do play for us, Miss Lithwick."

"And sing," Rudyard prompted.

There went those bubbles again, rising in her like champagne. "Perhaps a song or two." Lucasta eagerly approached the spinet tucked in the corner. "This is a Baker Harris," she said in surprise, glancing at Rudyard. "Did you visit his workshop?"

"Will it do?" Judith sounded anxious.

"It's a lovely little bentside." Lucasta pushed back the cover of polished mahogany and ran her fingers over the keyboard. "Practical for a small space, and very useful to learn on." She played a quick scale and leaned close to listen to the pitch. "It's perfectly tuned. I do love the sound of the spinet. It's richer, deeper than the harpsichord. Gloomier, one might say."

"You prefer gloomy?" Rudyard regarded her with a curious expression.

"I prefer rich and textured," Lucasta replied. She shook back her sleeves and warmed her fingers with a few more scales, testing the weight of the keys. "Shall I play a Welsh song, in honor of Mrs. Cadogan? I know an old love song that a friend at school taught me. It translates to 'Watching the White Wheat,' or something like that."

She launched into the song, a melancholy, resonant tune that suited her range and allowed for full-throated expression. The rest of the room drifted to the fringes of her awareness. For the first time that day, she was in her element, no longer plain Lucasta Lithwick but a vibrating chord of sound, a hollow reed for the air to move through.

Mrs. Cadogan sniffled from the doorway when the song ended. "Aye, but I love that air. *Bugeilio'r Gwenith Gwyn.*" She dabbed her eyes with the hem of her apron. "I haven't heard that in an age, Miss Lithwick, and never sung so lovely as you did."

"It's a sad story, I believe, about a girl who dies of a broken heart when she cannot marry her love," Lucasta said. "But I quite like the tune."

"Ann Thomas, the Maid of Cefn Ydfa, and her Wil," Mrs. Cadogan confirmed. "They're buried together at Llangynwyd, rest their souls."

"More," Starria demanded, inching her chair closer to the spinet. "Don't stop now, Miss Lithwick."

Lucasta moved on to some familiar tunes, "Soft Flowing Avon" and "The Trees They Grow So High," hoping her audience might sing with her, but they appeared content to listen. "Is there a song we all might sing?" she asked finally, turning about on the stool. The faces regarding her were rapt, Bertie's eyes filled with tears, Judith's face dreamy and far away.

Lucasta regarded the younger children, who stared back at her with wide eyes. "Do you have a favorite nursery tune, or a lullaby?"

"Our nurse will only sing hymns to us," Hannibal explained. "She's a Methodist."

"Jem, I wish you would sing with Miss Lithwick," Judith said softly. "We rarely hear your voice anymore."

Rudyard coughed. "I could not possibly do well enough for a voice like Miss Lithwick's." His tone sounded lower, rougher than usual.

"I confess I have been longing to hear your brother sing," Lucasta said to Judith. She wanted to hear his rich baritone put to use, but even that small admission made the tips of her ears burn with embarrassment.

Rudyard cleared his throat. "Jude—"

"Something simple, to please me," Judith coaxed. "The True Lover's Farewell?'"

Heat spread down the side of Lucasta's neck. The song was a

lovely, intimate duet. She rarely sang duets; she was never asked. "I know the tune," she managed.

"I have never heard you sing, Jem," Bertie said with a curious tone.

"Then you must," Judith said firmly. "To please me, Jem."

Lucasta drew in a deep, long breath as Rudyard moved closer. Heated awareness moved across her shoulders and down her arms as she felt his gaze settle upon her. She lifted her hands to the keyboard to begin the simple, familiar tune and let her eyes close for a moment as Rudyard began the first notes of the lover's duet.

*"Fare thee well, my own true love, and farewell for a while..."*

She blinked back sudden tears. His voice was untrained but steady and clear, with a rich, deep timbre that made her feel like she'd partaken of strong spirits. Her throat closed as she listened to him sing the melancholy words.

*"And the rocks may melt and the seas may burn, if I shall not return."*

She felt his eyes on her face, and a wash of heat filled and buoyed her. Lucasta swallowed, consciously relaxed her throat, and lifted her voice in the lover's reply.

*"Oh, do you see that lonesome dove, sitting on an ivy tree?"*

It was almost too much to bear, having him so close to her, his attention bent on her so completely, as their voices rose and blended. The emotions of these ballads that had always seemed so overdrawn and silly suddenly took on a new dimension as she sang. For the first time she could understand how it might physically hurt to be parted from a beloved, how that longing could feel so intense.

Singing with Jeremiah Falstead was a magic she had never known. Harmonizing with him as they began the final chorus was as intimate as twining their hands in a dance. As intimate as sitting side by side in a carriage. As intimate as a kiss.

*"I'm going away, but I'll be back, if I go ten thousand miles."*

Lucasta let her hands rest on the keyboard as the last note

faded away. Then she made the mistake of lifting her head and meeting Rudyard's eyes.

His brown-gold gaze was a deep well. She might never stop falling. He looked as dazed as she felt.

"I..." Her voice was a whisper. "I believe that's enough for now." Carefully she closed the lid of the spinet, grateful to look away from Rudyard's face.

She might fall as far as she wished, but then what would happen to her? A Lucasta Lithwick did not enchant a Lord Rudyard. Such things were not possible in the world in which she moved.

And she must, at all costs, protect herself from further exposure to him, for heartbreak was inevitable. He had already enchanted her.

# CHAPTER TWELVE

"You are silent," Rudyard observed as they retraced their route to town, past the Queen's Elm, past the tavern known as the Bell, back toward Knightsbridge. "Did we tire you?"

"Not at all. That was one of the most pleasant afternoons I've spent. Thank you." Lucasta turned to include Bertie in her gratitude.

Bertie smiled sweetly in return. "Judith liked you," she remarked.

"I like Judith," Lucasta answered, and said the next without thinking. "I hope I might see her again."

Though doing so would put her too near Rudyard's orbit, make her aware of his every move, his mere presence. Such foolishness fed infatuations, rather than throttling them in the least painful manner possible. She knew that from experience.

"I do not imagine my siblings would be considered good *ton*," Rudyard said, his mouth set in a grim expression. "I barely am myself."

"You? Smart Jeremy?" She saw his eyes narrow and understood. "You do not believe you are admired?"

He clucked to the horses to wait their turn at the Hyde Park toll gate. "I believe it amuses women like Clara Bellwether to admire me," he answered. "And then a new fancy will come along, as one inevitably does."

She had seen the truth of this for herself already this season. "But you have your business," she said. "You do not depend on the goodwill of the grand."

He raised a dark brow. "My business profits from the goodwill of wealthy patrons. Indubitably."

"You forget about Arendale, Jem," Bertie said from the back seat. "You will be our grandfather's heir."

"My father is the heir," he replied with a bitter twist to his mouth. "And I am likely to be my father's heir, in consequence of which I will inherit whatever my father chooses to leave of the estate and its various incomes, as well as the burdens and debt."

He did not think much of his father, that was clear. Lucasta combed her memory for information about the Falstead family but came up with precious little.

"Your mother?" she asked cautiously.

"Inherited the draper's business and died when I was young, and Judith younger," Jem said shortly. "Dixon & Co. continues under her family name, and will as long as I have breath. It is one thing my father no longer has power to ruin, since I bought out his shares long ago."

"And Lord Payne is now a governor in the West Indies," she ventured, trying to make some sense of his antipathy. "Does he— have a second wife?"

"Wife?" Jem turned his face to her, and she flinched, though his ferocity was not directed at her. "If only he would accord her that dignity. No, he brings Portia into his home and expects her to perform the duties of a wife at his board and in his bed, but on paper she is still enslaved. And so are her children."

He turned his face away, his jaw hard as granite. "That is why I have brought the older ones here. And I'll bring the younglings as well, as soon as he lets them leave."

"Because, thanks to the Somersett case, they cannot be

removed from England against their will," Lucasta realized. "How many others?"

"Two yet living, and I gather she is anticipating another happy event, from the steward's last letter. The child may already have put feet to earth, given how long it would take a letter to arrive."

Lucasta gathered her courage. She had already decided she must separate herself from Jeremiah Falstead, for her own peace of mind; she lost nothing by being honest. "What is it you despise, Rudyard? The institution of slavery, or the mixing of races?"

This time his furious expression was directed at her. Lucasta lifted her chin.

"You can still ask me that?" His voice sounded pained, rather than threatening.

"I'm afraid I must. You called my friend a zebra."

"Oh, Jem, that was true?" Bertie said with dismay. "I was hoping it was simply Clara Bellwether being vicious."

"I was remarking on her gown!" Rudyard shouted, jerking on the ribbons as the vehicle in front of them stopped abruptly. "Those stripes were an offense to the eye."

He turned his body to face her, hands clenched on the ribbons, and Lucasta drowned in a wave of heat as his eyes burned into her.

"Let me be very clear, Miss Lithwick, about what I detest. Not only do I regret that the vile institution of slavery has enriched the Falstead family to the violence and ruination of a great many human lives, but I find my father's behavior reprehensible. Even if Portia were a British citizen, I doubt he would do her the courtesy of marrying her and legitimizing her children. I have made my feelings clear to him with very little effect."

He turned back to face the street. "And since he knows I plan to get rid of the plantation and free its people the moment the title passes to me, he runs the estate for no other purpose than his own immediate enrichment. It is a belief my uncles before him held, and my grandfather still holds, I am sorry to say."

At Bertie's stifled moan, he threw a pitying glance over his shoulder. "Not you, Bertie. I know that."

"I still benefit," Bertie said, her tone hollow. "We all do." She looked down at the picture hat in her hands.

"I do as well," Lucasta answered. "I eat sugar. I wear cotton, which British ships will no doubt begin bringing from the American colonies again, now that hostilities have ceased."

Rudyard regarded her sternly. "You ought to wear linen, bought only from my shop."

"Perhaps I shall." Ah, another reason to draw near to him, stay close, live within his realm, and know whatever she might be foolish enough to long for could never come to pass. Lucasta tugged at the worn finger of a glove. "Thank you for introducing me to your family, Rudyard. I consider it an honor."

He kept his profile to her. "Enough to forgive me for being a dandy concerned only with the arrangement of my necktie?"

She allowed herself a smile, relieved at his lightening of the moment. "You may show great care for your neckcloth *and* still entertain other attachments. I see that now."

Again he shrugged, as if he were throwing off some unwanted touch. Lucasta studied the breadth of his shoulders beneath the finely cut coat. However thin the approval of the fashionable world might appear, he had it. In addition, he ran a successful business and was heir to a wealthy estate along with one of the highest titles in the kingdom. Add to that his physical stature, and Jeremiah Falstead was a powerful man, a man of presence and command in addition to his wealth.

None of that seemed like *him*. He'd seemed most authentic, most at his ease, in the tiny parlor of his Little Chelsea cottage, watching his family interrogate her.

Watching her sing. Singing with her. A shiver moved over her neck at the memory of his delicious voice. That sound would follow her into sleep and twine through her dreams.

As the sky began to glower with the smoke of civilization, Rudyard let Bertie down first at Arendale House. The two girls parted with a squeeze of hands, Bertie exacting a promise for Lucasta to visit soon. Rudyard steered the horses the few blocks to

Caroline Street and the town house the Pevenseys had rented, drawing up before the door with its scrubbed steps and large, ornate knocker.

"Bertie means it, you know," he said as he walked around to help Lucasta down from the vehicle. "She would adore for you to call on her."

"I should adore calling on her," Lucasta admitted, putting her hand into his. His grasp was strong, warm, firm. "But it seems out of place that I should make free at Arendale House."

"She needs friends," Rudyard said. "The loss of her brother has laid her quite low. Perhaps you could introduce her to the Gorgons."

"I thought the Gorgons were to be despised." Lucasta gathered her skirts with her other hand to begin her descent. "Thus the name, unless I am mistaken?"

A sedan chair jogged by them. The men carrying it shouted and jostled Rudyard's coach, and the horses stomped and jerked in their harness. Thrown off balance, Lucasta tumbled forward, only to collide with a firm surface. Rudyard's arms clamped about her and remained there as he lowered her feet to the pavement, well away from the muck accumulating in the street.

A lightning bolt fell from the sky, shearing through her.

She was encased in heat, like a jacket potato. He held her as if reluctant to let go, his face a hand's breadth away from hers. She stared into his eyes, overcome by a new and incomprehensible sensation. He was hard and yet yielding at the same time, solid as a wall and yet pliant. A man, a powerful man, as she had thought, yet with secret currents she had never guessed at before today.

The air between them crackled like a sky before a thunderstorm.

"I wonder, Miss Lithwick," he said, his voice a low, sensuous rumble, "if we have both been mistaken about a great many things."

She would touch her lips to his if she simply rose on her toes. His voice resonated in her chest, a rich, decadent chord. She had the insane urge to graze her teeth along the shadow of his jaw.

She could *not* kiss Jeremiah Falstead in the street. She ought not even *think* about kissing him, here in plain view of their house, the passing traffic, the curious eyes of the neighbors. Had she taken leave of her senses?

He released her and stepped back. Lucasta fought for balance. It was beyond her yet to attempt speech.

"I hope you will call on Judith as well. She gets lonely for company." His voice was rough and low.

"I..." His touch had left her light-headed, wanting air. "I should like to see her again," Lucasta gasped, her wits still at sea. "But I'm afraid I do not have means of transport."

It was beyond her funds to hire a chair and beyond her stamina to walk that distance. She could request use of the Pevensey carriage, but then she would have to explain her destination, and her aunt would have too many questions.

Lucasta already knew she had been drawn into a great secret. Jem did not talk about his family, and neither would she.

"I can arrange it," he said simply. "Send me word or tell Bertie when you are free. I shall drive you whenever you wish."

Leaving his business and his other affairs to follow her whim, and putting his large, distracting presence in proximity to her. What a lovely, treacherous thought.

Lucasta stepped back, hoping the distance would repair her presence of mind. The burning look in his eyes made her want to sway toward him. Had she ever thought this man a shallow, useless dandy? He was a mine of rich ore and she wanted badly to explore his depths.

She could not be in the pocket of Lord Rudyard. The complaints of Aunt Pevensey or the town gossips were the least of her worries. This man threatened her peace of mind.

"Th-thank you," she stammered, her eyes burning with the threat of tears.

She felt his gaze scald her like a torch as she clutched her shawl and hurried inside. She needed her music room, her refuge, to soothe and order her thoughts before she must face anyone. There were so many revelations, so many sensations of the day to sort through and put in their proper place.

"Lucasta. There you are."

The Baron stood in the hallway, blocking her progress toward the stairs. "A relief you've finally been able to tear yourself away from Rudyard. I'll have a word with him if he bothers you in future."

All the oversetting heat of her day with Jeremiah Falstead puffed away under the Baron's cool stare. Lucasta followed the hand he flicked toward the green parlor, resenting that he could so quickly drain away all her pleasure.

"There's someone you need to greet." The Baron herded her toward the parlor, and she stopped in her tracks at the doorway.

Lady Pevensey perched in her favorite chair, her expression strained. Cici's cheeks were flushed, her eyes sparkling with joy as she stared adoringly at the stranger in the room.

"Trevor," Lucasta whispered. "I mean, Mr. Pevensey."

"Of course he's Trevor to you," the Baron said with a slow, crafty smile. "Your dear, very dear cousin. He's finally come home."

## CHAPTER THIRTEEN

Something caught tight around Lucasta's throat and strangled. She made her living by her voice, by her expression, and she couldn't make a sound.

She'd met Trevor Pevensey on a few family occasions after Aunt Patience married the Baron. He'd been a pudgy, petulant boy with a pouty lower lip, prone to tantrums, cheeks always red from exertion. From all she'd heard of him since her arrival in London, he was much the same as a man.

She saw now he had changed a great deal.

The man before her was assured in his manner and fashion-able, but not flamboyant in his dress. He wore a single-breasted riding coat with broad lapels and a collar and cuffs trimmed with blue. Rows of large silver buttons lined the coat and the matching waistcoat beneath. A ruffle of white linen peeked from his cuffs, a black silk cravat nestled about his throat, and his lightly powdered hair was pulled back in a queue and tied with a blue ribbon. Rudyard would approve.

His was a younger version of the baron's face, with a broad forehead and pronounced chin, slashing black brows over lively blue eyes, and a nose that still looked masculine rather than overly large. Grooves about his mouth deepened into creases as he smiled.

"My cousin Lucasta, all grown up." Trevor swept her a graceful bow and rose with her hand at his lips. "Cici tells me you have been the most charming possible chaperone for her season." The corners of his mouth quirked upward. "But who has been chaperoning you?"

Unless she was mistaken, he squeezed her hand lightly before releasing her fingers. That made two men who had held her hand in the span of minutes.

"Trevor. Mr. Pevensey." She fumbled with the strings of her bonnet, flustered.

"Trevor," he and his father said at the same time.

"Trevor. How—how delightful that you are home. You enjoyed your Grand Tour?"

The gossip she'd heard belowstairs gave various reasons for his circuit abroad. Some said a scandal with a woman, some said gambling debts, some an affair of honor, and some thought all three. But whatever the reason, the effect of his foray on the Continent had been to mature her cousin. He had lost at least a stone of baby fat and acquired a degree of polish in its place.

"I've any number of stories I could bore you with," he said lightly. "I've already shared a few of the more amusing anecdotes with Cici and her ladyship." He turned his smile to Cici, and she glowed like a cat in the sun. Lucasta noticed that Trevor's warm expression did not extend to his father's wife.

"Show her the little trinket you brought her from Paris," the Baron prompted.

The strangling twist in Lucasta's throat inched lower. Her cousin, alone, would not have marked her existence. The Baron had warned him to return home ready to woo.

Trevor held out an exquisite enameled box not much larger than his hand. "I remembered you were musical."

Lucasta accepted the gift with caution. Trevor's hands were soft, the hands of a gentleman. Unlike Rudyard, he'd been born to leisure. And unlike Rudyard, he was not a man who would work when he had other expectations.

For instance, gaining a fortune through marriage.

The delicate scenes painted along the top and sides of the music box featured Marie Antoinette and her ladies in brilliant dress, lounging in the Queen's Petit Trianon. When Lucasta turned the crank, a clear, metallic song tinkled out. She recognized the short piece from a recent French comic opera. It was a charming tune, with the kind of melancholy undertone that she loved. She met Trevor's eyes, surprised that whether by insight or sheer luck he should stumble onto something that pleased her so well.

"I adore it." She tilted her head to listen to the tune again. "Thank you."

Trevor held her gaze. His was curious, amused, but veiled. He nodded his head in acknowledgement. "How fortunate for me."

Cici had contained herself long enough. She seized her brother's hand. "Can you imagine how wonderful it will be, Lucasta, now that we will have a handsome escort for our revels? I have already begged *belle-mère* to let us bring him to Mrs. Plimpton's tomorrow, and to Ranelagh Gardens the day after." She giggled at her brother. "You will make such a splash! I daresay you will outdo Lord Rudyard as the Season's most eligible bachelor. How I will adore watching all the girls go wild over you."

Trevor met this confession with a manufactured smile. The Baron laid a hand on the back of his lady's chair, clearing his throat.

"You may wish to consult with your brother, miss, before you fan the hopes of any of your friends. Trevor might already have his own match in mind."

Lucasta's heart slipped down to puddle in her stomach. The Baron's triumphant smirk said he would hold her to the devil's bargain she had struck. Her sly promise to entertain Trevor's suit, made when she thought he would linger on the Continent for the foreseeable future.

Now he was here. And she sacrificed her benefit concert if she let the Baron know how she felt.

The strangling vine slithered through her chest and wrapped tight. She must not let herself be trapped by these men. And she must not be a fool.

"Time enough to think of all that later, sir." Trevor directed a brotherly smile at Cici's adoring face. "You will first allow me to wash off the dust of the road, I hope, and look up a few friends before I go marching anyone up to the church door."

"I expect you'll find more than a few friends under the hatches or in disgrace," the Baron said. "Best to start fresh, son, and begin as you mean to go on."

Aunt Pevensey grimaced as though someone were sticking her with pins. "But we cannot think of marrying Trevor off when he has just returned to us. Besides, we are concentrating on Cecilia's marriage this Season. I daresay your son's expectations might be raised higher if his sister makes a worthy match, my love. Rudyard meant to take her driving today, before Lucasta pushed her way in."

"Rudyard?" Trevor frowned. "Do you mean Cadmus?"

"Your friend Cadmus died of fever," the Baron informed him. "Then his father died of a side of bad beef and passed the title of Earl Payne to his uncle. This new Lord Rudyard is no more than a draper's son who thinks himself quite a beau, and there are far too many who let him believe it. Worse, he'll be heir to the Marquess of Arendale. Sooner rather than later, if his father stays in the West Indies. Hardly a place for civilized men."

"They were out all day," Aunt Patience said. "Wherever could you have gone, Lucasta?"

Every Pevensey eye turned to her. The images came in a hot rush. Sunlight on green fields and blooms of color climbing the elegant cottage. Judith, Bertie, and the children chatting with her in a golden pool of light, weaving her into their life, their parlor filled with sweet aromas and enchanting song.

A rich baritone voice that had been imprinted in her memory, never to leave.

If Aunt Patience sabotaged the Baron's plot to match her with

Trevor, Lucasta would find her permission to host the benefit concert withdrawn with the snap of a finger.

"Rudyard means to engage me as a music tutor for his cousin," she said finally. His name left a soft hum on her lips, like the reed of an hautboy. "I give lessons, you know. That is how I support myself." Time to remind them all that she labored for a living. No fit match for a gentleman.

"But you won't need that now, with your Aunt Cornelia determined to make you her heir," the Baron said with a toothy smile. "She's sitting on a tidy sum, I wager."

Lucasta loosened her fingers before she crushed the delicate enamel music box. If the Baron convinced Trevor that she was some prize—

"I must confess, I do not stand in expectation of any inheritance from Aunt Cornelia. She will likely give away her fortune to one of her favorite charitable institutions. Or bequeath it to the current Viscount Frotheringale."

"She will!" Aunt Patience cried. "It is as I said, my love."

"Gale?" Trevor untangled his arm from Cici's. "He's plump enough in the pocket. He's no need for her boodle."

"A smart man would try anyway," the Baron replied. "But if there's expectation of a happy event, why shouldn't Lady Evers open the purse strings early?"

Cici linked her hands beneath her chin, glancing from Trevor to Lucasta with consideration. Aunt Patience looked as if she'd drunk vinegar. Lucasta didn't know where she drew the courage to say what she said next.

It had something to do with Jeremiah Falstead's expression when he introduced his half-siblings to her. With the way his rich baritone had supported and complemented her voice during their duet.

With the way his eyes lit when she practically fell out of his carriage into his arms and they stared at each other for a long moment, both of them, she was certain, feeling that strange sense that though they stood on a public street, the rest of the world had momentarily withdrawn.

She had always been inclined to speak her mind. But something about the golden light of his notice—of Jem's approval—was making her uncustomarily bold.

"Aunt Cornelia said she approves my being invited to get up a benefit concert for the Foundling Hospital," Lucasta said. "She adores music. And I expect I will be kept quite busy with that project in the coming weeks."

"Not too busy to have a bit of fun!" With a wave of his hand, the Baron swept her protestations aside. Lucasta couldn't recognize this hearty man who had replaced the tight-lipped, sullen Lord Pevensey. He behaved as if a weight had been removed from his shoulders, or a festering splinter taken from his side. "You'll enjoy squiring your cousin about, won't you, Trevor?"

It was a warning, one Trevor acknowledged by a tight knot of muscle in his cheek. Lucasta held her breath. If Trevor didn't want her, she would be free from the Baron's schemes. Trevor would face his father's wrath, but Lucasta could continue planning her concert. Or thinking about her concert, at least.

But if he fell in with his father's plans—she didn't know what she'd do.

"And Cici?" Lucasta asked. No one ever asked Cici what she wanted. She, too, was expected to fall in with her father's plans for her without a murmur of complaint. But if Cici wanted something better for her brother, she could be an ally.

"Oh, do marry my brother, Lucasta." Cici threw her arms around Lucasta's shoulders, a gesture that took her entirely by surprise. "I would adore having you for a sister."

Lucasta's head felt like a chamber orchestra all tuning to different scales, a discordant blur of noise.

"It seems my sister is as eager to welcome you into the family as is my father," Trevor drawled.

"Cici, why don't you show your cousin what arrived for her," the Baron said, narrowing his eyes at his son.

"Oh, you must see," Cici squealed, tugging at Lucasta's arm. "The first of your new wardrobe, and I hope you will be very pleased with it! Those awful things *belle-mère* gave you need never again see the light of day."

Lucasta followed Cici's bright chatter to her chamber where the dress box awaited. She wished she could escape to her music room and sort out the blaring riot of music in her head.

She needed to stop dwelling on that moment when Jeremiah Falstead might have kissed her.

She needed to hold the Baron's goodwill long enough to organize the benefit concert.

She needed to avoid being trapped into marriage with Trevor Pevensey. And she could achieve that by remaining no more than what she was: poor, plain Lucasta Lithwick.

But Lucasta had not reckoned on the consequence of being flattered by Smart Jeremy. Nor the effect of Mademoiselle Beaudoin's gowns.

~

LADY PLIMPTON'S rout was a crush when they arrived in Berkley Square. Sir Titus Plimpton was a nabob awarded his knighthood after he brought home a fortune from India and with it wooed the daughter of a shipping magnate who ran an empire in slaves, sugar, and rum. Lady Pevensey speculated that the Countess of Jersey, Horace Walpole, and the Prime Minister, Lord Shelburne, were all likely to make an appearance, given they lived in the neighborhood, and it was only too bad that the Devonshires had withdrawn to Bath for the summer, for the Duchess could not fail to make a pet of Cecilia, did she only meet her. Trevor gave noncommittal answers as his stepmother furnished a long list of ladies of birth and breeding who could be considered worthy of his attentions.

Lucasta looked for her friends, and as soon as she could make her excuses, she joined them before a study of classical sculptures clustered in the corner of one enormous drawing room.

"Queen Lucasta!" Annis cried. "Is this Mademoiselle Beaudoin's doing? How clever she is."

All three of them circled Lucasta, admiring her new gown. The seamstress had taken the patterned chintz Rudyard sent and turned it into a gorgeous open robe with just enough ruffles to make it seem the gown floated on its own, but not so many that Lucasta appeared drowning. For the front panel she had chosen a contrasting silk in blushing pink, the color of the inside of a grapefruit, and lined it with small flirtatious ribbons that cascaded over the bodice and down the skirt. Instead of a cap, the seamstress had insisted on a gauzy veil that looped Lucasta's head, showing off the color of her curls, and a slender collar of ribboned lace around her throat to make up for her lack of jewels. The effect was fresh, demure, sensual, and sensible all at once.

"It suits you exactly, my dear," Minnie pronounced. "I hope my creation is as marvelous."

Selina gave her a merry smile. "Have you forgiven Lord Rudyard at last?"

Lucasta squeezed her friend's hands and refrained, with an effort, from looking about the room for him. "I am taking forgiveness under consideration."

Aside from fancies here and there for various musicians known about Bath, and a short-lived period of pining for a concert-master's son, Lucasta had never entertained attachments to a man. Her friends would be astonished, and possibly concerned, to hear she might be developing a *tendre* for Smart Jeremy.

No, not Smart Jeremy—that was a creation of the gossip sheets and the man himself. She was going soft in the head over Jeremiah Falstead, a man who was devoted to his family and who helped young dressmakers trying to make their way. A draper's son with a discerning eye and a voice that made her weak in the knees.

"Did you get my letters from yesterday?" she began. "I—"

"Miss Lithwick." Ralph Plimpton, scion of the house, stalked toward them wearing a waistcoat of crushed silver with so much embroidery that the eye could look nowhere else. "If Mum asks, tell her I made you a leg, will you? She said I ought to do the pretty, though she also said I wouldn't have a chance with all the other bucks likely to be sniffing around you." He wheeled to glare at where the Pevenseys stood, chatting with their hostess. "Now tell me, who's that chap drooling all over your cousin? He's standing a good deal too close, if you ask me."

"That is her brother," Lucasta said. "Mr. Pevensey, just returned to town."

"It can't be." Annis turned with an incredulous look. "Who swapped Trevor for that gorgeous specimen?"

"Gorgeous?" Lucasta blinked. "Are we looking at the same person?"

"My word, he's turned delectable," Minnie observed. "Can the Grand Tour do that to a man?"

"What was he before?" Selina stared as avidly as the rest. "Remember I did not know him."

"He wasn't *this*." Annis gave Lucasta a shrewd look. "Does it change anything? For instance, how we feel about the Baron's wishes."

Lucasta worried her little finger between her teeth. Marriage was the way a woman secured her position in the world. Marriage to a baron's heir would grant her status security and protection. As an eventual baron's wife, she would have access to musicians galore. She could be a patroness to many, and she could perform as much as she liked for private audiences. She'd never be a leading lady on the public stage, but she could build her own.

"Currently, I am letting the Baron dangle me, or rather my supposed inheritance from Aunt Cornelia in front of Trevor, in return for permission to put on the concert to benefit the Foundling Hospital. And if you think it too sly in me," she added, glimpsing Selina's wide eyes, "believe me, I am repenting the bargain. But if I tell Trevor he has no hopes of me, his lordship may send me packing straight back to Bath, and I won't have the concert at all."

Or her friends. Or Cici. Or more time with Jeremiah Falstead, whatever fragile accord seemed to be growing between them.

"What do we do?" Selina asked.

"Help me persuade milord Pevensey I am an unsuitable match for his son. Or persuade Trevor of it. I am plain, I lack accomplishments, I am of low birth, and I have no real expectations. I am the last person he ought to be paying address."

"Him and every other unattached gentleman here tonight," Minnie murmured.

Lucasta straightened with a nod. "I must be a Gorgon in truth. Reviled. Unapproachable. Let men shudder at my very name."

Annis laughed. "A forfeit, girls, from the one of us who tonight who receives the most offers to stroll about and admire Lady Plimpton's art? I suggest she must pay our way into Leicester House so we may see Sir Ashton Lewes' collection of curiosities."

"Cox's Museum," Minnie answered. "He's a new silver swan among his automata I want to see."

"The Royal Circus," Selina suggested.

"A concert at the Hanover Square rooms managed by Signor Gallini," Lucasta began, but Minnie jostled her into silence.

"Be certain you can afford your forfeit for all of us, dear, for you shall be called upon to pay it," she said.

Lucasta returned her smile with a glower. "I am Medusa."

Annis laughed. "You fascinated Smart Jeremy, and now the gossips have put you in line for a fortune. The Baron may make his gamble, but if milady Plimpton has her son making a pitch, you may count upon it, Lucasta. You will be besieged." Her eyes danced with mischief. "We did establish a forfeit for the first among us to obtain a marriage proposal, did we not?"

~

"MY STEPMOTHER HAD NOT TOLD me you were the toast of the season," Trevor commented to Lucasta as Lady Plimpton's guests circulated in the small parlor where a light supper was laid on. "She had intimated that Cici had taken well, but she suggested you were—"

"A complete antidote," Lucasta said.

"Not in so many words." He glared as a gentleman to Lucasta's left placed a slice of cold ham on her plate with an ingratiating look. As the companion who had escorted her in, it was Trevor's duty to stock Lucasta's plate with delicacies.

She could see any number of young ladies in attendance who wished they were in Lucasta's place beside the beguiling new arrival. But any number of men glared at Trevor, too, clearly wishing him at Jericho.

"You are very much in demand," Trevor observed.

Lucasta didn't respond, for at that moment, Rudyard strolled in with Clara Bellwether on his arm. He wore a suit of midnight blue silk embroidered with a pattern that spread to the silver-gold waistcoat, and the matching lining inside the tails of his coat, contrasting the embroidered breeches, drew attention to his powerful legs. *He* was gorgeous.

Lucasta's mouth went dry as Lady Clara whispered to him behind her fan, inviting him to lean close to hear her.

The way her heart leapt at the sight of him was ridiculous. She did not have a claim to him. Lucasta tore her eyes away, looking anywhere else.

Selina was enjoying the attentions of Major Mallory, who had been beaten to Cici's side by Mr. Plimpton. Minnie had, with her unerring accuracy, located the one eccentric scholar in the crowd and was deep in a discussion of Old English syntax, pretending not to see Ashley's freezing stares in her direction. And Annis had been cornered by a fellow diplomatic envoy, who loudly demanded how much of a threat she thought this upstart Sheikh Mansur of Chechnya might pose to Catherine the Great's plans for expansion in the Caucasus.

"If I am in demand," Lucasta said, fixing her attention on the table laden with the night's repast, "I shall take advantage to find as many sponsors for my concert as I can."

"Sponsors and not suitors?" Trevor probed, scooping a pile of candied lemon onto Lucasta's plate.

She sneaked a spoonful of sugared almonds, debating how forward she was allowed to be. It was glaringly impolite of a young lady to presume a young man had an interest in her. But if Trevor was as unenthused as she was about his father's plans, her greatest fear could be laid to rest.

She looked about to see how likely she could exchange an unobserved word with him in the supper room, where couples hovered at side tables or small groups stood chatting and balancing their plates. The evening had been a constant stream of young men inviting her to stroll about the room, young women wanting to be seen with her, and gossipy matrons who wanted to know just what she had done to fascinate Lord Rudyard. Her face hurt from holding a polite smile for hours, as if she were sitting for a portrait.

"Your father," Lucasta began.

Trevor examined an oyster, then replaced it on the tray. "Yes?"

"I only hope you know I have no expectations. Of you," she rushed to say. "That is, I would not presume so high."

His eyes narrowed, and he swept a glance over the others milling about the refreshment table. "You mean to say you don't intend to settle just yet."

"I do not intend to settle at all," she said. "What I mean is…I will sympathize if you are not in accord with your father's wishes."

He moved on to a bowl of dried oranges. "He gave me to understand I would have no rivals. Yet I find that not at all the case."

Her heart thumped and she held her plate with both hands to steady it. Some men thrived on rivalry. None of the men here tonight had taken the least notice of her until Smart Jeremy made his careless remark.

No, not careless. Calculated. But she still wondered, why?

"Of course you should be at liberty to choose as you wish." She was careful to steady her voice, too.

Trevor's eyes were blue like Cici's, but a darker, stormier shade. "Picture a man who returns from the Continent ready to establish himself," he said. "Perhaps improve a somewhat soiled reputation. Then imagine he finds the most difficult choices already made for him: whom to take to wife, and how to support her. All that remains for him is to select a house in town, choose a club, and find a tailor." He lifted a brow, dark gold like his hair. "What man would not agree?"

It was as good as a declaration. And yet she could not, must not let him think she conceded. "As I said..."

She caught his scent first, then the warmth of his presence behind her, and then a familiar melting voice poured down Lucasta's spine.

"Miss Lithwick."

Trevor's face shuttered. Lucasta looked up into the deep gold-brown of Jem's eyes.

"Milord Rudyard." She wished she didn't sound breathless.

"The sun left us when I returned you home yesterday."

His eyes were not on her as he delivered this pretty compliment, but on Trevor Pevensey. There was something guarded in Jem's look—hostility? Annoyance bubbled. He had waited an awful long time to approach her.

"What a foolish thing to say," she answered, noting with alarm that she stood in the canyon between the two men's bodies. "The clouds have come in nearly every day of this month, and yet we still have no rain."

"You will honor me with a dance after supper? I have requested the musicians play the Duke of York's Cotillion. Though I notice," he added, and his eyes twinkled with mischief, "they are the same band as at Lady Clara's party, with the same wretched second violin."

She pursed her lips so she would not catch his grin. Trevor watched her face closely.

"How enterprising of you, Lord Rudyard, to invite me to tread once again on your toes."

"A small sacrifice," he murmured, and with a short bow moved away.

Trevor watched him move among the company, paying small compliments here and there. "M'father doesn't like that man," he said shortly.

"He'd accept in a moment did he offer for Cici's hand," Lucasta said in surprise.

"It doesn't appear to be Cici he's interested in," Trevor replied.

Lucasta's heart executed the most astonishing pirouette at that remark, and still had not settled when the music struck up and Rudyard claimed her. He was Smart Jeremy to this crowd, Rudyard to the rest of the world, Jeremiah Falstead to her, and fast becoming Jem. She must not, *must not* be a fool.

"I have secured my first performers for the Foundling Hospital's benefit concert," she reported as they bowed and began the country dance. "The Gorgons have consented to perform one of Haydn's string quartets."

"We shall sell out on that basis alone." He swept her through a turn, his hand firm and strong through her protective layer of chintz.

"I had a note from Judith today," he added. "She demanded I bring you to see her again."

"As soon as she would like," Lucasta said immediately.

"Alas, I have business tomorrow. The day next?"

"I believe I am free of obligations." She ought not seem too eager. Indeed she ought to spend all her spare time organizing the concert. The governor's board had set a date mere weeks away, wanting to take advantage of the nobility in town before Parliament concluded.

Rudyard watched her as the ladies *chasséd* to their places, his face arresting her thought, the stern nose and sharp jaw such a contrast with his sensual lips and melting eyes. She wanted his company as much as she wanted his sister's.

*Goose.*

"The violinist seems behaving tonight." He bent his head and spoke low near her ear as they came together for the promenade.

"He is much improved. I knew he was a fiddler and not a concert violinist. I wonder if he would sell me his Amati in that case."

Rudyard glanced at her face. "I suppose I ought not ask for a second dance."

There would be speculation if he did. Worse, there would be more danger for her. With his hands holding hers at her back and waist, his gloved fingers tight and firm around her own, his leg brushing her skirt, Lucasta had the strange sense that she'd stepped into a place made for her.

"I suppose not." Her voice came out husky.

"Everyone will think I am paying court to you." His fingers squeezed hers. She recalled how he caught her when she fell out of his carriage, the press of his body against hers. She felt faint.

"We mustn't have that." She barely breathed.

"And your escort, I think, is begging for a reason to call me out."

"Trevor?"

Her cousin watched them from the side of the room with a baleful glower. Her fellow Gorgons regarded them with considerable interest as well.

In fact, every eye on the room, save those of their fellow dancers and the musicians, appeared glued to Jem and Lucasta. Her stomach twisted in knots.

"I will call upon you in two days." They reached their place and completed the figure. As Lucasta executed her final curtsy, Rudyard caught her hand and kissed her fingertips. It was no more than a slight pressure on her glove, yet she felt as if she'd touched a live coal.

But then he raised his head and glanced about the room, as if confirming that every eye rested on them. Satisfied to find this the case, he held her hand a bit more than was proper, let his gaze linger on her face a beat too long.

The sense of betrayal nearly made her stagger. Her knees went liquid and her mind blanked.

Lucasta, though, had trained for performances. Smart Jeremy was putting on some sort of display, and though she didn't understand his intentions, she could guess her role. She smiled, nodded her head with cool politeness, and withdrew her hand.

And promised herself that, for the rest of the evening, she would not watch his progress, see whom he spoke with, take note of the least thing he did or said.

He wanted something from her. She had to figure out what it was.

But he didn't want *her*.

# CHAPTER FOURTEEN

"He's besotted with you," Judith declared. She sat before the spinet, Lucasta at her elbow.

Bertie looked up from the deep chair where she sat with her feet tucked beneath her, a novel on her lap and a dish of sweetmeats on the table beside her. "Indeed he is," she murmured in agreement.

Lucasta blushed. "I am sure I don't know who you're referring to. Now, this passage—"

"You know perfectly well." Judith smiled. "I've never seen Jem so taken with anyone."

"The only interest your brother has in me is as a music tutor," Lucasta said briskly. "And refurbishing my wardrobe, it should seem."

In the last few weeks, Mlle. Beaudoin had just so happened to come across several extraordinary fabrics which she made into gowns for Lucasta. As much as it embarrassed Lucasta to fear she might have become one of Jeremiah Falstead's charity cases—or whether it were right to accept the gift—the relief of having properly modish gowns to wear when she conducted charity concert business outweighed her reservations about becoming too much in his pocket, or in his debt.

"Shall I run through this exercise once more?" she asked, determined to distract.

"I have most of it." Judith played through the small piece, only pausing once or twice to ask Lucasta to clarify a passage or correct her fingering.

Lucasta sorted through the pages of musical scores she had brought, listening with pleasure. She had received a delightful response to her inquiry to Mélanie de Salignac, who promptly shared her system of using raised print in musical scores. While this meant Judith could use her fingers to read the musical notes, she really didn't need notation. The girl's ear was remarkable, better than Lucasta's, and she needed only play a piece through twice to have it committed to memory.

Judith added a final flourish at the end. "Has he declared himself yet?"

Lucasta fanned herself with the sheet music. The small fire, built in the fireplace against the cool day, made the room absurdly hot. "There is nothing to declare."

In all the time they had spent together the past several weeks, him whisking her from beneath Aunt Pevensey's pinched stare to bring her to Rose Hollow, or the dances or conversation they shared when their paths crossed at yet another card party or rout, they spoke of nothing more than his family's health, Mlle. Beaudoin's shop, her preparations for the concert, or what Lucasta thought of the evening's musical offerings.

There were no murmured compliments, no heavy-lidded glances, no pressing of fingers to suggest she meant more to him. She was not being wooed, therefore no reason existed for her insides to flutter like a flock of starlings taking flight each time she saw him. Absolutely no cause whatsoever.

"I suspect he has made a project of me," Lucasta said.

"Pygmalion fell in love with his project," Judith said.

"Galatea," Bertie agreed, popping a bonbon into her mouth.

Bertie was much more relaxed in her cousin's parlor than in her own. When Lucasta visited Arendale House for Bertie's musical lessons, she was received stiffly in a cavernous formal parlor by Lady Payne, who always managed to imply she was standing guard so that Lucasta didn't lift some priceless object off an occasional table.

In contrast, in the cozy parlor at Rose Hollow both Bertie and Lucasta were greeted with the warmest enthusiasm by the three younger Falstead siblings and the resident cat, a tray of pastries and tea whisked in by Mrs. Cadogan, and a lively go-over of absolutely everything that had happened in the intervening hours since they had seen one another. Judith hungered for tales of Lucasta's glittering social round, demanding details of dress, furnishings, music, and conversation, as well as a full transcript of conversations, especially with the men who vied for her attention.

Jem often lingered in the parlor on one pretext or another, eavesdropping on this gossip as if he wasn't also attending every function Lucasta did, watching with no doubt great amusement, and a great deal of self-congratulation, her absurd transformation into the Season's toast.

According to Clara Bellwether, no less a person than His Royal Highness Prince George, whom Lucasta had unexpectedly run across when she called at Carleton House with an errand having to do with the charity concert, remarked her a veritable diamond. Nothing more was needed to make Lucasta Lithwick an unquali-fied success.

This afternoon, Jem had taken his siblings off with the promise of fishing instruction. But how, Lucasta wondered, had a draper's son learned to fish? And how did a man with a business to run, a man whose taste ruled the current caprices of London fashion, find the time two or three afternoons a week to ferry about his sister's musical tutor?

She enjoyed their lessons and the easy rapport she had developed with the Falstead girls. Judith was steady and true, completely artless, though she had a buried sense of mischief. Bertie had been raised more conscious of her status as a marquess's granddaughter, and even out from under her mother's stern eyes, she moved as if wary of her apparent freedom.

And then there was Jem. He was a completely different man among his family than the dandy who strolled society drawing rooms with studied elegance, whose approval was sought, his reprimands crushing. The man she met and occasionally danced with at evening soirees was not the man she sat beside on their drives to Little Chelsea, snugged under a blanket to keep the dirt of the road from her skirts.

She could not, in good conscience, charge for musical instructions when she was being welcomed as one of the family. Not even she was that grasping.

Which meant she was not building her savings for the musical conservatory she would open when she returned to Bath. She was spending all her spare time planning the benefit concert. Time, that was, not spent parading around town on the arm of Trevor Pevensey taking Cici to her entertainments, while the Baron watched with sharp eyes, overseeing this courtship that was not a courtship.

Trevor was amusing, courteously attentive, and completely uninterested in Lucasta, who meant nothing to him beyond a foregone conclusion. She doubted he would make a stir to recover her once she made her feelings clear.

But if the Baron began pressing for a wedding date while Lucasta was still in London—while she still needed his goodwill, and her aunt's, to take part in the concert she was single-handedly planning—she would find her back to a wall.

And there was no accommodation in any of her plans for a brown-eyed, whiskey-voiced draper's son who kept a hidden family and ran a clothing empire. No room at all.

"Yes, Galatea." Lucasta located a simple Mozart concerto that Judith could try. "I've read the story. So disgusted was the sculptor Pygmalion by the changeable and unreliable nature of women that he made himself a companion out of ivory, kissed and caressed her, and draped her with silks and jewels because she pleased him as no mortal woman could. And when the goddess of love took pity on him and made his ideal woman take flesh, he adored her all the more because she was so innocent in mind and body that she depended entirely on him. Ovid doesn't tell us what happened if Galatea ever developed a will or desires of her own, or whether poor deluded Pygmalion could handle sharing his life with an actual living creature."

"Peace!" Bertie cried, laughing. "You are no man's creation, Miss Lithwick. God forgive us if we ever make such a suggestion again."

"I only mean to say that book ten of the *Metamorphosis* is devoted to doomed and painful love," Lucasta said. "Orpheus and Eurydice. Atalanta and her prince. Pygmalion and Galatea."

"But also about transformation," Judith said. She ran her fingers over the raised musical notes of the concerto, reading the music. "Have you secured the performers for your concert?"

"I have a roster beyond my wildest dreams," Lucasta said with a happy sigh. "Miss Harriet and Miss Theodosia Abrams have agreed to sing a duet. Margaret Kennedy will sing as long as she might wear a gown. She says she is weary of playing breeches roles —it's what most contraltos are consigned to. And Mrs. Cecilia Young has promised to make an appearance, though she does not sing in public anymore."

"And?" Bertie prompted.

Lucasta laid a hand over the neckerchief filling in the neckline of her day gown. "Signor Marchesi has consented to perform." Her heart pounded at the thought. "He had very kind words about my English version of his Italian song, which I arranged for the harpsichord. I sent him a copy, with my compliments."

"You should sing a duet," Bertie suggested.

Lucasta laughed. "I, sing with the great Signor Marchesi! You have taken leave of your senses."

"I hope you will sing, Lucasta," Judith said.

"I have no intention of doing so. I will conduct the choir of my foundling girls and accompany some of them in their smaller pieces, but otherwise, I shall be silent."

"Not to be borne!" Bertie cried. "You ought to shine as well. It is your night."

"On the contrary, it should look as if I were pushing in." Aunt Cornelia might have approved Lucasta's part in organizing the concert—a properly genteel pursuit, after all—but the grand chapel of the Foundling Hospital could hardly pass as an acceptable private venue in which Lucasta might perform.

However Aunt Cornelia chose to dispense with her fortune—and Lucasta did not for a moment credit the Baron's belief that it would all come to her—Lucasta owed her aunt for her support after her parents died, and her tuition and board at Miss Gregoire's. Which was to say, she owed Aunt Cornelia her life. Complying with her great-aunt's prohibitions on singing in public, while a hated restriction, was the least she could do to show her gratitude.

"You could sing a duet with Jem," Judith suggested. "That was such a beautiful air you performed when you first visited. You brought tears to my eyes."

Lucasta cleared her throat. "Perhaps I might ask your brother to sing. But certainly I cannot think of doing so myself. The night is for my foundlings, not my own display."

Her throat ached with longing around the denial. How she would love to sing. She dreamed of it.

Judith lifted her chin. "I'll play if you will perform a song."

Bertie, in her cushioned chair, opened her mouth in surprise. Lucasta shared the sentiment. Judith did not venture beyond her quiet street. This suggestion came out of the blue.

"I would accept in a moment if I thought there were any more chance of your brother allowing you to perform than of Aunt Cornelia giving me permission to sing."

Judith ran her fingers over the music, back and forth across the lines. "I don't wish to be put on display all by myself, the poor little blind girl. I couldn't bear that. But I am so weary of always sitting on the sidelines while life goes on around me. I want to help the foundlings, and I want you to sing. So, I will play if you take the stage with me."

Lucasta squeezed the girl's delicate wrist, fighting back the hot lump in her throat. Judith did not want her pity. "Jem—Rudyard—will never approve."

Judith tilted her head. "You don't wish to perform?"

"I wish it above anything."

The thought thrilled and terrified her, how much she wanted this. To stand on a stage, fill a room with her voice, tell a story with her music. To move and uplift, teach or embolden, to heal, or simply stir hearts worn by the toils of the world.

And it would be good for Judith to be seen and acknowledged. After all, she was the granddaughter of a marquess. Lucasta could choose a simple air, one Judith could learn quickly. A benefit concert for foundlings should be the one place in the world she could reveal herself and be shielded from censure.

And Lucasta could sing. In public. Her grand, too grand for her, dream.

Lucasta exhaled. Aunt Pevensey would never approve. Aunt Cornelia would make her feelings clear in some swift and soul-crushing fashion.

"I adore the thought," Lucasta said. "But I fear the consequences." Being laughed at, or simply though common and unimpressive, was the least of it.

A small smile curved Judith's bow-shaped lips. "Then let's not tell Jem just yet."

BERTIE WRIGGLED with the secret all the way home. Several times, as she turned to address her in the back, Lucasta saw the other girl press her gloved knuckles to her lips as though she were holding back words.

She dreaded Jem's response when she broached the subject. She had never seen him lose his temper, but he was excessively protective of Judith. No doubt he would have thoughts as cutting as Aunt Cornelia's about his family performing in a public venue.

He might forbid her music lessons with Judith when he learned what they were plotting. Cast out of the warm circle of Rose Hollow would be like being cast out of paradise.

"Are you attending the Countess of Calenburg's *converzatione* this evening?" Jem asked as they made their way through Knightsbridge, now a familiar trek. "Your diary seems over overfull of late, Miss Lithwick."

"I think you might call me Lucasta," she said with a laugh. "Yes, the Countess is a friend of Miss Gregoire's, and I am always interested to see what her artists are creating. If my diary is overfull, it is only because everyone of *ton* is still puzzling over what about me Smart Jeremy could possibly find *fascinating*."

Was she imagining an irritated twitch to his shoulders? "I am sure you have risen to notice on your own merits."

"You must be aware it is you who has made the Gorgons so admired," she said.

That, and the succession of sumptuous, splendid, well-fitted gowns delivered from Mlle. Beaudoin's, all with the gracious plea to wear with her compliments and, if asked, be so kind as to give Mlle. Beaudoin as the name of her modiste. The Gorgons were necessary at any social occasion whose hostess wished it a success, and Lucasta's gowns had turned her from an antidote to a fashion plate.

Cici delighted in the change as well. Major Mallory found many a young buck vying for the hand of the Pevensey daughter as she was swept along in the wake of the Gorgons.

"Your cousin seems particularly attentive," Jem remarked, his tone flat.

Lucasta studied the elegant mansions that lined the road, their gardens gray-green under the lowering clouds. Every time they stepped out the door to another evening's entertainment with the Baron's self-congratulatory smile and her aunt's unhappy glances, Lucasta looked for the snare at her feet. And she watched in apprehension for evidence that her cousin had taken up his old habits.

Trevor Pevensey spent a great deal of time at his club, out riding, and amusing himself with his friends, but every young man of his age and station was expected to gamble, drink, visit loose women, and amuse himself with the latest freak of fashion.

If Trevor stayed within his means, there was every chance they could both eventually free themselves of his parent's expectation. Lucasta suspected he had no strong wish to marry her, either. But if he fell into straits, lost pots of money, or brought down some other trouble upon his head, then Lucasta—or rather, her presumed inheritance from Aunt Cornelia—might look a good deal more attractive.

Unless Lucasta sang at a public concert and Aunt Cornelia, outraged, cut her off completely. Lucasta would be free of the Baron's machinations and her plague of suitors in one fell swoop.

Thrown entirely onto her devices, her meager savings, and the good graces of whatever musical students she could attract to her conservatory. Hardly a promising start.

The drifting mist turned to a gusty drizzle, then the low clouds opened for the first time in weeks, releasing torrents of rain. Lucasta gasped as a sheet of cold water swooped under her bonnet and slapped her in the face. Behind them, Bertie squealed in discomfort.

Jem, the wretched man, laughed and urged the horses to a brisker pace. "Now, that's bracing!" he shouted. "Makes a man feel alive."

"Oh, Jem, it will ruin my new hat!" Bertie wailed.

"Never fear, Bert, we'll duck into the shop and wait it out."

Lucasta was glad that the sheets of rain dimmed the outlines of traffic and other obstacles before them. She crouched under her woolen cloak as the cold rain furiously pelted them. "Your shop will not be open on Sunday?"

"No, and the draper's assistants will be out on their half day." Jem steered them toward the glass-plated front of a large, attractive shop on Piccadilly. "We shall have to shift for ourselves. Can you manage?"

"I was not raised as a marquess's heir," Lucasta said, stung that he should think her some poor wilting flower who could not abide the elements. The daughter of Laurence Lithwick was much hardier than that.

"I was not raised a marquess's heir, either," Jem replied.

They clipped down Piccadilly past the broad new expanse of Melbourne House, with its extravagant pedimented windows. Just past the tidy brown brick of St. James Chapel, Rudyard turned them down a side alley and into a courtyard behind. Securing the horses to a carriage post, he reached up to help Lucasta from the carriage, and she tried not to curl against him for shelter as he swung her down. She and Bertie clung together like bedraggled swans as he produced a key and let them in through the back door of the establishment. They stepped into a cool, dry storeroom that smelled, unaccountably, like fresh-made bread.

"Halloo?" Jem called, his voice carrying down the hallway that led beyond.

Bertie shook off the droplets clinging to her shawl. "It seems quite deserted."

"I work my lot rather hard, so I don't imagine they'd miss the chance for a holiday." Jem hung his greatcoat and hat on a set of pegs, then reached for Lucasta's cloak. As her cold fingers fumbled with the tapes, he swept her hand aside and, with swift economy, lifted the wet fabric from around her.

"I d-d-dislike being c-c-cold," Lucasta chattered.

"I'll build up the fire in the kitchen—it's that way." He pointed. "And perhaps we can cadge of a bit of what Mrs. Coolidge has set aside for supper."

"You've never brought me here before," Bertie announced. "I'm going to pry about."

"Don't steal anything!" Jem called as Bertie disappeared down the hall. Her laugh floated back to them.

"A housekeeper? Kitchen? I thought you were taking us to your shop," Lucasta said. While Jem went to the hearth and banked it with wood, she drew the wet, limp neckerchief from around her neck and unpinned her hat and apron. She stepped toward the fire, bringing her wet things, just as Jem stood and turned.

His eyes landed squarely on the expanse of bosom exposed by her fashionably cut open robe. It was one of Mlle. Beaudoin's creations, a creamy chintz block-painted with rose stripes and intertwining flowers. The damp fabric molded to her body, and the white petticoat clung to the shift beneath, which had already attached itself to her legs. He would be able to see the shape of her body and a great deal of décolletage.

Lucasta sucked in her breath as his eyes absorbed every inch of her. She held perfectly still, feeling her heart pound against her tight stays. She ought to cover herself. She ought to shy away. She couldn't move.

A curious heat flushed through her, raising the soft hairs on her skin. It was rather like the sensation she got when she heard a new piece of music that she would grow to passionately love. Jem's gaze tracing her body held her in the same breathless state of suspension.

The brown in his eyes turned darker, a beckoning shadow. She stepped toward him, drawn by an impulse she couldn't name.

"Ahem." Jem cleared his throat and stepped away from the hearth, letting her near the revived flames. "What did you say?"

Lucasta's mind had blanked of all but the image of his captivating eyes, the steam rising from the broad shoulders of his coat, the flex of his muscles in the breeches pressed wetly to his legs, the heat drenching her from his body—no, from the fire. *Gracious, girl! Take hold of yourself.* She looked for a place to drape her wet things.

"I—er, I am curious why your shop has a kitchen. And a housekeeper."

"My assistants live above the shop, and I have up to a dozen at any one time." Jem took her sodden neckerchief. His warm fingers brushed her cold ones, a startling touch. "There was always a kitchen of sorts—the building was one of the first houses built here, back when it was Portugal Street. After a while I noticed that my apprentices were spending most of their wages on dinners at the cook shop and saving very little for their own futures. So I expanded their pay to include room and board, and Mrs. Coolidge came on as cook-housekeeper. I'm afraid she can't resist mothering them now and again—she raised any number of children of her own."

The delicious smell of stew wafted from the huge pot on the back of the stove, combined with the fresh loaves wrapped in towels keeping warm in the oven, attesting to the fine meal waiting for the apprentices later. Lucasta's heart squeezed.

Jem was generous to his employees, a benefactor to orphans like Mlle. Beaudoin, and he had taken in his half-siblings as well as supporting his sisters, when surely that was his father's obligation.

And she had accused him of being a dandy concerned with nothing more than the perfection of his appearance.

"I expect your apprentices are glad for a bit of mothering," she said.

As if he were a man at ease in a kitchen, he poured water from a nearby pitcher into a kettle and set it on the stove. He raised his fingers to the elaborate buttons on his velvet coat, then caught himself.

"Do you—er—mind terribly if I remove my coat? It's damp, and I'd rather—"

"Of course. I mean, of course I don't mind," Lucasta hurried to say. She supposed she ought to turn around or look away. It was such an intimate act for a man to disrobe before her. It was this intimacy that kept her eyes riveted as his fingers worked the row of expensive buttons.

Carefully he peeled the tightly fitted fabric from his shoulders, tugging the sleeves over the lace at his cuffs, then arranged the garment over the back of a chair pulled up to the table. He untwisted his cravat as well, draping the length of linen over another chair.

It was such a domestic scene with their clothes steaming before the fire, the cozy warmth of the kitchen chasing away the chill of the rain, both of them in a state of undress. As if they were at ease with one another. As if they were man and wife.

Her heart tapped against her stays. She was not at ease. She couldn't take her eyes from the breadth of Jem's shoulders, the skin of his exposed throat, the shape of muscled arms through the sheer linen of his shirt. The way his waistcoat, so broad around his upper chest, narrowed around his waist. He was a splendidly made man.

She was entirely alone with him. "Where did Bertie take herself off to, I wonder?"

Jem shrugged, and Lucasta's eyes followed the ripple of movement across his shoulders. "Poking about. She's insatiably curious." His eyes rested on her, something warm and potent in his gaze. "Would you like a look as well?"

At first she thought he meant she might look more at *him*, and a heat blazed through her face and neck. Then she realized he meant she might see the shop.

"May I? It isn't open. It feels—illicit." The word sent a thrill through her, or perhaps the thrill was due to Jem, standing near her, partially undressed.

Lucasta Lithwick had done a daring thing or two in her life, usually provoked to it by one of her fellow Gorgons, but never in her life had she done something illicit.

Jem laughed, the sound rich, deep, smoky, wonderful. "Darling, it's my shop. We can do whatever we like."

He held out his hand, a well-shaped, strong-fingered, masculine hand, and Lucasta took it. As she did, she had the strange feeling of completing an action that had been set into motion some time ago and was finally coming to its sure end.

She had the stranger notion that whenever Jeremiah Falstead held out his hand to her, she would take it, every time, and follow where he led.

Where he led her was to the front of the shop, and poor, plain Lucasta Lithwick stepped into a fairytale.

# CHAPTER FIFTEEN

Jem could tell from Lucasta's face that she was seeing the shop as he had seen it for the first time. And found it as entrancing a place as he had.

He'd grown up in rooms above the shop in Holborn and as a child had free run of the Cheapside warehouse. His world from its very beginnings had been a swirling tapestry of color, texture, and fantastic prints. He'd watched over baby Judith, nestled into a basket in the corner, while his mother served customers at the counter or measured yards in the back. He had no doubt he'd taken his own turn in that basket, from birth watching the colors come into harmony about him.

From an early age he'd been taught the trade. There'd never been any doubt that Jem would one day take over the business. He understood his father was a gentleman and thus spent his days and most of his nights absent from the household, engaged in the pursuits of a gentleman, activities supported by the unceasing labor of his wife and her family.

Whatever it was a gentleman did, his father had not cared to teach Jem. He'd been left in the care of the women and clerks, and instead of chums at public school, he had apprentices for his fellows, boys and girls from poor backgrounds pressed by their families to move their way up in the world.

He'd loved it, and his childhood was happy. Instead of balls and wooden animals, his toys were scissors and measuring tape. Instead of riding ponies and rolling hoops, he'd learned to take apart spinning wheels and fix looms. No Latin or studying classic literature, but he'd learned to keep careful ledgers and balance the account books.

He knew how to budget for when a hot spring blighted a flax harvest, when a shipment was lost due to fire or shipwreck, when a new Parliament changed the customs tax. He'd honed an eye that could tell when a linen had the luster that meant the flax had been harvested on time, when a weaver was mixing his fibers with tow, or when a wholesaler was substituting pure linen with hemp. He could tell whether a red silk had been dyed using the madder plant or the cochineal insect, and he could sniff a dyer's vat and recognize if the mordant used to fix the color was aluminum, copper, or chrome.

And he'd never felt cheated that he was being raised a draper's son. Whatever world his father inhabited, Jem hadn't cared to enter. He'd seen early on that his parents' marriage involved his father having an income to fund his amusements and a wife he could trot out at formal affairs and trust she would behave adequately. He'd known his mother to dress up and enjoy the occasional gala or dinner, but Constance, like Jem, preferred the happy industry of her trade.

A true daughter of the merchant class, she'd rather invest money than gamble it away, and would prefer to sort and price a new shipment rather than shop for herself. If she wanted a gown made, she went straight to the wholesaler and bargained for the best silk at the best possible price. Instead of a carriage she drove the wagon that carted their wares from the London docks, and instead of a round of country houses in the summer and fall, she took Jem with her on trips to visit the Irish weavers and Belgian mills that supplied their warehouse.

Far preferable to Jem than the stiff, cold rooms of Arendale House, where he occasionally was compelled to call upon his forbidding grandfather the marquess, were the lofty echoing spaces of the Draper's Hall in Throgmorton Street, which had seemed a veritable palace to his eyes. The hall had burned in his youth and been rebuilt in fine style, but Jem missed the magic that had disappeared with the earlier building. The original Draper's Hall had belonged to Henry VIII's disgraced minister, Thomas Cromwell, and the apprentices spooked each other by pretending to see poor Cromwell's ghost, dragging chains through the guildhall and carrying his head.

Jem had tried to capture that bit of magic and that sense of medieval wealth when he designed his new shop on Piccadilly. He'd been to shops in the Netherlands that were relentlessly tidy and businesslike, all the fabrics pressed into tight neat bolts, tucked into wooden shelves and organized by color and cost. In the expensive shops in Paris, customers sat primly in a chair while an officious clerk selected fabrics for them and perhaps allowed them to touch a corner of it.

Jem wanted his customers to experience his fabrics, to see and smell and revel in them. He wanted shoppers to fall in love with the cloth they were taking home, and more than that, he wanted patrons of his shop to dress in ways that flattered them. He wanted the clothing supplied by Dixon & Co. to combine function and beauty. It was his small way of embellishing a world that often had too little beauty in it.

And so, he'd draped his shop in luxurious swaths, drowning the place in color and designs. Rich brocades in eye-popping patterns cascaded across the bow window like a waterfall of color. Metal hooks attached above the wooden shelving held unrolled gauze that swung through the air above their heads like garlands at a market fair.

Swatches of silk dangled from the corners of cabinets, and thick sample books stuffed with scraps of velvet and damask occupied the long counter. Out of habit Jem ran his eyes over the lighting fixtures, ensuring that none of the wall sconces, floor torches, or chandeliers were within distance of any flammable fabrics. The dull clouds outside dimmed the profusion of color that normally met the eye, but the dusky light made the space more intimate.

Lucasta turned in circles, gaping at everything.

"It's beautiful," she breathed. "I'm in a palace from *The Thousand and One Nights*. A place of enchantment."

Another piece of literature Jem had never read. "I'm glad you like it."

He wanted to lay bolts of silk damask at her feet, his finest and rarest weaves of moiré and lampas liséré. He wanted to drape her in bolts of duchesse satin dyed in deepest Tyrian purple and see if the color went with her hair.

"Josie has been doing well by you," he remarked, moving to a shelf of newer stock. He sensed that Lucasta Lithwick would shy away if he began too boldly. Best to lure her close with small quiet treats and slowly accustom her to the riches she deserved. He ran his fingers over a bolt of indienne, a floral-patterned chintz.

"Who?" She clasped her hands to each shoulder, hugging herself with her arms. Jem guessed the gesture had less to do with delight than with the temperature of the room. With no customers and no attendants, the braziers hadn't been filled, and it was scarcely warmer than outside. He lifted the bolt of indienne chintz from the shelf to the counter.

"You know her as Mlle. Beaudoin. Or has she asked you to call her Joséphine?"

Orphaned by the smallpox nearly twenty years ago, she'd been logged into the rolls at the Benevolence Hospital as Jo Baker, the last name taken from her father's occupation. Of her mother or the rest of her antecedents, nothing was known. She'd been raised in the Hospital, determined to make her way in the world, and she had an eye for what flattered a figure almost as good as Jem's.

Lucasta's teeth chattered lightly, and Jem beckoned her closer, draping the chintz around her shoulders and arms. She smelled like a wind from over the sea, fresh and damp and a bit salty. He studied the creamy fabric against her skin, the shades it brought out in her hair and eyes. Lucasta Lithwick was subtly, stunningly beautiful.

"You must tell her to stop sending me gifts." She stood quietly under his regard, under his hands on her shoulders, but she trembled, as if she might bolt at any moment. So different from the ranks of blushing debutantes who queued up at the balls and parties of the *haut ton*, hoping Smart Jeremey would take notice.

"She's been entirely too generous, and I'm certain she needs paying customers for her business," Lucasta added.

"You must allow her to send whatever she wishes. Including, I think, this one, which would make a *robe à la française* very suitable for day wear, if you paired it with a petticoat of taupe or beige. I have a beautiful linen that will do."

Her brow furrowed. Jem resisted the urge to finger a red-gold curl that had fallen free of its pin to dangle before one ear. "You've been sending the gowns? The way you sent those silks to the Gor— to my friends?"

"That was an apology," Jem said, unwrapping the fabric from around her shoulders. He let his fingers brush the curve of her neck. Her skin was satin itself. "Your gowns I consider your fee for so kindly tutoring my sister and cousin. I would recompense you directly, if it were possible, but I expect Lady Pevensey would object."

She turned her face away, regarding a display along the wall from a newer shipment, a sensible cotton with a rich carmine color and a checked print. "In that you are correct. Lady Pevensey does not discourage any attentions I receive from Smart Jeremey."

He hid his flinch at the name and moved to the cotton that had caught her eye, bringing an armful of fabric to her. "This might make a lovely *polonaise*. Suitable for performing in small musical entertainments among friends. Or when giving lessons to difficult young ladies."

Her lips curved in a smile, and something inside him tugged

upward in response. "Judith is a very quick pupil, and Bertie—Bertie is determined and tries very hard. I—" She bit her lip. "I wonder why you don't bring Judith out in company. She's lovely, and I think she'd like—"

"Not to be considered," Jem said, turning away. "It wouldn't do. People are cruel, and the *ton* would make a spectacle of her. She'd be a mockery."

"But perhaps in small situations, like calls, or a drive in the park when—"

"No, Lucasta. I won't have it."

He noted the silence behind him and was glad that for once she didn't challenge him. Perhaps she was outraged by his use of her Christian name—she'd invited him to use it, but that was in a teasing moment. He smoothed his expression and moved to a different shelf with the brocaded silks. The one he selected had a rich ochre background and a delicate pattern of twining golden vines.

"This for evening, a ball or perhaps to be seen at the theatre." He wrapped the rich, heavy fabric around her shoulders, tempering the harsh tone he'd let enter his voice. "You really have the most remarkable coloring. This ochre would wash out a pale complexion, but you..." He trailed off, realizing she might find his remark insulting.

"Am not a fair English rose," she confirmed. Her smile rose higher on one side of her mouth, amused, but not yet ready to forgive him. She lifted her chin. "I'm a Vlach."

"I beg your pardon?"

"My father was Romanian. From Wallachia."

"Romani?" he asked cautiously, not understanding. "Like the Gypsies?"

"No, Romanian. They're a different people."

"And now you will weave me some romantic story about a smuggled prince, raised in exile to return someday and restore his kingdom—"

She gurgled a laugh, her slim shoulders lifting beneath his

hands. He smoothed the fabric, tracing the fine weave of the golden sheaves, all an excuse to touch her.

"They were serfs," she said with amusement. "My grandfather had an enormous family, they were destitute and struggling, and there was no way they could have bettered their lot in their home country. Wallachia is ruled by the Ottoman Empire, so they escaped to Transylvania, which is controlled by the Habsburgs, and somehow they ended up in Britain. They changed their name from Ludovic to Lithwick to sound more English, and my father converted so he could attend university and be ordained into the Anglican church. He loved being a vicar, but he was always regarded as faintly heretical because he loved Greek and Roman history more."

"What did he convert from?" Jem asked, fascinated.

"Greek Catholicism."

He raised his eyebrows. "Your people are serfs. Romanian, Catholic serfs."

"Yes." Her smile was dazzling, her eyes dancing with light. "My grandmother, the Dowager Viscountess Frotheringale, went into an absolute pelter when my mother fell in love with my father. A daughter of the English peerage, setting her cap for a refugee Romanian! She nearly struck my mother's name from the family Bible. I think she would have, except my Aunt Patience—"

She faltered, that frown clouding her brow again. "My Aunt Patience, and I've never figured out why, championed the marriage. She lived with us for most of my childhood. And the Viscountess approved of Aunt Patience, though she rejected my mother."

Lucasta stared at the bow window facing the street, and he guessed she looked not at the dim shapes outside but some formidable if distant enemy. "My grandmother never had a kind word to say of Father, and never a thing to do with me. She refers to me, I understand, as the half-breed."

She said this so lightly that Jem's chest constricted. He understood. It was no less than what most British would call his siblings.

And he'd felt the cold indifference from the marquess all his life, treated like nothing, or less than nothing, because his father had chosen to marry into a middle-class merchant's family rather than a genteel but less financially provident member of his own class.

"I know what that feels like," Jem said softly.

"You said you weren't raised as a marquess's heir," Lucasta observed. She rubbed a corner of the silk brocade against her cheek.

"I wasn't. I was raised here." He pointed to the ceiling, indicating the room above their heads. "Well, not *here*. The original shop run by my mother's family is in Holborn, and has been there since medieval times. I grew up there, and running wild in the storehouse in Cheapside, where most of our fabrics are kept."

"It must have been a shock," she murmured as he took the ochre silk back. "On top of the losses to your family, that is. To find your station so changed."

"It was," Jem confirmed, rewrapping the bolt of fine fabric. "My father is the third son. The eldest and heir, my uncle— He clearly enjoyed his bachelorhood, but the family always assumed he would at some point marry a proper girl and provide the requisite heirs. He got carried away by malaria on his travels before he could."

"And Bertie's father became the heir. Earl Payne," Lucasta said.

He turned away from her, not wanting to let too much of his emotion show. "And Cadmus, her older brother, was Viscount Rudyard. The succession was assured. But then Cad fell ill with typhus, and—"

He stopped, his throat choked with grief. Cadmus had been his truest friend, the one member of his father's family who never cared that Jem was a draper's son. When his father died and Cad gained his courtesy title, he had kept Jem and Judith close despite his mother's feelings.

After Cadmus died, it was only the rage of his grandfather the marquess that could induce Jem to take up his cousin's title. Rudyard was Cadmus's name, a dead man's name. Every time he heard Rudyard he felt as if the ghost of Cadmus—like the restless ghost of the unlucky Thomas Cromwell—stood near his shoulder, flinching at every reminder of what had been taken from him.

"What I don't understand," Lucasta said, "is how you became Smart Jeremy."

Her scent drifted past his nose as she let him swath her in another silk brocade, a green background this time. It was the most expensive fabric yet, green being a difficult color to achieve as it required first several baths in yellow dye, then blue. Lucasta stroked the silk threads of the design, and Jem's groin tightened merely watching the caress. He was going to embarrass himself in a moment.

"That is Clara Bellwether's doing. She came in here fresh out of mourning and wanting to wear colors again. I advised her, and within a month the dashing widow had the *ton* at her feet." He rolled his shoulders, shrugging off memory. "She suggested I could advertise my shop if I showed myself about town in some of my own fine wares. She made it a fashion to consult my taste, as if I am some sort of oracle."

He pinched the edges of the fabric close beneath her chin, feeling the feathery heat of her breath over his fingers. "I suppose you think me unforgivably mercenary."

"Strategic, rather, if it enlarges your income," she murmured. "I shall be a tradeswoman too, or so I hope, when I open my music school. And you have a family to support."

Her eyes were extraordinary, a shadowy gray green, like a forest veiled in mist. He shuddered at the impact of her gaze, the understanding in it. She didn't revile him for being a grasping tradesman masquerading as a marquess's heir.

Jem's fingers tightened. She took a small step toward him and he realized he was pulling on the fabric, drawing her near. The way he had tried to draw her to him the night of their first dance together.

As if he wanted her in his arms. As if he knew she was meant to be there.

He had to break the moment before he did something ungentlemanly. "Sometimes I think I did better catering to the *bourgeoisie*," he said, gazing down into her face. "Aristocrats are terrible about paying their bills."

Her glowing expression, full of laughter, made heat coil in his gut. "The *bourgeoisie* seem to be better behaved in many respects. It is why I preferred being plain Lucasta Lithwick. But no, someone insisted on making me *au courant*."

The heat twisted and moved downward. He needed to confess. To admit he had meant to make a demonstration of his power, to see how much Smart Jeremy's pronouncements could do. And win her—and her possible share in the Frotheringale fortune—into patronizing his shop.

He wanted to be real to her, to put aside the façade of Smart Jeremy. But she could do naught but hate him when she learned how truly mercenary he was.

He should step away. But when she swayed toward him, he lifted a hand and pressed a finger to her delicate chin.

Her lips parted. She wanted him to kiss her.

Desire slammed through him. He wanted to kiss her as well. His scruples vanished in smoke, overcome by the spell she cast. He had dreamed of this night after night, Lucasta Lithwick in his arms. But the reality of her, her scent, her softness, was so much more potent than his mind could have conjured.

"You needed no making. Only for people to take a proper look." His voice scratched from his throat. He traced her soft, full lower lip with his thumb. "I don't suppose...you would permit me..."

"I might," she breathed, leaning toward him, and Jem was lost.

He intended a courtly kiss. A chivalrous kiss. A chaste meeting of lips. But when her lips parted beneath his, the sensation drove all thoughts of courtliness from his head.

He slipped his tongue into her mouth. She tasted divine, like tea and sugar and a hint of chocolate. She gave a small whimper, relaxing against him, and Jem caught her with a groan, hauling her up against his body as if she could quench the flames. The brocade rustled, and she made another noise deep in her throat that made him kiss her harder, more deeply, tipping her head back and twining his tongue around hers.

He ought not devour an innocent woman. He'd never devoured a woman in his life. But Lucasta Lithwick kissed him back, pressing her mouth against his, tasting him with her tongue. She lifted a hand to the back of his neck, sliding her fingers into his hair, and that welcome, that reaching out, was his undoing. He locked her to his chest and ran a hand down the silk encasing her, molding her body to his, cradling her to him, relishing her softness and warmth. She fit him perfectly. He'd have to tell her—

"Gracious, these stairs are steep." Bertie's voice floated from the back rooms, her voice unusually loud. "I shall have to go slowly so I don't fall down and break my crown like the boy in the nursery rhyme."

Jem broke the kiss and regretted doing so when he saw Lucasta's face, dazed, soft, touched by wonder. Her lips were red and full and her eyes smoky, and he wanted to kiss her endlessly. He wanted to unwrap the fabric that enclosed her and kiss the dusky skin beneath.

*Control, man.* He cleared his throat and with both hands set her away from him, holding her steady as she blinked. She swayed but then found her feet, and he lifted the green brocade from around her, trying not to touch her skin. When his thumb grazed the smooth swell of her bosom, they both sucked in a breath. He pulled the fabric away and saw the small hard peaks of her breasts beneath the bodice of her gown, and he had to turn away to hide the evidence of his own arousal.

"Oh, the robing room is so tidy and delightful," came Bertie's voice from the next room, again overly loud. "I shall linger here a moment and take everything in."

Lucasta wrapped her arms around herself and carefully wiped

her face clear of its dazed, soundly kissed expression. Jem attended to rewrapping the brocade, wishing he had the same self-command. The blood still pounded in his ears, leaving him dizzy.

Everything he'd thought about his life, his future, had just been torn up by the roots and turned widdershins, settling into a new place. One that had this woman at its foundation.

"Satisfied that you've seen every corner, Bertie?" His voice came out low, hoarse.

"Oh, very." Bertie entered the show room with a sunny smile. Her shawl was still damp, the clever fixings of her hat sadly bedraggled, but she looked none the worse for wear. "I see you started tea?"

"Perhaps you could take Lucasta—Miss Lithwick back to the kitchen and pour her a cup." He turned to face the women, his lower half hidden behind the counter. "I'd like to finish up here. Take a look-through. You know."

"Brr! Let's do warm ourselves before the fire. You're shivering like a leaf, Lucasta." Bertie drew her away, and Lucasta followed.

She didn't glance back at him, and Jem was glad of it. He might have done something ridiculous like leap after her, grasp her hand, and beg her to stay with him always.

He had kissed her. A gentleman would do something about that.

He pushed the bolt of brocade back in place and then surveyed his shop, this space as familiar to him as his own bedchamber. Everything—the shop, his business, the world—looked new-made.

He was an outsider to this world he'd been invited to enter, the world of the *beau monde* where address mattered more than intelligence, breeding more than skill. Where people who had no need to strive for resources or self-support competed to gain admiration and display their wealth. He'd hoped that his step into the fashionable world would elevate his business, expand his clientele, ensure an income that would support his family.

But he was aware every moment that he didn't have the innate training of those who had been bred to it from birth. He didn't know the proper degrees of bowing, how a gentleman entered a room, how to hand a lady to dinner. He'd survived this far by aping his blooded friends, Ashley and Plimpton, but he knew the eyes watching him sharply noted every flaw.

It was the latest fad to admire Jeremiah Falstead, Lord Rudyard, yet he had no doubt that laughter and snickers spread behind him every time he left a room. He'd begun to wonder where he belonged, whom he could trust. The draper's world was the world he knew, but the aristocratic world would be his, like it or not, when—many years hence, God willing—the marquessate of Arendale passed to him.

He'd never once imagined he would be fortunate enough to find a consort like his mother had been to his father, someone who could navigate both those worlds with him, with the style and poise to pass among wealthier circles, but the wit and sense to remain amused by the ostentatious display.

He'd never imagined there could exist a woman with passions that matched his, with the same love of beauty and a generous heart for the less fortunate, who would embrace his family as they were and never feel ashamed of his upbringing or his tastes.

He'd not thought the woman existed who could rouse his mind as much as she fired his blood. Whom he could imagine as a companion through all of his days, facing the world together, his world improved by her humor and warmth.

And now, suddenly, here she was.

# CHAPTER SIXTEEN

"But of course we must be Greek goddesses," Annis declared. "Why would we dream of being anything else?"

"How about saints? Famous female scholars? Medieval queens?" Lucasta asked. The Gorgons were gathered in Annis's parlor this time, keeping away the chill of the glowering spring day with a fire and an endless supply of tea. "That dress, at least, would provide more coverage."

"If you're to be out and about all the day, then we've to choose your costume when left to our own devices at Mlle. Beaudoin's," Minnie answered. She shook out a sheer length of linen that gleamed like a pearl. "You've never touched anything so fine, and we'll feel queenly wearing them."

Lucasta passed a length of the fabric between her fingers. She supposed, if it came from Mlle. Beaudoin's, the linen was from Jem's warehouse. She had indeed felt something this fine—the silk brocades Jem had wrapped her in that day in his shop. She'd reveled in the luscious weave sliding over her skin.

And he'd kissed her.

She hadn't yet managed to tell her friends about that.

"Which goddesses are we to be, then?" she said.

Annis nodded her head at the smallest girl. "Selina is to be our Aphrodite. Goddess of love."

Selina dimpled and giggled, which made Lucasta wonder if she had missed something. Why was Selina claiming the realm of love? Lucasta had been out so often, on calls with Cici, seeing to lessons with Judith and Bertie, that she'd neglected her friends. They'd chosen their costumes for the masquerade ball at Ranelagh Gardens without her.

"Annis, naturally, is Artemis, goddess of the moon," Minnie said. That made perfect sense for Annis, their astronomer.

"I plan to wear a bow and quiver of arrows," Annis said. "I'm not certain I won't be called upon to put an arrow in someone who deserves it."

"And you, Minnie?"

"Pallas Athene, goddess of wisdom. I shall carry a spear and my *aegis* with the head of Medusa."

"Then whom does that leave for me?" Lucasta wanted to be Athena, with her breastplate and spear, but she understood this was punishment for her absence.

"Hera," Annis announced. "Chief among goddesses, Queen of Heaven. Selina is going to fashion you a crown."

"Hera! The jealous wife who is always turning people into things?"

"Protector of women and of marriage," Minnie said. "It's Homer who makes her a nasty little termagant. She was revered in the Archaic period. Hera was ruler of the heavens first, remember. Zeus gained his throne when he married her."

The thought occurred to all four of them at the same time.

"If Trevor hasn't declared himself yet, he will when he sees you as Hera," Selina whispered. "He'll be reminded of all he stands to gain."

"Which might be very little, in the end," Lucasta pointed out. "Aunt Cornelia might live a score more years, which I sincerely hope she does. My grandmother the Dowager Viscountess might yet succeed in persuading her to confer everything on my cousin the current Viscount Frotheringale, which I believe is the sole aim of her existence. Aunt Cornelia might leave everything in an endowment for Miss Gregoire's, or for that secret society she's in, the Daughters of Minerva or some such. There's no point in wedding me for a fancied inheritance that might never come to be."

"He might simply like you for yourself, Lucasta," Selina suggested.

"Piffle," Lucasta replied. "I sincerely doubt he feels we'll suit any better than I do. I only plan to marry—*if* I marry, it will be for esteem. Someone like—well, never mind."

Her thoughts went at once to Jem. In the usual way of things, a gentleman kissing a genteel young lady led to a declaration and then an offer. He had kissed her in secret, true, with none the wiser. They had not discussed the impropriety—could not, with Bertie there.

And she did not want a declaration, did she? A draper, a tradesman from London did not fit in Lucasta's plans to open a music studio in Bath. A marquess's grandson and a vicar's orphan —that was the difference between heaven and earth, to be laughed out of thought.

He had told her why he played the Smart Jeremy. The role he assumed to gain custom. It made sense; the calculation did not offend her, not to someone who also made her own way, or tried to.

He had not, in the days since their time in his shop together, looked around the room after talking with her at a party as if he were taking the measure of who watched them. He had seemed completely absorbed in Lucasta.

And that kiss. Such a kiss gave a girl ideas. Unexpected, sleep-stealing, outrageous ideas.

Annis coiled her long form into an upholstered chair and glanced at Minnie. "It's time we told her."

"Oh, I'm sure it cannot be true," Selina protested.

"My source is not the most trustworthy," Minnie said.

"And it's just a malicious piece of gossip, after all," Selina added.

Lucasta scanned their concerned faces. "If it's malicious, you ought to tell me."

The others looked at Minnie, who straightened in her chair and looked Lucasta in the eye. "Ashley told me that Rudyard took up with you to make you the center of attention. In revenge for your epigram about his cravat."

Lucasta's stomach sank. "Lord Ashley said that?" Her mouth filled with sand at the words. Ashley was one of Rudyard's closest friends.

The man she knew could not be so petty.

Not Jem. But Smart Jeremy, the persona he'd fashioned as his shield and spear to carry him through the fashionable world—who knew what defenses he needed to keep his place on ground so hard-won, so tenuous to hold?

Annis released the rest of it in a rush. "Ashley said Rudyard only took note of you because Clara Bellwether said that Lady Evers means to make you her heir. He knew you would gain notice, with that gossip circulating. He meant to bring you to attention. And—" Here her friend hesitated. "Something Rudyard said led Ashley to believe he intended for you to be ridiculed."

Lucasta stared at the row of delicate porcelain vases lining the mantel above the fire, her face frozen. So now she knew. Rudyard— Smart Jeremy—had looked first at her because of spleen over her spiteful remark. But he had looked again—and pursued her—only because of that cursed gossip about her cursed supposed inheritance. Not for herself alone.

But to make a mockery of her.

"Why would Lord Ashley tell us this now?" she managed.

Selina leaned forward on the flowered chaise. "Because Rudyard has been spending so much time with you. I believe Lord Ashley did not want you to—misinterpret his intentions."

"Think Rudyard has designs on me, you mean."

"Oh, he has designs," Annis said in a hard voice, pouring Lucasta another cup of tea. "The angling cad."

Minnie hesitated. "Normally I wouldn't put the least value on anything Ashley has to say. But for once in his thoughtless existence, I believe he feels concerned that you might be hurt."

"Mr. Plimpton doesn't believe Rudyard attends you out of spite," Selina hurried to say. "He thinks it is because he—Rudyard, that is—wants you to be seen in his shop."

Lucasta slumped in her chair as if she'd gone boneless. Jem had taken her to meet his sister, introduced her to his half-siblings. He'd persuaded the governors of the Foundling Hospital to put her in charge of the benefit concert.

He had, indeed, brought her to his shop. In fact he'd been dressing her in his fabrics for weeks.

Her throat closed against the words. "So all this time—his attentions—because he wants to make fun of me, or he wants to make an example of me."

Because he knew, if she stood in line for an inheritance, she would suddenly be the focus of attention. He was drawn to her for the same reasons as everyone else.

Not for herself alone.

Why should she be surprised? He'd told her his one aim was to bring the *beau monde* to his shop. Clara Bellwether, a baronet's relict, had made him Smart Jeremy. What might a poor orphan connected to barons and viscounts do?

"We don't know that, darling." Annis reached over and took her hand. "But Ashley warned us that you should not put too much stock in Rudyard's attentions. He's not sincere."

Heat rushed over the face Lucasta had thought frozen. That kiss, that molten, shattering, world-spinning kiss. What had it been for, then? It was the kind of kiss that plucked at a girl's soul, whether she wished it or not.

The fire in the hearth felt hot on her face, and her back ice-cold.

"I am sure Lord Rudyard must see how wonderful you are," Selina said. "He may have begun with those intentions, but what if his feelings have changed?"

His own sister had thought he was besotted, and Bertie too.

Could he be playing her so deftly? But what did he stand to gain by toying with her heart?

Revenge, perhaps, for calling him Smart Jeremy. For thinking him as prejudiced as the rest of his class.

And to demonstrate that he could. That he had that power.

"Can you ask him about it?" Annis inquired. "Would he give you an honest answer?"

"I don't know." Lucasta picked up Minnie's costume spear and hefted it in her hands. Of a sudden she could understand the blind, aching rage that might make a goddess punish a poor mortal for a slight. "The masquerade is three days away, isn't it? Perhaps I'll speak to him then."

"And find out Ashley is just playing a cruel trick, which is just like him," Minnie said. "I'll box his ears if that's so."

"Why do you suppose Hera always tormented the helpless women that her husband pursued?" Lucasta mused. "Why did she never punish *him*?"

"Because she knew if she fought him directly, she'd lose," Minnie said soberly. "Even goddesses are subject to the will of the gods."

Impossible to think that kiss that had shattered her world could have been calculated. His face, when they'd parted, looked as pole-axed as she'd felt.

But he was more experienced, far more jaded than she was. It was entirely impossible it was all an act.

Lucasta's chest ached. The shaft of love had already gone deep into her chest. She couldn't deny it. And it was going to hurt terribly when she yanked it out.

THE DAY of the masquerade was as dry as the rest of the spring had been, and the evening promised to be clear and bright. The family dined early, as the doors at Ranelagh would open at seven and entertainments began at eight. The relative earliness of the proceedings, and the assurance of well-lit gardens and walks, were the reasons Lady Pevensey allowed the girls to attend events at Ranelagh when she absolutely forbade them Vauxhall. Ranelagh was appropriate for the well-behaved and staid, and kept out the riffraff with its higher entrance fee. Vauxhall was for mischief, which milady could not condone.

"Cici! What have you done to yourself?"

Lucasta entered her cousin's room to find the lady's maid scooping clouds of white linen onto Cici's tiny form. Over this she fitted a thick silk robe embroidered with gold and tiny red flowers. Cici giggled as the maid draped a tippet with equally lavish embroidery around her narrow shoulders.

"Can't you guess? I'm Pope Joan." She gestured at the papal miter unfolded on her dressing table and the stave with an elaborate carved cross leaning against the wall.

Lucasta clapped a hand over her mouth. "You are adorable. And so heretical."

The fabric, Lucasta was certain, came straight from the warehouses of Dixon & Co. Lady Pevensey had not yet given up hope, despite what the Baron thought of Lord Rudyard, draper's son.

Cici grinned as the maid pinned the embroidered miter onto her powdered, piled-high curls. "*Belle-mère* wanted me to wear one of my better gowns and a mask, like everyone else does, but I wanted a costume, like you and the Gor—your friends."

"We're Greek goddesses. I'm Hera."

"Your gown is lovely. And very daring."

"I'd catch the ague if I wore what Minnie wanted for us." Lucasta perched on the edge of a chair, watching Cici's toilette. "Mlle. Beaudoin won in the end."

The gown wasn't revealing, the skirt reaching to her ankles in a column of artfully pinned draperies, with a long purple cloak swathing her shoulders—more Roman, really, than Greek, but Lucasta didn't intend to complain. She'd left her hair unpowdered and much of it loose, only a few curls caught up and pinned into a chignon at the back of her head. She liked the look very much, and more than that, the freedom of moving about without panniers and pads and endless, inhibiting layers of fabric.

"Have you told Major Mallory how to identify you?" Lucasta asked.

Cici scrunched up her face. "I've no doubt he'll guess and be at my elbow all evening. Given that it's a masquerade, he's sure to attempt liberties."

"But you don't intend to allow them?"

Cici sighed. "I know *belle-mère* wishes it—more like, she insists —but I don't think I need be married bang out of my first Season, need I? It smacks of desperation. As if I don't have any other thoughts in my head."

This was a surprise. Lucasta had thought Cici meant to rush headlong into marriage to escape her stepmother's gimlet eye, establish a household of her own, and begin making babies as soon as possible. It was the done thing for girls of her station.

"There are no clear favorites on the marriage mart this year? Or are you enjoying being the Season's toast?"

Cici picked up the stave with its cross and regarded the sparkling effect of her gold trim in the cheval glass. "I think *you* are the Season's toast, my dear. It is marvelous fun for a while, all the parties and calls and drives and merriment, but...it all comes to seem quite frivolous, don't you think? I wish I had a hobby or an interesting pursuit, like you with your music. All I've ever been prepared to do is marry well."

She turned with a plaintive expression in her clear blue eyes. "And truly. How do you know when a man fancies you for yourself, and not for your looks, or your family, or your dowry?"

"Oh, my dear girl. I wish I could advise you. But since I have none of those things, neither dowry nor looks, I had always thought that any gentleman who offers for me—I mean, were any gentleman to offer for me, which I don't imagine will ever be the case—well, I might be sure the only attractions I have to offer are my sparkling wit."

"You have family." Cici reached out a small, ungloved hand and clasped Lucasta's. "You keep forgetting that. You have us."

"I have *you*." Lucasta wrapped her other hand around their clasped fingers. "And you are very good to me. Thank you for that."

The warmth of Cici's fingers, oddly, left a chill on her heart. Whatever the consequence of Rudyard's games, Lucasta's downfall would reflect badly on Cici. She'd come to London thinking she'd find one more cousin who scorned her for her mother's marriage and had instead found as good as a sister.

Trevor, waiting in the parlor, wore a draped tunic of white linen with a purple cloak. Lucasta stifled a moan of dismay. At a masquerade, matching costumes were nearly an advertisement of intent, as good as reading the banns.

"Cousin! Did you plan this?"

His eyes widened, the same clear northern-sky blue as his sister's. "I am Julius Caesar. Are you Calpurnia?"

*She* would never know when a man wanted her purely for herself, Lucasta thought churlishly, while she had the promise of Aunt Cornelia's fortune hanging over her head. Jem, Trevor, all the other beaux who vied for attention at parties—none of them would have paid the slightest attention otherwise to the orphan of an obscure vicar and the cast-out granddaughter of a viscount.

"I am Hera, queen of the heavens." Lucasta straightened her shoulders. "And I will turn anyone who displeases me into a cow. Or an insect."

The carriage bumped its way to Chelsea and Ranelagh Gardens, and Lucasta stared out the window, brooding. Her father, the immigrant vicar, had loved her mother terribly. He had risked her family's wrath and his own career to wed her. He would have followed her to the corners of the earth, and he let her know every day that the chief joy of his life was to be near her.

But those kinds of stories were fairy tales, rare, and men like Laurence Lithwick even rarer. Lucasta never expected to find devotion like that for her own. Trevor's artful comments, like the attentions of the other young men suddenly approaching her, were self-interested. They would vanish as soon as her expectations did.

But to think that Jem's warm interest was not, had never been sincere—that was a stab to the heart, with a twist of the blade for flourish. He had wanted to make a figure of fun of poor, plain Lucasta Lithwick.

And now the damage was done.

## CHAPTER SEVENTEEN

The masquerade was a crush by the time they arrived. After standing in line to present their tickets, they could scarcely move among the people thronging the path leading to the Rotunda. Despite the entrance fee, Ranelagh Gardens masquerades were hugely attended, even the outdoor summer balls. The bourgeoisie were delighted to pay for the chance to mingle among royals and the nobility, and the Cyprians were always in the market for new customers.

Lucasta had agreed to meet her friends by the Chinese pavilion, and she was grateful that Annis and Minnie were tall; there was a chance of locating them in the crowd.

Lucasta had been warned that some of the costumes would shock her, and that was true. Near the canal where musicians floated in an anchored boat and played a lovely little chamber piece, a woman laughed as a naughty devil snatched away the neckerchief covering her chest. Beneath she was completely bare, not even a shift to cover the bosoms spilling over her tightly laced stays. The woman wriggled her shoulders in a generous display, while the men in the vicinity hooted their appreciation.

Cici let out a *whoosh* of breath.

"That is—the most convincing devil costume I have ever seen," she whispered. "Pitchfork, horns, everything."

"I was hoping such antics would wait until after dark," Trevor said, a tight set to his mouth. "I meant to get you away before the worst started."

Trevor, turning prim? Lucasta would not have thought it. She had no intention of baring anything, of course, but the wild spirit of play infected her. She could see why moralists crusaded against masquerades, claiming they encouraged licentious behavior, upset the social order, and encouraged transgression. She very much felt like transgressing tonight.

She'd already been licentious, kissing Jem in his draper's shop. Her toes curled into her slippers at the memory of that kiss. There'd be no more kisses like that, now that she knew the truth of him. She'd had her one and only taste of passion.

"There you are! Yoo hoo! Queen Hera!"

The Gorgons had commanded one of the best spots, a railing along the perimeter of the Chinese pavilion. This elegant structure overlooked the canal and one of the walks, framed by the looming shadow of the Rotunda. They could observe the crowd on shore and watch the small boats punting over the water with their gaily dressed occupants. Lucasta clung tightly to Trevor's arm as they edged along the plank leading to the Pavilion, built in the center of the canal.

"Mr. Pevensey! Are you Zeus, to match our Lucasta?" Minnie laughed.

"If only I had been so wise as to inquire in advance. I am Julius Caesar."

Trevor didn't look delighted to see the Gorgons. They'd been cordial but cool to him, following Lucasta's lead, and he frowned as Selina drew Lucasta away.

"Miss Pevensey." Annis pounced on Cici. "Are you Pope Joan? How witty! I adore it." She winked. "Next time you will have to make her..." She rounded her hands before her belly. "*Enceinte.* For full effect."

Cici laughed. "I knew Trevor would never condone it."

"Indeed I would not," said her brother in a freezing tone.

"Lucasta, the strangest person has been asking about you," Selina said.

Lucasta's heart gave a foolish leap. "Je—I mean, Rudyard?"

"No, I think I would recognize Lord Rudyard, even in disguise. This was someone else, dressed in the most frightful furs and robes, with a mustache and a beard. I found him quite alarming. He quizzed us terribly on our relation to you, and when we expected you, and what company you were keeping. I think we ought to do our best to avoid him."

"That's him in the boat," Minnie said as one of the long, narrow wooden boats nosed up to them. "Do you know him?"

"Not in that costume," Lucasta answered.

The man in the boat wore enormous silk robes dyed the orange-yellow of costly saffron and over that what looked like a bear pelt, with claws dangling over a very broad chest. He seemed a stocky sort, not at all Rudyard's sleek build, and a drooping mustache and black beard disguised his face. The features beneath were not known to her, but there was something predatory, and familiar, in the gleam of his eyes as his gaze lit on Lucasta.

"Queen Hera! The goddesses of Olympus now assembled! Will you do me the honor of floating with me, o Empress of Heaven?" the stranger called out.

"Thank you, no," Lucasta called back. "I do not think it wise, o menacing one, to trust my divine self with a person unknown to me."

He wore a black wig and an odd kind of headdress with a furred rim and flaps over the ears, but something about his prominent nose teased her memory. She knew that nose, but from where?

He shot a scornful glare to the side as another boat on the crowded canal bumped into his, a jester and a lady in mask and domino laughing, and Lucasta's stomach twisted. He was definitely not a mild-mannered sort of man.

"Who should not wish to be in the company of the Ruler of Heaven?" her suitor bellowed. "Let me make myself known! I, o Queen, am Kubla Khan, great Khan of the Mongols and Emperor of China. The Venetian explorer Marco Polo served at my court for a time. My grandfather was the greatest conqueror the world has ever known, and my empire spans half the earth. Surely of all mortals I am fit consort to a goddess and queen?"

"Who is he?" Annis drew close, watching the stranger curiously.

"I haven't a notion," Lucasta replied. But he was making a spectacle of himself and her. Much like Rudyard had contrived to do.

She had a word or three she wanted to say to Smart Jeremy, milord Rudyard.

And also, if she were to be fully honest with herself, she wanted Jem to see her in costume. It was her most flattering gown yet.

Annis leaned over the rail, her draperies fluttering in the slight breeze. "You dare much, petty mortal! Great Hera has no other consort but mighty Zeus. Now begone, or I shall loose one of my arrows on you."

"Let's go look in the Rotunda," Minnie muttered. "You're right to mistrust this one, Lucasta. He'll ravish you or worse."

"What's worse?" said Selina grimly, putting her elbows to the task of cutting them a path. Minnie leveled her spear, which helped.

"A shame to leave when the musicians are playing Handel's *Water Music*." Lucasta sighed. "The G major is my favorite suite."

"There will be music in the Rotunda," Annis promised. "Come, come."

Trevor glared across the crowd as the girls pressed their way out of the Pavilion, but the crowd of Cici's admirers barred his way. The girls swept along one of the gravel paths, where liveried footmen were setting up the torches that would be lit as dusk descended. Lucasta lagged as the strains of a Boccherini quintet reached her ear. There were musicians set up all over the gardens, and the cello was particularly lovely.

All of this—the gardens, the music, the stately buildings, the gorgeous extravagance of the crowd—all was a treat she'd been looking forward to for weeks. She'd never experienced anything this lavish in Bath. Yet there was a pall over everything with the knowledge that Rudyard, by his own friend's admission, was making a game of her.

She wanted to hear him say Ashley was wrong. He'd put her name forward to the governors of the Foundling Hospital, not to make her beholden to him, but because he believed in her passion for music. That his praise about her being fascinating had been a true olive branch for naming them Gorgons, and that dressing her through means of Mlle. Beaudoin was not a way to display his shop wares, or not only a way to display his wares.

She wanted to hear him say he had meant all those trips to Rose Hollow, bringing her among his family as if she belonged there.

She wanted to know what he meant with that kiss.

Inside, the Rotunda was close and hot from the press of bodies, from the lights of the chandeliers dangling on long ropes from the ceiling, and from the many candles lighting the alcoves lining the wall. The niches along the lower level seated diners at small tables, and the boxes above held attendees who wanted to enjoy the spectacle without being jostled or trod upon by the crowd. The multi-story, tiered box with its carved wooden canopy was packed with musicians, and the familiar strains turned Lucasta's dark mood melancholy.

"Mozart's Paris symphony," she told her friends. "What a pity the acoustics in this building are so poor. Look, they even have the clarinets."

"Mr. Plimpton. We require you to settle a question for us, in all honesty, if you please." Annis marched up to a dashing Cavalier wearing a red sash over a leather jerkin, a huge, plumed hat, and a pair of knee-high leather boots with enormous cuffs. Plimpton lowered his wine glass, a look of alarm on his face.

Lucasta stifled a moan. All of sudden, she didn't want to confront Jem. She didn't want to know the truth.

She wanted the dream to linger as long as it might.

"Anything for a…" Plimpton's gaze flickered over Annis's cascading white robes, from the quiver of arrows over her shoulder to the leather sandals laced about her ankles. "Lady?"

"Is it true that Lord Rudyard set out to make Lucasta a diamond?" Minnie wanted to know. "On some strange fancy fashioned of his own pure brain?"

"Well. Ah." Plimpton sniffed his wine, as if he meant to hide behind it. "He—er—made a declaration to some of us that he wished to see Miss Lithwick become the reigning queen of the season." His eyes flicked to Lucasta, then away. "And it worked, I'd say."

Lucasta curled her hands into fists.

"Because he took some grudge against her," Annis said. "Or thought to make her the subject of talk."

"No, no. Out of esteem for her own admirable person, I'm sure," Plimpton said.

Lucasta narrowed her eyes at him.

"I suppose there were one or two reasons," said Lord Ashley, joining them. "He took some objection to Miss Lithwick's manner, and set out to improve it, or he took objection to Miss Lithwick's dress, and set out to improve that as well."

Minnie turned a fulminating glare on him. "Thank you for that information, though no one requested it of *you*. And who are you supposed to be?" She glanced over his red breeches, high boots, and the blue breastplate with a large white cross.

Ashley took off his black plumed hat, showing a small white powdered wig, and bowed. His sword knocked against Plimpton's legs. "A Musketeer of the Guard, in the Royal Household of the King of France."

"So it's as Clara Bellwether said." Selina spoke in a small voice. "He was making fun."

"Clara Bellwether." Jem's crony. She, more than anyone, was like to be in his confidence. There being nowhere to sit in the crush of people, Lucasta leaned on Selina.

She'd called it a shame he was no better than he was, hadn't she? He'd set out to prove her wrong. And in so doing, proved her right.

"I shouldn't see why it matters." Ashley curled his lip at Minnie. "You all seem to have benefited from the attention, and he's done your friend no harm."

"You went out of your way to inform us of Rudyard's stratagem," Minnie snarled back, "precisely because you wanted to do harm. Here, now," she barked as a third man joined them. "These two are expressing their secret desire for military accomplishment, and you, a genuine military man, are a monk?"

"Friar, actually." Major Mallory smiled. He wore a long brown cassock of rough wool and a large wooden cross hung from his neck. "I heard that Miss Pevensey was—somewhere about, I hope?"

"In the Pavilion," Annis said. "If you'll excuse us."

The three girls formed a guard around Lucasta. "Pay it no mind, Lucasta," Selina said immediately. "Whatever his intentions to begin with, it's quite clear to us that Lord Rudyard has come to value you for yourself alone. I am certain his admiration is real."

"He sent you all those beautiful gowns through Mlle. Beaudoin," Annis pointed out.

"To improve me," Lucasta said, striving to control the quaver in her voice. "And as payment for the music lessons I've been giving his—cousin."

She ought not feel riven through the heart by his betrayal. She had brought this on herself, had she not?

"He drives you about. He calls all the time," Selina insisted.

"He watches you at all the parties," Minnie added. "He knows every moment where you are and what you are doing. It's as though he can't keep his eyes from you."

"Waiting for me to make a fool of myself." Lucasta said. No, no tears—she would not cry. Not over this.

"His friends could be mistaken," Minnie said. "With those two dunces, it's likely."

Yet Ashley and Plimpton were Rudyard's closest companions, the most likely to be in his confidence. Jem had told Lucasta, on one of their drives back to London from Little Chelsea, how much these men, both sprigs of the nobility, had taught him about *ton* and the unspoken etiquette of the Polite World. They'd saved him on more than one occasion from using the wrong utensil at table or walking into dinner before a person of higher rank. They'd taught him how to drive, how to walk, and how to bow like a gentleman instead of a merchant. They would be aware if he took on some pet project to elevate a poor, plain vicar's daughter from wallflower to diamond.

"Miss Lithwick—Lucasta—are you quite all right?"

Lucasta swiped the moisture from her eyes, then looked up. "Bertie. I mean, Miss Falstead. Hello." She glanced about quickly —no Jem. A relief and a dagger, all at the same time. "How delightful to see you out."

Bertie offered a nervous smile. "Mama and I had quite a wrangle about it, but I insisted. I-I knew you all would be here. Are these your friends? The Gorgons?"

Lucasta flinched. Jem's epithet for them. They had adopted the title in fun, but it felt mean-spirited of him now. "Yes, allow me. These are Miss Selina Humby, Anastasia Voronska, and Wilhelmine von Luneburg. My fellow goddesses, the Honourable Miss Lambertina Falstead."

"You all look very fine. Greek goddesses, so clever." Bertie regarded their costumes enviously. "Mama insisted I might only wear a domino." Beneath the short black silk cape, Bertie wore a robe of yellow, which did not flatter her complexion.

"Friend or foe?" Minnie demanded, still bristling. "She's his cousin, after all."

"Oh, friend, no question." Surely, no matter what Rudyard was about, he would allow Bertie and Lucasta to remain friends.

He could bar her from seeing Judith, however.

"We pronounce you an honorary Gorgon," said Annis, tapping Bertie on each shoulder with her bow. "Which goddess do you wish to be?"

"Er—perhaps you might choose for me?" Bertie's smile turned uncertain. Lucasta had found that Bertie's education, overseen by her mother, was nothing like that given the girls of Miss Gregoire's.

"Hestia?" Selina proposed. "Goddess of the hearth?"

"Oh," Bertie said. "Domestic things?"

"Demeter, goddess of fertility and the keeper of sacred law." Lucasta grabbed a cluster of tall bound grasses from a nearby urn holding decorative foliage. "Here."

"Demeter. Yes. Thank you," Bertie said gratefully.

Selina drew Bertie to her side and engaged her in friendly, innocuous chat. Every fiber in Lucasta's body tensed as a tall man stalked toward her, dressed in an ermine cape and a crimson velvet robe of state, the regalia of the Britain monarch.

"King Arthur." She recognized Jem. "How quaint."

"I am Alfred the Great." His brown eyes glinted, austere and aloof. "King of England."

He had no right to look so majestic. Those eyes skimming her frame made Lucasta feel like her linen tunic was transparent. He might see her heart furiously beating, the blush spreading over her chest as she recalled their kiss.

That warm, enthralling man who had woven her into a spell of silk and seduction was gone.

"Alfred was King of Wessex and held back the invading armies of the Danes," she said. "The Anglo-Saxon kingdoms weren't united under one ruler until Alfred's grandson Æthelstan did so in 927."

The glint in his eyes turned dangerous. "Thank you for that history lesson. You and your friends represent the Olympic pantheon, I presume?"

That wildness reared within her. She wanted to bite something, to break through that cool façade of his and find what lay beneath. A living man with a heart, or a cold manipulator?

"Yes, we thought it would be too obvious to dress as Gorgons, and besides no one might identify us. The Gorgons are never fully described in the early sources, you know, aside from Medusa, known for her unusual hair."

His cool detachment was an arrow through her heart. Jem had been the one to pronounce her Medusa—Clara Bellwether made sure that witticism reached her ears. To think he had let her into the bosom of his family while esteeming her so little! She tried to swallow the painful catch in her throat.

"So which goddess are you?"

If only she were a woman of power. She would not feel so naked and vulnerable.

"Hera. Take care you do not cross me, or I might turn you into a cow and send flies to sting you."

He raised a brow. "I thought it was only the unfortunate mistresses of Zeus who incurred Hera's wrath."

"She's changing her methods. Why punish the poor women who are merely toyed with at the whim of powerful men?"

A muscle clenched in his cheek. "Will you walk with me?"

"Will you invite me onto a boat, tip me into the canal, and drown me?"

"I see the goddess is angry. With all mortals, or one in particular?"

He'd discerned her feelings, which was itself so surprising that Lucasta felt her ire waver for a moment. He was a perceptive man, one of the qualities she most admired about him. He must have known what it would mean to her to organize the benefit concert. He'd seen that his lonely cousin and isolated sister needed companionship, and he'd brought them all together.

He'd done her a service, really. Why was she stung over his motives, whatever they were or had been? She ought to simply take the opportunities—and the beautiful gowns Mlle. Beaudoin had made up for her—and take a dignified leave.

Be done with him entirely, leaving him the board of whatever game he was playing. The thought made a hole in her heart.

"Great Hera, goddess of Heaven, patron and protector of women. I beg leave to discuss with you that most sacred provenance of yours. Marriage."

"Ugh. It's the Mongol Khan again." Annis hissed through her teeth as the furred emperor, shouldering his way through the crowd around them, managed a deep and flourishing bow. His eyes didn't have the aspect of a suppliant; they held the gleam of the hunter. A sheen of sweat across his brow hinted that his layers of costuming, combined with the abundant light and heat within the Rotunda, did not contribute to his comfort.

"Who dares address the Queen of Heaven?" Jem stepped closer to her. The low growl in his voice sent a thrill down Lucasta's spine. That rich, velvety tone held a hint of menace. Was he jealous?

"I am Kubla Khan, great ruler of the Mongols and Emperor of—"

"Yes, yes, we know." Minnie angled her spear at the intruder's chest. "The Queen is otherwise engaged."

"She looks at liberty to me," the khan challenged, brackets of tension forming around his mouth. Lucasta had seen that scowl before. "I beg a moment of her time, to stroll among these fair gardens and enjoy the music floating on the breeze. Our Hera delights in music, does she not?"

Lucasta shivered at the alert stare directed at her. He knew her, but she could not fathom where she had made his acquaintance.

"How inconvenient," Jem drawled. "Hera has just agreed to accompany *me* on a stroll through the gardens."

He drew her hand into the crook of his arm, bringing him close to her body. Her glove extended over her elbow, leaving only a thin band of skin between it and her sleeve, but that skin erupted in gooseflesh as she recalled the last time she'd been this close to Jem.

Draped in gorgeous silk, caught in an embrace both reverent and hungry, feeling her world change and shift around this new information of what it felt like to kiss a man—not just any man, but Jeremiah Falstead, Smart Jeremy, Lord Rudyard. Jem.

So many names for him, and she still couldn't be sure the man she'd seen—the man, God save her, she'd let herself grow attached to—was real.

The crowd outside had grown in size and boisterousness, and torches studded the tall, slender trees lining the path as Jem drew her along. Light flickering over his face showed a set jaw, a muscle twitching in his cheek. He was furious. With her? The wildness reared again. Perhaps this was why proper young unmarried girls weren't to kiss men. That awakening, like the sleeping beauty stirred by the brush of the prince's lips, brought all manner of hitherto unacknowledged desires to life.

Besides, she was the one furious with him.

"The evening is very pleasant, is it not?" he asked after they had walked a good distance in silence.

"Exceedingly pleasant," Lucasta said in a stony voice.

The grounds were brightly lit and not extensive—one essentially circled the Rotunda when strolling through Ranelagh—but she was alone with him and unchaperoned. Young ladies, so she had been instructed by her lady aunt, were never to be unchaperoned. Not in the retiring room, not at the home of a friend, not ever. Aunt Patience lived in a world where unscrupulous men waited in shadows to fall upon unsuspecting girls and spirit them away to ruin, like Barbary corsairs.

But Jem, it seemed, had contrived to ruin her in plain sight. She clenched her teeth.

"The musicians seem competent," he remarked. "This group ahead, in particular, seems unobjectionable."

Was he *trying* to send her up in the boughs?

"They are playing one of Haydn's Russian quartets." The bright, singing strings were the antithesis of her aggravated mood. "I am particularly fond of Haydn's quartets. Four voices in counterpoint and harmony, blending together for a beautiful effect. How rarely one finds that in real life."

He stopped and turned to face her. Her eyes were on a level with his mouth, set in a determined line.

"You seem to have another eager swain."

"You are the one who set them upon me." She lifted her eyes to his. "All of a sudden I became *fascinating* to those of *ton*, and now I have crowds of people who know nothing about me vying to admire and pet me."

"You called me Smart Jeremy," he said.

"You called me and my friends Gorgons."

That muscle in his jaw twitched. "You accused me of thinking those of other races inferior."

"You were the one who said Selina looked like a zebra."

"Your uncle the baron threw his daughter at my head. For no reason other than that I am presumed heir to a marquessate, and the estate is known to be solvent."

"None of that was my doing," Lucasta answered, stung. "Perhaps you ought not so flirt so openly with Clara Bellwether if you don't wish to be seen as available."

"And now you've brought Bertie into your set." His nostrils flared as he breathed heavily through them. "When she is at a vulnerable moment, still grieving her father and her loss of status, and living with my horrible Aunt Payne."

"You brought Bertie to me." Lucasta's eyes filled with tears. She hoped the growing shadows hid them. "That's botched your plans, has it? You meant to make a cartoon of me, to see if poor Lucasta Lithwick could become fashionable all at a word from Smart Jeremy. Such power you have! Mongol kings and Chinese emperors now accost me wherever I go. Just what was your aim, Rudyard? To toy with people's emotions, simply because you can?" She faltered there, and bit off the rest of what she wanted to say.

"You speak to me of toying!" His anger unleashed. "When you have poured Judith full of stories of parties and balls, made her long for a world she can never be a part of, and let her think—"

He clamped his lips together, nostrils flaring again, and spoke the rest through gritted teeth. "You tried to persuade her to perform at your benefit. To play for others. *In public.* Do you have any idea what they will do to her?"

"She will be admired, as is her right," Lucasta retorted. "She has a skill she wants to share for a good cause, and she asked me—"

Abruptly she reined in the words. Just as she wanted to bring Judith out of the shadows, Judith was trying the same for her. She saw the shape of Lucasta's dream and wanted that for her, wanted to share it with her, a truly generous, warm-hearted act.

"You are trying to persuade her to expose herself on a stage, in front of people who would gossip and judge her and examine her for flaws. They will cut her terribly, make her the target of their mockery, and you'll give her hopes that she—when she can never—"

"She can do whatever she wishes, and much more, if you would allow her even the smallest breath of freedom." Lucasta stamped her foot. "Instead you keep her swaddled in cotton as though she is a fragile infant. She is a woman full-grown who knows her own mind. Why do you never let her make her own choices? You keep her on a tighter leash than you would a lap dog."

"Because they will hurt her!" Jem shouted. "I will not have her exposed to such cruelty. You have made her your pet, like your poor little foundlings, that blind girl you're so fond of—"

"Do not speak to *me* of making people projects! When you have played the Pygmalion with me, dressing me in gowns of your choosing, driving me about in your very smart and treacherous carriage, showing me in your box at the opera! For what purpose?" she cried. "What could you possibly hope to accomplish?"

He loomed perilously close, nostrils flaring again. "I have played the *what* with you?"

"You know very well what I am talking about!" She fought back the tears threatening to spill over. Except Pygmalion fell in love with his creation. The man who had notoriously scorned women burned with such devotion that the goddess of love granted him his deepest wish.

It was the wrong parallel to make, of course. Rudyard had not been falling for her; he'd been plotting her ruin.

No doubt he meant for her to fall into the same trap he thought she was laying for Judith. Become an object of fascination, all this attention paid to her, and turn into an object of pity and derision when the world saw the truth. Why would he be so angry at a simple invitation unless he'd meant for Lucasta to fall, and now was furious that she might bring his sister down with her?

"It must stop now, Rudyard." Her voice broke, and she cursed herself. She must keep control at all costs. The charade of his interest had to end, here and now, before she ended up heartbroken, wrecked by her own foolish hopes, gutted by his disdain.

"I agree," he said coldly. "Thank you for your services in providing music lessons for my sister. But I'm afraid that association is at an end."

He stepped back, the torchlight lending satanic shadows across his face, and Lucasta felt her heart break in truth.

"No," she choked. "You can't deny me Judith. She's learning so much. And I care for her—"

"As her guardian and brother, it is my duty to protect her from influences that might lead her astray," he said, and that voice she had thought sounded like velvet and brandy together had the quality of cold steel. "I am sure you can understand."

A new horror froze Lucasta where she stood. "The concert— the foundlings? Are you going to tell the governors to—" She couldn't even voice the idea.

"I think it is too late to change any plans." His face was as unyielding as a wooden mask. "I will not attempt to influence the board of governors in either direction. But I hope you will not count on my support or my contribution to the scheme. It will cause Judith distress if she knows I am involved when she cannot be."

"Cause Judith distress," Lucasta echoed. And Lucasta's distress mattered not at all.

She turned away, blinded by tears, hoping the path she chose led to the safety of her friends in the Rotunda, and away from him. This had been his plan all along: to hold out something tantalizing and exhilarating, to make her dream of something she'd never considered possible, then crush her dream in one careless fist.

"I shall escort you back," he said sharply. "You can't be left alone in this crowd."

"As if you care for my safety," she cried. "As if you care anything but your own pride."

She plunged into the crowd, glad she didn't have Minnie's spear, for she would have been tempted to ply it on anyone who prevented her from fleeing Jeremiah Falstead as quickly as possible. She felt him beside her, clearing the path as she fought her way back to the building and refuge, providing protection when he was the last person she wanted to be near her. When he was the one responsible for shattering her hopes and grinding them beneath the heel of his gleaming boots.

"Lucasta! Dearest, what is the matter?" Cici stood with the Gorgons by the orchestra box, and she held out her hands as Lucasta rushed toward them. "Has someone hurt you?"

The urge to tell everything was overwhelming, but Bertie turned to her as well, watching with alarm as Jem, stone-faced, shouldered his way toward them. Trevor stepped forward to block his path.

"What have you done, Rudyard?"

"Nothing more than a discussion about whom I approve of her associating with, and whom I do not," Rudyard said grimly.

His high-handed delivery did not go over well with his audience. "Cad!" Cici cried, then clapped a hand to her mouth in horror. She had never called names in her life.

"As if it is your decision to decide whom Lucasta associates with," Minnie exclaimed.

Trevor took another step forward. "It appears it has not been to her benefit to cultivate an association with *you.*"

The men were of an equal height, and equal mass when it came to that, both broad of chest and lean of hip, a shape approved by fashion but in their case not formed by it.

"Oh, don't start a mill here, Trevor," Annis snapped. "You can't call him out, and Selina's about to faint."

Selina and Bertie clutched each other, wide-eyed and trembling, like two frightened chicks clinging together for safety.

"Who says I can't call him out?" Trevor answered. "Did he insult you, Lucasta?"

Lucasta pulled away the hand she'd clamped over her mouth. Had he misled her? Yes. He let her think his interest in her was genuine, when he was merely looking for a weakness to exploit. And she'd shown him several weaknesses—all of them, in fact. But had he insulted her?

He'd intended for her to become the object of scrutiny; she understood that now. All the new attention and opportunities that had come her way from being an admired figure. All the people she had met who might in time become patrons of a musical school, or employ her for lessons, or in some other way support her dream; all the people who had extra smiles for Cici now that her cousin was admired by Smart Jeremy; all the famous singers she'd approached about her benefit concert who might have simply refused to see an obscure vicar's daughter, including Signor Marchesi, who had acted as if she flattered him by translating and making a new arrangement for his song—all of that had been so Jeremiah Falstead could watch in amusement as she foundered on the public stage.

It was cruel. It was beneath him. It didn't match at all with the kind, generous man he was with his family, the benefactor of foundlings and unprotected women, the orphaned boy and draper's son now thrust into Polite Society. He knew she came from the same place she did, the despised fringes of the aristocracy. He knew what it was like to stand in the unrelenting light of public scrutiny, and he'd meant for the same scrutiny to descend on her.

"He did not insult me." It took everything in her to compose her voice, but she was a singer, after all. She lived by controlling her voice. "I disagreed with him over the Foundling Hospital concert. But he did not insult me."

He'd only broken her heart.

There was something tense and furious in Jem's posture, but a guarded, almost plaintive look as well. Lucasta realized what it meant. What she knew about his family—his sister's blindness, his half-caste siblings—she could make public at any time. She could turn his secrets into a weapon against him, just as he had used his attention as a weapon against her. He was watching her very carefully to see if she'd try to hurt him in response.

When to do so would hurt his siblings more. And hurt Bertie, too. She'd come to care about them all. That he feared she might do something to retaliate against him, something that would hurt people they both cared about—that was the deepest wound yet. He didn't know her at all.

"Queen Hera! Goddess descended to earth again, I beg you will not flee me this time. I am your most humble servant."

The great khan was back, looking more flushed than ever, his face red with heat or exertion or drink, his breathing heavy. Again that sense of familiarity poked at Lucasta. The sight of his face brought dismay, annoyance, and even a touch of—fear? Who *was* he?

"You," Minnie shouted, raising her spear, "are a pestilence!"

"You do not recognize me, cousin?" The emperor threw his bear skin cape at Jem, who caught it. He unwrapped the turban and tossed that at Trevor, who also caught it out of reflex. Then he tore off the beard and mustache that had disguised his face.

The sideburns were his own, as were the heavy eyebrows and the brown curly hair that capped his head. He met Lucasta's eyes with a quizzical look, touched with mockery, and finally she recognized the nose.

"Gale!" Trevor spoke first. "Where in God's name did you come from?"

The other man held Lucasta's eyes. "I find my dear cousin has been spirited away from her proper home, and I've come to retrieve her. Miss Lithwick—dearest Lucasta—why did you ever leave Bath? This place—" His eyes flickered over Trevor's deepening scowl, then the transfixed faces of the other girls. "This company, clearly, is not for you."

"Who are you?" Annis demanded. "And how do you know Lucasta?"

The other man looked expectantly at Trevor, who set his mouth in a mutinous line. Lucasta opened her mouth, but she was still too stunned with surprise to speak.

"Very well," the man snapped, annoyed at the indignity of having to perform his own introduction. "I am Roland, the Viscount Frotheringale. This lovely apparition—this goddess in truth—is my cousin, Lucasta. My cousin, and—" His voice took on a warm, silken quality— "I hope, very soon, my affianced bride-to-be."

# CHAPTER EIGHTEEN

"Are ye all right, mum? It's Friday-faced ye are today."

"Aye, ye look a mite knocked up. Been dipping in the Blue Ruin?"

"No, Philippa," Lucasta answered, forcing a smile. "I do not drink gin."

"Well, ye look done to a cow's thumb. Ye've been trotting too hard, trying to get us into shape for the concert. We're such regular dunces, I can't doubt yer a deal fagged."

"You've been doing wonderfully, Camilla, working very hard to learn your songs. I'm quite proud of you all."

"It's 'im," Hester guessed. "The swell as comes to hear you sing wi' us. What's 'e done, then? Cutting shams? On the rocks? Found out e's a ladybird, or a side-slip somewhere?"

Lucasta coughed. "Do you mean J—Lord Rudyard?"

"Aye, 'im, the Corinthian. The one danglin' after ye."

"I can say with authority that he is not dangling after me, Hester." Lucasta's heart squeezed, and for the tenth time in an hour, she told herself to stop thinking of Jem.

"Well, 'e's a nonesuch, top o' the trees, and if he's trying to rivet ye, I say ye let 'im, even if 'e does have a by-blow stashed some-where about," Hester advised.

"Likely he does," Isadora agreed. "Why else'd he want to be a guv'nor here?" Her eyes widened. "D'ye suppose it's one o' *us*?"

"Don't be a gudgeon, 'e's trying to cut a wheedle with Miss Lucasta." Hester, one of the older girls who had won the coveted honor of giving a solo performance, fixed Lucasta with a grim look. "Mind ye don't take Spanish coin from 'im, now! A girl lets 'er guard down, and afore she knows—" She snapped her fingers— "she's leavin' a bundle at the gate with a note and a wee remembrance."

Many of the infants signed onto the rolls of the Hospital came with some identifier pinned to their blanket, a piece of fabric or a small token by which the surrendering parent hoped to identify their child when circumstances improved. The hospital staff kept careful records of these tokens, though they were rarely called upon. Most foundlings lucky enough to survive their childhood left the gates of the Hospital of their own volition, with a set of new clothes and a few coins donated by benefactors.

"It is time we focused on the task at hand," Lucasta said briskly. "The concert is a fortnight away. Eliza needs to practice her solo of 'Au claire de la lune.' Isadora, Camilla, Philippa, we'll run through your trio of 'The Trees They Grow So High.' And I'm very glad we can practice our hymn today with Mr. Handel's organ, which I have wanted to play my whole life."

"What about your solo, Miss Lucasta? Aren't you going to do 'The Bells of Aberdovey'?"

Lucasta's heart pinched again. That was the song Judith had wanted them to perform. She'd practiced for hours in the parlor at Rose Hollow, to the great delight of Mrs. Cadogan. But she might never see Judith or Mrs. Cadogan or the halflings, as Jem called the younger ones, again.

Her hands trembled at the thought. She'd not seen Jem since the masquerade, days ago. He'd seemed even more furious with the sudden appearance of Frotheringale than he had been with Lucasta, but she'd not had time to protest before Trevor whisked her away into a dance. Between the attentions of the Pevenseys, the

Gorgons, and Bertie, claims to her hand from no less than a dozen gentlemen who were fulsome in their compliments, and demands from nearly as many young ladies wanting to quiz her for information about Trevor, there had been no opportunity for either Frotheringale or Jem to approach Lucasta even if they'd wished it.

And Jem, she feared, didn't wish to approach her ever again.

"I'm afraid I won't be performing, girls." It took all Lucasta's training to keep her voice steady. "My accompanist, sadly, has proven unable to keep our engagement."

"Then you won't sing at all?"

"I have no plans to."

"That's a right shame, it is, Miss Lucasta. A *right* shame."

"The way of the world, girls, is that we rarely get what we wish for. Glimpses, sometimes, but that is all."

Lucasta turned her attention to the console of the great organ with its pipes stretching to the ceiling. The girls milled about her on the tiered seats of the balcony, enjoying this unusual view of the hospital's glorious chapel. At other benefit concerts, professionals performed for admiring crowds, and the children were allowed to listen. This was the first time any of the girls had performed. It was a dream they'd never thought to harbor.

Lucasta played the opening chords of the hymn they were rehearsing, "Come Thou Font of Every Blessing." The resonant, full-throated sound of the organ reached like a fist into her belly and pulled up every painful emotion swirling there, accompanied by tears. The layers of rich sound blasted open all the parts inside her that felt hopeless and miserable and stuck.

Lucasta's dream, fostered at Miss Gregoire's, had been to have a music conservatory of her own, a small school of dedicated students whose musical training was in her charge. She'd imagined a gracious room with windows, full of her favorite instruments, and when she'd thought further, perhaps a set of rooms above that providing living quarters for her and possibly a companion who also had no other place in the world.

Now, as she pressed a different keyboard and a new rank of

pipes mingled a fresh set of tones with the first, she permitted herself to acknowledge the new dream that had come into being. In this dream, she walked onto the stage of a beautiful opera house in a glorious gown and sang for a crowd there to hear her, just her.

She traveled wherever she was invited, filling palaces, theatres, country houses, and foreign castles with her voice. The studio where she practiced and trained students still had sets of windows and every kind of instrument she could afford. But her private rooms, which held her private life, held a different kind of companion than she had ever dared imagine for herself—a partner of the heart, someone with whom she shared bed and board.

A husband.

She released the keyboards, and the sound ended. Echoes reverberated through the chapel, bringing the air alive. The girls stared with wide eyes. Benedicta, who had been obliged to leave her wheeled chair on the first floor and let Lucasta carry her up the narrow stairs to the balcony, sat on a bench with her eyes closed, swaying as if she felt the music pass through her.

"They won't take this away from us, will they, miss?" Eliza, sitting close by her, spoke barely above a whisper.

"What do you mean, Eliza? You fear they will take the concert away from us?"

She nodded. The girl faced in her direction, though Lucasta knew that the clouded eyes had long since ceased to discern light and shadow. "If milord is angry with us. He won't take it away, will he?"

Eliza was the only one among the girls who had expressed no trepidation about how they might be perceived during their performance, or how she might dress. Her only care was that she perform her solo, a popular French children's song, with the correct pronunciation. She trusted no one but Lucasta to accompany her on the violin.

A shaft of affection pierced Lucasta's heart as she regarded the girl. Eliza's quiet strength and humor reminded her of Judith, though Judith, who had been sheltered all her life, tended more towards playfulness and mischief, while Eliza was more somber. Both girls faced their world with a dignity and courage Lucasta wished she could cultivate in herself. Neither were floored by obstacles, nor discouraged by what the world saw as their limitation. They carried forward, spirits high, making the best of what they had. And they never held a grudge when something was denied them.

Lucasta could do no less.

"We've engaged half a dozen very famous people to sing for our concert," Lucasta answered, "and I hope their names will help sell the rest of the tickets. The governors could not stop our concert even if they wished to, and if they try, I shall chain myself to this organ console until they let you sing."

Eliza's smile was beautiful. "Thank you, Miss Lucasta. For what you've done for me, and for all of us."

Lucasta walked home with a new firmness in her stride, determined to push back the gloom over her heart. So a man she respected had turned on her with disdain. So a friendship she cherished had been severed. So her term as society's brief toast was at an end; she always knew that was an illusion. She still had her music.

That would have to be enough.

"ALL RIGHT, then! What is Frotheringale doing here, that miserable worm? What does he want?" the Baron barked.

Lady Pevensey sat tense and distraught, the firescreen she was painting streaked with unruly blobs. Trevor was crisp and pressed in riding attire, but his hair was disheveled, and red spots on his cheeks looked as if someone had struck him across the face.

It was the Baron's glower that gave Lucasta a shiver. There was no fire laid in the parlor, and a damp chill pervaded the room.

Lucasta took a step backward at the Baron's fury. She was accustomed to quiet contempt. "I'm sure I don't know."

The Baron advanced, a vein in his temple throbbing. "Of course you know! Trevor says he declared himself before all your friends. Did you accept him?"

"I did not." Lucasta spotted the paper in his hand, the seal broken. The handwriting was familiar. "Is that letter for me?"

The Baron thrust it at her. "Your Aunt Cornelia writes that she is sending someone to you to settle a certain matter, as she calls it. Is she the one pressing the match? I suppose she thinks it a proper turn for Frotheringale to unite the name and estates with her income, after her father was ass enough to split it up."

Lucasta took the letter with trembling fingers. "You read my post now?"

This time her aunt's cheeks reddened. "We have the right to know about any correspondence of yours that affects us."

Lucasta lifted her chin. "How does my cousin's coming to town affect you?"

She glanced at Trevor, whose jaw was set mutinously. He refused to meet her eyes. How long would he be able to hold out against the pressure of his parents?

How long would she? It was easy to say that in this enlightened age, she could no longer be wed against her will. They couldn't sign her marriage lines for her; she had to give her consent.

But consent could be wrung from a friendless poor relation in any number of ways.

"Don't play dim, girl. Your one saving quality is that you have two wits to rub together," the Baron snarled. He directed a cutting gaze at his son. "You know our plans. Don't make my son a booby by prancing about with other men beneath his nose."

"Mr. Pevensey has made no declaration to me, sir." Lucasta's voice wobbled.

"Then it's time we got it settled, don't you think?"

Her ladyship gave a small cry, raising a hand to her mouth.

"I won't have my hand forced by threats, sir." Trevor was stony-faced, his back ramrod straight.

"It's not threats forcing you, by God!" the Baron roared. "It's a very simple equation. Do you want to continue with your fancy tailor and your horses and your shiny phaeton and your clubs? Or do you want to be a beggar with a hungry belly, cast out on the street? It's she—" He flung a hand in Lucasta's direction, stabbing at her through the air— "who will keep a roof over your head, if you want it!"

Her ladyship's cry broke free. "Peter! Is it so bad? Have things come to this?"

The Baron's face stiffened. "I will find a way for us to survive, Patience. The tradesmen's bills can be put off. We can shift houses if we need to. But my daughter will need to marry, and this one—" He stabbed a finger in Trevor's direction— "will need to make something of his looks and my investment in his education, if he wants to hold his head up about town."

"But Lucasta," her ladyship moaned. "Does he have to sink to Lucasta?"

Lucasta held back her retort. Her aunt was working in her favor, though she didn't appreciate the slight. "Indeed, sir," she said instead, appealing to the Baron's vanity. "There are any number of available heiresses this season who will make Trevor a better wife."

"Are there? Heiresses with their income assured, and no family to meddle with the use of their assets?"

"Gale will fuss if I take Lucasta away from him," Trevor said.

"Name another, then," the Baron accused Lucasta. "Name three."

Lucasta racked her brains. She could name one heiress of the season: Cici. Or at least, everyone assumed she came with a generous dowry.

Would Cici be able to marry where she wished if Lucasta refused Trevor?

She clenched her hand around Aunt Cornelia's note. The ornate touches of the formal parlor pressed in on her: the hand-painted wallpaper, the expensive rugs, the porcelain and marble and silver pieces scattered about, all the pretty and expensive orna-ments hiding a great emptiness.

"Where is Cici?"

"At Arendale House, calling on Rudyard's cousin, that girl you introduced her to at Ranelagh," her ladyship said sharply. "I told her to wait for you, but your friends came to collect her and bid you join them there when you were free."

"Your friends. The ones they call the Gorgons. They are all rich, are they not?" The Baron's voice turned calculating.

Trevor looked alarmed. "If I'm to put my head in the parson's mousetrap, sir, I'll decide who's holding the shackle."

"My credit is running out," the Baron said. "And so are your purse strings."

The look the Baron gave her made Lucasta feel an inch tall. She was nothing but a purse to him. She much preferred when she had been invisible.

She straightened her shoulders. It must be fury making her bold. She would never have dared oppose her uncle a few weeks ago.

"I find it curious that you are discussing my marriage, sir, when you have not yet procured my consent." As the Baron's eyes bulged in anger, she turned to Trevor. "Will you take me to Arendale House? It seems you and I have some matters to discuss, and fresh air will do us good."

A muscle flicked in Trevor's jaw. "Cici won't want to walk home in this chill. I'll order the carriage."

Lucasta walked out of the parlor with milord and milady Pevensey gaping after her.

Trevor helped her into the carriage and arranged the fur throw over her lap, shielding her against the damp breeze. Lucasta studied his strong, fine profile as he navigated them out of Caroline Street. Trevor was an attractive man, an observation she made with an almost sisterly tenderness. From what she had seen of him since his return, he would make an unobjectionable husband.

But not *her* husband. "Did you know of your father's financial situation?" she asked.

He flicked the ribbons, guiding the horses around the corner.

"He's been dropping hints. I think he received a report from his steward that brought matters to a head."

"You seemed—" Lucasta curled her fingers in her muff and breathed from her belly. "I had not gathered before that you meant to defy him." *Please defy him. Please, please.*

He avoided looking at her. "When he first posed the match to me, I presumed you had no other attachments. But I won't be saddled with a wife who hates me. Or is in love with another man."

"I'm not—" Lucasta swallowed back the words. She would not lie.

"I do not hate you," she said quietly. "But you are correct that I hate not being consulted about my own wishes in the matter."

Which were what? To pull off the concert with as much style as she could, and then flee to Miss Gregoire's to lick her wounds in private, count over her meager savings, and drown herself in music until she had come to a proper sense of things and all her newfound fancies had died for lack of feeding.

"We simply refuse, then." She lifted her chin.

"I can refuse," Trevor said, drawing the carriage to a halt before Arendale House. "But you'll need somewhere to go when he throws you into the street."

The girls had gathered in one of the smaller drawing rooms at Arendale House: Cici, the Gorgons, and Bertie, beaming at her role as hostess. The circle only wanted Judith. She'd adore being introduced to the Gorgons, feeling their fancy gowns and hearing talk of the events at Ranelagh while they sipped tea and nibbled cakes.

Trevor made his bow to Bertie, but left at once when he realized the conversation was about Frotheringale.

"And when he tore off his turban and threw it at Jem!" Bertie giggled. "I vow I thought I might faint in surprise." She paused. "He's rather handsome, d'you think?"

Cici's eyes were wide, round sapphires. "He was ever such a mischievous child. *Belle-mère* would take us on visits to Frotheringale House, and he tormented me till I cried. But when we last saw him after his father died, when he became viscount—He'd quite changed. Trevor hated him from the start, they're always in competition, but I do think he's grown up. To think he wants to marry *you*, Lucasta!"

Lucasta managed a crooked smile. "He doesn't want to marry me. He wants the inheritance he thinks my aunt Cornelia will leave me, which includes part of the Frotheringale properties that the old viscount, our great-grandfather, divided up among his children."

Along with the properties and incomes her aunt had acquired by her own means, through marriage and investment. Her aunt had still given no hint that Lucasta would be her heir of choice, which made her wonder why the Baron and Frotheringale both seemed convinced of it.

"It's rather unpleasant," Lucasta added, accepting the tea that Bertie poured for her, "to be wanted for one's presumed inheritance, and not one's own self."

Cici wrinkled her nose. "That's exactly what I've been saying all Season."

Her new worry struck Lucasta silent. Cici had begun the Season with vague thoughts of enjoying herself and entertaining proposals at the end. Now, it seemed she would have to marry. But who would have her if her dowry disappeared?

Lucasta could offer her a home once she had her studio established, but it would be a great fall for a baron's daughter. Pevensey's improvidence had thrown away his children's future and narrowed his own.

She hugged her muff to her middle. She'd never make enough as a music teacher to support Trevor *and* Cici. Perhaps Aunt Cornelia could be persuaded to help. Or the Dowager Viscountess Frotheringale might bestow something on Aunt Patience, her only remaining daughter.

Of course, if Lucasta *did* inherit something from Aunt Cornelia, she could provide for her cousins. Without having to marry any of them.

"Try being admired for one's father's rank." Minnie snorted and plucked another cake from the tray.

"Or whom he knows," Annis agreed, taking the cake Minnie passed her.

Selina bit her lip. "Better than not being wanted at all."

"Well, at least I had a bit of fun while I could." Bertie slumped on the settee, her ruffled gown mounded about her. "It seems I'll be back in mourning again soon. My grandfather arrived a few days ago. He was visiting the estate in Dorset but took ill in his travels. He's always said he wants to die at his seat in Arendale, but he's too weak to travel north. Jem's with him now, and my mother brought in his solicitors to make him review his will."

"Oh, what terrible news!" Cici cried. "We oughtn't be imposing on you at such a time."

"I need the cheering," Bertie answered, refilling Cici's dish of tea. "It's been terribly grim. Mama and I have prepared ourselves, but Jem— I think he's been trying to pretend our grandfather doesn't exist. And now he can't avoid it."

Bertie met Lucasta's gaze, then looked away. They both knew how Jem felt about his father. And when the present Earl Payne succeeded the Marquess of Arendale and returned from Barbados, what would happen to the rest of his family?

No wonder Jem had been in a temper at Ranelagh Gardens. It didn't excuse his unkindness to Lucasta, but fear for what would happen to his half-siblings still in Barbados—if his father would leave them, or bring them to Britain—had to be preying on his mind.

The room stilled as Jem appeared in the doorway. Lucasta's heart pinched.

He looked terrible. His face was drawn with fine lines, all pointing downward. His neckcloth drooped, and the gold buttons on his coat, waistcoat, and sleeves were dull. His breeches were creased from sitting, and with his hair drawn back in a simple queue, tied with a dark ribbon, he looked more vulnerable than Lucasta had ever seen him.

His eyes found hers as though there were no one else in the room. She was still furious with him, yet she wanted to draw him into her arms.

"Do you wish us gone, so your family may be alone together?" she asked quietly.

He scrubbed a hand over his face. "Alone, together, is the worst thing for us at this moment," he said in a tired, gravelly voice. "I am glad you are here—that you are all here—for Bertie."

He glanced at his cousin, whose expression turned miserable. "Should I—must I?" Bertie fretted, holding her dish of tea close, as if he meant to take it.

"No." Jem shook his head. "It cannot be long now. He is afraid and suffering, and— It is best you stay here."

As if lost for direction, he turned and left the room. Lucasta's ire at him fell away. She had never seen Smart Jeremy so rumpled and at a loss.

"He forgot his tea," Bertie whispered.

Lucasta rose. How could he have this power over her? He'd scorned her, taunted her, set out to humiliate her, and kissed her. Now he needed her, and she went.

"I shall take him a cup, and one for your mother, too, if you prepare it as she likes."

Bertie gave her directions to the master's rooms, and Lucasta balanced the tea tray carefully as she ascended the stairs and knocked. "What now?" Lady Payne called in an irritated voice as Jem opened the door.

The look of relief in his eyes assured her she had done right. Lucasta entered and set the tray on a small table, moving aside a clutter of parchment and broken quills. The marquess was working on his last will and testament, or rather, his secretary was.

The room smelled of illness, that thin, sour undertone that Lucasta knew from other rooms where doctors had bled and dosed a body past its endurance of pain. The Marquess of Arendale, a powerful peer of the realm, was a thin stick under a heavy quilt, his face starkly white, his breathing labored.

Others stood in the shadows, watching, waiting. Every eye was dry.

A man was leaving this life, and it was a business transaction, to be witnessed and formally documented. No one mourned.

"The entail," the marquess rasped, his weak eyes searching out Jem. "Promise me. You'll renew the entail. An heir of your body. It won't go…" He struggled for breath. "No bastards."

"You must leave the directive for my father." Jem's tone was as clipped as if he were shearing fabric. He might have been carved from wood. "All your holdings will fall to him."

"Insolent whelp." The marquess flailed his hands, clenched into weak fists. "Fancy boy…a draper's daughter…leave me this at least." His breath hissed. "Promise. Don't let him destroy my legacy."

"We will heed your wishes, sir." Lady Payne glared at Jem. "I will see to it."

"You." The marquess turned his eye on her, beady beneath cragged white brows. "You're not to take what you can get. Vulture." The eye closed, the fingers curved around the bed quilt growing still. "Make…sure," he breathed.

Lucasta's stomach turned over. His last moments, and the man could not rein in his bile. It was a miracle that Jem had not been poisoned by this man, or his father. Somehow, she would guess due to the influence of his mother, he'd become a man of warmth and humor. And the tenderness he showed his siblings and cousin could not be denied.

She'd watched him arrange bolts of cloth across his shop window, filling a space with beauty. She'd seen him come stomping into the cottage in Little Chelsea with his hands reeking of fish and his half-siblings frisking about him like puppies. Jem would never become this bitter and broken, not even on his deathbed. He was a better man in every respect.

"What do you want?" Lady Payne asked sharply, seeing Lucasta stood near the table, fixing Jem's tea.

Lucasta stirred in sugar with trembling hands. "I came to ask if

I may offer anything." She glanced at the impassive faces of the others in the room, the secretary scribbling at a desk, two men dressed as solicitors, and the last a doctor, lifting leeches from the Marquess's arm.

Lady Payne's face held stony. "What could you possibly offer?"

Jem stepped forward and slipped a hand around her arm. His grip was warm, firm, and yet she felt he drew strength from her. She gave it gladly.

Lucasta pressed her hands together, meeting Jem's eyes. "I— My father often liked for me to sing to him, when..." When he was at his most frail, and dying. "It...soothed him." She'd been a fool to come. She turned, ready to flee back to the parlor, but Jem's hand stayed her.

"I do not think there is much else we can do," he said, glancing at the still figure on the bed.

The thick hangings, woven with rampant dragons and swirling gold foliage, quite drowned the frail figure in the white linen bedgown and cap. The draperies at the window were drawn against the light, and the scent of a burnt pastille added an acrid odor to the room.

Lucasta swallowed hard, recalling too well those last days with her father. How precious every moment had been, and how terrifying the thought of losing him. She fought not to cry, for weeping would ruin her voice.

"It would help me to hear you," Jem said softly. "And it might ease him as well."

Lucasta nodded, unable for the moment to speak. His anger with her had not lessened, nor had she forgiven him for the May game he had set out to play with her. But around and within the exasperation she felt a deeper pull, the connection that had been building between them for months. This was not the moment to examine it.

"Arendale is in the north, I understand?" she asked.

"In Northumberland, above Newcastle. In fact near the Borders of Scotland," Jem answered.

"This is not the time to distress him your warbling," Lady Payne snapped.

Lucasta bent over the bed. "Would you wish a song or two, milord? I do not want to disturb any business."

A cold eye glared at her, slitted like a snake. "You," he rasped. "Jeremiah's ladybird."

"A friend," she said. "I'll sing a northern ballad I know, and if it distresses you, turn me out."

She folded her hands before her, squared her shoulders and filled her lungs, and imagined she was in the music parlor at Miss Gregoire's. A gracious if elegantly shabby room, filled with her favorite people. She sang to soothe Jem; she sang to calm Lady Payne; but mostly, she sang for the still, wracked man on the bed, to gentle his path into that bourn from which no traveler returns.

She sang of weary travelers, of Mary McCree, of the green mossy banks of the Lea. She sang a few Scottish tunes she knew, "The Flowers of the Forest" and "The Birks of Abergeldy." The Marquess breathed slowly, listening, his hand occasionally twitching, but the twist of pain in his face eased. The solicitors rustled quietly in their corner, the nib of the clerk's pen scratching steadily across the parchment, and the doctor wiped a tear from his eye at the end of a slow, sad air in Scots Gaelic that a friend at Miss Gregoire's had taught her.

Lady Payne sat with her head bowed, still as marble. Jem nodded when Lucasta drew a small wooden flute from her pocket.

"You always have a musical instrument about you, do you not?" His smile, though it brought out the lines about his mouth and the shadows of strain beneath his eyes, was unbearably fond. Lucasta's heart clenched again.

"Most times," she agreed, and took a sip of his tea to wet her lips.

The air in the room changed as Lucasta sang and played. Lady Payne dropped her head to her folded hands, her lips moving in prayer, and a few tears slid down her cheeks. She was a woman who had lost the protection of her husband and was now losing her father-in-law's protection as well, to be thrown on the mercy of a nephew she had never been able to like. It was a precariousness that faced all women who had no secure income of their own, and Lucasta understood it.

The doctor collected his leeches and sat beside his patient, monitoring his pulse. The secretary blotted dry his ink and passed his documents to the men of business, who reviewed them at length and nodded. They passed the copy to Jem, whose face tightened as he read, but he made no comment.

Lucasta played the lovely, haunting "The Rowan Tree," singing the lyrics written by the Baroness Nairne, as the doctor roused the marquess to sign his last testament. And she played the gentle, sad melody of "Hasten and Come With Me" when the doctor picked up the thin, white wrist for the last time and shook his head gravely, indicating that the Marquess had stepped through that thin veil between worlds, and the man on the bed was a man no more.

A brief flurry of activity from the men of business attended the doctor's verdict, a last ordering of documents and signing of signatures. Lady Payne, a grim set to her mouth, went to the clock on the mantel, opened its back, and stopped the hands. Then she opened a lower drawer in the bureau and withdrew a white sheet which the secretary helped her drape over the mirror. Lucasta felt the ancient thrill of superstition shiver over her skin, remembering how she had done the same when her father died.

As the woman of the house, it would fall to Lady Payne to prepare the body for burial and attend to all the other funeral and mourning preparations. Lucasta wondered who would sit with the Marquess tonight.

She had sat with her father's body that first night, before the rest of his family could arrive. While the candles burned down to nothing, she sat watch in those solemn, sacred hours. She knew the vigil for the dead came from an ancient superstition of not letting a demon enter a fresh body, but she herself had huddled in that liminal darkness like a shelter, knowing that when she emerged, she stepped into a world where her father no longer lived. In that threshold she had felt him, lingering, as reluctant to leave as she was to let him go.

Jem slipped out the door and Lucasta, returning her flute to her pocket, followed. She suspected he would, like a wounded animal, seek to be alone, and alone was the last thing he needed.

She found him before the tall window at the end of the hall that overlooked the street. The day's clouds had rolled away, leaving a last blush of golden afternoon light before evening fell. When she neared, her skirts swishing across the thick rug, he turned sharply, as if he might attack. But she held her hands out to him, offering, and he swept her into his arms, pressing his face into her shoulder.

His body was warm and hard, as it had been during their embrace in his shop, and as she slipped her arms around his shoulders, she felt again that deep sense of completion, as if she had arrived at some place she had longed for without ever knowing what it was she sought.

She must not give in to that dangerous softness. She offered the warmth of one human creature to another, no more. She did not forget that he had laid some plot against her and she had stepped into it like a trusting fool. She did not forget that he had brought her in friendship into his second home, acquainting her with his sister and the rest of the family he kept hidden from the world, then had slammed that door shut when he deemed her unworthy.

She did not forget that when he kissed her, the rest of her surroundings melted to nothing, and she kissed him back as if nothing in the world mattered save for him. That way lay a sure path into madness.

"It's all mine now," he muttered into her hair.

She paused in the act of stroking his shoulder. He had such fine, firm shoulders, taut with fabric but not padding. He was not a man who deceived others about who he was.

"Your father?" she said tentatively.

He rubbed his forehead against her shoulder as if trying to

erase a memory. "He will have the control but leave the running of it to me. I will have to carry out his decisions, distasteful as I might find them."

"Your grandfather has men of business. I saw them in the chamber."

"And they must be overseen as well," Jem said bitterly. "The marquess didn't trust them, and I do not either." He sighed, his shoulders heaving. "My shop—my business—there will be no time for any of it. And my family..."

"Bertie will hate to go into mourning again," Lucasta murmured. "But perhaps at the end you might have a grand come-out gala for her, and bring Judith out as well."

"Judith." His shoulders stiffened, and he drew back his head to stare at her. "Why are you so concerned to expose my sister to ridicule and shame?"

Lucasta's mouth parted. "I am only thinking of what she wants—"

"You know nothing of what she wants!"

Lucasta pulled away, stung by his obstinacy. He would do this now? "I happen to have spent many hours of conversation with her about her dreams. But it seems her wishes for her future do not matter to you. You have already decided what she will have, and what she deserves. You care only about what *you* want."

A dark glitter entered his eyes, and he leaned toward her. They were already very close, and the action made the large buttons of his coat brush against the scarf she had wrapped about her bodice.

"And what," he said in a hoarse mutter, "do you presume it is that I want?"

A thrill of alarm singed along her spine. The shadows in his eyes were the same gray as a cloud of smoke drifting past the window. She did, in fact, know nothing of an adult, healthy male's wants or needs.

But with his breath on her neck, his scent filling her head, the heat of his nearness raising a prickle of awareness along her skin, all that filled her awareness was this inexorable pull to be near him.

It was a deep, yearning ache in her belly that only eased when she touched him.

"I think you wanted to make a fool of me," she said, battling to steady her voice. She couldn't give in to her body's longings or the deeper desire to push away the haunted, empty look on his face. She must remember where she stood with him. "You meant to make me a figure of ridicule and fun. The Gorgon. The Medusa. Let Smart Jeremey show her a hint of attention and watch everyone run to pet and make much of her. I agree it would make an amusing spectacle."

He winced. "You did not deserve that."

"Oh, most likely I did, in part. I'm sure my pride and vanity could use pruning. But you took it too far." Her throat tightened, hurt threading her voice, and she drew a deep breath for strength. "You came to meet my foundlings. You introduced me to your brother and sisters and Mrs. Cadogan. You brought Bertie to me. You—dressed me."

Her voice hitched, and breath left her as she recalled standing in his shop, shivering with delight as he swathed her body in thick, luscious silks and brocades. "You—" He'd kissed her. An unbearable liberty. Even more unbearable to think he might never kiss her again. "You made me—" *Want you.*

She couldn't say *that.* Widgeon! He'd tricked her, manipulated her, made sport of her. How Ashley and Plimpton and all of them must have roared with laughter to see her go starry-eyed the moment Lord Rudyard led her out in a dance. "You toyed with me," she managed.

"I meant all of it," he muttered, his face growing haggard, taut, as if he harnessed his own emotion with great difficulty.

"To mock me?"

"I meant..." He raised a hand to touch a lock of hair at her temple, and the heat of his nearness sizzled her skin. "You bewitched me," he said hoarsely, as if the words were drawn from him against his will. "I wanted to hear you sing to your foundlings. I want to hear you sing every day of my life. I wanted you to meet my family because I knew you would love them as I do. I know it makes me a cad, when I made you no promises, no offer of marriage, but when I kissed you..." His breath was a rasp. "I could think of nothing else then, and I have thought of nothing else since."

That wasn't true, the rational part of Lucasta's brain wanted to argue. He'd thought very carefully about how to hurt her when he found she'd planned for Judith to appear in her benefit concert.

But the rational part of Lucasta's brain had very little claim on the rest of her at the moment. The rest of her was focused on the turmoil in his expression, the longing in his eyes, the firm, sensual shape of his lips and the persistent, begging ache spreading from her belly into her chest.

He stroked her temple, and the soft slide of his fingers along the side of her face made her breath stop. "Lucasta," he said, "forgive me." His face was so bleak, his brow furrowed with regret.

Oh, she was a foolish, foolish girl, to turn to treacle at his touch. So this was how a girl lost her head over a man. She forgot her hurt over his calculations, his designs. Before her stood the raw, real man, stripped of his elegance, his defenses, his mocking demeanor and the careful shield he held to the world.

She had slipped around his fortifications to find the real Jem standing before her. And everything in her leaned toward this man and his touch like a young sprout seeking the sun.

"Very well," she said huskily, trailing her fingertips across his jaw. "I demand a forfeit. A kiss. One kiss. And then we will shake hands and part, and there will be no more—toying of any sort."

His eyes flared, and something inside of her opened at the desire on his face. Wanton, shameless girl. When had she become so bold as to ask for what she wanted?

"I have made you no declaration," he said softly. "I am not in the position..."

She steeled herself not to flinch at that crushing admission. He didn't want her, not really. Not in the enduring, deepest ways she wanted him. She needed to step back now, take herself away, retrieve what she could of her heart and her self-respect.

*Go,* said her head. Lucasta always followed her head.

Except with him. The rest of her wanted to kiss Jem, more than she wanted self-respect, more than she wanted dignity. The ache would not be denied. The part of herself that stood before him just as raw and exposed as he was answered that desperate look in his eyes. She knew with certainty that he longed for her every bit as much as she longed for him. The space between them fairly shivered with the weight of that need.

One kiss goodbye. She would grant herself that. She curved her palms around his jaw, stroking the stubble emerging on his chin, the lines left by muscles tense from the trials of the day. She wanted to ease that weariness, and she wanted to revel in his desire, and she wanted to tell him she forgave him. She wanted to linger in his mind after she was gone.

"I did not ask for a declaration," she whispered. "I just want you. I suppose..."

She didn't know what she meant to say, and it didn't matter. His mouth swooped to hers like a hawk striking, as if he had been posed for just this, waiting hungrily to kiss her.

She fell against him, or he tugged, or she threw herself, perhaps all of it together. But there she was, pressed tightly into the wall of his body, falling headlong into a drugging, maddening, molten kiss.

Any rational part of her that was left sank without a murmur under the tide of obliterating sensation. Her entire being was heat and hardness and a high, wild humming. She felt him completely, and his need urged her to abandon. He kissed her as though she were the breath keeping him alive. He kissed her as though he would never stop.

And even as the whimper rose in her throat, the glad surrender to the drenching tide, she felt that restless surge in her belly shift and settle, like an anchor dropping into the deep. Like a prison door being thrown open, or the drawbridge to a fortified castle slamming down.

She wasn't just awash in a thrill of physical sensation. She was connected to Jem, this man that against her will she had come to love. She saw the deep goodness of his nature, his driving ambition, his fears for his family, the grief and frustration at his new responsibility. She felt his strength, his solidness, his need to seek her despite his reservations.

She felt the swirling depths of his soul laid open to her, as nakedly as she opened herself to him, and she knew with utter clarity that she wanted nothing in her life but to hold Jem, be with Jem, care for and live beside and laugh with and tease Jem to the end of their days, living one long kiss that went on and on and—

"Ahem."

The level of irritation in the throat clearing suggested the possessor of the throat had been trying to get their attention for quite some time. Lucasta swam to awareness through a fog of bliss, unwilling to open her eyes to the real world and leave the perfect dream she'd been building inside that kiss.

Cold air rushed in as Jem lifted his head and looked beyond her shoulder. He blinked, his pupils adjusting, and she thrilled to realize he'd been as lost as she was.

"Aunt Payne," he managed.

"Rudyard," his aunt said icily. "Though I suppose you will be Payne, as your father is now the Marquess."

Lucasta turned to face Lady Payne, who gave her a furious, scornful glance. The older woman's face was engraved with lines of despair and weariness.

"You are wanted," she said with great emphasis to Jem, "elsewhere."

"Of course." Jem tightened his arm around Lucasta's shoulder. He drew her toward him and she leaned against his warmth, not yet ready for the contact to end. "Lucasta—that is, Miss Lithwick and I..."

He trailed off. What they were doing required a great deal of explanation, but was also obvious.

Lady Payne turned her back on them, her dismissal a slap in

the face. "You may be forgiven an aberration, given the circumstances," she said. "Though I hope Miss Lithwick will not harbor hopes. I cannot think this behavior makes her a good influence for my daughter, especially in this difficult time."

Lucasta, stung, opened her mouth to protest, but Jem rushed in before her. "We were discussing the terms of our marriage."

His aunt recoiled as if taking a blow. "This is neither the time nor place," she gasped. "The very idea is beyond belief." She threw a withering glare at Lucasta.

Lucasta stepped forward, away from the sheltering circle of Jem's arm. She missed his warmth as if she'd been expelled from paradise, but she had to face the consequences her mad, wanton choice had brought her to. "Lady Payne. I am sorry for your loss. Believe me, if there is anything I might do for Bertie—"

Lady Payne cut her off in a freezing voice. "Miss Lithwick, I think it is time your visit ended. You've done enough."

That was the last humiliation she could bear. Lucasta's eyes smarted with tears. "Of course," she said numbly. "I'll go."

"Lucasta!" Jem called.

But she couldn't face him either, couldn't bear for him to proceed with the foolish straw he had grasped at. He told her he meant to make no declaration. She wouldn't use this unfortunate discovery to force him to one.

Now was the time to clutch at those last tattered shreds of pride. Ignoring his call, she hurried away, brushing past Lady Payne and nearly sprinting down the hallway.

Her throat ached from tears and the hours of singing, her head ached from the tangle of intense emotions, and her heart ached from the knowledge that her gift to herself, one last kiss with the man she loved, had made her a spectacle of shame and folly. Jem's power before to ruin her had nothing on the devastation to her reputation if Lady Payne made this known.

"Lucasta!" Jem's voice was a warning, a plea.

"Goodbye!" she sobbed, and flung herself toward the stairs.

# CHAPTER NINETEEN

"I wonder what he'll do now," Minnie said aloud. "Rudyard, that is." She pushed aside the frond of the potted palm brushing against the embroidered brocade of her skirts. They stood again in Clara Bellwether's drawing room, gathered for an evening soiree. Above them loomed a lovingly painted oil portrait of the departed Sir Egbert's favorite horse.

"Lord Payne now, isn't he," Annis remarked. "His father will be the Marquess of Arendale. Do they expect he'll return to England to be invested in the House of Lords?"

"I couldn't say." Lucasta wished her friends would take an interest in any topic of conversation but Jem and his family. If his father did return to England, what then of Portia and her children? The Marquess of Arendale's Black mistress would be an object of much wonder and speculation, and there would be no hope of hiding her children away in Little Chelsea, even if Jem felt it was for their own protection.

But this was none of her concern. She occupied herself with sipping from her tumbler of orgeat. She knew Clara Bellwether wished her in Hades and only extended the invitation because it would sink her as an admired hostess not to have the latest freak of fashion, the Gorgons, in attendance at her soiree.

And here, Lucasta could escape the frigid air pervading the Pevensey town house. The Baron was attempting by furious stares to bring Lucasta to heel. Lady Pevensey couldn't look Lucasta in the eye. Trevor had made himself scarce, as if he expected his father was lurking around corners waiting to throw a noose about his neck. Even Cici was subdued and had begun limiting her entertainments to one outing a night, instead of three.

Lucasta had not heard from Bertie, though she had sent a note of condolence. Neither had she heard from Jem, who was not attending this evening. It had only been days since his grandfather's passing; there would be much setting affairs in order, which fell solely on him.

"And Bertie shall have to hide away again," Selina said with a sigh. "Just when we had found a new friend."

What would this mean for Judith? Lucasta wondered. She had sent a note to Rose Hollow as well but received nothing in return, which was unlike Judith. Perhaps she too had much to do to prepare for the funeral. And what of Tressie, Starria, and Hannibal? Children would not attend the funeral in any case, but would they be allowed to openly grieve?

Judith had spoken of her grandfather's horror at what he thought her deformity. To one of the old Marquess's temperament, blindness, illness, and other debilities were punishments from God. Her own father might very well feel the same way. And if he had not felt obliged to recognize his new family as Earl Payne, what would the new Marquess of Arendale do with them now? His unkindness would torment Jem.

Lucasta's heart ached. She wished she could be a support and a help to him during this time. But he was too proud to send for her, and she was still too devastated by that kiss to have the courage to call at Arendale House, knowing what Lady Payne had seen.

She ought to be practicing for the benefit concert, a mere week away. She had rehearsals to oversee. She must review and correct a printed proof of the program, confirm the flowers were ordered for decoration, and check with Mlle. Beaudoin on the new embroidered aprons her seamstresses were making for the foundlings who would perform.

Her own gown needed a last fitting as well. Jem had produced a gorgeous saffron silk that Mlle. Beaudoin fashioned into an elegant open robe with lace at the ruffled sleeves and a stomacher set with embroidered flowers. She felt queenly in it, though her role for the concert would be largely backstage, ensuring performers met their cues and occasionally providing accompaniment.

But with the chapel to decorate, the instruments to check and double-check, the girls to reassure and settle, and seats yet to fill, the next week would be exhausting. They hadn't sold nearly enough tickets. Lucasta had neither the time nor energy to spend mooning over a man who had kissed her in a moment when he was beside himself with emotion.

And there was no use dwelling on the marriage he had proposed to assuage his aunt's sense of propriety. The look of scorn Lady Payne had given her, as if she were the worst sort of social climber, a contemptible garden slug—

"Do you want to marry him, then?" Annis regarded Lucasta curiously.

Lucasta's heart slammed in her chest, startling her. As usual, she and her friends stood in their own little group, the recipients of many stares. The difference from weeks past was that the stares were now speculating, rather than scornful or indifferent. Gorgons they still were, but the Gorgons had become feared and respected rather than objects of pity.

All thanks to Jem and his calculated remarks.

*I meant all of it*, he'd said. She couldn't dwell on how deeply those words thrilled her. But to offer marriage?

"I wouldn't—I don't—" Lucasta stumbled. "Wait, whom do you mean?"

Annis could not possibly know of Jem's insane declaration in the hall at Arendale House. She had been in the parlor with the other girls, chatting over tea, and when Lucasta came storming in with a white face and wild eyes to report that the Marquess had breathed his last, the girls had all taken turns to embrace Bertie, who burst into tears at the thought of being locked away in mourning once again, then had taken a polite leave.

The two days following, having grounds to excuse herself due to a female complaint, Lucasta had kept to the house. She had spoken of that kiss to no one, though she breathed it, brooded over it, relived the experience in her mind's eye every waking moment and then carried Jem's kiss with her into the realm of fantastic dreams.

"Which one? O Queen Lucasta." Minnie smiled with amusement. "Two men, a baron's heir and a viscount, vying for her hand. What was the forfeit we proposed for the first among us to receive an offer of marriage?"

"The forfeit was for whomever accepts an offer of marriage," Lucasta said. "I have accepted no one. I have not been made a proper offer, actually."

"Trevor is handsome," Annis noted.

"Bertie thinks Frotheringale is handsomer," Selina pointed out.

"Really, girls, what has happened to us?" Lucasta scoffed. "We used to spend evenings like this debating the accuracy of various translations of Homer. Now we are reduced to discussing which men we might marry?"

"It was worth a try, since everyone else does it," Minnie said with a shrug. "Though I admit the topic becomes tedious."

"Miss Lithwick." Clara Bellwether joined them, exquisite in a gown made of heavily embroidered royal blue silk that Lucasta guessed had been smuggled from France. She had been spending too much time in Jem's company, learning from his observations on fabric, cut, and style. She could not look around the room without seeing what each person's clothing said about them, their history, their tastes.

Clara Bellwether liked expensive, she liked fashionable, and she liked to be admired. She did not, judging from the glitter in her narrowed eyes, like Lucasta.

"How lovely that you could stop by my little gathering," Clara said. "No event is complete unless the Gorgons attend. I find myself quite honored."

"I was flattered by the invitation," Lucasta replied. It had come addressed to her this time. That was another oddity, receiving invitations on her own account rather than playing chaperone to Cici.

Her cousin stood across the way, captured by a rich older widower intent on explaining, through admiration of Sir Egbert's horse, how the Dutch masters achieved their canvas effects. The Baron must have impressed on his daughter the need to entice a solvent suitor who could support the family coffers, which might explain why Cici looked miserable.

Lucasta was waiting until after the benefit to inform the Baron that she would not be coerced into marriage. She needed this concert to establish her musical reputation. The sooner she could get her music conservatory off the ground and stocked with paying students, the sooner she could provide Cici a safe haven so her cousin would not be forced to marry for a roof over her head.

And if Lucasta had means of her own, she need not be forced into marriage herself.

"I do hate to draw you away from your clever group," Clara continued—she had just managed not to call them Gorgons—"but your friend asked me to tell you he's waiting for you in one of the carriages outside."

"Friend?" Lucasta cast a quick glance about the room. Trevor, who had been watching them while he chatted with Lady Cranbury, made his bow to the dowager and started in their direction. Lucasta shook her head. Did he think she had summoned him? But if Trevor were not waiting for her outside, then—

*Jem.* He and Clara Bellwether were cronies. She'd seen Clara commandeer his attention a hundred times at the parties she'd attended in the past weeks. Jem would entrust her with a message to contact Lucasta. But why would he not come inside to deliver it? Because he did not wish to be accosted by others?

If he wanted to see Lucasta here, now, instead of making an

appropriate morning call or sending a message, it must be something important. Lucasta made a hasty farewell to her friends and hurried to gather her wrap before Trevor bore down upon them. She did not wish to explain to him where she was going. She would make up an excuse later, when she rejoined the party.

Jem was waiting for her. She went as if he were the siren and she the doomed ship. There was no earthly way she could resist his call.

The row of carriages outside the Bellwether town home was long, and a clammy cold had descended with the dusk. It was a spring that didn't feel like a spring, dry and full of chill breezes. Lucasta pulled her elegant mink pelisse up to her chin—another gift from Jem via Mlle. Beaudoin—and looked for Jem's calash.

A thump came from a closed chaise some way down the line, a plain conveyance with no identifying arms on the door, and the driver called gruffly to her. "'Ere, miss."

She didn't recognize him as one of Jem's servants, but then, Jem had always driven himself. The pavement was cold against her silk slippers as Lucasta moved in that direction, making her way by the light of the carriage lamps on the various vehicles. The chaise didn't hold Jem's horses, either; she'd recognize the mighty pair he called Atlas and Hercules.

"M-milord?" she called, uncertain how he wanted to be addressed now. He was the new Earl Payne, by right of succession, but she wanted to call him Jem. He had kissed her, twice, throwing her world off its axis each time. Surely that allowed her some intimacy?

The door of the chaise opened, and a masculine arm clothed in dark wool reached for her. Lucasta took the hand and climbed in, but she knew before the door closed behind her that the arm did not belong to Jem.

"*You!*"

The Viscount Frotheringale sat in the dark confines, grinning. He rapped on the roof and the chaise jolted into motion. Lucasta tumbled into the seat, throwing herself to one side to avoid landing in her cousin's lap.

"At last, Lucasta! It is very hard to find you alone."

"What are you doing here? I did not give you leave to use my name."

The least of her worries, but the first indignation to rise to her lips. She'd decided she was not at home each time he called, and the footman who answered the door, loyal to Lucasta after all the time she spent in the servant's quarters signing to them, stood behind this message. Furthermore, whatever his wife might feel about her nephew, the Baron was not obliged to give Frotheringale access to Lucasta.

"Oh, but we are cousins! And soon, I hope, more than that. Indeed I plan for us to become very close." His grin broadened, and the threat in that smile made Lucasta shrink into her seat.

"Very well, then, Roland," she said crisply, "what do you want of me?"

"Gale," he said. "All my friends call me Gale."

He reached for her hand, but Lucasta drew away. The chaise tilted as the coachman swung around a corner. He was driving too fast for a city street, so often clogged with traffic. Lucasta braced her hands against the seat and wall, glad she was wearing gloves. The carriage had the musty smell of a hired vehicle. This couldn't be her cousin's own conveyance—and if it was, he was a desperate man.

Desperate enough to kidnap her?

She considered the possibility for escape. Overpowering him was a remote chance; he was much larger and heavier. The coachman was not likely to obey her commands to stop. She could open the door and throw herself from a moving carriage, and risk getting herself killed by the fall or trampled by traffic. Even if she landed somewhere soft, she would be in the cold, wet night alone and without company—a sure invitation for disaster.

"Where are we going?"

"Did your aunt not write that she was sending me?"

"She said she was sending..." Lucasta tried to recall the letter. It was brief and vague, much unlike her garrulous aunt, who wrote pages of letters crossed so many times that one needed a quizzing glass to read them. And this letter had been sent by penny post, when her aunt would have searched high and low to find someone to frank her letters, even when she knew the recipient could afford the postage.

"She said she would send someone for me," Lucasta allowed.

"And I am taking you to her."

"To Bath?" Lucasta said in alarm. "I am not equipped for travel."

The London-Bath route took three days, and Aunt Cornelia had taught her never to stop at a coaching inn without her own linens. "My benefit concert for the Foundling Hospital is next week." They could never post to Bath and be back in time.

"We're not going as far as all that." Her cousin lifted a threadbare drape from the window, then dropped it before Lucasta could make out the scenery beyond.

She dared not remove her hands to shift the curtain herself, for the rocking motion of the coach had become rapid and treacherous. They were on a broader thoroughfare now, and the coachman was applying the leather, as Jem would say.

Jem. Oh, why couldn't it have been he who summoned her? Why did it have to be her infernal cousin? She'd never liked him, on the rare occasions the Lithwicks had been invited to family events.

The Dowager Viscountess Frotheringale, their grandmother, had never got on with Aunt Cornelia. The break was confirmed when Aunt Cornelia stayed in contact with Felicity, Lucasta's mother, after she'd thrown herself away on a man of foreign birth.

Lucasta's uncle, upon succeeding to the viscountcy and marrying a delicate woman who shared the dowager's scruples about class and breeding, had never acknowledged Lucasta even when Aunt Cornelia insisted she be included at family gatherings. Gale, older and male and the obvious heir, had never taken any notice of her either, a state of invisibility to which she profoundly wished she could return.

"How far are we going?" Lucasta asked, hearing the cry of "Hyde Park Gate!"

Her cousin must realize her consent was required, even to marry over the anvil. He could not force her, and he could not hold her captive. She reached for the door as the driver paused to pay the toll, but her cousin's hand on her arm stopped her.

"We are going to my house outside of town. Aunt Cornelia wanted me to bring you to her in Bath, but with the Season at its peak, I told her you could scarce be expected to take that much time away from your entertainments."

"I do not care about entertainments," Lucasta said. "I do, however, care very much about the benefit concert for the Foundling Hospital, which I am in charge of bringing off. And Aunt Cornelia would never come this far. She dislikes travel."

"She felt it was time to settle one or two things with you," her cousin answered. "And she thought that with the Season and all its eligible bachelors, you might be besieged with offers for your hand. Which in fact I find is the case, is it not?"

"Hardly," Lucasta scoffed. Jem's offer—nay, that was a needle to the heart. A salve for his aunt's ire. He'd told her he meant to make no declaration.

"Trevor Pevensey is interested," Gale said, an edge entering his tone.

"Not in me," Lucasta replied. "He, or rather his father, seems to think that Aunt Cornelia means to settle some of her property on me. I have tried to persuade him he is misinformed."

"Have you succeeded?" Gale demanded. "Or has he exacted a promise from you?"

Lucasta lifted her chin. "I have made no promise. If I marry, it shall be where and when I will. I shall not be any man's means to extract himself from debt."

A gleam of light from a passing carriage caught in her cousin's eyes as he turned toward her. "How fortunate I am not in debt," he said softly. "Would you be persuaded to marry me, Lucasta?"

"I do not see the prospect very likely." Lucasta chose a strategic reply rather the firm rebuttal that rose to her lips. After all, it was dark within the carriage that still swayed dangerously, though at a steadier pace, and she was beginning to feel the chill. Gale was a near stranger, and he was spiriting her someplace unknown without her consent. She did not trust him, but it was not wise to anger him, either.

"My friends will be frantic when I do not return," she realized with a pang of worry. "And the Pevenseys—I cannot image how distraught Cici will be."

"Clara will tell them," Gale said.

"Tell them what?"

He turned from her, pulling the curtain away from the window. "Ah—here we are."

"Where?"

"Why, the house we are to be married from, Lucasta, dear." Gale's grin was wide and not at all benevolent. He took her arm as the coach clipped up the gravel drive and swayed to a stop before a tall set of doors. "My home, and yours as well, once you consent to become my wife."

"I will not consent." She started for the door as it opened, but the large form of the coachman filled it, holding the lantern as he unfolded the steps. Gale spoke as if he didn't care who heard his declaration.

"You will consent, my dear," he said confidently. "You have not heard yet all I can offer you. And all that you stand to lose, dear cousin? How sad it would be to never see your family, or your friends, ever again."

# CHAPTER TWENTY

She was a prisoner, well and truly caught. It mattered little that she was trapped in a gilded cage.

The house, which her cousin referred to as Deer Moor, had been modeled after the neighboring Syon House in its neoclassical design and airy elegance. High-ceilinged rooms with tall windows caught whatever light the cloudy day afforded, and the furnishings dated from the present decade, which was a far cry from the dark Jacobean mass of the Frotheringale seat, not far from Bath.

Lucasta stalked from one drawing room to another, glaring at the large footmen who hovered near each door. They didn't look like footmen. They looked like pugilists, rowdies that Frotheringale had brought in from the nearest village. As she tried anew to approach an outside door that let onto a formal garden, a large man casually moved in front of it.

"You have orders not to allow me out of doors, I take it?"

"Looks like weather rolling in, miss," the not-footman replied, tipping his head in the direction of a lowering cloud. "Best fetch a wrap and an escort."

"Frotheringale, you mean." Lucasta stalked away. At least this footman understood the King's English. The others had merely ignored her or given her curious looks when she railed at them.

Breakfast was brought to her room, a rare treat that somewhat foiled Lucasta's ability to sustain her ire. Her cousin didn't mean to starve her into submission, then. A light supper had been brought to her room the first night, shortly after she arrived, as if she'd been expected. The house had an air of disuse, as if it had not been inhabited in some time, but the housekeeper was perfectly pleasant. She'd brought in a maid—another unheard-of luxury in Lucasta's world—who brushed her hair, delivered a deliciously soft bedgown and wrapper in her approximate size, and even produced a toothbrush and tooth powder.

Perhaps her cousin was trying to woo her consent to marriage by spoiling her with comforts? It was a clever tactic. Deprivation would have stiffened her resolve; largesse confused her. If she were trapped into marriage, forced by law to live in a large, gracious house with servants to attend her, every need provided for—how bad would that be, really?

"At the price of freedom?" Lucasta muttered to herself. "Really, Lucasta, show some fortitude of mind. Miss Gregoire's girls do not succumb to shams nor idle flattery."

Her cousin and jailer had been absent all morning, but shortly after noon she was summoned to a small, bright parlor where a table was laid for a light nuncheon. Lucasta steeled herself against the elegance of the buttery yellow room, the lush paintings and draperies of thick silk damask interwoven with golden threads. She tore her eyes from the pretty prospect beyond the windows, where a paved path wound through tended flower beds to a delicate folly overlooking a small pond.

"Your footmen aren't allowing me outside," she challenged Gale, who put down the slice of bread he was buttering to rise politely at her entrance. The warm, yeasty scent made her stomach growl. "I am your captive, then?"

"You will have your freedom when you consent to be my wife." Her cousin passed the slice to her, then grinned. "Well, as much freedom as the law allows a wife, I suppose."

Lucasta checked the childish urge to throw the bread at his

head. She was a woman of wit and intellect; she would use those weapons. She seated herself in the chair one of the not-a-footman held out—the loquacious one who had prevented her access to the gardens earlier. Lucasta glared at him and pulled the serviette from his hand, spreading it over her lap herself.

"And when I do not consent?"

Gale looked genuinely surprised. "Why would you not? I offer much more than Trevor Pevensey can give you. His father has all but bankrupted his estate, and mine has been wise in his investments." He waved a careless hand in the air, indicating their surroundings. "This could be your home. Or Frotheringale House, or any number of villas and cottages. There's a set of apartments in Bath for town entertainments, and the hunting box in Yorkshire."

"You have nothing but Frotheringale House to offer, and that if the Dowager Viscountess permits, however much you are the heir and its proper possessor," Lucasta said. "The apartments in Bath and the villa in the Lake District are Aunt Cornelia's properties." She knew nothing of the hunting box in Yorkshire, so held her tongue about that.

"Yes." Gale bared his teeth. "And Aunt Cornelia will pass them to us eventually, or perhaps on our marriage, if we can persuade her sooner. And in time, her own manor and its incomes, along with her jointures, her annuities, and her investments will come to you—that is to say, your husband."

Lucasta played her trump card. "I cannot conceive that our grandmother, the Dowager Viscountess, approves of your marrying me. The half-breed? She must wish much higher for you."

Her cousin applied a thick slab of butter to his own bread with decided relish. "I don't think you comprehend how very wealthy our dear Aunt Cornelia is."

Aunt Cornelia was well-settled, that much Lucasta knew. Though Jem's empire out-rivaled Aunt Cornelia's for income, and Jem had built his successes with his own labor and skill, not by coercing landed relatives into marriage.

"I don't think *you* comprehend that her income is hers to

dispose of as she wishes. Her properties she owns in her own right, as a widow. A right married women do not have," she added bitterly.

"I won't trouble your head with talk of jointures and annuities and the rest of the legal terms. Nor of the obligation an aging widow might feel toward her favorite grand-niece, though our grandmother will freely admit she has never understood why you merit that distinction."

Gale smiled blandly and passed her a tray of cold cuts. He was perfectly cordial about it, and nothing else about him was offensive. His hair was neatly trimmed, if unpowdered, and the cut of his morning coat was flattering, the fobs across his waistcoat quite in fashion. Still, Lucasta wanted to bite him.

"All you need concern yourself with, dear Lucasta," he went on, "is that I will allot you a generous amount for your pin money and provide portions for our daughters and younger sons in the marriage settlements. My solicitor is drawing them up as we speak and will be here this afternoon for your signature."

"And if I do not sign?" Lucasta put down her fork before she gave in to the urge to aim it at him.

He bared his teeth again. "Why, I'm quite enjoying our little interlude. There's a village market close by, and the house has gardens. We shan't starve, and after a certain amount of time elapses, and certain assumptions have been made..." He shrugged, though the tight fit of his coat did not allow much range of movement for the casual gesture. "You'll find that marrying me is the best of the other options."

After it went about that she was compromised, her prospects of earning money as a respectable music teacher or governess of her own music conservatory would vanish. Marrying a man who wanted her properties would be the most attractive of possibilities afforded her, by far. Lucasta tried to swallow the burning lump of outrage in her throat.

"I am in charge of a benefit concert for the Foundling Hospital to take place next week." They'd been rehearsing for days. The girls were counting on her. The governors were counting on her to bring in money for new musical programs, new instruments to provide to the blind and disabled children who would not have much other hope for an income. "I cannot miss it."

Gale sank his teeth into a slice of ham, his eyes gleaming. "Then you had best sign those papers this afternoon, hmm?"

One brilliant, unthought-of hope exploded in Lucasta's chest, burning like a phoenix risen from the ashes. Under one condition she could see herself being persuaded to marry her cousin, one benefit that would override all that she would give up. "Would you allow me to sing? In public? On a stage?" she pressed. "For money?"

His dark brows rose to an impossible height. "Absolutely not. No wife of mine will ever put herself out to solicit another man's attentions. Going on stage is as much as advertising that you're for sale."

"It is not," Lucasta muttered, picking up her fork.

She could try to contact her Aunt Cornelia, but what recourse did her aunt have? She did not travel, and so the most she could do was send letters threatening Frotheringale to behave. Gale's mother was dead, and appealing to their grandmother, the Dowager Viscountess, would be of no use. The woman had used every family gathering to heap slights upon the head of her errant daughter Felicity, and then, after Felicity died, Lucasta. The Dowager had not even sent condolences on the occasion of Laurence Lithwick's death.

Jem?

All of Lucasta's being caught in a great gasp of despair at the thought of Jem. Heart, body, and mind, she longed for him to rescue her. But would he act, if she asked him?

He had kissed her senseless at Arendale House, madly, with complete abandon, and she had allowed it. And then she heard nothing from him. Nothing. The actions of a cad in truth, even if he did have the funeral of his grandfather to sort out.

Had she been hoping all along that Smart Jeremy was a better man than she had first thought him? No, she knew he was. She had seen him with the people he loved.

It was only that he did not love *her*.

Her maunderings nearly made her miss her opportunity. Gale excused himself and left, saying he needed to attend to a small matter, and she might wish to freshen herself before the solicitor arrived. He was out the door before Lucasta could find the most freezing way to remind him that, having been borne off without her knowledge and against her will, she was quite lacking in even the barest of necessities.

The maid came to remove the covers and dropped a tray, creating a ruckus. The enormous footman stepped away from the sideboard to lend his aid, and Lucasta lost full moments as she sat there, contemplating her confinement. Her foundlings needed her. Cici needed her. Her friends would be worried sick, and Jem...

Her heart clenched. Jem didn't need her. But she, in some way she couldn't yet define, needed him.

Even if she meant nothing to him, he had roused her heart to love and longings for things she had never thought possible for poor, plain Lucasta Lithwick. Like Pygmalion, he had shaped her, and his love had brought her alive. She wanted to tell him that before they parted for good.

Gathering her shattered wits, she rose, stepped quickly toward the door that opened to the gardens, and slipped out of it.

She was still wearing the silk slippers she'd chosen for Clara Bellwether's party, and she lacked a wrap. From somewhere a maid had produced a day gown, a simple open robe and a zone to wrap about her bodice, along with a cap to cover her hair. Lucasta wondered who the previous owner of the clothing had been, and why Gale should have a woman's frock in the current fashion to hand in one of his homes. Now she cursed the vanity of that unknown woman who had insisted on a tight bodice and voluminous skirts, which tripped her as she rushed down the garden path.

Where, where could she go?

Stables. Gale had brought her in a carriage, and a carriage

meant horses. She could take a horse and ride away—she didn't know where. Anywhere. Safety. Jem. No, Jem wasn't safety. But she could at the least find her way back to the Pevensey house where, if they too meant to trap her into marriage, they at least had not reached the point of holding her prisoner to achieve it.

She stumbled her way to the stables, bruising her feet on the uneven ground and clutching her neckerchief about her to ward off the chill. Then she stood frozen in the hay-strewn corridor of the dim building, blinking at the enormous animals that poked their heads over the half door of their stalls.

They were terrifying. She hadn't done more than glance at the horses when she approached the carriage the evening before, but they were enormous in size, their backs taller than her shoulder. How was she supposed to get herself atop one of these towering creatures? How was she meant to control it when she did? And what if the huge beast threw and crushed her, or worse yet, tried to eat her?

A boy with a grimy cap and the sleeves of his shirt rolled up to his elbows emerged from one of the stalls with a bucket in hand, then paused to gape at her.

"Miss?"

"I need a horse." Lucasta eyed the one closest to her. The gigantic animal, its black eye large and dark, eyed her haughtily in return.

"Ter ride, or to 'itch to th'carriage?"

Lucasta gulped. "To ride."

The boy looked her up and down and appeared as unimpressed by her as was the animal he'd been tending. "Dun 'ave a proper lady's saddle, miss."

She heard a shout from the direction of the house. Her escape had been discovered.

"I don't require a saddle," Lucasta said. "Only—how am I to get up there, please?"

The boy gestured toward the door she'd entered through.

"Mounting block, miss, but you don't mean to ride ole Heller bareback?"

Lucasta squeezed her eyes shut and said a quick prayer for strength. "I mean to ride him any way I must. Hurry!"

The boy led the horse out of his stall by his halter rope. "You 'as to wait, miss, so's I kin get a proper bridle on 'im," the boy said, clearly skeptical of Lucasta's abilities.

It seemed that riding a horse was far more complicated, and far more dangerous, than Lucasta had ever imagined. Oh, for a sedan chair, or a good pair of walking boots! But did she set out on foot, she'd be overtaken in a moment by Frotheringale or one of his buffoons, and she had little doubt that all of them knew how to ride.

"Quickly!" she gasped.

The boy held the animal by its head as Lucasta mounted the block and faced the broad, muscular back. It was covered with short dark hair and smelled feral. Gritting her teeth, Lucasta clambered, after many efforts and in the most ungraceful manner possible, atop its enormous back. The animal shifted and, stifling a shriek, she threw herself prone along the length of its back, clutching at the mane to hold herself atop it.

"All right! Let go!" she called to the boy.

"The bridle, miss!" he replied, astonished. "And I'm sure you want a saddle, then?"

A trio of men appeared on the path to the stable, running toward them. "Let go!" Lucasta shrieked. One of her flailing heels dug into the animal's side.

The horse leapt forward with a power and speed Lucasta had never imagined possible. She swallowed a scream of pure fear as her whole body jolted. She squeezed her eyes shut again, but when she started sliding, she had to open them and clamp her legs on either side of the horse, uncaring of who saw her petticoats. The jounce of the horse's gallop jarred her teeth.

The trio of men fell back as the horse hurtled toward them, and a flare of triumph and relief soared through Lucasta as she shot by.

She was free. She would ride to the nearest house she could find, call out for aid, find some way to transport herself back to London and safety and Jem and—

"Hi, Heller," Gale called. "Whoa, boy! Whoa, Heller."

One of the footmen flung himself into the horse's path, and the animal reared. Lucasta scrabbled for purchase as the world went vertical. There followed an extraordinary weightless sensation, a feeling of being completely untethered, and an astonishing euphoria that washed through her even as her body froze end to end with fear.

She slammed into the ground, her head bouncing off the gravel, and the air left her lungs. A great weight fell onto her chest. She couldn't breathe.

She was going to die here, die in this driveway, without ever hearing her foundlings perform, without ever telling Jem how much she loved him.

Dimly, as through water, her cousin's face appeared above her. "Lucasta!" he exclaimed. "You could have killed yourself!"

*I did*, she tried croaking, but only her mouth moved, not her lungs. She tried sucking in air.

"Here now, that's a high price for your freedom," he scolded, bending toward her.

*It isn't*, Lucasta wanted to say. Miss Gregoire's girls fought until there was nothing left in them. Then Gale bent to lift her from the ground, and she realized that she was not numb after all. A pain she had never felt plowed through her body like a burning comet, and Lucasta Lithwick, who had never been delicate in her life, fainted in her cousin's arms.

# CHAPTER TWENTY-ONE

Jem strode into the parlor of the Pevensey house without waiting for the footman to announce him.

"I've finally heard word of Lucasta," he said before he was fully in the room. He waved the brief, mysterious missive in the air.

Trevor was the only one present, and he tossed his newspaper onto a stack beside him as he rose. "One of your men found her?"

"No, a letter from herself. Or something like it." Jem held out the sheet of parchment, feeling a surge of possessiveness as the other man plucked it from his hands.

Trevor's brows lifted. "It's a poem."

For him. She had written to him. Jem could not check the feeling of jubilation that had filled him since the butler at Arendale House brought the post.

Trevor had, like him, been searching for days, and all her friends were frantic, writing letter after letter to everyone they knew, wearing down the Baron with their pleas to frank each missive in search of Lucasta. But she'd contacted him. Jem.

Though the letter held no information of her whereabouts, it was the first contact they'd had since she disappeared. The first clue.

A poem, by one Richard Lovelace, a poet he'd never heard of, with a brief introduction scribbled above it:

*Milord Payne: you asked once the provenance of my unusual name. It was invented by a poet my father loved, one of those they called the Cavaliers, who fought for King Charles in the civil war. I found it among my cousin's books and thought of you. –L.*

The poem was titled "To Lucasta, Going to the Wars." It was a strange, brief little ballad about a man who was leaving his sweetheart for the honor and glory of battle, and informing her that, rather than lonely or bereft, she ought to feel pleased by his choice and think the better of him for it.

"Tell me not, sweet, I am unkind," Trevor read aloud, his brow furrowing, "that from the nunnery / Of thy chaste breast and quiet mind / To war and arms I fly'—" He looked up. "Have you been corresponding in rubbish poetry, then?"

"No, I'm certain it's a hint. A code of some sort. She's trying to tell us what happened, but she isn't at liberty to speak freely."

Jem paced the parlor, which held the damp chill of the day, a fire not being laid. A poorly painted fire screen, not yet finished, stood in one corner. Jem clenched and unclenched his hands.

"If only his man would let us into the Frotheringale townhouse. I don't believe for a moment that your cousin has been indisposed all this time. I'm sure we could throttle information out of him, if we could only get inside."

"But the men we have watching the house have only seen servants coming and going," Trevor replied, returning to the note. "'A new mistress now I chase'— If it's code, I think she's breaking it off with you, old boy."

A lump like cold pudding quivered in Jem's gut. Lucasta had good reason to fly from him.

He'd behaved abominably when he discovered the agreement she'd made with Judith behind his back. His grandfather the Marquess had suddenly descended on the household, ill and quarrelsome, and the hours of grating lectures from the old man had left Jem so raw that he'd unleashed his unhappiness on Lucasta, punishing her as if she'd been conspiring against him when she'd done nothing but bring tenderness and light and joy to his family. To him.

And after she in graceful forgiveness had stood with him during his grandfather's last awful hours—after she'd gifted them all with that angelic voice, the divinest lullabies to their aching and fearful hearts—he'd lost his head and kissed her in the hallway of his home, making a display of her when any number of people in that over-populated house could come upon them. And one did.

He had much to atone for.

And he had not had her reply to his offer of marriage.

Lucasta was no coward. She would not run away, then pen him a letter telling him coyly not to pursue her. No, she had sent a letter asking for assistance. If she didn't want to consider marriage to him, she would tell him to his face.

His heart seized. She couldn't say no.

Besides, she wouldn't leave her foundlings so close to the date of the concert. Whatever she felt about him—and it tore Jem's insides to know he had not done much to win her esteem—she would not abandon Eliza and the others.

"She's been abducted," he insisted. "Someone scooped her away from Clara Bellwether's *soiree,* and I'm certain it was your mad cousin, that booby Frotheringale. I don't doubt she wrote asking for help in freeing herself from him."

"Then why wouldn't she write me or Cici?" Trevor said in a surly tone. "Her family? Why should she trouble you? No, old man, she's telling you to cut sticks. 'A new mistress now I chase / The first foe in the field.' I rather think she's referring to you as a foe."

"Whoever has her wouldn't let her write to you or your sister," Jem muttered, pacing the small parlor. "But what does she mean by foe? You're the one she doesn't want to marry."

After Lucasta disappeared, Jem learned from Bertie that Baron Pevensey was pressuring Lucasta to marry his son. But Trevor was just as baffled by Lucasta's disappearance as Jem, and when the

Gorgons came to his aid and described how Lucasta had left on the last evening they'd seen her, they had all gone together to confront Clara Bellwether. That good lady protested that she had merely delivered a message passed along to her and had no idea who was behind it, but, she suggested coyly, perhaps Lucasta was not running from marriage but toward it, and they ought to consider whether she had eloped.

As Clara said this while attempting to wrap a hand around Jem's arm, Jem had seen fit to dispense with the courtesies of an exit and merely stalked out of her house. The others followed.

"She doesn't wish to marry you either, if she'd rather have 'a sword, a horse, a shield,'" Trevor grumbled, turning the letter about as if searching for a hidden text.

"Foe—Frotheringale," Jem said. "She's naming him as her abductor."

"How could he have done it, if he's been flat on his back for the past week with an ague, as his butler claims?" Trevor argued. "And if he is behind this, why wouldn't she simply write 'Gale's got me, send help?'"

"Because he's reading her letters, you great sapskull," Jem snapped. "A shield, a shield—what's on the Frotheringale arms?"

"Two crossed swords," Trevor said slowly.

"The sword and shield. And he abducted her by horse." Jem resumed pacing. The exertion helped ward off the chill of the room. "But where would he have taken her? We already have the townhouse being watched. We'd have noted any unusual activity."

"'Yet this inconstancy is such / As you too shall adore,'" Trevor read. He shook his head. "A *congé*, old boy. You gave her a slip on the shoulder, and she's given you your walking papers."

"It can't be a *congé* if she swears she loves me," Jem retorted. He plucked the letter out of Trevor's hands. "'I could not love thee, *dear*, so much / Lov'd I not Honour *more*.' See? She underlined *dear*."

"She also underlined *more*." Trevor's frown cleared suddenly. "Wait. Dear and more—Deer Moor. That's the old villa out in

Fulham. Gale used to have such parties there, you wouldn't—" He cleared his throat as Jem leveled a steely glare at him. "Never mind."

"Then that's where she is." Jem strode into the small, circular foyer, already headed for the door. "She said she found the poem among her cousin's books. I told you this was a message."

"I'll have my horses brought round," Trevor said on his heels. "God's teeth, man, at least let me have a footman fetch my overcoat. It's cold as the devil's tit out there."

"We can take my calash, and your footman better run," Jem said. "He's had her for days, and the concert is Thursday. She must be mad with fear that she'll miss it."

"A benefit concert with a bunch of yodeling orphans?" Trevor slid an elegant walking stick from its holder in the foyer, then pulled both ends, revealing a slender hidden sword. "I fail to see the urgency."

"Then you don't know Lucasta," Jem said. "How far is this Deer Moor, and do you have another of those for me?"

"You are not calling my cousin out." Trevor shrugged into the greatcoat the footman brought him at dead run. Jem retrieved his own overcoat. "He's his mother's only son, the sole heir of that branch of the family, and only a gentleman can challenge—"

Jem waited for the realization to set in and had the satisfaction of seeing his companion scowl as they stepped into a whipping wind. "Damme, you *are* a gentleman," Trevor swore. "I keep thinking of you as the draper."

Jem leapt into his seat, checking that the contents of his interior pocket were shielded from the elements. "I won't bother with calling him out. If he's harmed her in any way, caused her even a moment of fear," he said in a chilling tone, "I'll run the man through on the spot."

"SHE'S NOT HERE!" Frotheringale yelped.

No sword drawing proved necessary. Jem threw the ribbons to the boy who ran to them as the calash bowled up the gravel drive to a neat neoclassical manor, and as he stormed through the door, Trevor beside him, Jem found servants running into and out of the foyer in varying states of distress. Frotheringale appeared on the landing of an upper stair, pulling his hands through his curly hair and making it stand on end.

"We know she's here," Jem said ominously. "She sent me a letter."

"She sent you a poem," Frotheringale said, looking baffled. "Did she write a message inside it? The minx!"

"The poem was the message," Jem said through gritted teeth. "She was here. If you don't produce her, I am going to forget that I lay any claim to civilized status and—"

"She escaped this morning!" Frotheringale blurted. "Sent the maid to say she'd taken ill. I believed it until I finally went up myself to fetch her for tea. She bolted, and the maid covered for her. Off without a character!" Frotheringale shouted into the foyer. "No one's to put in a word for that strumpet, hear?"

"Where," Jem said with deadly calm, "did she go?"

"The maid? Why should I care, when she double-crossed me? And here I'd promised them a bonus if they'd—"

"Lucasta, you bacon-brained idiot!" Trevor shouted. "We didn't pass anyone on the road that could be her. She couldn't have walked clear back to London. It's miles."

"Lucasta isn't afraid of walking," Jem said. He prowled the circular foyer, slapping his driving gloves against his leg. "Which are the main roads that would take her back to London? She'll be trying to return there by any means possible."

"Why wouldn't she take a horse?" Trevor wondered.

Jem eyed him with amazement. "Lucasta is terrified of horses. How can you not know that?"

"She most certainly doesn't ride." Frotheringale ran a hand through his hair again. "The scare she gave me when she fell, and the way she was limping about for days, I'm surprised she's hale enough to walk any—" He trailed off when the faces of both men swung toward him.

"She fell *how*?" Jem asked in a low, dangerous voice.

"She tried to steal a horse." The Viscount cleared his throat. "That is to say, borrow a horse. And—it threw her."

"She was injured?" Hot fury slammed through Jem. He couldn't recall ever feeling this angry in his life. Lucasta had not only been stolen from him, she'd been hurt, and he hadn't even known she was in danger. "Did you seek medical attention? How could you not at least contact her family—"

"Speaking of family." Frotheringale launched an accusing stare on Trevor. "You can't marry her, you clodpate. First of all, you haven't a feather to fly with, and second, I wrote to Aunt Cornelia and—"

"Roads!" Jem roared. "Footpaths! Anything! Where would she have gone?"

Frotheringale blinked and stepped away from the railing as if Jem meant to vault over it and throttle him, though he was still on the floor of the foyer below. "Well. Er. There's the road that goes through Little Chelsea up to Knightsbridge. She might have found some means of transport, a wagon or such."

"I told you, Lucasta does not mind walking," Jem tossed over his shoulder as he headed for the door, the capes of his greatcoat swirling about him. "It's best neither of you come with me," he warned as Trevor turned on his heels and Frotheringale hurried down the stair. "I can't promise I won't thrash the both of you."

"We all want to know she's safe, Rudyard," Trevor replied.

"Payne, now, isn't it?" Frotheringale asked, cramming a hat on his head as he followed them outside. "If you ask me, a royal pain in the—"

"There's not a seat in my vehicle for you," Jem snapped at him.

"I'll bring my own and be directly behind you," Frotheringale huffed. "Really, Payne, you've being awfully proprietary about my cousin, when I'm the man she's going to—"

"*I* am the man she is going to marry," Jem said firmly. "No one else."

He would see to that, he promised himself. Lucasta would marry no one but a man of her choosing. Somehow, he thought desperately, he had to persuade her that that man was him.

~

ROSE HOLLOW LOOKED as lovely as Jem had ever seen it, despite the gray veil of clouds. Something red and ebullient bloomed in the front yard, and the vines twining over the slate bricks of the house gleamed a lush, lovely green. Golden lamplight shone from the parlor window, and as Jem neared, he heard music.

He paused on the stoop. Trevor Pevensey stopped beside him, and Frotheringale, tossing the ribbons over the loop at the gate to keep his horses from wandering off, joined them.

"Where are we?" Trevor asked.

Jem cleared his throat. He hadn't thought this through, or he would have directed the other men elsewhere on their search. But some instinct had insisted he would find Lucasta here, and he had headed for Little Chelsea with no thought in his mind but making certain that she was in one piece. Now, he realized he was exposing both of these men—neither of whom could be called allies—to his precious secret.

"The inhabitants here are—dependents of mine," Jem said, his voice hoarse. "I will thank you to be civil to them."

"Your mistress's little nest?" Frotheringale smirked. Jem answered with a scowl, then lifted the latch on the door.

A siren's voice welcomed him, luring him inside, but not to his doom. Merely to the most beautiful sight he had ever beheld in his life.

Lucasta sat on the sofa where he had seen her perched many times before, but she was encased with children. Tressie sat on one side, Starria another, both so close that Lucasta could not have moved her arms. Hannibal sat on the floor, leaning against her knee, playing with a wooden toy.

Judith sat at the spinet, playing a tune. Mrs. Cadogan sat in a corner, smiling contently over her knitting. And Lucasta's voice filled the room, so clear, so true, so profoundly miraculous that Jem blinked tears from his eyes.

Judith turned toward the door, tilting her head, and beside Jem, Trevor Pevensey let out a low gasp at the sight of her lovely face with its scarred, white eyes. Frotheringale cleared his throat.

Jem ignored all of them. Lucasta broke off in mid-measure as the children's heads swiveled toward the door, and in seconds they sprang from the sofa towards him. But Jem walked through his siblings to get to Lucasta, pulling her with both hands to her feet and into his arms.

"You are in one piece," he said on a rush of relief so strong he thought his ribs might break from it.

"I am," she said, her voice muffled against his shoulder. "What are—"

"You are not hurt?" He slipped a hand into the knot of hair at her nape and gently coaxed her head up so he could scan every beloved line of her face. His heart thumped against his chest. There was a cut on the slope of one cheek and a dark bruise at her temple. She gave him a lopsided smile as he brought his hands to either side of her face, examining her intently.

"No, I—" But the rest of her words were lost as he lowered his head and kissed her.

Her soft, happy exhale told him all he wanted to know. All except one crucial bit of information. He broke off the kiss before he drowned in her and said raggedly, staring into her eyes, "You are not married?"

Those gray-green eyes of hers held the sheen of tears, but the puckering of her lips was an amused smile. "I am not married."

"Thank heavens." Jem sighed. "For you are to marry *me*." And he kissed her again.

"Good heavens, Jem, let Lucasta breathe, won't you?" Judith scolded. "She's had a taxing day, you know."

"Nonsense." Jem lifted his head but refused to release the woman in his arms. She felt so warm, so lusciously right. She was the piece of his life he'd been longing for without knowing what it was he was seeking. He would never let her out of his arms again.

"It's scarcely two miles from Deer Moor to here," he told Judith. "I doubt she even felt exercised."

"It would be a lovely stroll in fine weather." Lucasta glanced over his shoulder. "You brought us company."

"You lied to me!" Frotheringale exclaimed.

"You kidnapped me," Lucasta replied. "Jem, you received my poem?"

"Minx," Frotheringale mumbled. "You told me it was nothing."

"I can't see why you didn't write to me, Lucasta," Trevor said. "Your family. I would have come for you in a moment."

"Yes, and the Baron would have been right behind you with a special license, extorting the vicar that Frotheringale found to marry you to me instead of him," she answered. "I'm not of a mind to be wed yet, thank you."

Jem's heart clenched. Did that include him?

"I have more important things to be concerned about, as I told you again and again, Gale. And that reminds me." She performed brisk, proper introductions all around, then looked up at Jem with an expression that made his insides turn to mash, so eager and imploring was her face. "Can you take me home, please? The concert is tomorrow, and I don't doubt that my foundlings have been completely lost without me, if they haven't given up on me altogether."

"Of course I'll take you." Jem tightened his hold. "The Gorgons—that is, your friends have kept your plans going, but we've all been frantic, to say the least." He faced his sister. "Jude, I've no doubt Mrs. Cadogan whisked off to make up a tea tray, but I really must take Lucasta away at once. The concert is tomorrow and—"

"And I am attending it." Judith lifted her chin and faced him with the sternest, most stubborn look he had ever seen his sweet sister wear.

"Jude, pet, we discussed this—"

"I helped save her," Judith said. "She was wise enough to find us, and we took her in at once. I won't perform if you won't permit it, but I insist on hearing this concert, Jem. Lucasta has put her whole heart into these preparations, and I want to be there myself to see what a marvelous success she shall be."

"Us, too," Tressie said. And his siblings ranged themselves before Judith, in order of descending size.

In his arms, Lucasta grew very still. Jem blew air out of his cheeks.

"I appreciate what you've done, Jude, really, but—it's a very public event. It will be attended by crowds of people. I can't think..."

He glanced toward the men who accompanied him, knowing their reactions would tell him all the reasons he could not want to expose his siblings to polite society. The cruelty, the judgment, and sneers and whispers—he would do everything possible to protect Judith from that, and his other siblings as well.

Trevor was staring at Lucasta. Jem glanced down at her face to see that the two were engaged in some wordless conversation. Trevor's look went from outrage and annoyance to an expression of perplexed doubt. Lucasta answered with a raised set of brows and a tilt of her head in Judith's direction.

Trevor cleared his throat. "Miss Falstead," he said, watching Lucasta's face for direction. "I, ah, hope I am correct in addressing you as Miss Falstead? I wonder if I might escort you to the Foundling Hospital's benefit concert tomorrow night. Though it occurs to me I have yet to procure tickets—"

"I would adore having you as my escort, Mr. Pevensey," Judith said promptly.

Jem narrowed his eyes at her. "Lucasta," he warned.

She squeezed his shoulders. "I can procure tickets for Trevor.

And my cousin will behave in very proper fashion toward your sister. Very proper," she stressed, throwing Trevor a look.

"Of course." Trevor nodded, watching Judith with caution.

But without cruelty. Without any of the sneering or pity that Jem feared. He looked no more nervous than any young man might feel at offering escort to a young lady not known to him, when his cousin had coerced him into doing so.

"And you can escort us!" Tressie announced, striding forward to look up at Frotheringale. "The three of us! Can't you, sir? Whoever you are?"

"I-er-I..." Frotheringale flailed, looking helplessly at Jem.

"What a marvelous idea, cousin," Lucasta exclaimed. "How kind of you to offer. I shall procure the very best seats I can for all of you."

Jem winced. There would be no disavowing the identity of his siblings now. Unfair of her to take advantage of his temporary loss of judgment to achieve what he'd told her he wanted to avoid: thrusting his siblings into the public eye, exposing them to ridicule.

"Judith, you will be envied, you know, showing up on the arm of Mr. Pevensey," Lucasta said conversationally, though she searched Jem's face with her eyes. "He has come to be very much in demand at town events. And Gale, you will be much wondered at, being so cozy with the daughters and sons of a new marquess."

"I—er," Frotheringale managed.

"I don't like it," Jem muttered.

Lucasta squeezed him again, and the warm press of her lithe body against his reminded Jem of how much else he had to be grateful for that day. "You take risks in your business, do you not? You would not have made such a success of things, else."

"That's different."

"I cannot see how," she murmured. "If you prove right, then we will know the truth of the matter. But if I prove right—" She pressed her lips together. "We cannot know until we try."

"I do believe I would enjoy the foundling concert m'self." Mrs. Cadogan bustled in with an overladen tea try. "I don't expect you'll be able to wheedle a ticket for me as well, Miss Lithwick? But if you may, perhaps milord Frotheringale can take Miss Falstead and m'self and the little ones to Arendale House tonight so we may attend the concert tomorrow. I've already set Nurse to packing up some things. And Mr. Pevensey, I imagine you won't rest easy until you've gone with his lordship to deliver Miss Lithwick to her family, but surely you'll take a bit of tea and cakes before you set out?"

Jem released Lucasta with great reluctance as she went to distribute cakes while Judith serenely poured tea. His arms ached as her warmth departed, but the ache in his heart was worse.

He had let Lucasta Lithwick into his life, and she had changed everything. He didn't feel as confident as she was that exposing his siblings to scrutiny would be anything but a humiliating disaster. To trust anyone but himself to make a decision went so profoundly against the grain that Jem had to grit his teeth to keep from shouting them all down until they bent to his will.

But Lucasta was right. He couldn't let fear and bitterness rule him any longer. He had done something he'd swore he'd never do: go daft over a woman. And losing her was the one risk he was not at all willing to take.

# CHAPTER TWENTY-TWO

"Well, that tears it! She's ruined," Lord Pevensey pronounced. "Trevor, you have to marry her now."

Every head in the room swung in Trevor's direction.

There were more people in the Pevensey parlor than it could comfortably hold. Lady Pevensey sat in an upholstered chair with her skirts arranged around her, face as pale as milk. Miss Pevensey and the Gorgons sat in a cluster around Lucasta, whom they had torn from Jem's arms to fuss and fret over the moment the door blew open. He wished he could have kept her by his side, with her strong, quiet warmth.

Trevor lounged against the broad mantel of the fireplace, the boredom on his face a deceptive mask. Frotheringale stood in the doorway, wearing an expression that was angry and ruffled and, now that he was facing the older and far more worldly Pevensey, held dawning realization of the consequences of his acts.

The Viscount had seen Jem's siblings and Mrs. Cadogan safely deposited at Arendale House, though Jem wrestled with the urge to run there himself to shield Judith and his younger siblings from Aunt Payne. But he must leave that battle to Mrs. Cadogan for the moment. He couldn't shift from this spot until he knew Lucasta was safe.

From his position near the window facing the street, he kept trying to catch her eye where she sat on the settee surrounded by her cousin and friends, but she seemed determined not to look at him.

How could she kiss him as she'd done and then ignore him like this? Jem wanted to squeeze her to him until the answers fell out of her. And he wanted to kiss every inch of her weary face. She insisted that the fall from the horse had only left her with a few aches and bruises, and that her cousin, other than restricting her movements and monitoring her letters, had otherwise not been cruel. But to a woman as proud as Lucasta, he knew the enforced helplessness had grated.

And now that she was home, she had gone from the frying pan into the fire, as the saying went.

"Ruined?" Lady Pevensey cried. Her eyes looked wild. "Lucasta?"

His wonderful Lucasta lifted her chin. "I am not ruined in any sense of the term. The only way my cousin inconvenienced me was to keep me from rehearsals for the benefit concert. I scarcely know I'll pull it off now, even with all the work the Gor  my friends have done to move things forward."

The Baron fixed his son with a commanding glare. "Special license, I suppose," he growled. "I'll have to stand the expense, before word gets about."

"Oh, indeed?" Trevor looked as bored as if they were discussing the weather. "And where shall my bride and I live, and on what income?"

"I have not consented," Lucasta said. Lady Pevensey gave a low cry.

"Ask her Aunt Cornelia how, why don't you?" the Baron replied to his son as if there were no one else in the room.

A babble of voices followed this remark, Lucasta's clearest among them, but Jem broke over the noise with a carrying tone.

"Lucasta is contracted to marry me."

Every neck in the room swiveled toward him. Among them,

Lucasta looked most surprised, Trevor interested, Frotheringale outraged, and the baron furious.

The Gorgons exchanged a fleeting look that Jem could only describe as knowing, while Cecilia Pevensey's mouth fell open with astonished delight.

"You?" Lady Pevensey gasped.

"She cannot marry without the approval of her family," the Baron said coldly.

"On the contrary, I am past the age of consent and therefore at liberty to give my hand where I wish." Lucasta met the Baron's glare with one of her own.

"You'll marry Trevor!" the Baron roared. "Why else would I bring you here for the Season and spend money on your food and entertainment? You'll show some gratitude, you insolent chit, and you'll bring your fortune to my son, or by God I'll see you cast out onto the street! And you'll do it, you coxcomb, or find yourself without a roof over your head," he addressed his son and heir.

Trevor appeared unmoved by his father's blustering, though the Gorgons watched the Baron's tantrum with great interest.

"And what about me, Father?" Cecilia asked, her voice small and plaintive. "Must I marry as well to retain a roof over my head?"

Frotheringale broke in before the Baron could formulate a reply. "Lucasta will marry me. She spent a week at my house with no chaperone. You yourself said she is ruined."

"I am not ruined," Lucasta exclaimed. Jem watched her annoyance turn to alarm as she realized no one was listening to her.

He reached into the pocket of his beautifully tailored coat and withdrew a piece of parchment. "Lucasta and I are precontracted," he said. "I have the settlement papers here. They require only her signature."

Utter silence followed this revelation.

"Papers?" Lucasta said blankly.

He nodded, holding her eyes. "The afternoon we—that I proposed. The same afternoon my grandfather—" His throat tightened. The haste would betray how badly he wanted her. "The solicitors were already there, you remember. So before they left, I, er, asked them to draw up a marriage settlement."

The tightening around her eyes was not an indication of transports of joy. "How curious you did not discuss this with me," she said.

Because he'd been terrified she might refuse him. He'd spent days racking his brains for arguments as to what he could offer, and before he had gathered the courage to approach her, she was gone.

"Give me that." Frotheringale snatched the paper from Jem's hand and, before anyone could stop him, tore the parchment in half. "There." He tossed the pieces to the floor. "You are freed from your contract, Lucasta, and can now marry me."

"My solicitor of course retained a copy for his own records," Jem said. "With the date attached, so there will be evidence for the magistrate, if anyone wishes to inquire, that our contract precedes your abduction, Frotheringale."

"Trevor," the baron ordered, "stop him. Lucasta is contracted to marry you. Your agreement was far earlier—"

"Lucasta cannot marry Trevor." Lady Pevensey's voice shook with strong emotion. "Her birth is not—" She faltered, then clenched her hands in her lap as if giving herself strength. "Her birth is not equal to his."

"I don't care what sort of low immigrant her father was," the Baron exclaimed. "As your sister's daughter, she stands to inherit your Aunt Cornelia's estate. That one—" He flung a hand in Frotheringale's direction— "already has an estate of his own. No reason he needs to get the whole pudding."

"Lucasta can inherit nothing! She is illegitimate."

Every neck in the room swiveled toward Lady Pevensey, who covered her face with her hands.

Jem watched the color bleed from Lucasta's face.

"What?" She struggled to breathe. "Laurence Lithwick was—not my father?"

Her ladyship pressed her hands over her eyes. "He was your father," she said with a moan. "But I gave birth to you."

The stark, awful look on Lucasta's face made Jem want to pull her into his arms. He wanted her to never have reason to wear that look of betrayal and horror again.

Her friends, ringed around her, grasped her hands, forming a wall of support before he could step forward. Even Cecilia reached out and clung to her cousin.

If he wanted to win Lucasta Lithwick, Jem realized, he would have to prove to her that his love was as steadfast, deep, and true as that of her loyal friends. And that he, too, would do whatever he could to protect her.

Was his love true? In the stunned silence that pervaded the room, and the weight of what this revelation meant for Lucasta, Jem finally saw his own heart clearly. He could be forgiven his slowness, he thought, as he'd never been in love before.

His siblings brought him joy, and his obligations to them were no burden. His mother had provided him shelter, protection, and affection, and he'd loved her as only a son could. But his relationships with women had always been passing, fraught with caution and to some extent a masquerade on both parts. He'd never been willing to open himself heart and soul to a woman.

Lucasta Lithwick deserved nothing less. She herself would love whole-heartedly, an authentic, lasting, selfless love. She would be the companion he had never dreamed he might find. And she had his devotion for his whole life, whether she wanted it or not. He would never find another woman like her.

But could he, heir to a marquessate, marry a woman of illegitimate birth? He had an obligation to his family. Could he still claim the woman he loved?

The Baron groped for a chair, and finding none, sat down on a dainty stool meant for a much smaller person. "Lucasta is yours?" he said, horrified. "But that means..." His scowl deepened as he thought. "Trevor isn't related by blood. They can legally marry."

"It isn't as you think, Peter," his lady whispered. "Aunt Cornelia knows. A bastard cannot inherit, and she'll never leave her estate to a natural child. You may be sure of that."

"What possessed you?" The Baron stared at his wife as if he had never seen her before. His lip curled in contempt. "Patience! That ragtail vicar? Your sister's husband?"

His wife gave him a pleading look. "Must we discuss it here?"

"If you can make such a declaration before this lot, you can damned well explain yourself!"

Lucasta stared at the woman she had thought her aunt. Jem studied her as well, but aside from their height and perhaps a certain natural aloofness, he could see no blood resemblance.

Lady Pevensey's round face had turned doughy with indulgence and lined with an expression of bitter self-interest. Lucasta, in contrast, was refined and elegant, graceful in bearing and manner. Her straight, broad nose and the clean, firm line of her jaw reflected her strength of character and spirit, while the softness of her lips and eyes showed her compassionate heart and gentle nature. He had heard her speak of her father with adoration, but her mother—or the woman she had thought her whole lifetime was her mother—Lucasta had revered as a near saint. This would be a blow beyond fathoming.

"We can leave, if it will be helpful," the Luneberg girl offered, "but Lucasta will tell us everything anyway."

Lucasta, nodding, found her voice again. "That is true." Her hands grasped her friends' tightly.

"And me as well," Cecilia said, placing her hand atop those of the other girls.

Her ladyship looked only at her husband, her expression desperate and pleading. "You'd broken things off with me," she wailed. "You had told me when things began that since you had your heir, you and Cecily meant to go your separate ways. But then she found out about me and insisted you reconcile. I thought—" She gulped, the tendons standing out in her pale throat. Her eyes bulged with fear. "I thought, if there were a child...you could not cast me away."

"But my father?" Lucasta exclaimed. "He and my mother were married. Unless my birth date is a lie as well?"

Lady Pevensey shredded a ruffle on her skirt with nervous fingers. "I tricked him," she said, staring at the ruined lace. Her voice was low and hollow. "He was the nearest thing to hand, and I knew he'd never speak of it. Felicity and I looked much alike at the time, and in the dark, when I had encouraged him to tipple, which he never did..."

She closed her eyes for a long moment, then cast a look of piteous appeal at her husband. "When you wouldn't take me back, I had to crawl to Laurence and tell him, tell my sister what I had done. They promised to take me in and claim the babe as their own. Felicity was so desperate for a child, she would forgive me anything, and she always said it—it helped her that it was Laurence's child after all."

"You told me it died," the Baron said, still wearing a look of horror. "When I told you I would support it, but I could not divorce Cecily."

His wife nodded, her face crumpling. "I-I wanted to tell you the truth when you finally proposed to me, after Cecily died. But Felicity was ailing, and they thought of Lucasta as their own, and we could finally be together in the open... I saw no reason to make it known."

"No reason?" Lucasta echoed. "No reason *I* might have been told the truth?"

Her ladyship refused to look at Lucasta, addressing the baron in a pleading voice. "Aunt Cornelia visited once when I was... expecting, and she caught on. She guessed at the whole of it— You know what a fearful dragon she is for meddling. She promised to keep quiet, because of the shame, but I was never in her favor again."

"He never told me," Lucasta said, bewildered. "Not even on his deathbed."

"That was the condition upon which he let me live with them, when I had no one else to support me," Lady Pevensey said. "I couldn't tolerate my mother. She's a worse harridan than Cornelia. I won't apologize for that," she added, casting a look at

Frotheringale that held more spirit than she'd shown during the entire interview.

"No, you've got the right of it," Frotheringale agreed, wide-eyed. "Frightful harpy, m'grandmother is."

"I promised Laurence that I would regard the child as wholly his and Felicity's." Finally, her ladyship looked at Lucasta, or at least in her vicinity of her chin. "He didn't want anything to shadow her joy in having a babe of her own to cherish. It was no loss to me. I was never motherly." She shrugged.

"That is true," Lucasta said. "Felicity Lithwick was my mother in every way that mattered. A child could not ask for better parents than I had."

The baron, Jem thought, looked like he had just been given a facer. The man dragged a hand through his hair. "We'll say none of this to anyone," he said, glancing around the crowded room. His eyes lit on his son, still lounging against the fireplace mantel, and the Baron watched him as if he now questioned even Trevor's existence. "If we keep it hushed up," he said slowly, "perhaps we can persuade Cornelia to leave Lucasta something anyway..."

Trevor straightened. "What if I agree with your wife and consider her bastard child beneath me?"

"It doesn't matter to *me*," Frotheringale said while the Baron spluttered. "I'll still have you, Lucasta, even if you're to inherit nothing."

"Has everyone forgotten," Jem said finally, "that Lucasta is to marry *me*? If you force her into anything, Pevensey, I'll bring a suit against you." He fixed a sharp eye on the Baron and then his son, the look he gave merchants he suspected of cheating him. "And you as well, Frotheringale."

The Viscount paled under this threat, and the Baron gnashed his teeth. Trevor smirked. All three men understood that, with his deep pockets, Jem could wage a legal war that could last years and bankrupt them even if he didn't win.

Lucasta rose. She looked ashen, but she held her chin high.

When Jem went to her side she did not turn him away, but she didn't look at him, either.

"If you will all excuse me," she said, her voice steady and clear, though her lips trembled. "I have had a very trying—" She couldn't finish the thought. Jem slipped his hand beneath her elbow and felt her shaking like the whiskers on a hare.

Everyone rose but her ladyship, who sat with her eyes fixed on her husband, frantic fingers mangling the lace of her skirt. Cecilia went to her brother, whispering something in his ear, while the Gorgons walked with them into the small entryway.

"We must discuss your forfeit, Queen Lucasta," one of them said lightly.

"Not now, Annis," Selina scolded.

Jem, with effort, drew his gaze away from Lucasta's drawn, battered expression. "Forfeit?"

"For the first among us to accept a proposal of marriage," Annis said.

"She must sing. In public. For money," Minnie affirmed.

"No," Jem said instantly. "Absolutely not."

"Really?" Annis lifted her eyebrows in the haughtiest possible expression.

"You won't allow it?" Lucasta gazed into his face with a questioning frown.

She looked at him as if she could see everything inside: his tangled guilt and loyalties about his family, the burden of worrying about their fates, the constant wearying decisions to be made about the business.

The fear that, with this new revelation, he could not in good conscience give Lucasta Lithwick his honorable name.

And the deeper, larger fear that, after all they'd been through, she would not find him the man she wanted, nor the man she wanted him to be.

No better than he was. Hadn't she said that from the very beginning?

"Allow what?" Jem asked with apprehension.

"Allow me to sing. In public venues. Before an audience."

His heart sank, and he pressed on her elbow to encourage her to continue up the stairs, away from the others. She went, pausing on a small landing above. Through an open door he saw a small parlor filled with more musical instruments than he knew how to name.

The room breathed Lucasta in every aspect, from the soft watercolor landscapes on the walls to the way the drapes were thrown back to admit light, the bundles of music heaped in baskets and neat piles, with here and there a dried flower adding a delicate fragrance to the air. It was completely expressive of her mind, tidy but not rigid, and her personality, warm, gracious, welcoming, but also disciplined, ambitious, and possessed of a talent he couldn't begin to comprehend.

"Lucasta." He faced her, placing his hands on her upper arms. She was lithe and firm and strong, yet supple to the touch, and the urge to pull her against him was unbearable. "I will offer you the protection of my name. I will give you every material comfort you ask for. I—It matters not that your birth was irregular." How could he possibly hold that against her, when he had accepted his natural born siblings into his home and his life?

"But." He drew a deep breath.

She held her eyes steady on her face, her expression open and watchful, the green in her eyes catching the light. But all the same he felt the tension in her, as if she were bracing herself for news she could not like.

"I cannot allow my family to be subject to scrutiny or public ridicule," he said quietly. "I have explained all this to you before. Judith is so fragile, and my father's children— All they may depend on is the life I can give them. I walk a fine line already, being born a draper. If my wife were to be notorious, to be thought a public woman—you know what the perceptions are," he said desperately.

"I wish they were different, Lucasta, I truly do. But this is the world we have, and even if I am to inherit an estate someday, my business is our livelihood. If we are scorned or looked down on, if no one patronizes my shops, we are destitute, and my whole family will suffer. Please understand."

He rushed to say the last words, pleading for her not to withdraw. But he saw her face tighten, the lines around her eyes, her nostrils, her mouth, even the tendons moving in her neck as she swallowed. She drew her head back and looked him in the face. The expression in her eyes nearly killed him.

"I do understand," she said quietly. "I respect your devotion to your family, Jem. I do. I admire your dedication to your business. It is one of the many things I adore about you. So practical. So determined. You are a kind, deeply moral man, and your mind is as good as your eye for fashion."

She laid a hand against his cheek. She'd stripped off her gloves, and her palm was cold, the pulse in her wrist fluttering against the corner of his lips. He turned his head slightly and kissed the delicate skin, trying at the last to coax the words he wanted from her. She drew a deep breath and dropped her hand.

"I have had a week to think deeply about what I want from my life, Jem. About what marriage would mean to me. What *you* mean to me."

He reached for her hand, drawing it stubbornly to his chest so she could feel the wild beat of his heart. "You love me."

She nodded. "I do. I never expected to feel this way about anyone. I didn't know that I could. I adore you with everything in me. I suspect that I always will." She spoke in a low tone, steady and firm, but her eyes glistened with tears. "But I have also, in these past weeks, come to understand myself more clearly. And I need to use my voice."

"You may," he said, the words spilling out of him. "Of course. However you wish. Benefit concerts, and performances for our friends, and even now and then a private engagement. Your voice is a miracle. Your voice is what truly made me see you." He clasped her hand to his chest with both hands. "I want to use your voice. Always."

"But not as a career," she said quietly. "Not in public."

"It doesn't have to be that, does it? There are other ways."

She tugged gently at her hand. He refused to release her.

"It is my one great dream, Jem. It is the one thing that has always been mine, when everything else was taken from me. My music. It is not just my greatest pleasure—it is my purpose." She tugged more firmly, and the tears spilled from her eyes. "If you cannot share my great dream, Jem, then I cannot give my life to you."

"I can give you music," he insisted. "Lessons with friends, like you did for Judith and Bertie."

"A music conservatory of my own?" she asked gently.

"You won't need it. I will provide for you. A marchioness has no reason to have a music conservatory."

"But I want to teach. I want to help others pursue their passions and use their gifts. I want to share music with them. And I want to perform." She wiped the tears from her cheeks with her free hands. "I didn't understand how badly I want to sing in this concert with the girls until Gale kept me prisoner and I thought I wouldn't get back in time."

"I'll build you a stage of your own at Arendale House," Jem said wildly. "You can have a private concert every night."

"And sing only by your permission. I don't want to have to choose, Jem," she said, her voice catching. The tears fell freely. "But if I cannot have a husband and also sing, then I do not want a husband. Not even you." She held her hands over her face a moment, then faced him, wiping the tears from her chin.

"I love you, Jeremiah Falstead, upon my soul I do. But I will not dally with you, and I cannot marry you." She passed a hand over her eyes.

"I have one request of you, however." She took a deep, bracing breath. "Please do bring your family, all of them, to the concert tomorrow. I promised they might hear it, and I want to say a proper goodbye. I shall send over the tickets."

She went into the music room and closed the door. Though he stood for several moments, not a sound emerged.

His guts had been torn out of him and flung to the ground, like a traitor disemboweled before his execution, but his skeleton still worked. Jem walked down the stairs, each jarring step telling him that he did not dream, that Lucasta Lithwick had declined his hand and wounded his heart to a depth he could not even begin to fathom.

Her friends waited for him on the small landing, watching.

"Turned me down." His voice rasped like dried flax. "After all I can offer her..."

"Can you give her her great dream?" Selina asked quietly.

Jem stared at her with bewildered eyes. "To sing," Minnie explained.

Jem shifted his gaze to stare out the small window, where the sky had finally delivered on its miserable promise and released rain. "I cannot," he said helplessly. "In my position— I have more than my own wishes to consider."

Annis nodded, her gaze full of compassion. "Lucasta understands that."

Jem looked back and forth between their faces. These women understood something about Lucasta that he didn't, and might never. Perhaps it was a fundamental difference in the way men and women were built. He could give her a lifetime of ease and protection, his utmost fidelity and devotion, and she wanted something he couldn't comprehend.

He looked at the women once more. The Luneberg, the daughter of a German duke, was a foreigner and an outsider on British shores. The same with Voronska, daughter of a Russian count. Miss Humby, a mix of races like his younger siblings, at least had the benefit of married parents.

But all three of them were considered, by those of the highest *ton*, exotic oddities. They were watched, speculated about, insulted. All the things he wanted to avoid for his own siblings, these women endured.

And rose above.

"I never meant that comment about the zebra to be a slur," Jem said to Selina. "Those stripes were vile, and I never considered your parentage. I ought to have. I am sorry."

She gave him a sweet smile. "I accept your apology."

He didn't deserve her easy forgiveness. "But I would never have chosen to subject you to shame or ridicule."

She shrugged. "You didn't. Not from anyone who mattered, at any rate."

Jem blinked at this, taken aback by her indifference. To not care if she were not admired, to not be watching every moment to see if she were being accepted by people around them, conforming to those invisible but very firm lines about what was *ton* and what was not—

"I named you the Gorgons," he said slowly.

"We suspected it was you." Annis nodded.

Again he felt the need to explain himself. "Ashley was outraged by something you'd said, and you were calling yourselves Miss Gregoire's Girls—"

"Ashley," Minnie hissed.

"But none of you cared," Jem realized. "You went to the parties anyway and made your own group and enjoyed yourselves hugely, and you never cared what others thought."

He simply couldn't wrap his head around the idea that it was possible to step away from that dance of courting attention and acceptance. Perhaps it was the draper in him, a shopkeeper after all; he had to win customers, he had to be liked.

So many times he'd heard his mother weeping over a slight one of his father's acquaintances had dealt her. Eventually she stopped going to the parties and the balls and the theater and the pleasure gardens. She focused on the business and her children, and her husband went his own way, letting her hard work fill the family coffers while he enjoyed his status and her income.

Jem had courted society's approval telling himself it was for the sake of his business. He had said as much to Lucasta. But all along, he'd wanted to show that world that his mother really *had* been good enough for them. That he, as her son, was good enough for them.

He'd hidden his sister's blindness and his illegitimate younger siblings because he was worried *he'd* no longer be approved of, and if society rejected him, they were rejecting his mother all over again. He had been exerting himself to the utmost trying to please people who were never going to find him worthy.

He'd just let the most miraculous woman he was ever going to meet refuse him—the woman made for him in every respect, the woman he wanted to spend his entire life with—because he was worried what other people might think of her wanting to sing. When Miss Gregoire's girls, the Gorgons, didn't care whom they pleased. They followed some inner guide, and Lucasta, especially, followed some lode star that shone from within.

What was *his* great dream? Jem wondered. What was the one thing he would give up anything else for, approval and acceptance be damned?

The girls still stood on the landing with its inset alcove and the absurd little trinket on display there. Traffic moved along Caroline Street, tousled by the wind. The girls watched him curiously.

"You are attending the concert tomorrow, I presume?" Jem rasped.

Annis gave him a broad grin. "We are performing. We always perform in the concerts Lucasta organizes. We have since our first year at Miss Gregoire's."

Minnie preened, and Selina, gulping, nodded.

"I have no right to ask a boon of you, and you have no reason to indulge me." It took all his courage to say these words. "But my sister will be there. She does not move in society much, and—because she is blind and very shy, I fear she will not make friends. You seem to have taken in Bertie, and I hope—I may—introduce you?"

"We shall be very happy to make the acquaintance of your sister, Lord Payne," Minnie said politely. She shared a look with her friends that said, whatever question they had for him, it had not yet been answered. "And now, if we might ask you to remove yourself from the stairs, we need to see Lucasta."

"Oh. Of course."

They'd not been waiting on the landing to offer support as he groped his way to understanding. They waited because, given how narrow the stairs were, they couldn't get past him. His heart turned to pulp, Jem located his hat and cloak and a boy to bring round his carriage. He needed to go to Arendale House and tend to his family.

He wanted to be upstairs in the music room with Lucasta. But her friends had the right to comfort and console her and hear every detail of her captivity, the details he was certain she'd kept from him.

Jem didn't have that right to her comfort and confidence. Her friends had earned her trust and loyalty.

He hadn't. The knowledge brought him lower than anything had since his mother died, taking away the last person in the world he had to depend on.

# CHAPTER TWENTY-THREE

"Miss Lithwick." Benedicta leaned around the partition that separated the door at the top of the stairs from the benches surrounding the magnificent pipes of the chapel's organ. The girl had appointed herself junior stage manager and had been moving throughout the chapel all day, seeing that Lucasta's orders were carried out.

People filled the lower and upper galleries of the beautiful wood-paneled room, and all fell silent as one of the Hospital's governors took the pulpit and welcomed their guests. There were more people than Lucasta could have dreamed. Enough people to make her concert a resounding success if the performers pleased, and enough to make her a memorable failure if anything went awry.

Lucasta bent to hear the girl's message and had to ask her to repeat it. "Someone wants to request a change to the program," Benedicta said again.

"What? Now? We've nearly begun!" Lucasta hissed. "It will be impossible."

"It's the governors asking," Benedicta explained. "Some special guest. They want to insert two pieces after the intermission."

Lucasta's heart twisted into a knot of worry. A change to the program would be taken in stride by the experienced performers, save perhaps Signor Marchesi, who had proven very exact about the accommodations he needed in order to perform. But a disruption might confuse her foundlings and throw them into disorder.

That was the reason that, earlier that day, when it had come time to ask for a change in the program for her own benefit—so she might perform along with her foundlings—Lucasta's courage had failed her. There was simply too much fuss already, with her being gone so long and having to make so many decisions at the last minute. In all fairness, she couldn't burden everyone who had helped her with a request to showcase her vanity.

There would be other times to perform. And she would. Performing was all she had left to her now, after she'd sacrificed everything else. She wouldn't have Aunt Cornelia's inheritance, not that she'd hoped for it anyway, but most certainly not now that she was revealed to be illegitimate. Trevor and Gale had both agreed there would be no more talk of marriage. She was free of their pursuits at least.

And she had already rejected Jem, though it made her feel she'd drunk acid. Every other minute, she regretted her decision and wanted to send him a note vowing she didn't know what had possessed her and she'd be happy to be his bride. She'd turned down the opportunity to spend her life with the man she *wanted* to spend her life with, and for what? Nothing but speculation and the fear that she might grow bitter and resentful if she gave up her ambitions to marry him.

How foolish could she be? The chances that she would make her living on the stage were slim to none. Competition was fierce, that life was difficult, and she had no highly placed patrons to use their influence on her behalf. She could indeed found a music conservatory, and with no husband to concern her she could run it as she wished. She might always be poor and struggling in that life; would she really choose that struggle over ease and comfort and wedded bliss with Jem?

But when she opened her mouth to say the words that might

bring him back to her, she couldn't force them out. Something in her *knew* that she was not the kind who could nobly self-sacrifice to make others happy. She could say she would give up her dream of performing in order to marry him, and any girl with two wits to rub together would.

But Lucasta knew herself. She knew, lamentably, her own inability to bend. And she also knew what she believed, and what —and whom—she loved.

Her Aunt Patience had confessed openly that she was Lucasta's mother, but Lucasta's heart had not softened toward her, other than to pity the actions of a desperate woman, grasping to keep the man she loved. The news changed nothing about her childhood nor her feelings about it.

Felicity and Laurence Lithwick had been her loving and devoted parents. Felicity Lithwick had been the tender bosom Lucasta sobbed her childhood woes upon. Felicity Lithwick had held her infant hand as she learned to walk. Felicity Lithwick had taken Lucasta to the church and waited patiently for hours, knitting and talking with fellow parishioners, while Lucasta practiced on the church organ.

Felicity Lithwick had sewed Lucasta's clothes, blistered her cuts and bruises, cooked her favorite pudding for her birthday, sat up with her when the night terrors came, and gave her a mother's sacred blessing on her deathbed, before the fever left her insensible. Nothing about the reality of her birth made Lucasta feel any closer to Patience Pevensey, who had been a distant, disapproving, unpleasant part of their household for so many years.

And if she couldn't find a bit of softness in her heart for the woman who had given her to her true parents, Lucasta knew she was right in believing that she would eventually come to resent giving up her musical ambitions for Jem. She loved him and she would love their family, but something in her would sicken and die if she could not reach for her heart's deepest desire.

She would become spoiled and bitter, unable to fully appreciate or enjoy anything around her, just like Patience had in the years when the Baron had rejected her. And she would be no fit mother, no true wife for Jem, if she begrudged what she had given up.

Knowing she'd hurt Jem made her limbs heavy and she moved as if in a fog, but the preparations had been finished, and the concert was beginning. All she needed was to keep moving until the night was over, and then she would deal with the next day when it came. The distractions of the concert held off the full realization of the blow she had dealt her own heart. In spurning Jem she had cut off a limb, and in time the full pain would hit her.

Yet she had been right to sever herself. She couldn't offer him what he truly craved, acceptance and belonging in the *haut ton*. She was the daughter of an immigrant vicar and now she wasn't even of respectable birth, the bare least he could ask for in a wife. She would struggle to become a hostess and a marchioness and a peer's wife with causes and influence of her own.

He would be disappointed and he would come in time to resent her for these things, when he put so much stock in the opinions of society. She couldn't bear losing his regard. And if she wasn't willing to make one small sacrifice—of a possibility only, not even something she possessed already—to be the wife he wanted and needed, then she didn't deserve him.

The knowledge hurt, and it would hurt all the more deeply when she had time to analyze it. For now she walked about with the blade buried in her heart, suspecting that blood and pain would follow when she had time to yank it out.

Signor Marchesi strode onto the balcony overlooking the chapel and the crowd gasped to see him. He nodded and dipped his head, acknowledging the prolonged applause. Lucasta took the opportunity to whisper to Benedicta, "What instruments will we need for the new performers?"

"The pianoforte only, they said. The pieces aren't long. But the guests are special."

Lucasta sighed. "Very well. We'll have one of the governors

announce the change to the program after the intermission. The news will go over better coming from one of them."

Signor Marchesi began to sing, and for all the hurt that awaited her later, the calm joy that flooded her told Lucasta she'd made the right decision. Music was her life's blood.

Being part of this performance, even in the smallest way— seeing the joy on the faces of her foundlings, who lined the benches of the organ balcony with their neat gowns and caps and white scarves pinned to their bodices—seeing the expressions on the faces of the audience visible within the circle of golden light cast by the many-candled chandeliers—Lucasta knew that everything she'd sacrificed was worth it to have her music. Jem had told her it would be a sin to hide her gifts from the world, and he was right.

She would miss Jeremiah Falstead, that she knew. Not a day of her life would go by that she wouldn't regret losing the chance to be with him. But giving up her voice to be the quiet, mannerly lord's wife, to be constantly concerned over what would make her talked about, to pursue her music only as a hobby or an entertainment and put it aside as if it were not her breath and her soul—that would hurt worse. At least she had spared them all that.

She applauded more loudly than anyone when Signor Marchesi finished, and did she imagine that he looked directly at her and grinned? No, more than that: the great castrato who had thrilled Europe and entertained kings looked at Lucasta and *winked*.

He was enjoying being the centerpiece of the concert, and he accepted Lucasta's undisguised admiration as his due. She had scheduled him to sing again, opening the second act after their intermission, so she hoped mightily he would not be put out by the sudden change to the program. She was sure he was preparing an encore as well, fully expecting that some fans in the audience would call for his return at the end. He had even suggested he might sing her English arrangement of the Italian solo he had performed at the end of *Ifigenia*, to Lucasta's great delight.

She pushed Benedicta's chair to the keyboard of the great organ, for the girl had designated herself the turner of pages. The girls who were singing took their places, and Hester, tallest among them, filled her lungs with air. She had a short solo at the end of the next song, an honor she had fought for fiercely.

Lucasta played the opening chords of the hymn they had rehearsed and the vibrations of the great organ blasted away the fog that had descended around her heart. She was where she belonged, and she knew it. As her darling foundlings lifted their voices in the first verse, all of them singing their hearts out and most of them in tune, she didn't even try to stop the tears that traced down her face.

Oh yes, she would miss Jeremiah Falstead. That loss would be a constant ache. But she had her friends, she still had some family, and she had her music. It was more than any woman had a right to dream.

Benedicta sang mightily into her ear, turning pages at just the right time, and as soon as she could steady her voice, Lucasta joined them in song. And in blending her voices with theirs, drawing the full-throated sounds from the organ that vented straight to heaven, Lucasta felt she stood in one of the moments of complete enchantment that came so rarely in life, but made an impression on the memory that would never fade. Whatever else she lost or was denied in her life, she had this perfect, fleeting happiness.

The time came for Hester to sing the last verse, and the girl froze. She turned wide and terrified eyes on Lucasta, her voice a thin and nearly inaudible thread. Fabric rustled as people shifted on the benches, and Lucasta, without thinking, leapt into the breach. She repeated the measure and began the verse, smiling in encouragement, and the girl's eyes shone with relief. Hester relaxed and they sang together, Lucasta's stronger voice twining and lifting around the girl's younger, untrained one. The poignant beauty of the stanza and the soft sounds of the organ carried the rich sound throughout the room.

The applause when their piece ended was nearly as enthused

as it had been for Signor Marchesi, and the looks of amazement on the faces of her foundlings turned to delight as they realized the accolades were for them. Whatever the society papers had to say about the evening, for her and for her orphans, the night was a success they would never forget.

Jem was wrong to put so much stock in what the *haut ton* had to say. Lucasta understood that his livelihood depended on pleasing his customers, but she couldn't live to please others. She wanted to uplift people through her music, of course, but the music she created would be her own. This she had learned from Laurence Lithwick and Miss Gregoire. She would live by her own light and take the consequences as they came.

Eliza stepped forward to bring Lucasta the violin and bow, trailing one hand along the railing until she reached the center of the gallery. The room fell completely silent and, as she turned to face the audience, the girl's face went white. She had taken care with her gown and her neckcloth was neatly tied, and one of the older girls had done her hair up in curls beneath the plain white cap.

"There are an awful lot of people here, Miss Lithwick," Eliza whispered.

"Yes, we have sold a great number of tickets," Lucasta whispered back. "And if some of them make extra donations, as the governors may request, just think of the benefit to the Hospital. And you, my dear, have a part in it."

"I shall do my best, then," little Eliza said, and lifted her chin.

Lucasta tried to focus on the girl, but the tune was a simple one she could play in her sleep, and her eyes wandered over the audience, as much of it as she could see. Jem and his family were out there somewhere.

Eliza's voice was small but lovely. Lucasta saw a few people, realizing the girl was blind, nudging their neighbors and pointing. But the audience maintained a respectful silence, listening, and the applause when Eliza ended her simple tune filled Lucasta's heart.

Eliza gave a brief curtsy, then took Lucasta's arm to walk away. The girl's face glowed with delight.

"I did all right, Miss Lithwick?" she whispered as she took her seat.

Lucasta swallowed down a rush of tears. What a watering pot she was tonight! But her heart swelled to see the audience so generous and attentive. No one had booed Eliza or thrown fruit, as often happened in the theater houses. They were being kind.

If this night was even a moderate success, which was as much as she dared hope, Lucasta would have the beginnings of a reputation upon which to start her conservatory. She would have some chance at the future she was meant to have, a future in music.

The audience murmured as a vision of operatic splendor swept onto the balcony. Margaret Kennedy, who on stage was often consigned to play breeches roles because of her singing range and her build, had chosen to wear a gown overwhelming in its ornateness. A green bodice and overskirt shot through with silver thread caught the candlelight and shimmered as she moved. The intricate embroidery covering the overskirt matched that of the satin underskirt, thick with gold, red, and blue. The arms of the gown were lavishly covered with rosettes and ribbon, and three ostrich feathers atop her head, dyed gold, red, and blue, added at least a foot to her presence. Once she'd paused at the balcony to assure she was the cynosure of all eyes, the famed actress turned and sought Lucasta.

"Before I begin," she said in her thick, purring contralto, "I wish to thank Miss Lithwick for giving me the opportunity to appear before you in women's garb. I was not sure I would remember how to sing in a frock." Murmurs of delight and some laughter met this remark. "Miss Lithwick," she asked curiously, "was that your voice accompanying our little friend in the last verse of 'Come Thou Fount of Every Blessing?'"

Heat scorched her face as Lucasta nodded. Every eye that had been contemplating Mrs. Kennedy's splendor was now focused on her.

"Well, my dear!" the actress said. "When I retire, Covent Garden may be in need of a new contralto. I hope they will think of you when the time comes."

Lucasta, too overcome to speak, nodded again. The very idea robbed her of speech. Mrs. Kennedy had performed at the Haymarket Theatre, the Royal Opera House, Ranelagh Garden, and Vauxhall as well as Covent Garden, and she was in demand for festivals around the country at other times of the year.

Lucasta might never be as well-known as Mrs. Kennedy, but to at least try for a place on these stages— That was the reason she had denied Jem.

The actress signaled her accompanist and launched into "A-Hunting We Will Go," a song from John Gay's *Beggar's Opera*. She had created quite a stir playing the lead in that play—a woman in a man's role!—and the fuss had drawn curious audiences for weeks. Mrs. Kennedy was not a woman who bowed to society's dictates. Lucasta would not, either.

Jem would never know this pleasure, this freedom, of defying expectation. The thought was a slice to her heart, just as the thought of him would be, she supposed, for a long while. Ears attuned to Mrs. Kennedy's performance, she scanned the galleries and the pews below for sight of the Falstead family, sure she would be able to pick out Judith and her siblings among the crowd. But there was no sign of any of them.

Jem would not have persuaded them to forego the concert altogether, not even if he resented her rejection. But she might never see his beloved face again. Her heart twisted until she thought she might not be able to breathe through the hurt.

When intermission came and Mrs. Kennedy swept regally away, Lucasta turned to her self-appointed stage manager. "Benedicta, who requested the change to the...program..."

Jem stood next to Benedicta's wheeled chair. The girl stared up at him adoringly.

"Him," she said. "The governor as comes to hear us sing when you're there." Her cheeks turned a delicate pink.

"You're here," Lucasta said stupidly. The breath left her body. She wasn't sure if the sensation rushing through her was agony or joy.

He nodded. He looked thrillingly handsome in a formal suit of deep red linen. The cut was severe in its simplicity, offsetting the elaborate silver embroidery and the thick silver buttons on his coat, waistcoat, and the cuffs of his breeches. His stockings were bright white. A fall of blonde lace at his throat replaced a cravat, and he wore a small white powdered wig. No other man in London could wear such a dandified ensemble and look so elegant and commanding in it.

She'd missed what he'd said, too busy staring at him. She'd been struck senseless yesterday when he showed up in Judith's drawing room, had fallen into his arms and his kisses. She felt like doing the same again.

"I beg your pardon?"

"Judith wishes to perform with you." He reached behind him and pulled his sister forward. "She wants to play 'The Bells of Aberdovey,' as you practiced, if you will sing."

Judith wore a simple but elegant gown of silver satin, and her lightly powdered hair was pinned in an elaborate coiffure. The feathers in her headpiece framed a face wearing a tremulous smile.

"I understand if it's too late to make such a request," she said shyly. "But I would not let Jem rest until he asked you."

"But—to perform—" Lucasta looked at Jem in bewilderment. "There are so many people here."

"I want to support the foundlings," Judith said stubbornly. "And Eliza did very well, didn't she?"

Lucasta took a deep breath and met Jem's eyes squarely. "I would be deeply honored if you would play, Judith," she said, pressing back the tremor in her voice. She would not weep again tonight; she would *not*. "And I would be even more honored to sing for you."

Judith smiled a beatific, rather knowing smile and allowed Jem to lead her to the small spinet that had been set up in the gallery for the occasion. The foundlings on the benches jostled each other, their eyes round as shillings, muttering about the fancy lord and his very fancy companion.

Lucasta heard not a single snigger or exclamation. This lot were accustomed to disease, wounds, scars, and challenges; it was the rare body, in their world, that was hale and whole. Judith in her blindness was immediately one of them. It was her dress causing the marvel. Several girls whispered appreciative comments about her gown as Judith seated herself at the instrument.

"Hey now, is that his wife then?" Hester exclaimed. "And here we thought he was danglin' after you, miss!"

"That is his sister, Hester," Lucasta shushed her. "Mind you address her as Lady Judith, as she is the daughter of a marquess."

"Ooooh." Hester looked appropriately impressed. "And 'e's still fixin' to marry you, then, ain't 'e?"

Lucasta stepped to the instrument and took Judith's hand. It was small and cold. "I am so very glad you are here."

Judith's smile grew enormous. "I knew your concert would be a success if you would sing, Lucasta. And I told Jem I could make you."

Jem bowed and withdrew to whisper a word in the ear of the governor who was announcing. After some throat clearing, the other man settled the audience with an introduction. "Performing on the spinet, Lady Judith Falstead, sister to one of the members of our governing board and daughter of the new Marquess of Arendale," he said pompously. "And performing 'The Bells of Aberdovey,' the organizer of tonight's concert, Miss Lucasta Lithwick."

Judith, with the serenity and concentration of a professional, flexed her fingers and began to play. And Lucasta, her heart overflowing with joy and gratitude, sang.

She couldn't begin to comprehend Jem's motives, but she didn't need to. She let the music lift and carry her. Judith played with ease, from memory, and Lucasta poured her heart into her voice.

It lifted into the great room, winding around the pillars of the first-floor gallery, trilling along the cornices outlining the ceiling, resounding off the polished wooden panels and arched windows. It wasn't a song that required gusto, but Lucasta gave it anyway. It felt so good to sing, to fill a room with her voice, to be a part of the music. She had found herself earlier in a moment of complete happiness; this was profounder, more perfect.

But Jem's gift wasn't complete. After their song, Judith remained seated at the spinet, flexing her fingers once more, and Jem stepped forward, joining Lucasta at the balcony. She gazed at him with questioning eyes.

"Judith had one more request," he said. His eyes on her, filled with amber lights, made her feel as if the music still poured through her, a current of liquid gold. "She asked if we would sing a duet." One corner of his mouth lifted. "Demanded, actually."

"Performing 'The True Lover's Farewell,'" said the announcer in a wondering tone, "one of our governors, the new Lord Payne, and Miss Lithwick."

"But you—these people," Lucasta tried telling him. "All watching. What you feared."

She didn't understand. He didn't want eyes on his family, but he had let Judith play. And now he was going to sing. With her.

He held out his hand. "Some things," he said simply, "are worse than gossip."

She grasped his fingers, warm and firm and strong, and the music inside her came to life. The sound of this throaty, rich baritone swirled through her to her very toes as Jem began the duet they had sang at Rose Hollow.

*"Fare thee well, my own true love, and fare thee well for a while—"*

There was no more thought, only music. And each note of the melody, each chord from the instrument drew them together, binding them with a tether invisible to the eye. They were tuned to the same pitch, Lucasta thought hazily, as far as thought was allowed her. They vibrated at the same frequency. They were a perfect harmonic unit.

She heard the strangest vibration when the last notes of the duet faded, and she wondered why the floor quivered. Judith stood and stepped toward them to take her curtsy, and the gallery shook with thunderous applause. Through blurred eyes Lucasta saw that the audience was on its feet, and her foundlings clapped and whooped with glee. Judith, slipping an arm through each of theirs, sank into another graceful curtsy, and then, still smiling that saintly smile, waved and took her leave.

Lucasta stood rooted to the floor. Signor Marchesi, who was slated next, stepped into the adoring applause, lifted Lucasta's hand and kissed it with a cheeky wink, and then launched into his aria from *Ifigenia in Aulide.* Though the song was his alone, he performed it with the gestures from the opera, addressing her as if she were the doomed Ifigenia, and Lucasta collected just enough wit to remember the postures the actress had assumed: her adulation for the posturing Achilles, her despair as she realized her fate.

It was almost too much. She had sung with Judith, and with Jem, before an audience of hundreds. It was her first public performance of this magnitude. And now the great Signor Marchesi was performing next to her. *With* her. She might very well die of happiness and be taken straight up to heaven in the chariot of the gods, just like another version of the play. It would be a fitting end.

The night lasted forever, and it was over in moments. The foundlings held up beautifully. Her performers were stellar. The Gorgons had a surprise for her as well: a Boccherini quintet, the one she had heard performed at the Ranelagh Gardens masquerade, with Cici on the cello. They, too, received a standing ovation.

The Abrams sisters, Miss Harriet and Miss Theodosia, brought flowers raining down upon their heads with their transcendent voices. The trio of Philippa, Isadora, and Camilla, with Hester playing the spinet, went off without a hitch. And at the very end, amid another ovation, with calls of *encore, encore!* Lucasta heard her name being chanted: "Miss Lithwick!" the audience called, amid shouts for Signor Marchesi. They were being called for together: the great Marchesi, and poor, plain Lucasta Lithwick.

Marchesi took the balcony, throwing his arms wide. "I will sing for you!" he cried, projecting his voice to the far end of the room. "A song I wrote myself, in Italian, but as arranged by Miss Lithwick, who will please me, I hope, by singing the English version she has so admirably translated for me?"

Lucasta moved to the harpsichord in a daze, praying she would not die of happiness until after she had performed a duet with Signor Marchesi.

She knew better than to try to overshadow the famous castrato. Rather she let the English be an echo of his Italian, her voice counterpoint to his, a delicate, supple lilt to his acrobatic contralto. As he repeated the last stanza, he signaled for her to sing the Italian with him, and Lucasta felt her chest would burst with joy as she harmonized with one of her heroes, using her voice to enrich and surround one of the most beautiful sounds she had ever heard.

As the echoes of the song faded into breathless silence, Lucasta closed her eyes and hugged herself, her heart breaking open. This was what she had denied Jem for. It would have to be enough. It *would* be enough, in time.

Then there were flowers being shoved into her arms by Selina, and suddenly all the Gorgons were on the balcony, Cici too, distributing flowers to the foundlings. The orphans curtsied and smiled as Lucasta had never seen them smile before, the simple roses the crowning beauty of an evening they would never forget. Lucasta curtsied as well, again and again through the rolling applause, until Annis finally took her arm and dragged her away.

"Let the staff clean up and tuck your foundlings into bed," she said in Lucasta's ear. "We are gathering at Arendale House. Jem will bring you."

"Judith?"

"Will come with us," Minnie said firmly. "Between Trevor, Ashley, and Frotheringale's carriage, we're all accounted for."

"Ashley," Lucasta murmured in surprise, but Minnie said airily, "I won't allow him to stay. It's just us girls, at Bertie's invite. Don't malinger, now, even if you are the star of the evening."

Jem waited for her at the bottom of the stairs, holding her cape and hat. People moved around them, staff taking the instruments away and the nurses herding their foundlings off to bed, where they would no doubt stay awake well after the lights were doused, whispering about their triumph.

One after another they hugged Lucasta as they passed, and she hugged them back, praising them all for their accomplishment. When at least she turned to Jem, her smile stretched so wide it hurt her face, and her heart was dangerously close to bursting.

"You let Judith perform," she whispered, leaning toward him as he slowly, gently, settled her cloak about her shoulders. His hands lingered, brushing down her arms, and she breathed in his scent, so familiar, so heady, so potent. There was no force on earth that would make her able to step away from him again. He would have to do it.

His eyes were dark and full of emotion, his voice husky. "I asked myself, why would I allow the possible displeasure of a few small people to keep her from her great dream?"

Lucasta smiled. "And you sang," she breathed. "You were glorious."

"And untrained. No match for you, my dear. But I knew no other way to show you I'd come to my senses."

"What do you mean?" She could barely manage air around the lump in her throat.

He clasped his hands around hers. As always, a tingle darted up her arm, curling around her heart. "Lucasta Lithwick," Jem said in that voice that was heaven and promise and seduction all together. "Will you sing with me every day of my life?"

Her lips trembled. "In private, you mean?"

"There are many duets I hope we shall have in private," he said, and his wicked look sent trills of pleasure along every nerve. "But I hope you will sing in public, too. You were a marvel tonight, Lucasta. A revelation. I don't think you comprehend how you enchanted everyone. To deprive the world of your gifts would truly be a loss. But as I also want you as my wife—" Here he drew her so close that she felt his breath against her ear— "I suppose I shall have to learn how to be the husband of a famous musician, and bear whatever slings and arrows of outrageous fortune result."

She lifted her chin and brushed her lips along the strong line of his jaw. He shivered.

"Jem," she said, "I want nothing more. But I would have so much to learn as your wife. There will be attention. There will be —opinions. All my failures will be public and will reflect on you. Your family. I know you don't want that."

"I don't wish it," he said slowly, wrapping his arms about her. "But Judith is stronger than I thought. So are the others. So are you. I shall have to learn to be equally resilient, and stand rooted in what I know to be true. That is all."

She raised her hands to either side of his face. She forgot they stood in a dark alcove in a building full of strangers. She couldn't tell if her feet still touched the earth.

"Jeremiah Falstead. You are the strongest, bravest, most generous, most protective, most—*giving* man I know."

"And you are the most *fascinating* female." His lips curved as she giggled, and his breath across her lips made her gasp. "Lucasta Lithwick. Will you be mine?"

"I already am," she whispered, and fell into his kiss.

# CHAPTER TWENTY-FOUR

The parlor at Arendale House was missing Jem's friends, but Lucasta was glad to see it held all of hers: the Gorgons, Cici, Judith, Bertie, and the younger Falstead siblings, who tumbled about with excitement over their evening out.

"I've done it," Jem announced as he ushered Lucasta inside. "I've persuaded Lucasta Lithwick to marry me."

His proclamation was met with cheers of delight and more applause. Bertie burst into tears of joy.

"A wedding!" she cried in rapture. "Please tell me you will wait until we are out of mourning, so we might have a proper celebration."

"It won't be as soon as I could wish." Jem sobered as he turned to Lucasta, taking her cape from her shoulders, letting his fingers brush her neck and collarbone as he did. She shivered. The saffron gown had held up beautifully, the fabric catching the light every time she moved, and the style flattered her frame. She warmed under Jem's appreciative glance as he met her eyes.

"Now that the funeral is over, I must go tell my father he is the Marquess," he said. "And I will insist on bringing Portia and the children to England. They must be free. I cannot allow him to let my brothers and sisters be treated as property."

Lucasta decided not to mention that, as his wife, by English law she too would be considered his property, under his complete legal control. Being a wife was a far cry from being enslaved. Her throat was sore tonight, not from singing, but by the many times she'd forced back powerful emotion. Her heart moaned at the thought of being away from him, but he was right.

"I agree," she said quietly. "We shall marry when your family— *all* your family—can be present."

"Lucasta! Lucasta! Lucasta!" Tressie and Starria whirled up to her, hugging Lucasta again and again, until Hannibal pushed them aside for his own embrace. "You were brilliant."

Lucasta soaked in their attention, hugging them back. In marrying Jem, she would gain a raft of siblings and a new cousin just her age. To one raised an only child, the thought was thrilling and slightly alarming.

Tressie gave a happy sigh. "And that gown is perfectly lovely. Jem, when shall I be allowed to wear long skirts, like a real lady?"

The butler hovered, clearing his throat. "Milord," he began, looking distinctly nervous. Lucasta had noticed before that Jem's butler did not have the stiff indifference that was prized among his occupation. She liked him better for it. "There is the matter of the town coach."

"Yes?" Jem asked, distracted by the children romping around him.

"It has been dispatched, sir, at the request of—"

"How now!" cried a booming, authoritative voice. "Have we come to our senses yet, or are we all still foolishly petting my niece?"

Two women appeared in the wide doorway leading to another of the formal staterooms. The first was Lady Payne, wearing an expression for once more bemused than harried.

Holding her ladyship's arm with one hand, supporting herself on a walking stick with the other, was an imposing figure of a woman wearing a gown whose panniers placed its age in a previous decade and whose powdered wig was doubled in height by a structure that looked like a bowl of fruit with feathers. Her face was lined, powdered, patched, and staring sternly at all of them, but a twinkle surfaced in her eyes as she gazed at Lucasta.

"Aunt Cornelia!"

Lucasta rushed across the room and gave her aunt a deep curtsy. Aunt Cornelia, Lady Evers, adhered to the manners of an earlier epoch as she did the dress. "What brings you to London?"

Her great-aunt grumbled and let Lucasta lead her to the largest and most comfortable chair, which Annis yielded to a greater dignity. Cornelia settled herself with enormous fuss, arranging her panniers and letting her yards of skirts sweep elegantly around her. Then she clasped both hands atop the golden knob of her walking stick and fixed her stare on Lucasta.

"Frotheringale, that fool, was making noises about coming here, and I suspected his intentions were no better than Pevensey's had been all along." She scoffed. "I sent you the note warning I'd come for you, didn't I? Yet you fell into his clutches like a peagoose. Thought you had more sense, gel."

"I do!" Lucasta exclaimed. "I didn't marry Gale."

"Good." Cornelia snorted. "If I wanted you for him, I'd have told him so myself ages ago, and Almira, that harridan I call a sister-in-law, can go hang herself with her garters. And I would never have allowed Pevensey to rivet you to his hey-go-mad rapscallion of a son, either."

The sound of choked laughter from Annis made Cornelia turn her head. "How now, and here you are as well, the fearsome foursome! The count's daughter, the duke's daughter, the soldier's daughter, and the vicar's get."

Her eyes moved over each of the girls in turn. "Who is it named you the Gorgons? Olympe will fall down laughing when I tell her how Miss Gregoire's girls are being admired in the highest circles. I always told her to rein in those radical Enlightenment ideals of hers at her school, but she's French, and there's no fixing that."

"Jem named us the Gorgons." Lucasta cast him an impish

glance. "Indeed I believe he pronounced me a veritable Medusa at the occasion of our first meeting."

Aunt Cornelia raised a set of glasses tied to her bodice by a gold chain. "You've brought him to heel good and proper, and fixed the leg shackle, too?"

Jem cleared his throat. "I have the honor," he said, "of having my hand and my suit accepted by your grand-niece. With your approval, of course," he added in a tone that implied he would marry Lucasta no matter who objected.

"Yes, we all heard you trumpeting your way in here like a green schoolboy," Cornelia answered, a smile playing around her carmine-red lips. "You suppose you're good enough for my Lucasta?"

"Son and heir to the marquessate of Arendale?" Lady Payne gasped. "Good enough for the daughter of a vicar?" She laid a hand over her heart, truly shocked.

Jem gave a short bow. "I will endeavor every day of my life hereafter to be worthy of her esteem, your ladyship."

"Aunt Cornelia to you, Payne," the lady answered. "I knew your mother, you know. Constance had her season in Bath before your father lured her away. I always hoped he'd prove worthy of her." She inspected Jem from head to toe. Her smile grew broader as she progressed.

"Too handsome by half, lad, just like your father, but not a dirty dish like he is, I'd guess." She tucked her glasses away and gave a decisive nod. "I mean to leave everything to Lucasta, you know. Have your solicitors get in touch with me when you draw up the settlement."

"Aunt Cornelia—" Lucasta faltered. Then, looking around the room, she realized that everyone else here knew her secret, for she doubted Cici had wasted a moment in informing Bertie of the dramatic scenes at Pevensey house yesterday. Only Lady Payne was unaware, and frankly she didn't care a ha'penny for Lady Payne's opinion. But Jem might.

"Aunt Patience said you know the full story of my parentage," she said instead.

"Eh, what's that?" Aunt Cornelia's voice grew booming once again. "My Felicity doted on her daughter, and you were the best thing Laurence Lithwick ever gave her. I never had a thing against the man myself, foreigner that he was. You've his coloring, no doubt about it, no one will mistake you for an English rose! But you're not as dark as these 'uns," she said, looking curiously at the younger Falstead siblings.

Fascinated, they lined up for introductions.

"Children of my father's second...wife," Jem said. "Er—common-law wife, as it were."

Lucasta held her breath. This was what he most feared: his siblings being exposed to the judgment and ridicule of the arbiters of society. Aunt Cornelia might live in Bath, and in her final marriage might have condescended to wed a mere knight, but she possessed a formidable network of contacts and a great deal of influence. Jem's face tightened as he awaited the blow, and Lucasta took his arm for support.

Cornelia applied her glasses again. "I've never seen more beautiful children," she announced. "If you ask me, mixing the races makes for more robust blood. Look what William the Bastard did for our isle when he infused our Saxon blood with some good staunch Norman stock! I told m'brother so when he had fits about Felicity marrying your father, and I'll stand by it. Look at our dear Selina, here—that skin will never freckle in the sun! You ought to consider marrying dark, for the sake of your children, dear," she addressed Cici, whose blue eyes were round as marbles and standing out against her pale skin. "Maybe a Turk for you, or a nice sturdy Greek? I've always had a taste for the Greek Isles, m'self."

Lucasta only barely managed to stifle a half-laugh, half-groan at this lecture, and the look on her friends' faces as they choked back their own reactions nearly did her in. Lady Payne's mouth moved in wordless protest. But Aunt Cornelia hadn't finished her assessment.

"Lambertina, is it?" she addressed Bertie next. "You're a good stout girl, and I like that. It never stopped me catching a husband that I couldn't cinch my waist in, and I've had four so far. But I don't know this little blind girl." She turned her glasses in Judith's direction. "Scarletina, was it, or smallpox?"

"Measles," Judith answered serenely, though her mouth twitched with a smile. "Lady Evers, Bertie tells me you are wearing the most astonishing headdress."

"Aunt Cornelia to you, too, if you're a Falstead," her ladyship answered, "and come over here and see for yourself, girl. I must say, you played beautifully tonight."

Lucasta gasped. "Aunt Cornelia! Were you at the concert?"

"Indeed I was. Demanded Frotheringale get me a ticket at the last minute, and he had a devil of a time doing it. Sold out, they were, and I think he had to wheedle one out of a governor."

Lucasta shot Jem a quick look. He was watching Judith's expression of absorbed rapture as she explored Cornelia's elaborate headpiece. "Then you heard me sing. In public. In front of a great many people," Lucasta said.

She caught the eyes of her friends, who looked as worried as Lucasta felt. She'd sobbed to all three of them many a time about Aunt Cornelia's strictures about performing. Cornelia straightened and gave Lucasta a level look.

"Indeed you did, and I don't see any reason why you can't sing or play wherever you wish, from here on."

"But—" Lucasta floundered for words. "You said it was vulgar. An embarrassment. That no member of our family would perform on public stage, before common crowds."

Cornelia snorted again. "A vulgar display for a vicar's daughter, lass. But you're to marry the heir to Arendale. There's less than two dozen dukes in these blessed isles, and what, half a dozen marquesses? Won't be many below the royals who can tell *you* what to do. And our sanctimonious Queen Charlotte might not let her girls step a toe in public, but I don't see why *I* should be so small-minded," Cornelia said loftily. "Though you'd best beware how you let men like that Marchesi fawn over you. Castrato or no, people will talk."

Lucasta bit her lip on a swift defense of Signor Marchesi. Aunt Cornelia would allow her to perform, and so would Jem. She scarcely dared breathe for wonder.

"What's a castrato?" Starria asked.

"A type of singer," Jem said quickly, and no one else dared elaborate.

Minnie spoke. "It seems to me we must acknowledge that Queen Lucasta is the first among us to accept an offer of marriage. She has already paid her forfeit, but it remains to be settled where the wedding breakfast shall be, and what colors she will make her maids of honor wear."

"I do hope you'll ask Mademoiselle Beaudoin to design them," Cici said hopefully. "And one for me as well?"

A shadow moved across Lucasta's happiness as she turned to face Jem. She didn't know how long a voyage to the West Indies might take, nor how much time he might require to collect his errant father. It might be a year or more before they could wed, and what would she do with herself in the meantime? The last day and a night without him, after his declaration and her refusal, had been a needle thrust through her heart. Would she ache this much each day without him, for months, perhaps a year?

"The matter of the town coach, milord?" The butler inserted himself into the group, making a desperate appeal to Jem.

"Yes, of course." Jem turned to him courteously. "What of it?"

"It was dispatched, milord, to the docks, at the request of—" Words failed the poor man, and he cast about in panic as every eye in the room turned upon him.

"Of whom?" Jem prompted.

"Of—that is to say—" He looked at Lady Payne, who scowled.

"It was not *my* idea, Payne," she said stiffly to Jem, "but when the message came, that housekeeper of yours insisted—"

She trailed off as a group appeared in the doorway.

"Hallooo, milord," Mrs. Cadogan called softly. "I was at the wharf just now and found one or two things that will interest you."

Lucasta, along with everyone else, stared in blatant curiosity. The housekeeper held the hands of two small children whose faces gleamed as if the wind had nipped their cheeks, and whose hoods were pushed back to reveal tufts of tightly curled black hair.

Beside her stood a tall, dark-skinned woman in a cloak spotted with rain. She was blindingly beautiful and looked very weary. A swaddled form in her arms chirped and shifted as if the babe within were kicking to get free.

"Portia?" Jem said incredulously.

"Mama!" Three little bodies flew past Lucasta in a blur, launching themselves at their mother.

"Starria. Tressie. Hannibal." Portia knelt and held out her arms, staring as if she saw three angels descended from heaven. "Oh, my heavens, you've all gotten so big!"

She greeted the children with swift kisses, then rose to face Jem with a steady, watchful gaze. The children, too, stared solemnly.

"Milord," Portia said in a quiet voice, "I regret to tell you your father is dead. I came to bring you his things and, because—" Her voice caught as if with strong emotion, and for a long moment Jem didn't move; he looked frozen in shock.

"Then you are the marquess," Lady Payne whispered. "Jem, you are Arendale now."

"Your lordship." With the babe in her arms, Portia made a brief curtsy. The bundled babe squirmed and gurgled. "It was not safe for us," she said, a note of desperation entering her voice. "I did not know where else to go."

"You did the right thing," Jem said firmly, stepping toward her. "You are free here, Portia. It is the law of this land. No one can take you anywhere against your wishes, neither you nor the children."

"Praise be to God," Portia whispered, closing her eyes to compose herself as she received this news. The expressions that chased across her face pierced Lucasta's heart. She could not imagine the horrors and indignities this woman had endured.

"Not in this house." Lady Payne's strangled voice came from behind them. "Not *here!* In my house?"

Slowly, working to contain his rage, Jem turned to face her. "I think you forget this is *my* house, Aunt," he said in a soft, warning tone. "I shall offer shelter to whom I please beneath this roof. My family will always be welcome." He paused. "But I understand if circumstances will not permit you to continue residence here."

Lady Payne turned and fled the room.

"No steel in *her* spine," Aunt Cornelia snorted. Hands folded over the golden knob of her walking stick, she watched the unfolding tableau with great attention. "Think she'll come round?"

"I doubt it," Bertie said flatly. She had risen as well, but she gave Lucasta a cautious look, as if questioning which of them should assume the role of hostess in Jem's house. She was his cousin, but Lucasta was to be his wife.

And she, Lucasta realized, was meeting the mother of her husband-to-be's siblings, who would become her family as well. Three more siblings, more family than she could have dreamed. Lucasta reached out to Portia with both hands.

"Please, come be seated, and take off your wet things. If I am not mistaken, Mrs. Cadogan has rushed off to the kitchen to find us refreshments, and she makes the most heavenly treats. Is it proper for me to call you Portia?" she asked self-consciously. "We have not been introduced."

"Portia, this is my intended wife, Miss Lucasta Lithwick," Jem said with great courtesy. "Lucasta, my father's wife, Portia."

"Wife," Portia said softly. She allowed Lucasta to take the babe from her arms, searching her face with large, deep brown eyes. "But we never—"

"We can present you as his widow," Lucasta suggested, looking to Jem.

"Hey, now! Present her to me, and you can rehearse." Aunt Cornelia banged her walking stick on the floor. Lucasta turned with the swaddled babe, feeling more nervous about presenting Portia to her aunt than she had at any point during the concert. Jem had feared exposing his family to the polite world, and now his secret was to lie in the hands of Aunt Cornelia?

But she had kept Patience's secret for all of Lucasta's life, and she had made certain it would go no further. Lucasta met Jem's eyes, and her heart softened at his nod. He had said he would be strong enough to take the risk of exposing his family, and he hadn't batted an eye at the revelation about her birth. How had she been so lucky to find him?

"Portia, may I make you known to my Aunt Cornelia, Lady Evers, daughter of the third Viscount Frotheringale," Lucasta said.

Cornelia acknowledged Portia's graceful curtsy. "And what title shall we address you with, then?"

"Title?" Portia startled. "My—if we are calling him my husband, his title was Lord Payne, but I—"

"I believe there's a Lady Payne who just removed herself from the room,"

Aunt Cornelia said, "but I am confident she will accept her dowager status with dignity, eh?" A smile lifted one side of her mouth. "We shall address you as Portia, Lady Payne, and leave it at that."

"Lady?" Portia looked dazed. In the span of a day she had gone from being a captive of the Falstead family to possessor of one of their courtesy titles. The jump would be near as dizzying, Lucasta thought, as her going from poor, plain Lucasta Lithwick to the Marchioness of Arendale.

"The children will take the name Falstead, if Lady Payne consents," Jem added.

"And they will be free," Portia whispered fiercely. "Free."

Jem nodded. "I will have papers drawn up saying as much, and we will record their births in the parish register at Arendale."

Portia sat up. "This is Selene," she said, indicating one of the exquisite children who stood beside her, "and this is Hyperion," indicating the other. She nodded to the babe. "And you are holding Phoebe."

Lucasta looked wonderingly at the babe in her arms, who was mere weeks old. A bubble formed between the tiny bowed lips, and when it popped, Phoebe's eyes widened in surprise. Lucasta laughed, but there was an ache in it.

Portia had traveled for miles with two small children and a babe who looked as if she might have been born aboard ship. An act of infinite bravery. And desperation.

"We wish to be made known to Lady Payne," Annis announced. Lucasta looked up in surprise to see that the other girls had gathered around the settee, Judith holding the hands of the two new arrivals, getting acquainted with her new brother and sister.

"And I should like to hold my cousin." Bertie held out her arms.

Mrs. Cadogan bustled into the room flanked by the butler and two footmen carrying trays of refreshments. The group sat long, laughing and talking and making arrangements for Jem's marriage, Portia's future, and provision for the Falstead children. Portia hugged Judith and shed tears on her shoulder when Judith welcomed her into the family. It was late when Lucasta helped Aunt Cornelia withdraw to her room, for Jem insisted that Lady Evers put up with them for the night.

"I'll remove to Frotheringale House tomorrow," Aunt Cornelia said with a yawn, "and that fool nephew of mine won't say a word against me." At the door to her room, she took Lucasta's hand in both of hers, and her smile was sweet and sad.

"My little Lucasta," she said. "Singing in the Foundling Chapel and playing Handel's organ. How proud your father would be of you. And your mother, too."

For the hundredth time that day, Lucasta's eyes welled with emotion, but for once she didn't mind being buffeted by the currents. It was the measure of her joy.

"Make certain your young marquess consults me about settlements." Aunt Cornelia yawned again. "I won't simply give him everything. I want some put in trust for your children."

"Good night, my favorite aunt," Lucasta said fondly. "And thank you for welcoming his family, for they will be mine now as well."

Jem waited for her at the end of the hall when she turned from her aunt's door. Lucasta recognized the same alcove where they had embraced the afternoon of his grandfather's death, the same niche with its marble bust, the same portrait of some stern ancestor on the wall.

A deep warmth surrounded her when she stepped into his arms. Safety, wonder, passion, and something she groped to name —a sense of stepping into a place that had been shaped and ready for her. Waiting for when she was brave enough to enter.

"My condolences on the loss of your father," she murmured. She gathered that Jem did not much admire or respect his father, but it must be a heavy blow nevertheless. She had been devastated to lose her parents, and still missed them both.

"Naught but good can come of it," Jem said, stroking the back of her neck. "Portia is here and the children are safe. I can start at once to repair the ills he has wrought."

"And you are the Marquess. Do you still mean to travel to the West Indies?"

"Not unless I must. I should be able to make out the manumission papers here for all the people on his estates. I will direct my father's solicitors to break the land into parcels and gift a portion to each family, so they have a place to live and means to support themselves." He moved his lips along her ear, and she shivered.

"We can wed in unseemly haste," he went on. "Or wait a few weeks to allow Josie to make up your wedding clothes."

"We ought to make some allowance for mourning," she answered, resting her head on his shoulder. "What is unseemly is the season's most eligible bachelor, compelled to surrender his hand by one unadvised kiss."

"That was a *very* advised kiss." He rubbed his cheek over her hair, which was quietly shedding powder on his beautiful coat. "I was courting you from our first dance, Lucasta. I don't think you knew that."

"That was a courtship?" She lifted her head to gaze inquiringly at him. "Engaging me to give music lessons to your sister and cousin?"

"A brilliant tactic which I would advise all ardent suitors to adopt," he confirmed. "And I rescued you from your errant cousin, did I not? Both of them, in point of fact."

She sighed with happiness. "And you sang with me. In public. For money."

"Indeed I did. What more do you require as assurance of my regard? Flowers? Poetry? A wedding trip to Italy or France?"

"Poetry is never out of place." She rested her chin on his chest and gazed up at him expectantly.

"To Lucasta, who is going to the stage." He struck a dramatic attitude, and Lucasta chuckled. "Tell me not, sweet, I am unkind, if from the warehouse of linen drapery to, um, your arms I fly."

"My arms," she said, sliding these around him, "and none other's, I hope."

"Oh, more? Second stanza. A new mistress I now chase—" He tightened his hold about her. "The, um, something in the field."

"Gorgon," Lucasta supplied.

"Hardly. Now what is my line: A stronger faith I now embrace —a stage, a career, a—vicar's daughter."

"Yet this inconstancy is such that I too shall adore," Lucasta murmured.

"Mmm." A silence fell as their lips met. "I must change the last lines," Jem said huskily in her ear. "I love nothing more than you. Not honor, not respect, not society's approval. Nothing."

"And I you," Lucasta whispered, framing his face with her hands. His eyes glowed with steadfast love, reflecting her own. "I was wrong about something. I thought I wouldn't survive if I gave up my hopes of a musical career. I thought it would hurt less to give you up rather than my dream."

"But?" He moved his lips along her jaw to the sensitive skin beneath her ear, and Lucasta melted in his arms.

"I have my whole life to sing and perform," she told him. "But when you came to the balcony with Judith and asked if she could play, and then you sang with me— I realized that even if I could have my dream, it wouldn't be enough. I want, and will always want, you."

"And now you have me," Jem swore, and gave her a kiss promising a lifetime of harmony, in their lives and in their souls.

# AUTHOR'S NOTE

Dear Reader,

Luigi Marchesi was indeed one of the most famous and revered singers of the late eighteenth century. He graced theaters all over Europe and was known for what critics called his "vocal acrobatics." While the fashion for *castrati* was fading, Signor Marchesi was considered one of the most accomplished and charismatic of his class. It is true that, as an encore, he would frequently perform an additional song that he had written himself. It is also true that *castrati* enjoyed reputations for sexual prowess.

Charles Ignatius Sancho was, in addition to being a writer and prominent abolitionist, a composer and music theorist. After establishing his shop in London and acquiring property, he was one of the first British Africans allowed to vote. He died in 1780, leaving a wife and four surviving children. He wrote often about the abuse he received for the color of his skin, but he was well-known, much admired, and had important friends.

The Foundling Hospital in London, established in 1739 by Thomas Coram, was indeed a fashionable charity. The well-born went to promenade around its grounds, and its board of directors were often important citizens. Frequently, foundlings who were blind were taught musical skills, as it was less likely they would be hired as domestic servants or apprentices to a trade. The hospital kept and catalogued the notes and remembrances that parents pinned to their surrendered child. Georg Frederic Handel conducted a performance from his *Messiah* oratorio to mark the installation of the new organ in the hospital chapel in 1750, and the work thereafter became a beloved annual performance.

John Stanley, Maria Theresia von Paradis, and Mélanie de Salignac, mentioned in the book, are real-life musicians who also happened to be blind. Stanley was a governor of the Foundling Hospital, a musician who frequently performed on Handel's organ, and who was likely responsible for teaching music to many of the blind students. Maria Theresia was a composer who was friends and co-performer with the likes of Mozart and Haydn. Long before Braille was invented, Mélanie de Salignac taught herself to read using a system of raised letters and devised her own notation of raised symbols to read music.

Somersett's case, a judgment handed down by Lord Mansfield in 1772, ruled that a person of enslaved status could not be forcibly removed from English soil and returned to captivity. While this judgment did not altogether end the practice, it was a landmark in the long, hard-fought battle to end the practice of enslavement on British soil.

If public opinion toward professional women singers seems two-faced in the story, that reflects contradictory strands of opinion in the historical record. It was generally more accepted on the Continent for high-born women to create and share their music. For many English critics, however, women performing on stage was tantamount to a declaration of sexual license. Actresses were, by many, assumed to be sexually available. A woman had some safety from public opinion if she were married. Margaret Doyle, who was Mrs. Kennedy by the time of the story, was a famous actress and singer, well known for her breeches roles (contraltos were often called upon to play men). The Abrams sisters were stars of the London concert scene in the 1780s and enjoyed pristine reputations, but I imagine it took some doing on their part.

If you've read other books in the Ladies Least Likely series, you'll have heard about Miss Gregoire's Academy for Girls, that quietly radical institution in Bath at which Olympe Gregoire and her staff are teaching young girls to follow their passions. My novella in the Suffragette Uprising series, *Miss Gregoire's Beginning*, accounts for the origins of this remarkable woman, and the love story she keeps a secret from the world. All the books in the Suffragette Uprising series celebrate women fighting for independence, much like the Ladies Least Likely are always going against the grain of convention.

I hope you've enjoyed meeting the Gorgons as much as I've enjoyed introducing them to you. May we all have many more delightful adventures together, and may your days, and your nights, be filled with music and joy,

Misty

# ABOUT THE AUTHOR

Misty Urban fell in love with stories at an early age and has spent her life among books as a teacher, scholar, editor, writer, and bookseller. Her favorite stories take you new places, teach you new things, and end with a win. She especially likes romances about unconventional heroines who defy the odds and the unexpected heroes who woo them, so that's mostly what she writes. When she puts down the book she likes to take long walks, drag her family to new places, or hang out around water, dreaming up new stories.

Visit her at mistyurban.com
Join author's newsletter